Jo... ...impeccably dressed.

Kat's eyes traveled over a broad chest and wide shoulders, up a tanned neck, to a strong jaw covered with two-day-old stubble. A mouth that was slow to smile but still sexy. Rich, successful and hot.

He had a rep for being a bit of a bastard, in business and in bed. That fact only dropped his sexy factor by a quarter of a percent.

"Mr. Halstead, welcome back to El Acantilado," Kat murmured, ignoring her jumping heart.

"Call me Jonas."

It wasn't the first time he'd made the offer, but Kat had no intention of accepting. It wasn't professional, and formality kept a healthy distance between her and guys in fancy suits. Like her ex-husband, and sadly, just like her father, those kinds of men were not to be trusted.

But it really annoyed Kat that a thousand sparks danced on her skin as Jonas's smile turned his face from remote-but-still-hot to oh-my-God-I want-to-rip-his-clothes-off.

No. Sexy billionaires were *not* her type. She'd married, and divorced, a ruthless and merciless rich guy.

But it sure felt like she had the screaming hots for a man she shouldn't.

And it was all Jonas Halstead's fault.

* * *

Convenien...
is part of the Se...
When you have it all...

D1076864

CONVENIENT
CINDERELLA BRIDE

BY
JOSS WOOD

First Published in Great Britain 2017
By Mills & Boon, an imprint of HarperCollins*Publishers*
1 London Bridge Street, London, SE1 9GF

© 2017 Harlequin Books S.A.

Special thanks and acknowledgement are given to Joss Wood for her contribution to the Secrets of the A-List series.

ISBN: 978-0-263-92836-5

51-0917

Printed and bound in Spain
by CPI, Barcelona

Joss Wood loves books and traveling—especially to the wild places of southern Africa. She has the domestic skills of a potted plant and drinks far too much coffee.

Joss has written for Mills & Boon Modern Tempted, Mills & Boon Modern and, most recently, the Mills & Boon Desire line. After a career in business, she now writes full-time. Joss is a member of the Romance Writers of America and Romance Writers of South Africa.

One

Another month, another breakfast. How many of these business breakfasts had they shared? Jonas Halstead had been the CEO of Halstead & Sons for five years… He did the calculation. Sixty Wednesday breakfasts.

Sixty three-hour meetings with the man commonly known as "The White Shark of the West Coast." Jack was reputed to be the most ruthless, occasionally morally ambiguous, businessman on this side of the country. He was also Jonas's grandfather, and Jonas would rather be water-boarded than sit through this monthly meeting.

When he'd first started as CEO he'd banned his staff from dealing directly with the chairman of the board because few people could deal with Jack's harsh manner, his interrogations and his dire warnings about possible disaster situations. Few, even those who were corporate animals, could handle Jack's aggression and his pursuit of perfection. Jonas had long ago realized that if he wanted to keep his key staff then he had to shield them from Jack.

But that meant it was his ass in the hot seat.

Jonas was a big boy, being paid the big bucks. He could deal with Jack. But, hell, he could not wait for the day when he could run Halstead & Sons without Jack's constant input and criticism. Thanks to Jack's ruthlessness and Jonas's father's reputation for cutting corners, the Halstead name was not one to be trusted, and while that didn't bother Jack in the least—*Let the bastards fear us, it's good for business!*—Jonas hated having his word doubted, his integrity questioned. He was a hard, tough businessman. He drove a hard bargain. But when he gave his word, he kept it. Always.

His family had a reputation for doing legal but morally dodgy deals, for losing their integrity in pursuit of the mighty dollar. Promises were broken; lies were told. Seeing the instinctual mistrust on the faces of his investors, suppliers and competitors burned a hole in his stomach and still, quietly and secretly, embarrassed the hell out of him. He was determined to rehabilitate the company's reputation and was just as committed to establishing his own reputation as a man whose word could be trusted.

He thought, maybe, that he was making progress, but it was taking a hell of a long time.

Having Jack still serving as chairman of the board didn't help. But, dammit, it was Jack's company, and until he decided to release the reins, Jonas could only manage the old man. And keep his treasured staff away from him.

Jonas walked up the steps to Jack's palatial, beachside home on the prestigious Palisade Beach Road in Santa Monica. The house had been in the Halstead family for many generations, long before Hollywood's elite had discovered the area. Jonas had grown up here. Well, in this house and the one next door, spending his time between his father's and grandfather's mansions, a motherless boy looking for attention from his disinterested father and demanding grandfather.

Jonas entered the spacious hallway and greeted Henry, his grandfather's man-about-the-house. Wanting to get this meeting over with, Jonas made his way through the Spanish Colonial Revival mansion to the outside entertainment area with its one-hundred-eighty-degree view of the beach and the ocean. The wind was up and the waves were high, perfect conditions for a bit of surfing or kitesurfing. Jonas jogged down the steps from the entertainment area to the tiled patio at the edge of the property, which held comfortable chairs and expensive outdoor furniture. Despite the distance from the kitchen, this tree-shaded spot was Jack's favorite place to dine.

His grandfather sat at the head of the table, his hand wrapped around a coffee cup, his glasses perched on the end of his nose, reading the business section of the paper, a daily habit of his. Jack liked his habits, in business and in his personal life. He wasn't fond of people—sons, grandsons, colleagues and staff—coloring outside the lines. Jonas's fluid, going-with-his-gut way of managing Halstead & Sons was a constant source of irritation to his grandfather. Jack could be as disapproving as he liked, but he couldn't argue with the numbers; since taking over as CEO of Halstead five years ago, cash flow and profits had steadily increased.

Jonas noticed Preston McIntyre. Why was Jack's lawyer eating with them? Jonas shook Preston's hand and slid a glance in Jack's direction. He immediately recognized the stubborn I'll-get-to-it-when-I'm-ready expression. There was no point in pushing; the old man was as stubborn as a mule. Which grated, since Jonas was a get-it-done-now type of guy.

Jonas pulled out a chair from the table. "Morning, Jack."

He'd been Grandpa Jack when Jonas had been younger, but it had been a while since he'd called his grandfather anything but his given name. Jack wasn't the sentimental type. "Jonas. Have some breakfast."

Jonas reached for the fruit salad.

"How is Cliff House coming along?" Jack demanded, his eyes flashing.

The Cliff House was their newest project, a rambling, neglected property that had once been the most luxurious hotel in Santa Barbara. That had been in the 1920s and it was now just a mess and a money pit. But it had awesome views and potential, and, best of all, Jonas had bought the property out from under Harrison Marshall's nose. Harrison might be a world-renowned chef, restaurateur and family friend, but going onto his turf and snagging a property he'd desperately wanted had been fun. And it had been a clean snatch; a simple offer of more money that the owner had quickly accepted.

"On time and on budget," Jonas replied, knowing that was all Jack wanted to hear. And it was the truth. He ran a tight ship.

"That's the least I expect," Jack snapped, eyes flashing. "Elaborate."

Jonas gave Jack his verbal report, his eyes flicking to the smaller but still impressive house next door. The windows were locked and the drapes were closed. That meant his father was in Europe looking for art that could be added to his already extensive collection.

Such wealth, Jonas thought, was attached to his surname. The houses, the cars…the option not to work another day in his life—that's the choice his father had made.

Jonas shuddered. Work was what gave his life meaning, how he filled his days. It provided the context of his life, the framework that kept him sane. For him, having nothing to do would be a nightmare.

He was too driven, too intense, too ambitious. In that way, he was like his grandfather. A focused workaholic determined to grow the family company under his stewardship. Besides, what else would he do with his time? He didn't have—didn't want—a wife and kids, and he didn't play golf.

Jonas wondered, as he often did, if he would be as driven if he'd had a gentler upbringing, if he hadn't had his father and grandfather riding him to do better, to be better. They'd both assumed he would be the future of the company, the fifth Halstead to run their multigenerational empire. A lot of emphasis had been placed on his performance; success was praised, failure was disparaged and a perceived lack of effort ignited tempers. Jack had encouraged independence of thought and deed, and winning at all costs. Lane, his father, didn't believe in expressing any emotion. As a child, Jonas had learned to suppress his feelings. They were tools his father used to mock or denigrate him. It was easier, he'd discovered, to avoid emotional neediness in both himself and others.

Jack asked him another series of questions and Jonas concentrated on the here and now. There was no point in looking back, it didn't achieve anything. And since Jack was, technically, Jonas's boss, he needed to concentrate. His position was reasonably secure. He'd pulled the company into the twenty-first century and both stocks and profit margins were up. He had the Halstead name, but he didn't own the company. Yet.

Jack leaned back in his chair, asked Jonas to pour coffee and Jonas complied. Preston had said nothing for the past half hour and Jonas wondered, again, why he was there. Preston gave him an uneasy look, and Jonas knew he was about to find out. And he wasn't going to like it.

What was his wily grandfather plotting?

Jonas watched his grandfather, who was looking down the beach.

Jack's deep green eyes, the same color as Jonas's, eventually settled on his grandson's face. "I am rewriting my will."

Jonas felt his stomach knot. Dammit, again? They went through this every five years or so. As far as Jonas knew, he would inherit Jack's shares in the company and his father would inherit a massive life insurance policy and most of Jack's personal properties, excluding this house.

"This property and my shares in the company will all be yours."

Good. He'd be pissed if he'd worked sixteen hours a day for more than a decade for nothing. "Thank you," he said, knowing that was the only response Jack wanted or would tolerate.

"But…"

Oh, crap.

"…only if you marry within the next ninety days."

What the hell?

It took every iota of Jonas's self-control not to react. He wanted to leap to his feet, slam his hands on the table and demand that Jack explain his crazy statement. He wanted to ask his grandfather if he'd lost his marbles. But the only gesture of annoyance he allowed himself was the tightening of his grip around his coffee cup.

"That's a hell of a demand, Jack," Jonas said, danger creeping into his tone. "Does it come with an explanation?"

"You're pissed," Jack said, and Jonas caught the note of amusement in his voice.

"Wouldn't you be?" Jonas countered, straining to keep his tone even.

"Sure," Jack agreed. "You can be as pissed as you like, but I'm not changing my mind. You're going to marry or you lose it all."

Jonas rubbed his forehead, not quite believing how Jack had flipped Jonas's life on its head in the space of five minutes. Jonas turned to Preston. "Is this legal?"

Preston sent him a sympathetic look. "They are his assets. He's allowed to disperse them any way he likes. It's blackmail but its legal blackmail."

Preston narrowed his eyes at his client and Jonas's respect for the lawyer increased.

"I've made up my mind," Jack said, ignoring his lawyer's comment. "Marry in ninety days and I will sign over everything to you, giving you complete control of the company and ownership of this house. That way we'll avoid paying the state a ridiculous amount of money in estate tax. All you have to do is marry."

"And if I don't?"

"Your father will inherit my shares. He wants them and feels they're his right as the next in line." Jack's voice was as hard as nails. "He has expressed his wish to return to the company."

Jonas struggled to look through the red mist in front

of his eyes. He hastily bit back the words *over my dead body*.

"He is a Halstead, Jonas. He says he's bored, that it's time for him to come back and take his place as the next Halstead to run our company."

But Lane stole from the company to support his gambling habit! The words were on the tip of Jonas's tongue but he couldn't voice them. Who was he protecting by keeping Lane's secret? Jack? His father? Himself?

"He walked away, Jack." It was all he could say in protest.

"He's still a talented businessman. And my son."

"And all the work I've done in the years since he left has meant nothing? You'd do this without my consent?" Jonas saw the answer on Jack's face and shook his head. "You're a piece of work."

Jack just shrugged. "My first priority will always be what I think is best for Halstead."

Of course it was, God forbid that he put his grandson's wishes before his company. "You have done a reasonable job with the company," Jack continued, "but what, or who, comes after you? In your twenties, you dated extensively and I wasn't worried. I believed you needed time to sow your wild oats. But you're about to turn thirty-five, you've never brought a girl home to meet me and I'm concerned you will never settle down."

"You've been single for more than fifty years, so I think it's a bit hypocritical for you to judge my lifestyle," Jonas pointed out.

"I was married. I produced a Halstead heir and Lane did the same. You have not. You should be married. You should have had a child or two by now."

"These days, people are marrying and having children later in life, Jack!"

Jack glared at him. "I want to see you married. I want to see your child. I want to be assured that the Halstead fortune will not pass out of our bloodline."

"I'm surprised you didn't demand that I produce a child in three months, as well," Jonas snapped.

"I'm not *that* demanding. That being said, if you marry, then there's a good chance children will come from the union," Jack said, stubbornness in every word he spoke. "Eventually. And I know you well enough to know that you'd hate, as much as I do, the idea of Halstead money, generations of effort and hard work, benefiting someone not of our bloodline."

Bloodline? Jack sounded like a medieval lord talking about his estates. "This isn't sixteenth century England, Jack. And I do not appreciate you meddling in my private life!"

"Pffft! Arranged marriages have worked for hundreds of years before love clouded the issue. It's simple, Jonas. Marry and I will give you Halstead. Do not and deal with your father."

Jonas muttered a low curse. Jack knew exactly what buttons to push; he knew Jonas would do anything to keep his father out of the company and that he wanted complete control of Halstead & Sons.

But there was a price to that freedom and the price was marriage. The one thing he'd planned to avoid for as long as possible.

But Jack had left him without a choice. It was Jack's way or the highway.

Jonas pushed his chair back, tossed his linen napkin onto the table and leaned across to shake Preston's hand. He ignored his grandfather, too angry with him to speak. He started to walk away but Jack's voice followed him.

"Well, what are you going to do?" he demanded.

Jonas relished the note of uncertainty in his voice.

He slowly turned and eyed his elderly relative, his smile cold. "I'll guess you'll find out in three months. You can wait until then."

Katrina Morrison slid her hand beneath her hair and, discreetly, pushed her finger under the seam of her dress, moving the still attached price tag in the hope that it would stop scratching her skin. How she wished she was in the position to yank the tag off and be done with it. But Tess, her best friend, who happened to be the manager of The Hanger—a downtown Santa Barbara boutique selling designer dresses—would slap her silly if she did that. Tess still had to sell the dresses Kat had "borrowed."

God knew what Tess would do if she ripped the dress or spilled wine or food on it. Katrina would probably be tarred and feathered at dawn.

Or, worse, she'd have to pay for the dress. And she didn't have a thousand-plus dollars to spare. Even if she did have that sort of cash lying around, Kat doubted she'd spend it on a mid-thigh, sleeveless, pleated dress that was so understated it screamed "expensive." But appearances, especially when you were the host at El Acantilado, the award-winning and flagship restaurant owned by America's favorite chef and entrepreneur, Harrison Marshall, were everything. El Acantilado's patrons expected a unique and expensive dining experience. Kat was the first person to welcome them into the restaurant, and her first impression had to be favorable. Hence the designer dress, expertly applied makeup, glossy lips and black suede three-inch heels.

She was happiest in a pair of faded jeans and a

T-shirt, her nearly waist-length hair in a ponytail or a braid and her face makeup-free, but this job paid the bills. If dressing up like a fashion model was what was required, she'd do it.

Kat tapped her pen against her leather-bound reservations book and looked into the wood-and-steel restaurant to watch the waitstaff. The newest waiter, Fred, seemed stressed, his hand wobbling as he placed Harrison's iconic roasted duck between the solid silver cutlery in front of Senator Cordell. Thank goodness he wasn't serving Elana Marshall, Harrison's daughter, who was sitting at the best table in the house with Jarrod Jones.

Hmm, Elana wasn't dining with her long-term boyfriend Thom. Jarrod's wife, the feted Irish actress Finola, was also missing.

God, Kat could make a fortune selling celebrity gossip to tabloid newspapers. They'd made her offers before, promised her anonymity, and she'd desperately needed the money.

Kat sighed. Selling gossip would be an easy solution to her financial woes. Damn her integrity and self-respect.

Kat smiled as Fred walked passed Elana's table, his gaze sliding sideways. The waitstaff was expected to turn a blind eye, to not notice a damn thing, but Fred was young and a little starstruck. And, really, since Elana Marshall looked like the millions of bucks she was reputed to be worth in that barely there dress highlighting her cleavage, how could Fred not notice that impressive rack, that fabulous face and those pouty lips?

Hadn't Kat, when she'd first started as a waitress years ago, been equally impressed by the star power that lit up the room? She'd stuttered when she'd first spoken to Angel Morales, the hottest and most talented celebrity around. She'd blushed when the younger Windsor brother had thanked her, very nicely, for a wonderful dining experience. She'd nearly fainted when a table of Oscar nominees had left her a two-thousand-dollar tip.

After serving so many wealthy and famous people, she was no longer easily impressed, and that was why she'd been promoted to the position of hostess a year or so ago. Harrison Marshall had personally promoted her, his decision based, he'd told her, on her popularity with his well-heeled clients. She was polite and personable, but she didn't fawn or simper. His clients, Harrison had said, liked that. They, apparently, liked her.

Kat looked down at her book and then at her watch. The Henleys were late, but then, they always were. Jonas Halstead and guest would be arriving within five minutes, and he was always on time.

Kat idly wondered who Jonas would be with tonight. By her calculations, the blond pop sensation he'd been dating for the past three months had reached her sell-by date, and there would be another girl on his arm tonight. Jonas, the billionaire property developer specializing in hotels and casinos, was a repeat visitor to El Acantilado over the past year. He'd recently bought Cliff House and was renovating the iconic Santa Barbara hotel. Rumor had it that he'd out-negotiated Harrison Marshall for the property, which suggested that Halstead was a hell of a businessman...or a shark.

Kat sighed. Tough businessman or not, his was the world she wanted to be in. The one she'd been destined for. The one that still beckoned to her. But, at twenty-eight years old, she was still working here and the closest she'd come to the world of finance was to show billionaire businessmen like Jonas Halstead to his table.

God. How sad.

"Katrina."

Kat's head snapped up and she silently cursed when she realized Jonas was standing in front of her, impeccably dressed in a black designer suit worn over a rain-gray, open-necked shirt. Her eyes traveled up, across a broad chest and wide shoulders, along a tanned neck, to a strong jaw covered with two-day-old stubble and a mouth that was slow to smile but still sexy. He had a long, straight nose and deep green eyes under strong brows. Rich, successful and hot.

He had the reputation for being a bit of a bastard, in business and in bed. That fact only dropped his sexy factor by a quarter of a percent.

"Mr. Halstead, welcome back to El Acantilado," Kat murmured, ignoring her jumping heart and squirrelly stomach. Yeah, he was built and so damn handsome, but geez, she wasn't a twenty-two-year-old waitress anymore.

"Call me Jonas."

It wasn't the first time he'd made the offer, but Kat had no intention of accepting. It wasn't professional to call him by his first name, and not doing so kept a very healthy distance between her and the Jonas Halsteads of the world. Like her ex-husband and like her father, rich guys in fancy suits were not to be trusted.

Then again, what man could be?

But it really annoyed Kat that Jonas did funny things to her stomach and made her heart jump.

Fast, furious sexual attraction had led to her falling in love with and marrying Wes, and since he'd ended up using her heart as a Ping-Pong ball, she didn't trust her pheromones' ability to pick men wisely.

But every time she saw Jonas, her libido loudly reminded her that she hadn't had sex in a very long time. Jonas Halstead would be damn good at sex. He'd had, it was said, a lot of practice.

But tonight he was here alone. "Is your guest not joining you tonight?"

Jonas placed his hands in the pockets of his suit pants. "Rowan will be joining me shortly."

Kat widened her eyes in surprise. He was dating Rowan Greenly? The actress had just separated from her very volatile husband after a domestic abuse charge, and the hot-tempered rock star had threatened to kill anyone who made a move on his wife.

"You're brave. I suggest you wear a bulletproof vest," Kat couldn't help murmuring, even though she knew she was being indiscreet. "Rock likes his guns."

Jonas frowned, confused. Then his austere face softened as he released a low chuckle.

A thousand sparks danced on her skin as his smile turned his face from remote-but-still-hot to oh-my-God-I-want-to-rip-his-clothes-off. Kat placed her fist under her sternum and resisted the urge to scrunch her eyes shut.

No. God, no. She couldn't have the screaming hots for Jonas Halstead. She'd married, and divorced, a ruthless and merciless man. A competitive and cutthroat billionaire should be the last person to interest her. She was avoiding the male species in general, and the hot and sexy ones in particular.

Jonas was not her type.

The front door to the restaurant pulled open and all six feet and five inches of the best basketball talent in the country stepped into the restaurant. Rowan Brady. God, of course it was.

Kat glanced at Jonas, who lifted one dark eyebrow. "My date."

Rowan joined them, clasping Jonas's shoulder as he did. "Joe, we've known each other since we were kids and I keep telling you you're not my type."

Kat heard the teasing note in Rowan's deep voice and blushed as his dark eyes settled on her face. "And I'm curious as to why you'd want this gorgeous creature to think that I am."

Jonas slid Rowan a droll look. "Katrina thought I was meeting Rowan Greenly."

Rowan shuddered. "You have more sense than that. She's hot but her husband is psycho."

Jonas pulled his hands from his pockets and placed his forearms on her counter, the fabric of his suit bunching around impressive biceps. Kat lifted an eyebrow of her own, annoyed that she could easily imagine pushing that jacket off his shoulders and down his arms, ripping that shirt apart to find out whether his skin was as hot as she imagined.

She swallowed a moan. It was time to do her job. "Let me take you to your table, Mr. Halstead."

"Since you felt comfortable enough to make assumptions about my love life, you should be comfortable enough to call me Jonas. Or Joe."

Kat walked around the podium and gestured to the already full dining room. She deliberately ignored his provoking statement and his friend's amused expression. "I've placed you by the window. It has the most wonderful view of the beach below. This way, gentlemen." Kat started the familiar walk into the restaurant, forcing her expression into one of calm serenity.

Please don't look at my ass, Kat thought as Jonas fell into step behind her. *Or, if you do, please like it.*

For God's sake, Katrina! What is wrong with you?
"You have a—"

Thankful they were at his table, Kat turned and waited for his cocky comment.

But Jonas said nothing. He just moved to stand behind her, his height and width dwarfing her. He lifted his hand to her neck and Kat felt the tips of his fingers graze her skin. He barely made contact but suddenly her feet were glued to the floor and every cell in her body was set to vibrate. If he kissed her she'd spontaneously combust. She was sure of it.

Jonas twisted his hand and quickly snapped off the tag to her dress and held it up. "You obviously forgot to take it off. Here you go."

Kat's eyes bounced between the tag in his hand and his eyes, horror smothering the burning attraction she felt for the man.

Oh, crap, oh, crap, oh, crap. He'd ripped the tag when he pulled it off and she wouldn't be able to reattach it.

Oh, God, Tess had made it very clear that the bar code had to remain intact, that it could not be reproduced. Kat wouldn't be able to return the dress.

Her stomach climbed up her throat and lodged behind her tonsils. She was quite certain the air in the room was fast disappearing.

"Are you okay?" Jonas asked from a place far away. "Katrina?"

His voice pulled her back from the abyss, just a foot or so, enough for her to get some air into her lungs and oxygen to her brain.

You can't faint. You can't yell at him. You can't even react.

You need this damn job.

But she couldn't speak. She was unable to command

her tongue to form even the smallest response. Intellectually she knew he thought he'd been doing her a favor, but his assumption had just piled another suitcase of stress onto the load she was already struggling to carry. Was this the straw that would break her back?

Kat suspected it might be. She snatched the tag from Jonas's hand and spun on her heel, praying she made it to the staff restroom without throwing up.

She now owed more than a thousand dollars on a dress she couldn't afford and it was Jonas Halstead's fault.

God, sexy man or not, if he had been eating with Rowan Greenly, Kat would have called Rowan's psycho husband and told him where to find Jonas.

And she would have suggested he bring his biggest gun.

Two

Kat, reaching her desk at the entrance of the restaurant and its adjoining bar, looked at the rows of liquor above the bartender's head and wished she could order something long, strong and alcoholic. Her eyes danced across a group in the corner, a girl and four guys, all pierced and tattooed. They were drinking the Mariella, the world-famous cocktail named after Harrison's wife. She could do with a Mariella, or three, right now. Actually she could really do with one of Mariella Santiago-Marshall's limitless, solid black credit cards or access to her bank account.

Crap. What the hell was she going to *do*?

"Please, *please* tell me you'd left the tag on the dress as a mistake—that you weren't planning on returning it in the morning."

Kat spun around and blinked at the multicolored creature standing in front of her. Her dress was a slinky cocktail number with a plunging neck and spaghetti straps the color of lemon sorbet. It was the perfect foil for the ink on her body. Pulling her eyes up from the amazing artwork, Kat looked into an elfin face dominated by a pair of warm brown eyes. The woman had a series of piercings in her lower lip and along her eyebrow; she had a tiny butterfly tattoo on her temple.

"You look amazing," Kat said. She sighed. It was obviously her night for allowing her mouth to run away with her.

"Thank you. But you didn't answer my question. Were you returning the dress?"

Kat looked into the restaurant and scowled in Halstead's direction. She never discussed one customer with another, but this woman would join her equally inked friends in the bar—birds of a feather—and she didn't see the harm in answering her question. Kat could spot a trust-fund baby at sixty paces and this woman was not one of them.

She lowered her voice. "Yes, it's borrowed. I was returning it in the morning. Now I'm going to have to pay for it, which was never the damned plan." Not sure what it was about this painted fairy that had her spilling her secrets, Kat continued, "God, I could just kill him. I don't have a thousand dollars to spend on a dress! I don't have a thousand dollars, full stop!"

"Thirteen hundred." The girl bit her lip. "It's a Callisto. Thirteen ninety-five, including tax."

Kat resisted the urge to bang her head against her desk. She swore, softly. "Dammit. I swear, I don't care that he's as sexy as sin and hotter than the sun, he's a stupid, idiot man!"

Before the painted fairy could reply, Elana Marshall interrupted their conversation by placing a hand on Kat's shoulder.

Kat spun around and smiled at the youngest Marshall and prayed that Elana hadn't heard her last emphatic statement. "Hi, Elana, did you have a nice evening?"

The dimple in Elana's cheek flashed. "I did. Thanks, Kat."

Elana looked at Pixie Girl, her eyes bouncing from tat to tat, her mouth curving upward. "Love the angel on your arm." Without waiting for a response, Elana turned her attention back to Kat. "So who is the idiot man?"

Kat wanted to scrunch her eyes shut in mortification. She and Elana were friends, sort of, in a "hey, how are you" sort of way. Elana was an heiress and Kat was Elana's father's employee. Kat's eyes darted to Pixie Girl, silently begging her not to answer. She didn't want Elana Marshall, who was the ultimate trust-fund baby, to know that her dress was on loan.

Pixie Girl smiled. "Aren't they all, at one time or another?"

Elana nodded. "Pretty much. And here is one of mine." Kat smiled at Elana's date and thought that Elana could do a lot better than the married casting director. She could also do better than her fiancé, Thom, who was really nice but…not for Elana. She needed someone with a personality as strong as hers.

But Kat had bigger problems to worry about than her boss's daughter's complicated love life. She had a job to do…a job she needed now more than ever.

Kat said good-night to Elana and turned back to the vision standing in front of her. "I am *so* sorry, you've been standing here forever. Let me walk you to the bar."

Pixie Girl grinned. "Actually, I'm joining Jonas Halstead's table."

Kat groaned and wondered if there was any way this night could get worse.

"Yeah," said Pixie Girl. "I'm meeting my boss and his friend for dinner."

"Please tell me that you work for Rowan Brady," Kat begged her.

She smiled, giving Kat a flash of her tongue stud. "Nope. I'm Sian and I work for Jonas Halstead."

Well, she had wondered whether this evening could get any worse.

Yep, Life answered her, *challenge accepted.*

The next morning, after a night long on worry and light on sleep, Kat heard the sound of a key in a lock. She brushed her hands across her wet cheekbones and rubbed her hands over her thighs, transferring her tears onto her old yoga pants. She heard the familiar thump of Tess's heavy bag hitting the floor and then her friend, with copper hair and freckles, stepped into Kat's small sitting area, holding—bless her—two cups of coffee.

"Yay, you're awake. I didn't know if you would be," Tess said, handing Kat a cup. "I got your text message this morning so I thought I'd pop in and see what the 'catastrophe' was." Tess sat next to Kat and peered into her face. "God, have you slept? At all?"

"I got home after midnight and I was too wound up for sleep." Not wanting to delay the bad news, she nodded at the designer dress lying over the chair. "I need to pay for the dress."

Tess's mouth dropped open. "Oh, crap, why?"

"Last night a guest, thinking he was being helpful, pulled the tag off," Kat told her, her voice flat. "The tag is toast."

Tess softly swore and wrinkled her nose. "Dammit,

Kat, if you'd spilled something on it we could've had it cleaned. If it ripped, I would've had it mended, but I can't give a reasonable explanation as to why the label was ripped off."

Kat held up her hand. "I get it, Tess, I do. Stupid Jonas Halstead."

"The property mogul and one of California's hottest bachelors?" Tess's eyes widened. "He's an idiot for pulling the label off but, oh, my God, he's so sexy."

"He might be but he's put me in a hell of a position," Kat grumbled. "How soon do you need the money?"

Tess thought for a minute. "Miranda is away on vacation in Cancun for a month. So, basically, you have that long. And if you give me the money, I'll buy it and that way you'll get the staff discount. It's not much, only ten percent off, but it'll help."

Kat squeezed her knee. "Thanks, Tess." She rested her head on the back of her couch and closed her eyes.

"Or I can pay for it from my savings and you can pay me back," Tess added.

"Ah, Tess." It was a sweet offer. It didn't matter that Tess was her oldest friend. She couldn't accept her help. Thanks to her father and her ex-husband, Kat had massive issues around money. And trust.

It was easier, safer, cleaner, to go it alone.

Tess placed her coffee cup on the battered table with a thump. "You can't keep this up, Kat. You can't keep trying to do it all. You've even dropped weight. Are you eating?"

She ate at the restaurant most nights, with the chefs at the end of a shift. In between she lived on coffee and fresh air.

"Kat, something has got to change," Tess insisted, sitting on the edge of the seat.

"But what, Tess?" Kat demanded, resting her elbows on her knees. "The house June lives in is mine but my evil stepmom has the right to use it for the rest of her life and, in the terms of the will, I have to pay for the utilities and the upkeep. I have to carry the costs on a property I can't sell or use to get a loan."

"Why the hell didn't your dad leave you any cash?"

"Because he thought that, by the time he died, I'd have a kick-ass, high-paying job. He also knew I had a rich husband to take care of me. He thought that if I couldn't pay for the house, Wes would pay for what I needed. I had someone to look after me. June did not."

"Your ex was such a psycho," Tess muttered, her expression dark.

Yep, beneath that charming all-American-boy exterior lived a sardonic, selfish narcissist who thought the sun disappeared when he sat.

"Okay, there's nothing you can do about the house but I don't understand why you are taking on the burden of Cath's medical bills," Tess stated, taking a sip of her coffee. She waved her hand. "I understand why you feel obliged to—when your mom died and your dad remarried Cruella, your aunt was there for you— but Cath is financially stable."

Kat pushed her hands into her hair. "She's really not, Tess. She has insurance but it's limited. Her cancer is rare and complicated and requires treatments her insurance doesn't cover. She's also paying for a full-time caregiver, which has wiped out the little disposable income she has." Kat shrugged. "So, between June's demands on the repairs to the house and sending cash Cath's way, I'm flat broke."

"Is she getting better?"

Kat felt her heart spasm as she shook her head. "I

need her to see a specialist, but even if there wasn't a ridiculously long waiting list, they always seem to want money up front to cover the cost of her tests."

Kat rubbed the back of her neck and looked around her small but cozy apartment. It was her favorite place in the world, a haven of color, the place where she could relax. After leaving the restaurant last night she'd returned home and spent a few hours crunching numbers on a spreadsheet.

One column held a list of expenses: rent, utility bills and food for herself; the repairs, maintenance and utility bills for the home her stepmom occupied; projected figures for Cath's medical expenses.

The other column, woefully small, held her income. There was a massive shortfall between the two amounts and she'd had yet to include paying for the damn dress.

God, how she wished she could roll back the years. She wished she hadn't taken a gap year between school and college to travel Europe. She wished she hadn't met and—in a haze of lust—married Wes. She'd managed to complete her degree in business administration, but there were lots of people with the same degree. She needed her MBA to earn the big bucks that would keep her head above water.

Over the past four years she'd managed to scrape together enough money to earn some credits toward her postgrad degree, but she still had a few courses to do. And she had to write her Leadership and Corporate Accountability exam in a few months. God knew when she was going to get time to study for that.

Yesterday she'd been treading water financially, but with a designer dress to pay for, she was now sinking below the surface. Tess was right. Something had to change, and fast. But what?

"I'm going to have to move," Kat reluctantly stated. "I'd save some money if I did. I can move back in with Cath."

Cath would love to have her and would refuse to charge her rent. If she did move back in, she could keep a better eye on Cath and monitor her health. But… damn, this apartment was her bolt-hole, her escape, the only place that was completely hers.

"This apartment block is owned by Harrison Marshall. Can't you ask the company to give you a break, to carry you for a month or two?" Tess asked.

Not possible. "They already give me a subsidy on my rent as part of my salary. I can't ask for more."

"So, essentially, you have a month to find the money to pay for the dress and to try to keep this apartment."

A month? God. "When you put it like that I want to bang my head against the wall," Kat muttered.

"Maybe something will come up. You never know."

"And I believe in unicorns and fairies…" Kat murmured, feeling utterly defeated. "God, Tess, for the first time ever, I'm totally out of ideas. What the hell am I going to do?"

Tess's eyes were full of compassion. "You're going to keep on believing that something amazing will happen. You're going to use your big brain and find a way because you are the smartest woman I know." Tess stood, took Kat's coffee from her hand and placed it on the coffee table. Pulling a throw off the single chair and then patting a pillow she placed against the arm of the sofa, she said, "But right now, you're going to sleep for a couple of hours."

"I've got stuff to do," Kat protested, her eyes heavy at just the mention of sleep.

"You need to decompress and you really need sleep,"

Tess insisted and watched as Kat curled her legs up onto the sofa and rested her head on the cushion. "You can't think straight without sleep, my darling. When you wake up, you'll feel so much better and you'll think of a solution."

God, she hoped so, Kat thought, closing her eyes. She was just about to drift off when she heard, once again, Tess's footsteps on her floor. "What did you lose, Tess?"

"Uh...it's not what I lost but what I found on your doorstep."

Hearing a note in Tess's voice that was a curious combination of both surprise and confusion, Kat forced her eyes open. She saw his feet first, trendy navy sneakers worn without socks. Indigo denim slacks covered muscular, long legs and a leather belt encircled a trim waist and what she suspected might be a washboard stomach. A striped blue-and-white shirt was tucked in and made his chest seem wider, his shoulders broader. The cuffs of his expensive shirt were rolled up to reveal tanned forearms and a Rolex encircling a strong wrist. His cotton shirt pulled tight across his big biceps and the collar of his shirt opened in a V to reveal a hint of his chest covered in a light dusting of hair.

Green, green eyes, messy hair, that sexy stubble on his strong jaw. Man, what had she done to deserve Jonas Halstead standing in her apartment at 8:05 a.m.?

Kat slowly sat upright and frowned when she saw Tess backing away. Huh, so Tess wasn't sticking around for moral support. She frowned at her friend, who shrugged. "I have to get to work. I'm late as it is. Sorry," Tess explained, walking backward into the hall.

Sorry? She didn't look sorry at all. Kat slapped her bare feet onto the floor and stood, wishing she didn't look like a bag lady on a bad day. She ran her tongue over her teeth and pushed her hand into her hair, sighing when her hand snagged on a knot. Really? This was now her life?

Kat forced herself to meet Jonas Halstead's amused eyes. "What on earth are you doing here? How did you find me?"

He reached into the back pocket of his pants and tossed a check onto her coffee table. "Fourteen hundred dollars. It's to pay for the dress I ruined."

Bloody Sian. Kat had thought she'd keep her mouth shut! Dammit. Kat looked at the check, sighed and decided to lie her ass off. "I have no idea what you are talking about."

Jonas jammed his hands into the pockets of his pants and narrowed his eyes at her. "The hell you don't. You borrowed a designer dress. You were going to return it. I pulled the tag off, which, as Sian told me, was a stupid ass thing to do. You are now on the hook for fourteen hundred dollars. I'm taking you off the hook."

Kat looked at the check, back up to his determined face and back down to the check again. God, it was so tempting to take his money. It had been his fault. He had pulled the tag off and it wasn't like he couldn't afford the donation. He was Jonas Halstead, billionaire.

But it was still a donation and she didn't accept charity, ever. She especially didn't take handouts from sexy men who threw cash around like it was confetti. Nothing was simple when it came to money and motives should always be questioned. Nobody, especially hard-assed businessmen, handed out money without wanting something in return.

Between her ex and her father, she was sick of men and the games they played with money. Kat folded her arms across her chest and shook her head. "I'm not going to cash your check."

Shock ran across his face, through his eyes. "What?"

"I'm not taking your money." Kat spoke slowly, as if she were her explaining her position to a three-year-old. "I chose to wear the dress, even knowing that I couldn't afford to pay for it if something went wrong. Something did go wrong, but it's my problem, not yours."

"The hell it is!" Jonas snapped back, his green eyes flashing with frustration. "I should not have been presumptuous enough to take the tag off."

"Maybe not, but I'm still not taking your money," Kat told him, feeling stubborn.

"Consider it a tip," Jonas suggested, matching her bullishness with a healthy dose of his own.

"Too late for that," Kat said. "Thanks for the offer but…no."

"You are the most infuriating, annoying, frustrating, sexy…"

Kat hauled in a breath when he said the last word and their eyes clashed and held. One little word and something hot and crazy buzzed between them. The air around them seemed to thicken and tighten, filling with electricity. God, he was as attracted to her as she was to him. She saw it in the way he clenched and unclenched his fists, in the green fire in his eyes. If she took one step toward him she'd be in his arms. She'd feel the heat and strength of him. She would know whether his sexy lips felt as good as they looked, whether sparks would jump from her skin under the warmth of his hands.

She wanted him. Annoying, cash-on-the-table cretin that he was, she wanted to taste him, feel him, make love to him. She was losing her mind; she was sure of it. Too much stress and not enough sleep…this crazi-ness was the result.

Kat heard Jonas snap out a swear word, heard his "This is insane" mutter. Then his hand breached the space between them and his fingers encircled her wrist. He held her lightly, giving her the opportunity to pull out of his grip if she so wanted.

She didn't.

Instead Kat allowed him to pull her in. She didn't step away when his hand rested on her lower back and jerked her hips into his, allowing her to feel the hard length of his erection pushing into her stomach. His other hand covered her right breast; his thumb finding her nipple with deadly accuracy. He hadn't even kissed her yet and her panties were damp.

If he didn't kiss her she would die. From want, need, sheer frustration. Kat stood on her tiptoes, her mouth aligned with his. Not bothering to be coy, she slammed her lips onto his, her tongue darting out to trace the seam, to tempt him to open up.

This wasn't her, Kat thought from a place far away. She waited for men to make the first move, to kiss her, to lead. She followed. But not today.

Jonas swiped her nipple with his thumb, held her tight against him and let her kiss him. When he didn't open his mouth or kiss her back, Kat, unsure of what she was doing or whether she should be doing this at all, started to pull away. Jonas growled a harsh *no* against her mouth and moved his hand from her breast to the back of her head to keep her in place. She wasn't going anywhere, Kat realized, and when his mouth started to move, she also realized she didn't want to.

Jonas Halstead was kissing her. It was candy floss and crack, sunshine and sin, pleasure and pain. He took command of her mouth, his tongue tangling with hers in a sexy dance. Kat, senseless, pulled his shirt from the back of his pants and put her hands on his hot, masculine skin. Jonas groaned his pleasure and she ran her palms over his gorgeous ass, annoyed at the barrier of clothes between her fingers and his flesh.

Jonas kissed the corner of her mouth and trailed his lips over her jaw, down her neck. It had been a long time since a man had kissed her liked this, touched her like she was something infinitely precious and incandescently gorgeous. She'd missed this. His teeth scraped across her collarbone. The tiny sting and the wave of pleasure made Kat's eyes fly open. Her gaze landed on the dress.

The one he'd just offered to pay for.

Kat stiffened in his arms as dismay swamped desire. Oh, God, did he think she was taking the money and this was her way of showing her gratitude? Did he think she was so easily manipulated? Did he think she was desperate, so eager to be with a man who was supposed to be brilliant at business? And in bed?

What the hell was wrong with her?

Kat jerked away from him and wrapped her hands around her waist.

"What did I do?"

Cynicism returned and Kat snorted, convinced he'd practiced that expression of puzzled surprise. "I'm not taking your check and, to be very clear, I'm not sleeping with you."

Jonas's eyes turned frosty. "I didn't make that assumption," he said, his soft voice holding an edge of danger. "And sex is not what I came for."

"Really?" Kat whipped out the words. "You didn't take very long to kiss me."

Jonas jammed his hands into the pockets of his jeans, those clever lips now thin with anger. "I'd like to point out that you didn't fight me off." He pulled on the tail of his shirt before tucking it back into his pants. "This shirt didn't pull itself loose."

Kat blushed, dropped her eyes and released an irritated sigh.

"Why are you mad, Katrina? Because I kissed you or because you liked it and wanted me to do more?"

Neither. Both. *Crap.*

Kat, feeling thoroughly off balance, brushed past him, deliberately connecting her shoulder with the top of his bicep before storming toward the hallway. Her attempt at intimidation had as much impact as a fly trying to move a cow.

When she reached her front door, she pulled it open and, when Jonas reached her, she gestured for him to keep on walking. "Just go."

"No. You're obviously upset and I want to know why."

She could never explain. For the first time in four years, for a few minutes in his arms, she'd felt protected, not so alone. She'd felt like the world wasn't conspiring against her, that life would get better, that things would eventually be okay. It had nothing to do with the check but everything to do with his strength, the power that radiated from him. He made her feel stronger...

God, he made her want to lean, to ask for help, to think that maybe, someday, she could trust someone again. Love someone again. He made her remember what attraction and pleasure and, dammit, what affection felt like. She'd deliberately pushed all of that away, locked all those emotions and memories in a box, refusing to look at them. Memories hurt, dammit.

But one kiss from Halstead had snapped that lock like it was made of spun sugar. She couldn't allow herself to look back; she couldn't afford to remember. It hurt too damn much. And, worse, it might tempt her to make the same mistakes she had before.

"Please go."

"Katrina…"

Kat was quite convinced that her head was one minute away from exploding. Anger rolled in—so much easier to deal with than fear. "My name," she yelled, "is Kat! I'm twenty-eight years old. I haven't had sex in four years. I'm flat broke and I've done no work to prepare for my LCA final! I'm exhausted and I don't need this! I have exactly one nerve left and you're friggin' standing on it. Go away!"

Kat felt her lungs pumping, heard the buzzing in her head and knew that if he attempted to speak again, she would kill him. Slowly. With her bare hands. It didn't matter that he was twice her size, she had so much adrenaline and unused sexual energy pumping around her system that she could take on a herd of angry hippos and win. Jonas Halstead didn't have a chance in hell.

Jonas sent her a you're-bat-crap-crazy look and walked into the hallway.

Kat slammed the door closed behind him and stomped through her living room into her bedroom. Climbing into bed, she pulled the covers over her head and wished she could just stay there for the rest of her life.

Because, dammit, Jonas Halstead's check was still on her coffee table. And because she was now, more than ever, tempted to cash it.

Three

Jonas looked up when Sian walked into his office and slammed the door behind her. He lifted his eyebrows, leaned back in his chair and waited for her to offload. He knew, from experience, that it wouldn't take long.

She went into all they had to do in their temporary office in Santa Barbara. The builders at Cliff House had found mold in the basement, the masons rebuilding the stone walkways were behind schedule and the anchor tenant destined for their new mall in Austin, Texas, now had cold feet. The investors for a ski resort in Whistler were uneasy—global downturn, less disposable income, global warming—and their head of human resources was moving to the East Coast.

Yet all Jonas could think about was the hot kiss he'd shared with Katrina—Kat—and the fact that she had yet to cash his check. Damned stubborn woman.

Walking away from her instead of taking her where

they'd stood had required every bit of self-control he'd possessed. He'd never become so lost in a kiss, so carried away in a woman's arms. He'd loved kissing her, touching her, and would have loved to have done more.

So much more.

That was all well and good but he didn't like the fact that Kat Morrison, hostess at the best restaurant in Santa Barbara—flat broke and currently celibate—had the ability to make him forget his own name.

He didn't like that at all.

But he couldn't stop thinking about her, remembering how soft her skin had felt under his hands, the spice of her mouth, those breathy sounds she'd made in the back of her throat. And her smell, something clean and natural, seemed lodged in his nose. He was also—and this was worrying—curious and, worse, concerned about her. She had a good job, why was she broke? Why didn't she have a boyfriend? She'd mentioned an LCA final and, as he remembered from his college days, that stood for Leadership and Corporate Accountability—part of the MBA program. He could handle her beauty and her sex appeal but if she was as bright as he suspected, he was in big trouble.

There was nothing more dangerous than a gorgeous, brainy woman.

Sian's small hand slapped his desk and he snapped back to the present. Talking about brainy, sexy women, this one was looking vastly irritated. "Will you please concentrate?"

Jonas nodded and quickly issued a list of instructions to, hopefully, address all the issues she'd raised. "Did I get them all?" he asked.

Sian nodded. "That is so annoying, especially since I didn't have your full attention."

"I can multitask."

Sian threw her pen down and linked her hands around her knee. "Want to tell me what's going on with you? And don't tell me nothing—you've been acting like a bear for the last two weeks."

"Jack," Jonas stated, making his grandfather's name sound like a curse.

"Oh, dear." Sian stood, walked over to the small fridge in the corner of the room and pulled out two ice waters. She handed one to Jonas, who cracked the lid for her before taking the unopened bottle for himself.

"So, what did the old buzzard do this time?"

"He told me I have three months—two and three-quarter months now—to marry or else he is disinheriting me."

Sian smiled, thinking he was joking. When he held her gaze, her mouth opened in shock. "You have got to be kidding me!"

"I so wish I was," Jonas replied. He'd spent the past week trying to convince himself that Jack wasn't being serious, that he was jerking Jonas around, but then Preston had sent him an official letter stating his client's position and assuring Jonas that his grandfather was deadly serious about him finding a wife.

Jonas had to marry or he'd lose everything he'd worked for, everything that made sense to him. He felt the burn of a rumbling ulcer and took another sip of water.

And even if he hadn't received a letter from Preston, he would've sensed Jack's displeasure from the cold telephone conversations they'd shared since that breakfast, Jack's terse and snappy emails. When circumstances went his way, his grandfather was congenial and charming, occasionally affectionate. When he was thwarted, he grew arctic cold and withdrew. Trying to stay on Jack's good side was like trying to herd cats, futile and exhausting.

After five minutes of thoughtful silence, Sian lifted a shoulder and the scales of the inked dragon covering her skin rippled. "Well, it seems like you don't have a hell of a lot of choice," Sian said. "Marry someone."

"Okay, pencil it in my diary and I'll meet you at the courthouse."

Sian's laughter danced on the sunlight. "Ha, ha, funny man. Garth has been asking me to marry him for a year and I keep telling him hell, no! So the chances of me marrying someone I don't love, even you, are less than zero. Besides, if you married me, Jack would definitely disinherit you."

Jack, narrow-minded as he was, couldn't look past the tattoos to see the razor-sharp brain Sian possessed. "Crap, Si, what the hell am I going to do? I need a wife. Where will I find someone to marry before the deadline? Maybe if I grovel, Gigi would take me back."

Sian shuddered. "You wouldn't need to grovel, you'd just need to crook your finger in her direction and she'd come skipping back. No! I absolutely refuse to let you do that. You'll be divorced within six months."

And why would that be a problem? If he went through with this crazy scheme, he intended to be married to his temporary bride for the least amount of time possible.

Sian stood and walked around so that she sat on the corner of his desk, facing him. "C'mon, Joe, there's got to be someone else you've met lately who would be a better bet than that whiny, vain actress."

Katrina's face immediately popped into his head.

"You're thinking of someone." Sian pushed a finger into his chest. "Tell me! Who?"

Jonas shook his head, sending a glance at his monitor. "Nobody. C'mon, Si, back to work."

Sian crossed her arms and glared at him. "No. Tell me who you are thinking of."

He felt like he was ten years old and had been caught with his hand in the cookie jar. "It wouldn't work. We're too different."

"Jonas! Who?"

"Kat. Katrina Morrison," Jonas finally admitted, meeting her eyes and daring her to laugh at him. Hell, he wouldn't blame her if she did. If he wasn't feeling so damn morose and confused and terrified, he'd be laughing, too.

But Sian just cocked her head and slowly nodded. "Yeah, I could see you marrying her. She's really nice and, despite only meeting her once, I really like her. You'd also, might I point this out, make spectacular babies."

Jonas felt like she was gripping his windpipe and squeezing. "Okay, let's get one thing straight, I am not looking for a wife."

Sian lifted a thin, cocky eyebrow. "I'm sorry, did I misunderstand you? Didn't you just say... 'I need a wife'?"

"A temporary wife. A pretend wife. Not a *wife* wife," Jonas snapped.

"*Wife* wife?"

This conversation was getting ridiculous. Jonas gripped the bridge of his nose, trying to control his temper. Sian was treading on dangerous ground, teasing him about this. "I plan on keeping her around long enough to satisfy my grandfather. As soon as I get the company shares transferred to me, she's out of my life."

A small frown appeared between Sian's eyebrows. "Isn't that a bit calculating?"

"Hey, I didn't make the rules. I'm just playing the game!" Jonas retorted. "I want a woman I can stand being around for less than a year, someone who doesn't think this is forever. But I don't want a gold digger."

"Talking of…did you see the three-page spread in *People*? Sara is divorcing husband number five—"

"Remind me, husband number five is the Hollywood director?" The tabloid press was how he kept tabs on his mother, and Jonas liked it that way. Actually, he'd prefer it if Sian didn't even tell him what she read, but she liked to torture him.

"Yep. Apparently she's having an affair with Mervin Kline."

Sara, so faithful.

"Kline is said to be the tenth richest man in the country…"

"Ah." Now Sara's actions made sense. Her main ambition, Jonas was sure, was to be the wife of the richest man in the world. His father, Sara's first husband, had just been a practice run. She hadn't even stuck around long enough for him to be a practice child. She'd just bailed, saying that motherhood wasn't her thing. Seducing and then marrying rich men—that's where her talents lay.

It shouldn't hurt that the last time he'd spoken to her was when he'd turned thirty, five years ago. He'd called her on his birthday, not the other way around. Jonas was pretty sure she'd wiped the memory of giving birth from her mind. After all, you couldn't say you were in your early forties when you had a son in his midthirties.

"We need to get back to work, Sian, so get off my desk."

"Oh, touchy." Sian saw something in his face and she winced. She held up her hand, her expression requesting his patience. "Why don't you ask Kat out to dinner, see if you like her enough to temporarily marry her?"

He couldn't get Kat to cash his check. She'd yelled at him after they'd kissed. She was a basket of complicated. She had issues, and Jonas tried, whenever possible, to avoid issues. He needed this search for a wife to be complication-free, easy, businesslike. An emotion-free zone.

Kat was independent, mouthy, annoying—sheer hard work. She was trouble. He should be running from her as fast as he could. She was the last person he should marry.

But he thought that, probably, he was going to anyway.

Sian, reading his mind, patted his arm. "Good luck, boss."

He was going to need it. Jonas rose and bent to drop a kiss on her cheek, grateful that he had her in his life, standing in his corner. He rested his forehead on hers. "Are you sure you won't marry me?"

Sian patted his cheek. "Darling, not even for you."

Kat was glad for the madness of Friday lunch service. It kept her from worrying about Cath, from thinking about her money problems and the fact that she was going to have to leave her beloved apartment.

But mostly, being busy kept her from thinking about Jonas Halstead and how she'd felt in his arms. Kat stared down at her reservations book and tried to concentrate on who she would seat where. She had reservations for both the current and ex-wife of a famous producer, former best friends, and, in the interest of peace, she needed to keep them on opposite sides of the restaurant and out of each other's sight…

Kat's thoughts wandered back to Jonas.

He knew exactly how to kiss her, how much pressure to apply to her nipple with his thumb. His kisses had been pure magic… He was all heat and power. Six foot two of pure masculinity. Broad-shouldered, muscled, powerful, he just had to look at her with heat in those smoky green eyes and she felt the urge to strip and climb all over him.

What the hell was wrong with her? Okay, sure, she'd been celibate for a while, but she wasn't the type to go all dizzy over a man. With the few lovers she'd had and even with Wes, getting naked had required a mental shift, a deliberate decision. With Halstead, her much-neglected libido had been calling the shots. Her body wanted to be against his, skin to skin.

Why him? Why now?

And why couldn't she get him out of her head?

Kat glanced at her watch, saw that she had another ten minutes before the restaurant was due to open and mentally allocated clients to tables, trying to keep her mind on her much-needed job. It wasn't as if she would see him again anytime soon!

Unless he came back here.

Crap! Kat bit her lip and quickly flipped through the reservations book. She hadn't booked a table for Jonas, but she was one of four hosts and he could've spoken to any of the others. Kat ran through the reservations for the next month and didn't see his name, but she knew there were many women who'd booked a table for themselves and a "guest." It wasn't an impossibility that Halstead could be a dinner companion. A model, an actress, the lead singer of an indie pop group—these women were his type. Actually, Kat suspected that any woman breathing was his type. Halstead made no bones about his disinterest in settling down.

On that score, Kat couldn't fault him. Marriage and commitment were games for fools and she'd never play again. Wes had ruined vows for her and ruined them well. She'd gone into their marriage in a starry-eyed haze, flying on a magic carpet of attention and compliments. The sex hadn't been great, but having someone so solidly in her corner, so deeply supportive, had more than made up for the infrequent, fumbling, lets-do-it-with-the-lights-off sex.

Their sex life would get better after they were married, she'd told herself. She'd been wrong. Nothing improved. In fact, everything had started sliding downhill a scant week after they'd returned from their two-week honeymoon. They might be married, Wes had informed her, but he had no intention of carrying her, financially or emotionally, anymore. He expected her to pull her weight.

Since she was now living with him, he'd said, all expenses were to be split equally. The fact that she was a full-time student and he had a corporate position held no bearing on the situation. She believed in women's rights, didn't she? Well, it was time to stand by her principles.

Not recognizing the man she'd married, and determined to keep up the pretense of being happy, Kat had taken two part-time jobs to cover her financial obligations, thinking that one day soon things would improve. They were getting used to each other, she'd thought. Everyone said the first year of marriage was the hardest.

Then her father had died. Six months later she was divorced and one month after that Cath was diagnosed. Kat's world fell to pieces.

Her dysfunctional marriage—and her father ignoring her in his will—created a pit inside where cynicism flourished. Kat was unable to trust a person's words, knowing actions were what counted. No, it was better to be independent, to sort out her own problems, to do it herself. That way no one could disappoint her and no one could hurt her.

But, damn, Jonas reminded her that she could really do with some hot, messy sex. A man's hard body on hers, strong fingers pressing into her flesh, masculine lips kissing her lips and throat and heading lower to suck her nipples, to make tracks over her stomach, to—

"Hey, Kat, are you going to open? It's time."

Kat jerked her head up and snapped out of her daydream, embarrassed that she was fantasizing about Jonas Halstead at work. God, this had to stop, she thought, walking over to the front door to slide it open. Jonas was out of her league. He was a billionaire and she was a restaurant hostess, someone who was only noticed when things went wrong.

Besides, he'd forgotten about her already. He'd handed her a check, appeased his conscience and moved on to his next blonde. It was time she moved on, too...

Kat put her shoulder to the heavy wood-and-glass door and frowned when it easily slid on its track. She felt the heat of a masculine body behind her, inhaled the scent of lime and sandalwood from an expensive cologne and looked up to see a strong hand on the frame above her head, cuffs rolled back and a Rolex watch she immediately recognized.

"Hello, Kat."

Kat leaned her forehead against the wooden frame of the door and counted to ten and then to twenty. Jonas was back. He didn't have a reservation, so the only reason he could be there was to see her.

What could he want? Kat stood straight, turned around and looked at the man who'd invaded her dreams over the last ten days or so.

"What do you want, Mr. Halstead?"

The corners of this mouth tipped up at her formal tone. "God, I love that prissy voice of yours."

Kat didn't know how to respond so she just folded her arms and tapped her foot.

"Are you working tonight? Would you like to have dinner with me?"

"I'm not working," Kat replied, walking back to her hostess's desk. Scooting behind it, she reached into the narrow cupboard and yanked out her bag. Opening the zip, she removed an envelope.

"Okay, so I'll collect you at seven thirty," Jonas said, supremely confident.

"I might be free, but I'm not going to dinner with you," Kat told him, wishing she was brave enough, bold enough, to tell him she didn't want food but she wouldn't say no to a night of no-strings, blow-her-socks-off sex. But she'd never been a girl who could so frankly state what she wanted.

Besides, as hot as that fantasy was, she wasn't really the one-night-stand type.

"Why not?" Jonas demanded, frowning.

Kat looked at him, amused by the confusion on his face. Obviously he didn't hear the word *no* very often, and why would he? He was good-looking, rich, successful and smart. When he asked a woman out, the default response was probably "Yes, yes, God, yes."

But for Kat, there were so many reasons to say no. *I don't have time to date. You're so out of my league. We have nothing in common. But, mostly, I hate that I'm so crazy attracted to you that there's a good chance I'll jump you as soon as we're alone.*

Unable to tell him the truth, Kat used an old standby. "I'm not allowed to fraternize with clients, Mr. Halstead. I could lose my job and my job is very, very important to me." It wasn't a big lie. Dating clients wasn't encouraged, but neither was it forbidden.

"Because you're flat broke."

Damn him for remembering that! "I need the money, yes. Most normal people do need a salary to keep the wolf from the door," Kat replied, her tone implying that he had no concept of what it felt like to live from hand to mouth.

"If you're in such dire need of cash, then why didn't you cash my check?" Jonas demanded. "After all, it's not like I'd miss fourteen hundred dollars."

"I don't take charity, Mr. Halstead. Not even from rich, smug billionaires."

Kat handed the envelope to him and watched as he took it, the paper white against his tanned hand.

Jonas slid his finger under the flap, lifted it and frowned when he saw the contents. She'd cut the check into pieces as small as confetti and she'd planned to post the envelope to him, care of the Halstead & Sons head offices in Santa Monica. Seeing his annoyance in person was so much more satisfying.

"Did you enjoy doing that?" Jonas asked, his tone bland and his expression now inscrutable.

"I did," Kat admitted.

Jonas tucked the envelope into the back pocket of his stone-colored slacks and nodded once. A small smile hovered around his lips. "Are you sure you don't want to have dinner?"

"I'm sure," Kat said, trying not to look at his mouth and failing.

"Your mouth is spouting one thing but your eyes are telling me you wouldn't mind getting naked and crawling all over me."

God! This man! His ego! But was it ego when he was telling the truth?

Kat, feeling flushed, deliberately looked at her watch, a knockoff Tag she'd bought off a street vendor. Then she sent him a glance meant to stop him in his tracks. "You've wasted enough of my time, Mr. Halstead. I'm sure you've got better things to do."

Jonas shrugged, the muscles of his shoulders rippling under his white dress shirt. "Not really. But I'll let you go."

Kat rolled her eyes. "You speak as if you can stop me."

Jonas's eyes dropped to her mouth, to her breasts and back up again. He stepped toward her and raised his hand, cupping the side of her face. He stared down at her, his green eyes cutting through her bravado.

"Katrina, we both know that if I kissed you right now, you wouldn't know your name in ten seconds."

Before she could stutter a response, Jonas dropped his head and oh, so gently kissed the corner of her mouth.

A rush of electricity skittered through her body. Damn the man.

Jonas stepped back and tapped her nose with his finger before walking out of the restaurant and down the flight of stairs to the circular driveway. Kat watched as he walked toward his SUV. She'd expected him to drive a low-slung sports car, something flashy, but the expensive SUV was a surprise. It was more down-to-earth than she'd expected.

Well, huh. Kat bit her lip, her fingers lifting to her mouth, where she could still feel the imprint of that sexy kiss. He was right, damn him. If he had kissed her, she would've forgotten her name in seconds.

And that annoyed the hell out of her.

It had been a long, frustrating day and Jonas knew he had two choices. He could throttle the next person who screwed up or he could go for a run. He decided to take his bad mood to the streets of Santa Barbara.

He'd been too busy to explore the town since he'd arrived. He was staying at a boutique hotel in the heart of downtown and he made his way to State Street, mentally running through the directions the manager had given him. After doing a few stretches, he started to run, cruising past the eclectic shops, artsy cafés and small theaters.

This was Harrison Marshall's town, he thought. Harrison, his friend and competitor, was a local boy, but he hadn't come from the same income bracket as his highborn wife. Harrison had scrambled for everything he had and Jonas rather liked that about the man. Jonas hadn't had to struggle but, unbeknownst to many people, Jack hadn't made it easy for his grandson to take over the company.

During Jonas's vacations from college, Jack had put him to work as a low-paid laborer, doing whatever grunt work the site manager needed. When Jonas graduated college with a business degree, he'd spent years proving himself to Jack. After spending time in supply chain management, human resources and project management, he'd been promoted to vice president.

He'd worked directly under his father, who'd been the chief financial officer at the time. Those six months had been pure torture. Jonas had realized Halstead only had space for one of them, and after a life-changing fight, he'd stayed and Lane had left.

He'd taken over from Lane as CFO and then secured the job as Halstead & Sons' CEO. And, even if he said so himself, he was doing a damn good job.

Of course, he'd worked insane hours to grow the company, but Jack still wasn't satisfied. His grandfather still wanted another few pints of Jonas's blood, another ten pounds of his flesh.

Damned Jack. He'd only be content when Jonas was married and Jack was dangling the next generation of Halsteads on his knee. But, knowing Jack and his demand for perfection, he might not be satisfied even then. It seemed to Jonas that whenever he reached one goal, Jack moved the finishing line. No matter how hard he worked, Jonas would never fulfil Jack's expectations.

He wanted to draw his own damn line, march to the beat of his own drum, be judged on his own merits. He wanted to stand apart from Jack. He wanted his company, his family name, to be one his investors trusted. He wanted to prove he could make tough calls while avoiding the dodgy business practices his father had engaged in. Jonas wanted to do it his way, the *right* way.

But to do it his way he had to marry.

Jonas ran under the freeway overpass, crossed over a bridge and soon saw the Dolphin Fountain and, beyond it, the wide beach. He took a moment to watch the sea. He liked this town. He decided to run to the end of Stearns Wharf instead of along the beach. His feet slapped against the pier as he watched the anglers and sailors unload their gear. At the top of the pier he headed back and wondered if Kat ever came down here. Did she walk or run this route?

Kat. He frowned, remembering his shredded check. Why hadn't she cashed it to pay for the dress? It made no sense to him. She needed the money and it was his fault she now owed so much since he was the one who'd ripped off the tag. It wasn't like he'd miss the cash.

But she'd still refused. And, damn, that made him respect her. He couldn't remember when a woman had last refused his offer to pay for anything. Whether it was dinner or drinks or a cab or a handbag they fancied— one woman he'd dated had asked him to pay for silicon butt implants, for God's sake—he was their access to easy cash. Sometimes he handed over his card, most times he didn't. He simply could not recall a woman passing up a chance to spend his money.

Neither could he remember when a woman had refused to have dinner with him, when one had brushed him off. Kat's reaction was definitely a first. In the world of dating and casual hookups, in the world of getting what you want with the least amount of effort, Kat was...well, a freak.

She didn't play by the rules. Hell, she wasn't playing at all. She was an unknown quantity. And that had to change. Seeing a bench ahead of him, Jonas slowed and then stopped. He pulled his cell phone from the pouch on his arm and found the number he was looking for.

"Jonas Halstead, you bastard."

Jonas grinned at the familiar voice. So Harrison still hadn't forgiven him for stealing Cliff House out from under his nose. Harrison thought he'd had the deal sewed up. No deal, as Jack frequently reminded Jonas, was concluded until the ink on the signatures was dry.

"Since I've known you so long, I thought you

might've had the decency to keep your hands off my deals."

Jonas grinned. "Would you have tried to steal it from me?"

"Damn right!" Harrison readily admitted, laughter in his voice. "So, my friend, what can I do for you?"

"Katrina Morrison," Jonas stated.

Jonas heard his swift intake of breath. "I can cope with you stealing the Cliff House but I will be super pissed if you steal my best hostess, Jonas."

"Relax," Jonas told him. "I'm not going to steal her." Not that it was a bad idea. "Not today, at least."

He heard Harrison's growl and grinned.

"Why do you want to know about Kat? You interested in her?"

"Maybe."

"Don't bother, son. I keep an eye and ear on key staff at my restaurants and Kat has refused offers ranging from dinners to apartments from a variety of men."

"She says it's against company policy."

Harrison was quiet for a few beats. "Kat knows that if she met a man at El Acantilado, I'd trust her to keep her work and personal life separate. She's just not interested, as far as I know."

"She's young and gorgeous, why not?"

"No idea. All I know is that she's a hard worker and she has some money issues. She's not as tough as she looks. If you cause her any pain, I will not be pleased."

Harrison spoke in a flat, don't-doubt-me voice Jonas was unaccustomed to hearing from him. He was obviously protective of Katrina. Since Harrison had the habit of meddling in his friends', family's and employees' lives, Jonas wondered why he hadn't waved his magic wand and sorted out whatever was troubling

Kat. Rumors swirled about just how far Harrison's reach went. He'd supposedly squashed negative reports around a friend's daughter's drunken rampage in Cancun, kept a chef out of jail and saved a good friend from a revengeful mistress. Helping Kat shouldn't have been a problem.

Curious, Jonas asked him for an explanation.

"She won't let me," Harrison grumbled. "She's the most independent, stubborn woman I've ever met. She's determined to sort out her own life in her own way and she consistently refuses my help."

"So annoying when they do that," Jonas murmured, amused that Kat had the guts to refuse one of the wealthiest and most powerful men in California. Amused and, despite himself, impressed.

"All Kat will accept from me is a discount on her rent since I own her apartment block. Though I hear she's leaving at the end of the month because she can't make the rent, something about an unexpected expense that sideswiped her."

That damned dress.

Even as he scowled, he realized her independence was attractive. Since she was so determined to go it alone, she would be the perfect wife, not interested in his money or what she could get from him. Maybe they could strike a deal.

But an out-of-the-blue marriage proposal wasn't something he could dump on a stranger. He'd need to establish some sort of relationship with her first. A friendship at the very least. While he did that, he had to keep his hands off her. Their blistering sexual attraction was a complication...for now.

But if they were to be married for ten months, a year, that attraction could be a fun way to pass the time.

"If she's got money issues then I'll cover her rent for the next few months," Jonas told Harrison.

"Even if I allowed you to do that, she won't accept any charity," Harrison told him.

"Tell her that it's another raise. She needs the job, so she'll listen to you," Jonas insisted. "Come on, Harrison…"

"Are you going to hurt her?" Harrison asked, his tone full of doubt.

"Believe it or not, I'm trying to help her," Jonas told him and it was true. He needed a wife; Kat needed money.

Harrison agreed to offer Kat's rent as a salary increase, told Jonas he'd eviscerate him if he messed with Kat and Jonas responded by thanking Harrison before disconnecting the call. He placed his phone back into the pouch on his arm and started to jog again.

It would take some quick and smart work to get what he wanted, but that was okay. He was smart and hard work didn't scare him.

He was definitely going to marry Katrina Morrison, Jonas thought, grinning.

God help them both.

Four

It was past midnight. Kat had worked a double shift and she was so tired she wanted to cry. Harrison Marshall had run the kitchen tonight and his wife, Mariella, had also been in-house. She was joined by her nephew Gabe, who were their right-hand man and, Kat suspected, somewhat of a power behind the Marshall throne. The presence of the Marshalls changed the atmosphere within the walls of the establishment; it ramped up the staff and put them on edge. Kat included.

As a result, by the end of her double shift, Kat had a tension headache that threatened to split her skull open. Slipping out the back exit of the restaurant, she headed for the staff parking lot, her feet aching.

Kat stopped to pull off her three-inch heels. Opening her bag, she looked for the pair of flips-flops she routinely carried for moments like these. Dammit, she must have left them at home. Well, she could either walk to her car in her bare feet or slip her heels back on. Squeezing her feet back inside those shoes would hurt like hell, so Kat walked across the swath of lawn barefoot, enjoying the feel of the cool grass between her toes.

Kat heard stones rattle and looked up to see the outline of a big man leaning against the hood of her small car. She should be scared. His face was in shadow and he looked menacing. But she wasn't scared. Thanks to her thumping heart and her tingling skin, she immediately recognized Jonas. He was waiting for her. Why?

Kat slowly walked toward her car, desperately trying to ignore the little voice inside reminding her how good it felt to have someone waiting for her and even better that he was big and brawny and oh, so sexy.

She stepped off the grass and picked her way over to her car. Ignoring Jonas, she opened the passenger-side door, tossed her bag and heels onto the seat and slammed the door to the rust-bucket car closed.

"Hi, stalker," she drawled as she walked around the car to the driver's door.

"Hi back."

Kat tipped her head to the side. "Why are you here?"

"I was thinking about you and the next thing I found myself here, waiting for you. It's utterly bizarre."

Of course it was bizarre because she was the last woman in the world he should be interested in. Like most rich, single men—and married men who thought they were single—he had a type. She'd seen his type over these past few months: gorgeous and easily able to navigate the world he lived in.

Jonas was only interested in her because she'd turned him down. Kat knew people craved what was just out of their reach. He could buy anything he wanted. He snapped his fingers and people jumped. Her refusal to date him was a novelty, made more exciting because she'd said no. He wanted to be the guy to wear her down, to have what he thought others could not. She was his goal and he didn't give up easily.

She had no time or energy to play his games, to stroke his ego. She had a complicated, crazy life and she didn't need the added stress of diving into a fling with a guy who, once they'd slept together, would quickly become bored of her and move on.

Kat leaned her butt against her car door and ran a hand over her face. She couldn't deal with this much sexy, not tonight, not now. Blinking at the burn in her eyes, she stared at her bare toes. "I'm not good company, Jonas. All I want to do is climb into my car and head on home."

"Tough day, huh?"

"Double shift, big bosses in the house, annoying guests, hotshot property developers who won't leave me alone," Kat said, trying for flippant but sounding sad instead.

"That bites. Headache?"

"A bitch of one," Kat replied, frowning when he pulled her away from the car so he could stand behind her. Kat whimpered when his strong thumbs and fingers dug into the taut muscles below her neck, beneath her shoulder blades. God, if he kept doing that she was going to dissolve into a puddle at his feet.

But, damn, it felt like heaven and she never wanted him to stop. Jonas moved his thumb up her neck to push it into the hollow at the base of her skull, and she whimpered as the sweet, sweet pain drained away her stress.

"You are crazy tense," Jonas whispered, his mouth

directly above her ear. Kat shivered, this time from pure arousal. "Every muscle in your body is tight."

Kat managed to lift her shoulder. "It's been a rough few days."

Jonas dropped his arms over her chest, his forearms pressing into her breasts, creating a solid, warm X across her body.

Kat allowed him to take her weight, annoyed that he made her feel safe and secure and not so alone.

Jonas didn't speak, he just held her against him, his big body providing a place for her to rest. She wanted to burrow into him, to suck up some of his strength, both mental and physical. She wanted some of his confidence, his street smarts, his I-always-know-what-to-do attitude.

Because she didn't want to want him, she got pissy. "Isn't this where you ask me to come back to your room and promise you'll massage every inch of me until I feel boneless?" she asked, wincing at the bitchy note in her voice.

"I make an effort not to be predictable." Jonas's silk-over-steel voice rumbled in her ear.

Kat pushed her bottom into the hard length of him and wiggled against him. "That tells me different."

"You're a very sexy woman, Katrina, and that's what my body does when I'm holding a sexy woman. It doesn't mean I am going to jump you."

"Then what are you doing?" Kat asked, genuinely confused.

Jonas released his arms and gently turned her around. "Who, or what, have you been dating, Katrina? Neanderthals?"

Close. She'd married one.

"You looked like a woman who needed her neck

rubbed, who could do with a hug," Jonas explained. "Someone who needed a friend."

"Oh," Kat said. She rubbed her forehead and squinted up at him. "So, you didn't come here to hit on me?"

Kat heard the note of disappointment in her voice and when Jonas laughed, she knew that he did, too. "Do you want me to?"

Kat shook her head and opened her mouth to issue a sharp retort, but Jonas's hand on her wrist made the words die on her lips. Without warning, he dipped his head and his mouth covered hers, his lips begging her to open up. She did and his tongue invaded her mouth, robbing her of coherent thought.

Kat could only grab his shirt, a T-shirt this time. She wrapped her hand in the fabric and held on. Jonas pushed his leg between her knees and pulled her closer, the full skirt of her dress allowing her to ride his hard, denim-covered thigh. Kat groaned and Jonas's hand moved up her leg, past her knee and under her dress to grip her thigh. His fingers were inches from the small triangle covering her.

God, she wanted him to touch her in the worst, best way.

This was insanity... They were in a parking lot and she was pulling herself across his leg, trying to get off, hoping he'd rocket her to an orgasm.

Jonas pulled his mouth off hers and rested his forehead against hers, his hot hand still gripping her thigh. "I promise that isn't why I'm here. Though I'm damned if I'll apologize for wanting you."

"I keep promising myself I won't kiss you again," Kat murmured. Promises aside, the reality was that she wanted more of those drugging kisses, the way he made her heart pound, her skin blister. She wanted him. But because she felt so out of control, she backed away.

Jonas swore, ran his hand across his lower jaw and swore again. He placed his hands on his hips and stared up at the black sky.

"Can I feed you? Buy you a drink? Coffee?" Jonas eventually asked, his voice back to normal.

"Sorry. It's late." And she was feeling fragile and unable to resist temptation.

"Tomorrow is Saturday. Are you working?" Jonas demanded, casually adjusting his tented pants before raking his hand through his hair.

"The lunch shift."

Jonas picked up her hand and slid his fingers between hers. "Tomorrow night, I'm going to feed you and we're going to have a chat."

Kat vehemently shook her head. "I'm not going to date you, Jonas." Was she trying to convince him or herself?

"Actually, I want to talk to you about a business proposition, something you might be interested in."

Kat frowned at his unexpected reply. "What kind of business proposal?" she asked, suspicious.

Jonas shook his head as he lifted his hand to brush his fingers across her cheek, into her hair. "You're tired and I can still see the headache in your eyes. We'll go into it tomorrow."

Kat, even more suspicious now, lifted her hands. "I'm not going to do anything illegal, Jonas."

Jonas pulled his fingers from hers and stepped back.

Despite the dim light of the parking lot she noticed his eyes had lightened, turned icy. Crap, her words had hurt him; she could see the sting in his eyes.

"Why would you think I would ask you to do something that wasn't aboveboard?" Jonas asked, moving out of her reach.

"I—" Kat started to lie then decided he deserved the truth. She bit her bottom lip before forcing the words through slightly numb lips. "I read the financial publications, follow the business news. Your family isn't known for playing by the rules."

"I do," Jonas snapped, his voice as harsh as a Siberian winter.

Kat saw him hunch his shoulders, dig his fists into the pockets of his jeans. She waited for him to speak again or to walk away, the chances were fifty-fifty.

"I'm my own man, Kat, so don't judge me by what they do. Or did. See me for what I am. Judge me on my words and actions."

Kat folded her arms and nodded her head.

"I need the words, Katrina."

"I'll judge you on what you say or do, not on your relatives' reputations."

Kat saw him expel a long breath, saw his tension dissipate. She lifted a shoulder. "So, are you still going to feed me tomorrow night?" she asked, wanting to know if she'd torpedoed their plans. She was curious to hear about his business proposal and, yeah, she wanted to see him again. She shouldn't but she did.

Jonas nodded. "Yes, I am. Do you want me to come pick you up or do you want to meet me?"

"Uh…you don't want to just chat at my place?"

"If I go to your place, not a hell of a lot of talking will happen. In our case, privacy would be distracting," Jonas said, his tone dry. "Meet me at the Dolphin Fountain by Stearns Wharf at six thirty."

Kat nodded. "Okay. Are you going to offer me a job?"

Jonas bent and dropped a kiss on her temple. "Tomorrow, Kat." Jonas placed his hand on the handle to her car door and frowned when it didn't open. He gave it another jerk and it popped free. "Kat, this car. It's... diabolical. Is it safe?"

"Safe enough."

"I'll follow you home."

Independence made her protest. "I'll be fine, Jonas."

"You have a splitting headache and have had a rough day. I'll follow you home to make sure you get there safely. Or you can leave your car here and I'll drive you. You can argue until dawn breaks, but those are your options."

Bossy man. Kat ducked under his arm and slid in behind the wheel. She jammed the key in her ignition, turned it and cursed when the engine spluttered and died. She cranked the engine again but nothing happened.

Kat muttered a small prayer, turned the engine again and smiled when the engine spluttered to life.

"It sounds like an asthmatic old man," Jonas said, his tone mournful.

"Do not diss my car. She's classic."

"She's scrap held together by rust, wheels and an engine," Jonas muttered, tapping the frame above her head. "I'll follow you home. Of course, I might be gray by the time we get there...if we get there at all."

The next night Kat approached the Dolphin Fountain from Carillo Street and scanned the people milling around the beachfront landmark. It was just after six thirty and Jonas was a little late. Kat, feeling nervous, sat on the edge of the cement ring and reminded herself that, in a little while, she'd have all the answers to the questions that had consumed her thoughts since she'd watched him drive away in his SUV.

Business proposition?

A deal?

Why was she so very attracted to him?

That last one was an easy question to answer, Kat thought, watching him walk toward her like he owned the town. He was sexy in his expensive suits and designer shirts, but dressed in cargo shorts, an olive green T-shirt and brown boat shoes, expensive, trendy glasses covering his eyes, he looked fantastic. Billionaire meets beach bum, Kat thought.

So hot.

Kat looked down at her outfit, glad she'd chosen to go casual. Her tangerine-colored, crocheted, off-the-shoulder top over a white camisole and battered, ripped denim shorts meant they would be avoiding the rarefied air of luxury establishments.

Jonas stopped in front of her and sent her a slow smile. "That's the first time I've seen your hair down." He looked down her back and whistled. "It really does hit your waist."

Feeling self-conscious, Kat gathered the strands in her fist, rolled them into a long strand and dropped it again. "I keep meaning to get it cut but I need it to be a little longer before I do."

"You need it to be longer before you cut it? That doesn't make sense."

"If I cut it when it's another half inch they can make two wigs from the length instead of throwing a lot of the hair away."

Jonas frowned. "Wigs? Are you selling your hair?"

Kat smiled. "My financial situation isn't that dire,

Halstead. I donate the hair to an organization that makes wigs for cancer patients, specifically children."

"Oh." His face softened and he looked ten years younger. "That's amazing. How did you hear about them?"

Through Cath first, but Kat wasn't ready to talk to him about her beloved, dying aunt. "I heard about the program and found a stylist who works with them. I grow my hair, Marcie cuts it off… It's a mutually beneficial arrangement."

Jonas pushed his sunglasses into his dark hair and stared at her, amusement and respect in his eyes.

Kat didn't like the warm feeling that rolled through her body.

"That's a nice thing to do, Kat. But I'm trying to imagine you with short hair."

"Short, edgy pixie cut." At his blank look, Kat smiled. "You don't know what a pixie cut is?"

"I understand 'pixie' and 'cut' but the two words together? No."

Kat stood and patted his arm. "I go from lots of hair to having not much." Kat couldn't believe they were discussing hairstyles when there were more interesting subjects to discuss. Case in point…

"So, want to tell me about this business deal?"

"I will." Jonas gestured that they should walk in the direction of Stearns Wharf. "Let's get a drink at one of the restaurants on the wharf and we can chat."

"Why not tell me now?" Kat demanded, impatient.

"It's complicated." Jonas looked down at her. "And I'd like to get a few drinks in you before I do."

It sounded like he was joking, but Kat suspected he wasn't. Oh, Lord, what was he going to ask her to do?

Before she could demand more information, he changed the subject.

"Tell me something… That LCA exam you mentioned you were studying for? Is that part of the MBA program?"

Kat nodded. "Yeah."

"You're studying part-time?"

"I'm doing it one subject at a time, taking far too long for each. It's hard, I won't lie to you."

"Why didn't you finish it at college?" Jonas saw the expression on her face and grimaced. "Ran out of money, huh?"

"Yeah, between the divorce and my dad's death, staying in college wasn't an option."

Jonas placed a hand on her shoulder to stop her and Kat turned to look at him. "You were married?"

Kat nodded. "For a year or so."

"What happened?" Jonas asked, his voice gentle.

"I expected him to support me when my life fell apart, asked him to help me through a rough time. He chose not to."

"Asshat."

Wes really was, Kat silently admitted. "It was over four years ago and he taught me a couple of useful lessons."

"Like?" Jonas asked.

He might as well know, Kat thought. "Well, he taught me that the only person I can rely on is myself."

"That explains your rabid independence. What else?"

"Oh, just that I'll never get married again."

"Ah, crap," Jonas muttered, looking like he was gritting his teeth.

"And that would be a problem for you why?" Kat asked, her heart rate inching upward.

"Because I need you to marry me. And I need you to do it soon, like in the next two months."

Kat thought she'd heard Jonas suggest they get married. She shook her head and stared at him, not sure if he was joking.

He looked heart-attack serious but he had to be joking. Had. To. Be.

Kat, not knowing what to say to such an outrageous statement, allowed Jonas to take her hand and lead her into a restaurant on the edge of the water. In a daze, she followed him to an outside table, gratefully sinking into the chair Jonas pulled out for her. When he sat, he ran his hand through his hair and leaned back in his chair.

"Want a drink?" he asked.

"Hell, yes. I *need* a drink," Kat murmured and ordered a margarita. Icy, tangy and full of liquor, she was going to need one or three to navigate this conversation.

Jonas ordered a beer, and when the waitress skipped away, Kat drummed her fingers on the tabletop.

"Yep," Jonas said before she could speak. "I kind of, sort of, asked you to marry me."

"Was it a serious question?"

"Yes."

"Have you been drinking?" Kat demanded. "Are you high?"

Jonas shook his head. "I genuinely do need you to marry me, before the end of May."

"Why? Because you've fallen madly in love with me and you can't live another day without me?" Kat asked, her tone extra flippant.

"Would you believe that?"

"No. I don't believe in fairy tales," Kat stated, feeling calmer. She leaned forward and rested her forearms on the table between them. "Right, so why do you need to get married?"

Jonas looked at her, obviously debating how much to tell her.

"Jonas, I work at Harrison's flagship restaurant, it's filled with celebs every single night. I see husbands eating with their lovers. I see wives kissing the tennis pro. I see secret business meetings between sworn enemies. I could've sold those stories a hundred times over. I know how to keep my mouth shut."

Jonas nodded to the approaching waitress and waited until after she'd left before speaking again. "My grandfather is threatening to disinherit me unless I marry."

Kat couldn't believe what she was hearing. "That sounds positively medieval!"

"That's what I told him!" Jonas exclaimed.

"So...why?"

Jonas grimaced, looking uncomfortable. "When I was younger I dated a lot—"

"You still date a lot," Kat pointed out.

"Fair enough. But my grandfather was a lot more tolerant of my social life in my twenties than he is in my thirties. I should be married, according to him, preferably having sired male children to take over the business."

"God, I can't believe what I am hearing," Kat murmured.

"Believe it. My grandfather wants to ensure there will be more Halsteads after me and to do that I must marry. He's prepared to blackmail me to get me to take that first step."

"Is this legal? Can you challenge it?" Kat asked, taking a large sip of her margarita and sighing with pleasure as the lime and tequila slid down her throat.

"As it was pointed out to me, Jack can leave his stake in the company to anyone he likes and, if I don't dance to his tune, that person might not be me. In fact, he told me it would *not* be me. I stand to lose the company I've devoted the past fifteen years to if I don't marry."

Kat rubbed the back of her neck, utterly out of her depth. "But why me, Jonas? I mean, there must be a bevy of beauties out there who would be happy to marry you."

"Maybe. But they want the real deal. They want the white wedding and an actual marriage and access to my bank accounts."

So cynical, Kat thought, but she supposed he had a right to be. With his wealth, he was a catch. Add sexy and, yeah, nice to the package and Kat could understand why many women would be happy to hitch themselves to his star.

Kat would prefer to ride her own star, thanks all the same. "Still, why me?"

"With you, I can make this a business deal. I know you need cash, and I know you need it quickly. I would be prepared to pay you. This…arrangement wouldn't last more than ten months, a year at the most. I would make that year of marriage to me worth your while."

She should shut this conversation down but she was—damn her curiosity—intrigued. "Worth my while how?" Kat asked, her heart in her throat.

"I'd pay you five hundred thousand for each month you were my wife, with the agreement that it will be a minimum of ten months, maximum a year."

Kat's fingers tightened around her glass and she had to remind herself to breathe. "That would cost you six million dollars," Kat whispered, gob-smacked.

"I'd expect you to sign a prenup. This would be a legal agreement."

Jonas had said it was a business deal, and he was discussing it that dispassionately. He needed a wife. He was prepared to pay for one. Kat needed money; he had it.

It would be the solution to so many of her problems.

"You could go back to college, finish your MBA. Get a job where you can use that brain of yours for more than allocating table seating."

Kat's mind raced. She could stay in her apartment. She could buy a new car, pay for that damn dress. She could help Cath find the care she needed. God, Kat would be free.

It was tempting.

It was insane.

"C'mon, Jonas, this is nuts. You can't be serious." Kat hoped he'd tell her he was joking. Then they'd laugh about the amazing prank he'd played on her.

Instead, Jonas just lounged in his chair, his finger tapping his beer bottle, looking far too calm for a man who'd just rocked her world.

Kat drained her margarita in one long gulp and banged the big-bowled glass onto the table. "Can you order me another?"

Jonas held up his near full bottle of beer. "You slammed that down. How about something soft before you pass out?"

Kat wanted to protest but knew he was right. Her head was already spinning from the combination of desire, tequila, six million dollars and a marriage proposal. Kat placed her elbow on the table, her chin in the palm of her hand. "So what would you expect from me?"

"Out of this marriage?"

Kat nodded.

Jonas looked away from her to a lithe blonde standing on a paddleboard just off the pier. But he wasn't actually seeing the woman, Kat realized. His thoughts were far away. "I don't know, I hadn't really planned that far ahead. I haven't thought beyond my showing my grandfather the wedding certificate and seeing his shares pass into my hands."

"Well, maybe you should think beyond that. Whether it's me or someone else, you'd have a woman in your life on a semi-permanent basis. Would you expect her to live with you? Where do you live, by the way?"

"I have an apartment in LA, not far from the Halstead headquarters. Currently, I'm renting a suite in a boutique hotel not far from here."

"Why are you here, in Santa Barbara? Don't you have people to oversee your projects? Aren't you needed in LA?"

"I work virtually and go back to headquarters for management and board meetings. I move from project to project. The Cliff House captured my imagination and I wanted to be around to watch the renovation."

"So where would your wife live?" Kat asked.

"Anywhere she wanted to. I'd rent a house or an apartment and pay for her living expenses, her car."

Kat gathered her courage and asked Jonas the question burning a hole in her stomach. "Sex?"

"What about it?"

Kat rolled her eyes. "Would it be part of the deal? Would you expect your fake wife to put out?"

"No... I don't know." When he saw her annoyance bubble up, his eyes flashed with anger. "All I mean by that is that I hadn't thought that far. Of course sex wouldn't be part of the deal. Will you please stop assuming the worst of me?"

God, even pissed he was sexy. His features became starker and his green eyes flashed. Man, she wanted him. So damned much.

And what did it say about her that she was feeling a tad disappointed that sex wasn't part of the deal?

"The marriage agreement would be totally separate from whatever happened in the bedroom." Jonas tapped the bottom of his beer bottle against the edge of the table, looking rattled. "I cannot believe I need to explain this!"

She'd hurt him, Kat realized. She hadn't meant to, but it had happened all the same. She had wanted to think badly of him. It was a defense mechanism. Pushing him away would keep her from feeling too much, from not just lusting over him but liking him. Lust she could handle; it was easy to dismiss. But liking him? Liking him was deeply problematic. Liking him led to love and love wasn't somewhere she was prepared to go. Not again.

"Sorry," Kat softly said.

Kat saw Jonas's hand tighten around his beer bottle and watched, fascinated, as he flexed his fingers. The tension and annoyance faded from his face after her apology. When his eyes met hers again, they were free of anger.

"I want you, you know that as well as I do. But sex is not part of the deal. If we end up in bed together, that would be a separate discussion. Clear?" Jonas asked, his tone even now.

"Clear," Kat responded.

Jonas waited awhile before picking up a menu and

handing one to her. "What do you want to eat? Are you hungry?"

Marriage, sex, six million dollars and he was asking her what she wanted to eat? Kat had a quick mind but she was reeling. "You want to eat?"

"Sure, I'm starving."

Kat rubbed the space between her eyebrows with two fingers. "We were discussing marriage."

Jonas flipped his menu open and sent her a sympathetic look. "I've dropped a bombshell, Kat. I don't expect you to give me an answer today, or even tomorrow. Take some time to think about it."

He kept surprising her. She didn't like it that she didn't have him pegged. "I'll probably say no," Kat warned him. "I'm more of a bust-my-back than a take-the-easy-route type of girl."

"I know that." A small smile hit Jonas's lips. "Trust me, you saying yes right away would be the biggest surprise of my life. But sometimes, very infrequently, miracles do happen."

Five

Of course she couldn't marry Jonas Halstead.

The idea was ridiculous, ludicrous.

Sure, marrying him would make her life easier. Money could do that. But accepting his offer would make her feel like a commodity, as if Halstead owned her the way he owned his expensive cars and his fancy suits.

She belonged to nobody; she never would. No, dammit, she'd do what she had to do on her own terms, by marching to the beat of her own drum.

Six million dollars. Six million reasons to say no.

Kat parked outside Cath's small house in San Roque, pulled her keys from the ignition and slid out from behind the wheel of her rust-bucket car. She squinted down at the wheels, thinking they were looking a little worn. The devil on her shoulder started to whisper, *One month being married to Halstead would do more than fix your tires.* It would change her life, flip it up-side down, make it new and bright and shiny. One little ceremony, one signed contract and she'd be rescued.

Kat's stomach lurched and she swallowed once then twice. As Jonas's wife, she'd be able to forget the nights she'd spent wading through bills and trying to stretch one dollar into ten; the hours she'd spent making money to finish her postgrad degree; the arguments she'd had with her stepmom, begging June to release some funds so Kat could finish school.

Memories rolled in like an acidic, chemical tide. She'd screamed, cried and begged, but June had re-mained unmoved. Her father had left all his assets to his wife—cash, insurance policies and the contents of his house, including his first wife's personal possessions—and June had no intention of parting with any of it.

"Go ask your husband for cash," June had told Kat. "When you married, you became his responsibility." Wes, the tight-fisted bastard, had said no to money for school and not many weeks after that, he'd hurt Kat in the worst way possible.

Her father's sudden death, and his shocking will, had left Kat feeling unloved and unworthy. Sure, from day one she and June had fought, mostly because June deeply resented sharing her husband with his daugh-ter. As a result, Kat's relationship with her dad had be-come strained. But Kat had never thought she would be cut out of his will. He could've, at the very least, left Kat her mother's photos, jewelry and mementos. The last time Kat had seen June she'd noticed her wearing Kat's mom's favorite pair of diamond studs. Kat had barely restrained herself from ripping the jewels from June's ears.

Kat wasn't sure if she could forgive her dad for that.

Jonas was also facing disinheritance, albeit on a larger scale. He stood to lose hundreds of millions, possibly billions, if he didn't marry, but Kat sensed he was less concerned about the money than he was about the company. Curious, she'd done some research on Halstead & Sons and there was no doubt that Jonas had, in recent years, turned the company around.

Pre-Jonas, Halstead had been rocked by scandals involving shoddy building practices, low wages, labor unrest and questionable business practices. Jonas had changed all that; business journalists frequently said he was as smart and tough as his predecessors but had a streak of integrity that seemed to be missing in the previous generations of Halsteads. Building practices had improved, safety practices were adhered to—and Halstead now paid some of the best wages in the industry.

Jack Halstead might own the shares but it was Jonas's company. She couldn't blame him for wanting to seal the deal.

But *marriage*?

Could she trust him to keep his word, to do what he said? He'd spoken about prenuptial agreements, about legal contracts, but, as she well knew, documents could always be challenged. It was the actions that followed the words that mattered. Her father had said one thing— *I'll pay for your education, your mother's possessions will be given to you when the time is right*—and gone back on his word. Wes had promised to love, protect and care for her and he'd quickly forgotten those vows. He'd promised to be her husband, her best friend, her lover and her supporter. He'd turned out to be a bully with a low sex drive.

And she was considering marrying again? She couldn't, wouldn't…shouldn't. Offers like Jonas's were too good to be true. There had to be a catch somewhere. Yes, she would be a lot richer, but she knew that, with their combustible sexual attraction, they wouldn't be able to keep their hands off each other. They'd be sleeping together in no time. And if those lines between business and personal blurred, they'd end up with a complicated mess on their hands. Six million dollars wasn't worth the loss of her self-respect. Or her heart.

Besides, to marry him, she'd have to trust him, to a certain extent at least. She was still coughing up water because the two men she'd loved and adored had left her to drown.

And she was thinking about stepping into that murky lake again? She couldn't do it.

She used to be a trusting daddy's girl, a naive young wife. She was now smart and independent. She'd clawed her way back to solid footing and she refused to depend on anyone. But she was also, she thought as she walked up to Cath's front door, still broke.

"Honey, I've been checking out hotties on that dating app!"

Kat, standing in the doorway of Cath's living room, dropped her bag to the floor and gave her aunt a once-over. Cath didn't look any worse than she had last week. That had to be a good sign.

They were waiting for the results of the latest blood tests, which would tell them if Cath would see her sixtieth birthday or not. So young, Kat thought, and so full of life.

"Find anyone you want to hook up with?" Kat asked after dropping a kiss on Cath's cheek. She sat on the edge of her aunt's armchair and looked down at Cath's tablet and into an admittedly handsome but far too young face. "Thirty-five years is too much of an age gap, darling. Even for cougars like you."

Cath's laugh was not as strong as it usually was. "Not for me, you twit, for you!"

Kat pulled away to frown at her aunt. "Are you trolling a dating app looking for a date for me?"

"Absolutely! I've had to hold myself back. I've only swiped right on twenty guys and most of them swiped back and fifteen of them want to meet you."

Whoa! What? Kat jumped up from her seat to glare at her aunt, slapping her hands on her hips.

"You registered me and now you are picking my dates? What the hell, Cath?" Kat yanked the tablet from Cath's hand and saw the thumbnails of, yep, twenty guys on the screen. One was licking the handle of his mountain bike.

Kat spun the tablet around and pointed at the photos of men she'd never date. "These? What are you thinking? This one has his tongue frozen to a lamppost!"

"Oh, I think I must've swiped right when I was falling asleep once or twice."

"Or ten times!" Kat shook her head. "I am not meeting any of them!"

"Why not?"

Kat looked at the tablet again. "Too young. Too vain. Too in love with his motorbike. Psycho. Sociopath. Gym freak!"

"You're too picky," Cath grumbled.

Kat tossed the tablet onto the cushion of the sofa and blew out a frustrated breath. "Cath, I've got enough on my plate. I do not need to date weirdos."

"I'd be happy if you just dated someone, had some fun. Sex is an excellent way to relieve stress."

Kat opened her mouth to speak, realized she had

nothing, and snapped it shut again. After a minute she shook her head. "Mom was such a lady. How is it possible that the two of you were twins?"

"Oh, I was swapped at birth. I'm actually the daughter of a billionaire."

If she never heard the word *billionaire* again it would be too soon.

Kat watched as Cath pulled in a deep breath, a sure indication that a wave of pain was about to contract every muscle in her body. Cath panted slightly, closed her eyes, and Kat watched, helpless, as her aunt fought the pain. After a minute Cath finally relaxed, but she looked pale and defeated.

The pain medication wasn't strong enough, Kat realized as she knelt in front of Cath and placed her hands on her aunt's knee. "You're not getting better, are you?"

When she was first diagnosed with pancreatic cancer, Kat and Cath promised each other to always be honest. "No, I'm not." Cath picked up a strand of Kat's hair and wrapped it around her finger.

"And there is nothing else they can give you? Nothing else they can try?"

"This is the strongest medicine my insurance will pay for. After this, the next step is experimental drugs, clinical trials, being a human guinea pig."

Kat nodded. Right, then that's what they would do. Her mother's twin, her soul mother, would not succumb to this disease. Not without a fight and not until she'd tried every option available.

This was the woman who'd held Kat as she'd cried over her mom's coffin, whose house she'd run to when the walls of her own seemed to close in on her. Cath had taught her about the birds and the bees, taken her shopping, to the prom. Cath had taken the role of mother of the bride at Kat's wedding. Cath had dried Kat's tears, nursed her through her first hangover and breakup, held her hand through her father's death and through her divorce. Cath had stepped into her mom's shoes when June had refused to.

Cath was her home, the one place where Kat felt truly loved. Cath was the center of Kat's world and she couldn't lose her. She'd lost too much already...

"Right, then we'll do that. Who do I contact?"

Cath let out a small laugh. "My darling, Kat, so gung-ho. That's not going to happen, honey. Those trials are all taking place overseas, there's one happening in Switzerland, and it costs... God, the cost! Put it this way, between us we can't afford an air ticket let alone the cost of that treatment."

"I'll find the money," Kat stated, Jonas's face appearing behind her eyes.

"Kat, I'm not talking about ten thousand dollars, or even twenty. I'm talking big money. This is something I have to accept, darling girl, and so do you."

She didn't have to accept a damn thing. As long as they had options for Cath's recovery, or even just improvement, Kat wouldn't allow herself to imagine a world without Cath in it. As long as she had breath left in her body, she'd do everything in her power to keep Cath in her life.

She knew what she had to do.

She couldn't think about this, she just had to send the text message and get it done. If she wavered, if she hesitated, she would lose her courage and Cath would die. Maybe not today or tomorrow, or even in a year, but sooner than she should. Kat would not be able to live with herself if that happened. Especially if she could prevent it.

Hi, it's Kat.
Is that six-million-dollar offer still open? If it is, then I'm
interested. Call me.

There, it was done. It seemed, she thought, tears
burning in her eyes, she was getting married. For
money.

Kat climbed to her feet and tucked her phone away.
"Want some tea?" she asked.

"I'd prefer a double whiskey," Cath grumbled.

"Along with me meeting any of those men you
swiped right for, that's not happening," Kat said, pulling her phone from her back pocket.

He'd replied already.

Kat,
I'm in Toronto. There's a problem on a project here that
I need to resolve. The offer's still open but let's talk. I'll
call you when I get back to town.

Decision made. Marrying Jonas would net her all
the money she needed—but, oh, God, what would it
cost her?

After her father died and she and Wes divorced, Kat
made sure to always have a plan B…and a plan C. She
never wanted to be caught off guard again. But if Jonas
rescinded his offer, which was highly possible since she
hadn't heard from him in four days, there would be little—nothing—she could do to help Cath. How would
Kat live with that?

Kat slammed the door to her car shut and carried her
bag and heels up the concrete path to her front door. She
was exhausted. She'd taken every shift she could and

that meant double shifts all week. Instead of sleeping, she'd spent all her free time on her computer, scouring the internet for information relating to the treatment of pancreatic cancer, hoping for a miracle treatment and praying that said miracle would be free.

Cath hadn't done enough research into the clinical trials in Switzerland and it turned out they had very strict criteria for who entered the program. Cath was too old, too sick, and her disease was too far along for them to consider her.

Kat stopped to pull a stone from the bottom of her flip-flop, thinking of the information she'd found earlier. There was a California-based doctor who was also doing a similar treatment and, if Kat had access to cash, he might be an option. It all came down to money, as so much did.

"Kat, it's me. Don't scream."

A black shadow moved at the top of the stairs. Kat looked up and saw Jonas sitting on the step dressed in jeans and a plain black T-shirt. In the light from the corner of the landing she could see the stubble on his cheeks and jaw, his tired eyes.

"God, you have the survival instincts of a moth," Jonas grumbled. "You see a shadow, you run. At the very least you scream."

"I knew it was you," Kat said. She couldn't explain it, but she knew that if it had been anyone else but Jonas lurking around she would've screamed and run. It was like her subconscious, her soul, recognized him on a deeper level. How? And why him?

She was utterly exhausted but just seeing him gave her a bolt of energy; he was like a particularly potent elixir. And, as tired as she was, he still managed to stir her juices, to ratchet up her breathing and jump-start her heart.

He was such a man, Kat thought. Uncompromisingly masculine, hard-bodied and sharp-eyed. And she just wanted to crawl into bed with him and let him feed the hunger that raged inside of her.

Since that wasn't going to happen, she was happy just to stand here and stare at him, soaking him in.

"Get up here, Kat."

Kat walked up the stairs and sat next to him, dumping her bags and shoes behind her. She stretched out her legs and arched her feet, groaning at the pure relief.

"Long night?" Jonas asked, his shoulder against hers.

"Long couple of nights and days," Kat replied. "When did you get back?"

"This morning. I've been trying to call you all day but every time I picked up my phone I was slapped with another problem. By the time the calls stopped, it was after ten and I knew you'd be at work. So I went for a run, had something to eat and thought I'd wait for you here." Jonas nodded to the street where her car stood under a streetlight. "There's something seriously wrong with your car. I could hear it rattling long before you turned down the street."

Kat pulled a face. "I'm just grateful it's still running."

"Two words. *Scrap yard.*"

"Another two words. *No money*," Kat replied. "Are you happy to sit here? It's such a nice night and my neighbor is away for two weeks, so talking out here won't disturb anyone."

Jonas leaned back and placed his elbows on the step behind him. "Okay."

Kat wiggled her toes and wondered how to address the big, sparkly elephant sitting on the steps with them.

She was about to ask him if he'd changed his mind when Jonas spoke. "I was incredibly surprised to get your text message. I thought it would take a lot more persuasion to get to yes."

"I had every intention of saying no, I really did," Kat admitted, playing with the hem of her cobalt blue shift dress.

"Then why did you change your mind? What happened?"

Could she tell him? Could she open up a little and share why she was now prepared to forgo her independence and do this deal? Did she have a choice?

"I'm an only child and my mother died when I was fourteen. My dad remarried six months after her death and June, my stepmom, is…difficult. Before my mom's death, my dad and I were best friends, but June didn't like how close we were and she drove us apart. I ended up spending most of my time with my aunt Cath, who is my mom's twin."

"Is your dad still alive?"

"He died five years ago. He had a heart attack." Kat's voice dropped and she felt that familiar anguish and grief close her throat, burn her nose.

Jonas placed his hand on the back of her neck and immediately she relaxed. How did he do that?

"He left everything he had, every cent, to June. He did leave me my childhood home, but June has the right to live in it until she dies and I have to pay for its upkeep."

"Ouch," Jonas said, keeping his hand on the back of her neck. She was grateful. She felt anchored, centered. "Your stepmom won't help you out?"

Kat let out a low, bitter laugh. "If I were on fire, June would add some gas."

Not wanting to get bogged down in that swamp of past hurts, Kat quickly moved on. "Cath, on the other hand, is a gem. She paid for my last semester at college so I could get my degree."

"She sounds like a winner," Jonas said softly.

"She is. She's been my rock, my best friend, my second mom."

Jonas's thumb rubbed the cord in her neck. "But?"

She could tell him this; she could explain. He'd understand. "Around the time she paid for me to complete my undergrad degree, she was diagnosed with a rare form of pancreatic cancer. And it's hit her hard. She's a vibrant, funny, crazy, free spirit, but now she's chair- and bed-bound and it's killing me." Kat released a sad laugh at her accidental choice of words. "I mean it's killing *her*. Anyway, there's nothing more the doctors can do for her here in Santa Barbara. My lack of cash and their lack of experience dealing with this form of cancer are both stumbling blocks.

"But there's a doctor, working out of a private clinic in Malibu called Whispering Oaks. He's a researcher and he's looking for test subjects who would be willing to give something ridiculously unorthodox a try. He's had some fantastic results using a combination of homeopathic remedies and hard drugs."

Kat stared down at the street, her shoulders slumped. "It sounds like the answer to our prayers. It's expensive, but if you…um, paid me to marry you, I could swing the cost."

"And pay for the dress."

Kat didn't smile at his attempt at humor. "Money is the first problem, but there are others."

"Like?"

"The waiting list is a thousand deep and filled with

younger people, people with families, teenagers, children. Intellectually, I understand the doctor choosing those younger patients, but this is Cath. I want them to choose her! She might be an unlikely candidate on paper but she's everything to me!"

Jonas pulled her to him, his arm around her shoulders. "Shh, honey. It's okay."

Kat found herself turning to him, burying her head in his neck, unable to stop the tears she'd been holding back for months, years. She shouldn't be crying. She couldn't afford to show him she was weak, needy. But the more she tried to stem her tears, the harder she tried to stop her sobs, the more they demanded to be released.

We've been strong for too long, her soul and her heart whispered. *Let us weep. We'll be strong again later. We'll pull ourselves together, pick up our broken pieces, but for now, just let us cry.*

So Kat did. She retreated from Jonas, wrapped her arms around her knees and silently sobbed. Tears wet her knees and ran down her legs, dropped onto the mosaic-tiled steps below. And Jonas allowed her to weep, his broad hand drawing circles on her back, giving her an anchor when grief threatened to wash her away.

Eventually her tears lessened and her sobs quieted. He held out the hem of his T-shirt, lifting the fabric to run the soft cotton over her cheeks, down her chin. He held the fabric in front of her nose. "Want to blow?" he asked.

Kat reared back, shocked. "I am *not* going to blow my nose on your T-shirt!"

"Thank God." Jonas smiled, dropping his shirt. He cocked his head. "Better?"

"Yes, thanks." The heat of embarrassment dried the tears Jonas had missed.

"I'm sorry about that." Kat pushed her hair back, lifted her shoulders. "I'm just so tired, so utterly wrung out. It's difficult being strong, day after day, night after night. I'm so tired of the responsibility. I keep waiting for the next wave of trouble to hit me, wondering if this one will finally drown me."

A sob, one of the few she'd suppressed, escaped.

"Shh, Kat." Jonas's hand drifted over her head as he pulled her closer. "Stop crying now, you're going to make yourself sick."

"Can't afford to get sick," Kat muttered into his neck, her arms wrapped around him. He smelled so good, like sunshine and comfort and heat. If she could stay there until she felt better, stronger, she'd be so grateful.

Jonas slid an arm under her legs and, without any effort, stood while holding her cradled against his body. "Where's your key, Kat?"

Kat opened her hand to show him the key she'd been holding since she'd left her car. Jonas nodded and walked to the entry. He balanced her across his lifted knee and managed to unlock the front door. Without turning on any lights, he walked through her apartment and into her bedroom, and gently placed her on her bed. He looked down at her as he pulled her flip-flops off her feet.

"You need to sleep, Kat." Jonas gently lifted her dress, pulling it up and over her hips and chest. Kat, too tired for embarrassment and feeling utterly safe, lifted her arms. After Jonas tossed the dress onto a chair, he put a big hand on her shoulder and pushed her down. Kat snuggled her head into her soft pillow and felt her eyes closing. Forcing them open, she tried to make eye contact with Jonas. "We need to talk. About getting married. About your offer."

"We will, but not now," Jonas told her, reaching for a cotton throw at the bottom of the bed and draping it across her legs and hips. "Sleep now, Kat. We'll sort it out later. There's time."

Kat, feeling safe and secure for the first time in years, closed her eyes and drifted off to sleep.

Six

Shortly after lunch the next day, Jonas stepped into the expensive lobby of El Acantilado and looked into the restaurant, wondering if there was ever a time the place wasn't hopping. He stood off to the side, watching Kat walk swiftly back to her station, her nice-to-see-you smile on her lips.

That smile didn't reach her eyes, Jonas realized, pushing the lapels of his black jacket aside so he could put his hands into the front pockets of his stone-colored chinos. She'd slept but it didn't look as if it had been a restful sleep. Her eyes were red-rimmed and makeup didn't quite hide the twin stripes of pale purple beneath her lower lashes.

The guests coming to eat at the famous West Coast restaurant wouldn't give their hostess a second thought. But to him, Kat was worth more than one thought, or even ten. Unfortunately she was pretty much all he thought about from the moment he opened his eyes.

And not just in the "I need to marry her soon, let's get this done" way. He'd had many thoughts of her naked, of course. He was a male who liked sex, a *lot* of sex. But in between those hot fantasies of kissing her from tip to toe and everywhere in between, he remembered her laugh, her silky hair between the tips of his fingers, the sadness and vulnerability in her eyes. He wanted to hold her, protect her, make her life easier, dammit.

What had happened to viewing his marriage as a business deal? When did this become so very complicated? Since meeting her, Kat Morrison had made steady inroads into his mind and, somehow, crept under the wall surrounding his heart, and she was lodged in there, walking all over his soul. This wasn't good, Jonas decided right then, and it certainly was not to be tolerated.

He was marrying Kat only because Jack said Jonas had to marry *someone*. This arrangement wasn't about happiness or death-do-us-part. This was a hard, simple business deal. That was all it ever could be.

He didn't do emotions and he didn't do entanglements. He certainly had no intention of doing either with his bride-for-hire.

Maybe it would be easier to marry Gigi or one of the other many women who'd crossed his path recently. None of them had ever caused his stomach to flip or his heart to stutter. Around them he could easily keep his emotional distance.

No.

No way would he marry one of those vapid women. Jonas shuddered. He'd prefer Jack shoot him.

Kat caught Jonas's eye, flushed, looked at the crowd of people waiting for her attention and held up a finger, asking him to wait. He nodded and he couldn't help a small smile at her embarrassment, knowing she was more ashamed of her tears than she was of him seeing her in her underwear.

Plain white. No frills. Sexy as hell. Walking away from that smooth skin and those long legs and that slim but curvy body had taken an enormous amount of effort.

He wanted her.

He was going to marry her.

He was going to have to keep his hands off her.

Jonas pushed his shoulder into a steel-clad wall and stared down at the floor, his thoughts in turmoil. They had to keep sex out of the equation, as difficult as it would be. The more he came to know her, the more she intrigued him. Fantastic sex would amplify those emotions. He couldn't afford to think of her as anything other than a business partner, a means to an end.

She needed cash from him, and she needed his connections. He needed a wife in name only because, as he'd checked and double-checked, Jack had never once mentioned that love had to be part of the deal. Love would *not* be part of the deal. He didn't want it and he didn't need it. It was a cunning and dangerous emotion.

He wanted no part of it.

He could deal with no sex. He wasn't a kid anymore. Lack of sex wouldn't kill him…

But trying to keep his hands off Katrina might.

"Hi. Sorry to keep you waiting but it's been crazy busy."

Jonas straightened and looked over at Kat, standing behind her modern, free-form desk, her eyes reflecting fear and confusion. They needed to talk, to nail down this arrangement. Jonas looked around and saw that the lobby was empty. "Can you take a break?"

Kat looked at her watch and nodded. "I've already asked my manager to watch my desk and answer my phone."

Jonas walked out of the restaurant. Once in the sunshine outside, he shrugged out of his jacket. He looked down to the beach below, enjoying the sun on his face as he waited for Kat to join him. When she did, she gestured for him to turn right. "Let's walk in the vegetable garden around the back. I often take my breaks on the benches under the trees."

They walked to the back of the restaurant and into an area he hadn't known existed. The garden consisted of raised beds edged by zinc sheets, glinting in the sun. He saw fat, purple eggplants and bright red cherry tomatoes, and he inhaled the scent of lavender as Kat pulled her hand through the leaves of the herb as she passed it. Under the cypress tree, as she promised, was a bench. Kat sat on the edge, her hands tangled together.

"I'm sorry I lost it last night. I never cry and I don't know why I did."

Jonas noticed her flushed chest, the red tide creeping up her neck. It was a sure sign, he was coming to realize, that she was upset or embarrassed.

"Don't worry about it." Jonas sat next to her and stretched his arms out along the back of the bench, tipping his head to look up into the branches of the cypress. "This is a pretty spot."

"Yeah, it is," Kat said, running the palms of her hands on her pencil skirt. "Jonas—"

He wasn't sure what she was about to say but he wasn't going to give her a chance to back out from their deal, to have second thoughts. "Your aunt has an appointment at Whispering Oaks in a month's time. It was the earliest time they could fit her in."

Kat looked shocked, hopeful and confused all at the same time.

"But... *What?* There's a long waiting list!"

Right, time to explain how life worked in his world. "I know people, Kat, I know influential people. One of the benefits of money, and having the Halstead surname, is the ability to get what you want when you want it. I called someone and he called someone and an appointment was created."

"But who has that sort of clout?" Kat demanded, looking absolutely flummoxed.

This was going to be interesting. "Your boss."

"Jose? The restaurant manager?" Kat sounded skeptical.

"No, sweetheart. Harrison Marshall."

Confusion turned her dark blue eyes smoky. "I don't understand any of this."

He could see that. Jonas sat up, leaned forward and rested his forearms on his knees, allowing his hands to dangle between his legs. "In certain circles, Harrison has a reputation for being a guy someone can call when they want something done. Harrison collects contacts and connections like hoarders collect trash. He also likes doing favors for people."

"But Harrison is your direct competitor, why would you call him of all people?"

"He's a competitor in business—we sometimes bid for the same projects—but he's more than that. He's known me since I was a kid, so I felt comfortable asking him for a favor."

And, hopefully, Jonas thought, he wouldn't ask for ten pounds of flesh when he called in his IOU.

"But how and why would Harrison have the clout to get Cath an appointment?" Kat cried, trying to make sense of the bombshell he'd dropped in her lap.

"Does it matter?" Jonas asked. Harrison and his wealth of contacts was a conundrum and Jonas's gut instinct demanded he not look too closely at his old friend's actions. He wasn't sure he wanted to know...

Kat frowned at him. "Does Harrison know about Cath?"

Hell, no. Harrison was a friend but he wasn't that good a friend. Nobody was. "He doesn't. After I assured him that this favor wasn't for Jack, myself or anyone he knew, I asked him to get the appointment. I didn't tell him who it was for."

"Harrison knowing Cath was related to me would complicate the matter, so thank you. He recently gave me a raise by refusing to let me pay any rent on my apartment, so I'd feel uncomfortable if he knew he was helping me out again."

"This situation is plenty complicated enough," Jonas agreed. "Your aunt has an appointment with someone who should be able to help her, Dr. Cranston. He requires a deposit. He wants her to book into the clinic for a battery of tests and to monitor her condition. It will be very expensive."

"And the only way I can pay for it is if I marry you," Kat said, her voice bleak.

"Pretty much." Jonas felt frustrated at her despondent tone. "Kat, look, I'm not any happier about this than you are! I don't want to get married, but the situation is clear. I need a wife, you need money. It's a business deal—"

maybe if he said it often enough, he would start to believe his own words "—so…are you in or are you out?"

He still thought there was a chance she'd say no, so he held his breath, waiting for the ax to fall. He was surprised when she nodded her head. "Yes, Jonas. We have a deal."

Well, hell. He'd just officially acquired a fiancée. His company was almost in his hands…

"Okay, good. Great," Jonas stated, his voice harsher than he'd intended. Why did he feel bleak, like something was missing?

God, catch a clue, dude! Concentrate on what matters…

He needed a marriage certificate, the transfer of shares into his hands. He couldn't risk Jack changing his mind again. He needed to tell Jack, to tell the world, that he was marrying. Once the story was in the public domain, it would be a lot harder for Jack, or Kat, to back out. "Today is Thursday, what about Saturday?"

Kat blinked, gasped and blinked again. "To get married? Are you insane?"

Probably. "Not to get married, to host an engagement party. We can host it at the Polo Club."

Kat shook her head as if to clear it. She held up her hand, her gesture telling him that he was getting carried away. "It's the Polo Club, Jonas. It's booked up for months, years in advance for weddings. And we don't need a fancy engagement party."

Yeah, he kind of did. "It's expected, Kat. And I spoke to Mariella Marshall, who, as you know, runs the event planning arm of Harrison's company. She can do a party for a hundred people in the smaller of the two ballrooms any Saturday this month. But only if I give her a free hand with regard to the flowers and the food."

"But how did you explain the haste, the lack of a firm date?"

Jonas grinned. "I told her the truth. I told her that I was working on getting a girl to marry me and that I needed to move fast once she said yes. She said that no girl she knew would consent to a hasty engagement party or wedding and I told her mine would. And then I told her that if she didn't think she could arrange the party or the wedding on such short notice, I'd bring someone down from LA."

"And she took offense at that and told you she absolutely could handle a last-minute event. You played her," Kat stated.

Jonas wasn't sure if her expression was a reflection of her horror or her admiration.

Yeah, he'd had the balls to manipulate Mariella Marshall. God, after maneuvering his father out of the business, dealing with Mariella Santiago-Marshall was a walk in the park.

Jonas shrugged. It was what it was. "So, do we have a deal?"

Kat was scared, he could see that. But she was going to say yes because she was prepared to do whatever she could for someone she loved, someone who obviously loved her. Lucky Kat, to love and be loved like that. He wondered what that felt like.

Being loved by Kat, who was loyal, honest and courageous—someone who had so much integrity—would be a hell of thing. Not that he knew how to handle unconditional love. He was more familiar with approval that had strings attached. In his family, that wishy-washy emotion ebbed and flowed with his performance. He wasn't perfect and he frequently did things his way, so Jack's approval was often withheld and love was never part of the equation.

Jonas had learned to live with it, but sometimes, when he was faced with someone else's example of real love, he wished he knew what it felt like.

But if wishes were horses and all that crap...

It was what it was. He couldn't change Jack. Jonas had no interest in his father's attention and his mother was, at best, crazy.

He'd drawn the short straw with regard to his family. Having to organize a hasty engagement party with a woman marrying him for money wasn't, sadly, even a surprise. It was just another example of his dysfunctional family life.

Lots of money? Lots of problems.

"We have a deal," Kat told him, and Jonas noticed the tremble in her voice, her shaking fingers, "on one condition."

He braced himself and mentally tried to work out what her angle could be.

"I need the world to think that we met and fell in love, that we can't wait to get married. I am going to lie my ass off to Cath. She's an absolute romantic and needs to hear that I am happy and settled and in love. I am also going to tell her you used your connections to get her into the trial for free...I don't want her worrying about who is paying for her treatment. I expect you to back me up in that lie."

That was her additional demand? Easy enough.

But there was more, he could see it in her eyes.

"And I will only take the money I need for her treatment, down to the last dollar. If you pay Whispering Oaks, I will stay married to you for a minimum of ten months and a maximum of a year."

Jonas heard the determination in her voice and scratched his head. She wanted less money, not more?

It was honorable but it wasn't going to work. "Kat, you need to look like my wife, act like my wife. And that means me spending money on you. Dresses, car, apartment. You're going to have to give up your job."

Kat sent him a look full of steady regard. "Oh, hell, no, I'm not giving up my job. When you walk out of my life, I need an income to pay the bills."

"Finish your damn degree and get a proper job in a field that excites you."

Kat shook her head. "Not on your dime."

"You're being ridiculously, stupidly independent."

"You can pay for the dress you ruined, if that makes you feel better."

It didn't. "Kat—"

Kat looked at her watch and rose. "I need to get back to work. I've taken more time than I should have."

"What will everyone think when my wife carries on working as a hostess?" Jonas demanded, following her to her feet.

Kat shrugged. "Then you should not have chosen me as a wife, Jonas. I need your money for Cath. That's all I'm prepared to take. I can't take more."

Jonas shook his head, frustrated. Of all the women in California, the one he wanted to marry had no interest in having access to his limitless credit card? "Then we don't have a deal."

Kat spun on her heel, her eyes shooting blue fire. "Excuse me?"

Whoa…*hot*. He'd seen tired Kat and professional Kat, even sexy Kat, but the fire in her eyes sent a bolt of arousal straight down his spine and into his junk. He was, suddenly and ridiculously, turned on. What he wouldn't do to slide his hand up and under that dress, to feel that creamy skin under his fingers, to taste her spicy mouth.

Business deal, Halstead, he reminded himself. *Bus-i-ness.*

Jonas worked hard to pull his attention back to their argument. "I pay for your clothes, your expenses, whatever you need for the next year. Take it or leave it."

"Are you really going there, Jonas? You need *me*," Kat said, folding her arms across her torso.

Jonas gave a little shrug. "I need a woman to marry me, Kat. Any woman. I like you, but you're not the only fish in the pond. How many rich men do you know who are prepared to pay you to marry them?"

Kat narrowed her eyes and tapped her foot. "You're bluffing."

He was and was surprised she'd picked up on it. "That's the deal, Kat."

"Asshat," Kat muttered, annoyed. She lifted a finger and Jonas knew he had her. "I want a contract. I want detailed expense reports kept. No expensive jewelry, ridiculously priced dresses and shoes. Buy me a car and I will disembowel you."

Jonas just held her hot stare. "A contract, yes. I'll agree to keeping the jewelry simple. Designer clothes are a necessity—"

"Then you have to buy them from my friend Tess at The Hanger so she can earn the commission," Kat argued.

He nodded. He was, reluctantly, touched by her generosity to her friend. "The car goes." Jonas held up his own finger. "Not. Negotiable. It's a death trap."

"Something small, inexpensive, and you'd better run the make and model past me before you buy it. It gets sold when we divorce," Kat countered, her color up and her eyes flashing. She was enjoying the negotiating, Jonas realized with a smile. Her blood was up and she wanted to win.

"Anything else?" Jonas asked, entertained.

"I'm sure there is," Kat retorted, her brow furrowed in concentration.

"We'll add all we've discussed to the prenup."

Kat raised her eyebrows. "So you don't trust me?"

She didn't need to sound so damn happy about it. He did actually trust her, and that scared the hell out of him. He didn't usually trust anyone. "It's standard procedure."

Kat released a panicky laugh. "Oh, Jonas, nothing about this is standard procedure!"

Jonas lifted his hands to hold her face, her skin soft under his rough fingers. "It'll be okay, Kat." He dropped his head to kiss her temple, not trusting himself anywhere near her mouth.

"I hope so." Kat pulled her head back and held his wrist, her eyes locking on his. "Is having complete control of the company worth this, Jonas? Is being in control worth all this drama?"

Jonas took a long time to answer her. "No, maybe not." He saw the flash of disappointment in her eyes, tinged with sadness. "But making sure that someone else doesn't take control is worth every penny."

He'd said too much. Jonas dropped his hands and stepped back. "I'll let you get back to work and I'll do the same. I keep forgetting that I have a hotel to renovate, a massive company to run. We'll speak later, okay?"

Kat nodded and turned away, her hips swaying as she walked up the steps to the restaurant. When she reached the top, Jonas spoke again. "Kat?"

Kat turned around, lifting her hand to shield her eyes from the glare. "Yes?"

"Thanks." It was inadequate but he meant what he said. He was grateful. Profoundly.

"Ditto, Jonas. I wouldn't be doing this unless it was important. Cath means the world to me."

He knew she was trying to justify her actions, hoping he wouldn't think less of her because she was prepared to marry a stranger for money. Strangely, he wanted her to understand that his mission was just as important, that this wasn't all about shares and stocks and his inheritance. "I have other reasons, too, Kat. And they are equally valid."

Kat looked like she was going to demand what they were and he wondered whether he could trust her enough to tell her, shocked that he wanted to. How could he tell her that until he freed himself from Jack, from his father, from their lack of integrity, that he couldn't feel like his own man? Would she understand or would she think him weak for pandering to Jack's wishes for so long?

Jonas was confused by the sudden urge to open up, to reassure this woman that he wasn't the cold, hard-hearted businessman the world perceived him to be. He actually wanted to let her peek through a crack in the wall.

Jonas shook his head, feeling discombobulated and off center. Time to go…

"I'll call you," Jonas told her, turning away.

He would. But only much, much later—when he got his rebel heart back on its leash.

Jonas waited impatiently for Kat at the bottom of the main stairs of the Polo Club. Pushing back the cuff of his tuxedo jacket, he glanced at his watch and decided that if he didn't see her on the stairs in two minutes he'd barge into the penthouse and drag her out by her heels.

Jonas, his hand in the pocket of his pants, fiddled with the engagement ring he'd spent far too much time choosing. If it had been any other woman, he would've bought the biggest, boldest, most expensive ring in the store and be done with it.

Judging by her arguments about money—her new car was still a point of contention between them; she'd also objected to dressing at the Polo Club, saying that hiring a room for her at the venue was a waste of money—he knew she wouldn't appreciate a big, flashy ring.

But she did deserve something unusual, exotic, classy, and he'd eventually settled on a fire-orange opal and diamond ring. God help him if she didn't like it; he wasn't going to spend another afternoon looking at tray after tray of rings.

Once was enough.

Right, he was going after her. Jonas put his foot on the first stair when he heard movement above him, and he slowly raised his eyes. God, she looked...

Stunning. Amazing. Fantastic...

None of the adjectives adequately conveyed the sensation rumbling around his chest. She was dressed in a structured white crop top and full ball-gown skirt the exact orange of the fire opal in his pocket. She'd pulled all that glorious hair back from her face and up into a style that reminded him of those animated princesses in Disney movies. Earrings dangled from her ears and she'd kept her makeup natural.

She looked... God, she looked sensational. And nervous. She rested her hand on the banister, closed her eyes and Jonas saw her lips move, as if in a silent prayer.

"Kat."

Kat's eyes flew open and Jonas saw worry flash in her gaze, uncertainty. She stared down at him, her fear tangible.

"What the hell are we doing, Jonas?" she softly asked and her words floated down to him.

"It'll be okay, Kat. I promise." Jonas's own hand gripped the banister as if it were a life buoy in a turbulent sea. If he let go, he'd race up the stairs, march her down the corridor and take her straight to bed. That was how much he wanted her, how desperately he wanted to slip off that tiny top, how much he wanted to see that skirt in a froth of fabric on the floor. He wanted her naked and panting and he wanted her now.

"Are you okay?" she asked, concerned.

Jonas managed a small smile. "Just trying to get my heart to restart. You look spectacular. Dazzling."

Kat's mouth tipped up at the corners as she started to walk down the stairs. "Thank you. You look pretty good, too."

He was wearing a tuxedo, a white shirt, a black tie. Nothing special, but he appreciated the comment. Jonas waited for her to reach him and when she did he leaned forward to kiss her cheek, needing to make a connection with her, however small. Her scent was delicious and Jonas felt his head swim. What was wrong with him? He'd dated and slept with some of the most beautiful women in the world, but none of them had ever made him feel this off balance.

"You're very late, Katrina," he murmured, trying to get a handle on the situation.

Kat winced. "Lunch service ran over, my car wouldn't start, traffic was hell."

"Give up work, choose a damn car and I offered to send a driver for you."

Kat smiled and his heart stopped. Before the end of this evening Jonas suspected he might need a defibrillator. Kat smoothed her hand down his tie, over his chest. "I am not going to argue with you, Halstead. Not tonight."

Jonas smiled and lifted her knuckles to his lips. "Thank God for small mercies." Dropping his hand, he hooked his index finger in the band on her skirt, wishing he could lick the strip of bare skin between the skirt and her short top. "I'm glad you wore this and not the black-and-white dress."

Kat narrowed her eyes. "There's nothing wrong with that dress but Tess told me she left it behind and, because I was late, I had to choose between the three dresses she brought from the boutique."

Kat didn't need to know that he'd told Tess to make sure she left the dress behind. He smiled. "So, did you like the other two dresses?"

"I did," Kat reluctantly admitted. "The gold dress is fantastic."

"Good. The tags have been removed from all three so don't even think about returning them. You now have dresses for the next two formal functions we attend, so we won't have to have the don't-bother-buying-a-dress argument for another two weeks or so."

"You are diabolical," Kat told him, unhooking his finger from her skirt and squeezing his hand.

Jonas twisted his fingers so they linked with hers. "Nope, I just like getting my way. And not arguing about money."

"Spoiled rich boy," Kat muttered, but she saw the smile in her eyes.

"Ridiculously independent, financially challenged girl," Jonas responded.

"Financially challenged?" Kat asked, her words coated with laughter. "You can just say poor. I'm not easily offended."

Jonas felt his heart stutter, told it to calm the hell down. He couldn't stop himself from kissing her mouth, one gentle touch of his lips against hers, a light flicker of his tongue. It was all he would allow himself or that dress was coming off, here at the bottom of the stairs.

Since that would be desperately embarrassing, Jonas eased back and wondered who this sap was who seemed to have taken over his body. God, he was acting like a kid, not like a grown man who had a deal with this vision—with this *woman*, he hastily corrected himself.

An outrageously sexy woman, but that shouldn't have any bearing on the subject. They were going to wed in a marriage agreement that was advantageous for both of them. *Keep your eye on the end goal, Halstead.*

That reminded him. He shoved his hand into the pocket of his pants, keeping his eyes locked on Kat's exquisite face. "I have something for you."

Jonas held the ring between his thumb and forefinger and watched as pleasure danced across Kat's face. "It's a fire opal, set with diamonds, and it's not expensive, so don't start on at me about the cost."

Kat didn't say anything. She just took the ring and examined it from every angle, seemingly fascinated by the irregular shape of the stone.

"It's unusual, I grant you that, but I thought you might like it," Jonas said, uncomfortable with her silence. Damn, he'd really thought she would like it. "I can take it back if it doesn't suit you. We'll just tell anyone who asks that your engagement ring is being designed—"

Kat lifted up on her toes and dropped a quick, hard, openmouthed kiss on his lips. It shocked him. "Shut up, Halstead. I absolutely love it! It's perfect."

"It is?"

Kat slid the ring onto the appropriate finger and held her hand up to look at it. "It's amazing, exactly what I would've chosen! Did you pick it to match my dress?"

Thanking God that she'd finally asked him a question he could answer without stuttering, Jonas smiled. "That was a happy coincidence."

"Thank you for listening to me," Kat said, her voice dropping in volume and increasing in intensity. "Thank you for not buying a whopping diamond or an expensive stone that I would've felt uncomfortable wearing."

"It was my pleasure," Jonas replied, not knowing what else to say. How did one respond when a gorgeous woman thanked you for not spending too much money on her?

It was one of the many mysteries he would have to unravel now that Kat Morrison had walked into, and upended, his life.

Seven

It was exhausting being the center of attention, Kat thought, edging behind a huge palm tree in the corner of the room. She just needed a moment or two alone, to catch her breath, to understand that this was now her life. Through the thick palm fronds, Kat looked across the ballroom to where Jonas was talking to a group of men. One of them was Rowan Brady, who'd shared Jonas's table that fateful night three or so weeks ago. Three weeks? Was that all the time that had passed? Sian was also here, flaunting her tattoos, much to the endless fascination of the guests and the disapproval of Jonas's grandfather.

Jack Halstead looked exactly how Kat imagined Jonas would when he reached old age. A thick head of hair, a craggy face dominated by fiercely intelligent eyes. When she was introduced to him earlier, Jack had acted like an absolute gentleman, nothing in his manner suggesting that he'd blackmailed his grandson into marriage. Actually, she rather liked the old man. He was charming and genial, but she knew he wasn't someone to be messed with.

In contrast, Kat did not like Lane, Jonas's father. At all. He'd kissed the back of her hand with fleshy lips that made her skin crawl. Kat felt like he had X-ray eyes that were mentally stripping her. It also interested Kat that Jonas seemed to dislike his father as much as she did. Jonas treated Jack with respect but his body tensed when he had to interact with Lane. He sounded genial but Kat could sense the angry currents swirling beneath their polite conversation. Kat wondered if anyone else knew that father and son loathed each other. Jack certainly seemed to be oblivious to the tension.

Not your business, Kat told herself. *You're in this dress and wearing this stunning ring for the bucks, remember? Do not get sidetracked by your curiosity about your sexy fiancé.* Kat darted another look at Jonas and sighed. It should be illegal for a man to look so good in a basic, albeit shockingly well-tailored, tux.

Dragging her eyes off Jonas, Kat realized that Jack and her boss were on the other side of the palm, both oblivious to her presence. Kat stood statue-still, hoping neither would notice her.

"Jack," Harrison said, tapping his crystal glass filled with expensive whiskey against Jack's beer glass. Kat rather liked the fact that Jonas's grandfather drank beer at a black-tie event. Maybe the Halsteads weren't as stuffy and snobby as she'd expected them to be. "I'm glad to see that you managed the Jonas situation without my help."

"Your help is expensive," Jack said, his tone amused.

"That it is. But young Jonas has made a good choice," Harrison said. "Katrina is the real deal."

"This is only the engagement. Nothing changes until I see them say I do," Jack replied and Kat heard the steel in his voice.

"Are you sure this is the only option?" Harrison asked.

"It's the only way I can protect the company. Jonas is the only person I trust implicitly."

That was a hell of a thing to say, Kat thought. She wondered if Jonas knew how highly his grandfather valued him.

"Well, call me if you need me to do what I do," Harrison said before they walked off together in the direction of Mariella Marshall, who looked amazing in an emerald-green sheath dress.

The gentlemen's conversation was puzzling. What did they think Harrison could do to help and why would Jack pay him for that help? Jonas had noted something similar when he'd gotten Cath the appointment in Malibu. Weird, Kat thought. So weird.

"What are you doing, Kat?"

Kat snapped her head up at the words and looked into Jonas's handsome face and amused eyes.

"Hiding out," Kat told him, placing her hand in the one he offered her, allowing him to draw her out of her hiding place.

"Are we that bad?"

"No. Not bad, it's just that remembering all the names and answering all the questions is exhausting." The warmth of his hand sent sparks up her arm. How those sparks ended up between her legs, God only knew.

"Tess is having fun," Jonas said.

Kat looked across the ballroom to see her friend, in

an ice-blue gown, openly flirting with the very married mayor of San Luis Obispo. Tess was reveling in the attention she was receiving as the BFF of Jonas's love-at-first-sight fiancée, openly and gaily telling everyone that of course she'd known Jonas and Kat were dating, that she and Kat were exceptionally close.

"I guess I should go to the rescue," Kat said as the mayor's hand landed on Tess's hip.

Tess tossed her hair and lowered her eyes, going into full flirt mode. Oh, dear, trouble was on its way.

"She doesn't need rescuing," Jonas told her, placing his arm around her waist, his mouth resting against her temple. He'd been super affectionate all night and Kat had to keep reminding herself that it didn't mean anything, that it was all an act to sell their story.

"I was talking about rescuing the man she's flirting with."

Jonas laughed and the deep rumble caused her hormones to jump to their feet and start to boogie. "He's harmless. Besides, his older, rich wife keeps a beady eye on him and will break up the cozy tête-à-tête soon enough. You, however, need to dance with me."

"I do?" Kat asked as he pulled her to the small dance floor in the middle of the room.

"You do. It's expected."

Damn, Kat thought as Jonas placed his hand on the small of her back and guided her into a smooth two-step. And here she was hoping he wanted to dance with her because he wanted his hands on her as badly as she wanted to put her hands on him.

It's an act, a con, a story you need to sell. It is not real life. If you carry on thinking like this, you're going to get your heart smashed!

A smashed heart hurts like hell, remember? If you

*don't, then we should spend some time recalling the
tears, the humiliation, the feeling of being stabbed in
the heart, over and over again.*

You only get to be that stupid once in your life, Kat.

As per her directions, Jonas pulled his SUV into
Cath's driveway. Kat watched as he walked around the
big car to open her door. Kat saw the twitch of curtains
in the front room and smiled. Cath was sitting in her
favorite chair, anxiously awaiting their arrival. Having
missed out on attending their engagement party, Cath
wanted to meet the man of the hour. Since hearing about
the engagement, Cath had asked Kat on a daily basis to
bring Jonas by. Jonas easily, and readily, agreed to meet
Cath, but finding the time when both Kat and Jonas
were free had turned out to be a challenge.

She worked odd hours and Jonas worked long hours,
and days could go by without them meeting or even
talking. Such was the life of two fake-engaged people,
Kat thought as Jonas opened the door for her.

Her hand slid into his and she sighed as those spar-
kles danced over her skin. She looked up and into his
beautiful green eyes and her heart, predictably, stum-
bled. Thanks to her job she was immune to the power
of gorgeous eyes in a handsome face and a hard body,
but Kat noticed everything about Jonas—his strong
tanned neck, his broad, ring-free hands, the tiny scar on
his bottom lip—and was attracted to every inch of him.

And she had yet to see him naked. Damn, she was
in so much trouble.

Their attraction was a living, breathing entity and
when they came within twenty feet of each other, the
urge to throw off their clothes was a constant temptation. She suspected that was why they'd, since the en-

gagement party, used their busy schedules as an excuse to avoid each other.

Sex, they'd both agreed, was not part of the deal. It was a complication they did not need.

But she still, desperately, wanted to know what making love with Jonas felt like. Kat wondered if Jonas lay awake at night fantasizing about what they'd do to each other. She hoped so. She'd be pissed if she found out he was getting a solid eight and she was a hot mess of horniness.

Kat climbed down from the car and tipped her head to the side. "Don't look now, but we are being watched."

Jonas kept his eyes on her face and the corners of his mouth tipped up. "Then we should give your aunt something to see."

Jonas cupped her face in his big hands, placed his thumbs on her jaw and dropped his mouth to meet hers. *Yes...this.* His lips were hard and masculine and, damn, so skilled.

Kat immediately forgot this was a demonstration kiss, a way to reassure her aunt that she was happy and in love. She fell into the moment, the rest of the world fading away. Her senses amplified and Kat could feel the prickle of warm sun on her back. With every breath she remembered to take, she inhaled traces of Jonas's cologne. And his mouth was a revelation—a whisper and a storm, a fervent prayer and a banshee's howl. It was heat and comfort and excitement and danger and home...

Confusion.

She wanted him. But she didn't want to want him.

Kat stepped back, pushing her hand into her hair. She saw her own confusion echoed in his eyes. She touched her fingertips to her lips and Jonas's eyes followed her movements. She knew that if she gave him the slightest hint, the smallest encouragement, he would kiss her again.

Strip her naked and slide on home.

But hopefully not on her aunt's lawn.

That little bit of silliness brought her back to where they were and what they were doing. Kat started to walk up the driveway, pulling her fractured thoughts together. How would Cath be today? She would be alert, she always was, but the length of their visit depended on Cath's levels of pain. Right now her doctor and caregiver were managing and monitoring the pain. There wasn't anything more they could do. Within the week Cath would be transported, by private ambulance provided by the clinic, to Whispering Oaks and she would be put on a new medical regime. Hopefully the new cocktail of drugs would provide an immediate improvement.

But that was for the future. Right now Kat had to convince her eagle-eyed aunt that she was madly in love with a sexy billionaire. Not so hard to do, Kat realized.

"So, Cath thinks you swept me off my feet," Kat told him as they approached the front door. Only her aunt would paint her front door that virulent shade of raspberry.

"Interesting color," Jonas said, his tone bland.

"She's an interesting woman," Kat replied, using her key to open the front door. "I wish you weren't meeting her when she feels so unwell. In her prime she was funny and loud and off-the-wall. Most afternoons my friends and I would end up at her house, just to hang out with her. She was…well, cool. She was everything my stepmother wasn't."

"Meaning?"

Kat shut the door behind her and kept the palm of her hand on the doorknob. She hadn't meant to say so much, but with Jonas, the words tended to flow out of her mouth without much thought. "June, my evil step-mother, was uptight, very concerned about what people thought about her. What they thought about her home, her marriage, her stepchild. My father did everything possible to make her happy and that included living far beyond their means. My home was filled with tension. This place was filled with love, acceptance and laughter. Here I could just...be."

Jonas took her hand, his long fingers linking with hers. "I'm glad you had Cath in your life."

Kat darted a quick glance at his face and noticed sadness in his eyes. "I know that your mother left you when you were a baby, but did you have a Cath in your life?"

Jonas looked past her to an oil painting on the wall behind her head. "I wasn't that lucky."

"I'm sorry," Kat whispered, wishing she had the courage to hug him, to offer comfort even though she knew he would not appreciate the gesture.

"Hey, you two, get in here! Stop kissing in my hall-way!"

Kat rolled her eyes, turned away from Jonas and crossed the hallway to walk into the sunroom. Cath, her dark hair turned gray and cut super short after her bout of chemo, sat in the armchair by the window, her tablet on her lap.

She'd lost more weight, Kat immediately noticed, and it was weight she could not afford to lose. Kat placed her hands on the arms of the chair and bent to kiss Cath's cheek. "We were not kissing in the hallway," she told her aunt, sotto voce.

"Why not? He's a great-looking man. Is he a good

kisser?" Cath demanded, laughter in her blue eyes and coating her voice.

Kat narrowed her eyes at her namesake. "Behave yourself, Catherine."

"Well, am I?" Jonas asked from the doorway.

Cath laughed and Kat thought it had been a while since she'd heard genuine amusement in her aunt's voice. Kat was grateful to Jonas for making Cath laugh, but the question made Kat blush. He was an amazing kisser. They both knew that. Just as they both knew that if they got naked they would leave scorch marks on the sheets. Or on the wall. The floor.

It was time to get off that topic, so she deliberately ignored his question. "Cath, meet Jonas Halstead. Jonas, Cath Long. Cath and my mother were identical twins."

"I was the prettier one," Cath told him as Jonas crossed the room to take the frail hand she lifted.

"That, I can believe." Jonas took both her hands in both of his. "It's so nice to meet you."

"It's much nicer to meet you," Cath told him and nodded at the chair next to her. "Take a seat. Let me get to know you."

Kat sat on the arm of Cath's chair as Jonas lowered his long body into the chair. "Cath, you promised not to interrogate him."

"I promised not to grill him. I didn't say I wouldn't ask him any questions."

Kat groaned. "Oh, God."

Jonas stretched out his long legs and rested his linked hands on his flat stomach, looking utterly relaxed. Damn him. "Relax, Katrina. I'm pretty sure I can answer any question your aunt throws at me."

"I like him already," Cath said. "Why are you marrying her?"

Kat held her breath as she waited for his response, staring hard at the frayed hem of her jeans. *If you tell her that you are in love with me, Cath will see through the lie.* "Because I think she's the most interesting woman I've met in a long time."

Kat lifted her head and her gaze slammed into his. That was the truth, she realized. He did think she was interesting. And that was...well, *interesting.*

"Are you going to buy her a new car?" Cath demanded, changing course.

"I'm trying to, but your niece is stupidly stubborn. I've run a few options past her but she keeps refusing them."

"Two sports cars and a high-end sedan," Kat snorted. "Too big and too expensive."

Cath leaned forward, ignoring Kat's statement. "I know how stubborn she is. It's so annoying! She hates asking for help. She sees it as a weakness."

Kat felt a headache building at the base of her neck. "Cath! Really?"

"Don't 'Cath! Really?' me," Cath retorted.

Kat looked at Jonas and saw that he was trying not to laugh. Yep, he and Cath were now in cahoots, damn them.

"And have you persuaded her to give up her job and go back to school?"

"Working on it," Jonas answered her, keeping his eyes on Kat's face.

Kat lifted a warning finger. "Don't start."

"You really should do that, Kit-Kat. You can get your degree and then you can do what you want to do for a change."

"Which is?" Jonas asked, leaning forward.

Kat looked from his expectant face to Cath's smiling face and back to Jonas again. If she didn't tell him, Cath would. "I know that you'll probably think this is a line, that I'm saying this to impress you—"

"If you are, then it would be a first," Jonas smoothly interjected.

Kat wrinkled her nose at him. "I'd really like to do what you do. Projects. Developments. Building or renovating something. If I had lots of cash, then that's what I'd do."

Cath glanced from Kat's face to Jonas's, her eyes brimming with excitement. "Maybe after you are married, Jonas can bring you into the business. She's smart, Jonas, so smart."

Jonas's deep green gaze didn't leave Kat's face. "I know she is, Cath. Brains and beauty, it's a killer combination."

Kat tipped her head to the side. The problem with being smart was that she knew what was hidden beneath the words people said—or beneath the words they didn't say. Like sex, working with Jonas would never happen.

The image of her and Jonas working together flashed in her head and Kat smiled. She could easily imagine them arguing, then laughing, then arguing again. But, like making love, like their marriage being anything more than a business arrangement, it would never happen and she shouldn't let her imagination fly away with her.

Life didn't work like that.

Cath changed the subject and Jonas turned his attention to her. Cath, enjoying the conversation, peppered Jonas with questions about his childhood, his education, his hobbies and interests. Kat sat and listened and absorbed.

Her father would've liked him, Kat realized. He

would've liked Jonas's no-nonsense way of speaking, his lack of snobbery. Wes, on the other hand, had always needed to point out to the world that he was someone, that he was successful.

Her father, like Kat, would've appreciated Jonas's don't-give-a-damn-what-you-think attitude. She could really like him, Kat thought. She could like him a lot.

If she let herself.

Needing to put some space between them, Kat stood. "I'm just going to say hello to Moira. She's Cath's caregiver."

"Bring Jonas back a cup of coffee when you return, darling." Cath patted her arm. "Jonas will stay here and we'll get acquainted."

What had they been doing for the past fifteen minutes? Kat placed her hands on her hips and glared down at her aunt. "Behave yourself."

"Pfft." Cath waved her away.

Knowing this was a fight she couldn't win, Kat walked toward the door, praying Cath wouldn't bring out the photo albums. If she did, Kat was out of there.

Kat was about to walk into the hall when Jonas called her name. Keeping her hand on the frame of the door, she turned to look at him.

"You didn't answer Cath's question."

Kat frowned, puzzled. "What question?"

The mischief in his gaze, the crinkle around his eyes suggesting laughter, the fact that his mouth tipped up at the corners—all of that—should've given her a clue he was about to torpedo her. "You didn't tell her whether I was a good kisser or not."

Cath's laughter filled the room. Kat flushed and tipped her face up to look at the ceiling. When she looked at Jonas again, all amusement had fled from his expression. He seemed desperate to know the answer to his question. How could he not know that his touch made her burn? That he just had to look at her and her inhibitions, and common sense, melted away.

Saying he was a good kisser was like saying Michelangelo was an average painter.

Kat lifted her fingers to her lips, recalling the feel of his mouth on hers. She had to answer him, but how? How did she tell him that no one had ever managed to take her breath away until him? That he just had to sit in a worn chair and look at her and she couldn't find any air to inhale? His kisses were magical. His arms felt like home. His voice made her feel undone.

Kat opened her mouth to say something, even though she had no idea what words her tongue was trying to form, but before she could speak she heard the jovial voice of Cath's caregiver behind her. "Kit-Kat! I've been reading about your engagement in the society pages! So exciting!"

Kat pulled her gaze away from Jonas's and turned around to walk into Moira's hug. But, unfortunately, Moira's ample bosom didn't muffle Cath's sassy comment.

"Oh, you two are going to drive each other crazy. What fun!"

Not surprisingly Cath's definition of fun and Kat's own were wildly different.

Eight

Kat sat on the edge of Cliff House's wraparound third-floor balcony, her arms on the railing and her feet dangling off the concrete. Jonas had asked her to meet him there, and when she'd arrived he'd taken her on a tour of the once iconic hotel. He'd explained to her, in great detail, his plans for restoring the hotel. He'd seemed to enjoy having her input, encouraging her to make suggestions and really listening when she spoke.

She'd been hesitant to share her ideas at first, but when she forgot that he was a billionaire developer and she was a restaurant hostess, their conversation turned lively and engaging. It had been so nice to have a conversation that didn't involve celebrities and table seating and wait times and overindulged guests.

God, she wanted to do this, to do what she loved. And speaking of her future plans, she was going to have to postpone the writing of her LCA exam. With her crazy life as the Cinderella Bride of California's Hottest Billionaire—as she was now being called by the tabloid press—she hadn't even glanced at her books. If she sat for the exam now, she would fail and her time and money would be wasted. Dealing with Jonas, working at the restaurant and dodging the intrusive and downright annoying paparazzi left little time and energy for studying.

Kat felt her phone vibrate and she pulled it out of the back pocket of her denim shorts. She opened the text message and saw that Tess had sent her a link to a website. Tess found Kat's current celebrity status hysterical and kept track of the more outrageous stories about Kat and Jonas.

Kat clicked on the link and raised her eyebrows at the headline that appeared on her small screen: How an Average Santa Barbara Restaurant Hostess Snagged a Billionaire. Follow These Ten Easy Steps!

Kat rolled her eyes and scrolled down. "Step one. You've got to be where the rich men are. Kat Morrison works as a hostess at the fantastically exclusive El Acantilado restaurant and we bet that's where she plotted to snag Jonas's interest."

Kat rolled her eyes. What rot. Refusing to read any more, she was about to close the web page when she saw a link to an article titled "The Younger Marshalls, West Coast Royalty."

Kat skimmed the article probing into the love lives of Harrison Marshall's children. Apparently Dr. Luc, the prominent plastic surgeon, was keeping company with Rachel Franklin, a congressman's daughter. Daughter Elana was still linked with a very married Hollywood producer, Jarrod Jones.

There was a picture of stylist son Rafe walking with

a handsome man in Calistoga, their fingers brushing. The article went on to speculate on who Rafe's companion was. Why did it matter and who cared?

Fame, Kat thought, had never been so easy to achieve as it was these days. She was now semi-famous herself, simply for becoming engaged to a rich man. The Marshall children were famous because they were the offspring of America's favorite chef. It was crazy, Kat thought, that so many people were utterly fascinated by what the rich and famous, or infamous, did.

Kat felt Jonas's hand on her shoulder and was surprised when he sat beside her, his designer pants on the dusty balcony, his feet dangling off the edge. In front of them the Pacific Ocean was a perfect mix of blue and green and the setting sun tossed confetti sunbeams on the water's surface. The end of the day was approaching and soon the hotel would be empty of construction workers and she and Jonas would be its only occupants.

"I spoke to my project manager about changing that flooring in the ballroom as per your suggestion and he said it's doable. It's a cheaper option, also a lot less labor intensive so we'll save both time and money. This project is already over budget and running out of time, so I appreciate your input."

Kat felt pleasure, warm and delightful, unfurl inside her at his compliment. "You're welcome."

"You've got a good brain, Kat," Jonas said, his voice quiet. "You should be completing your degree so you can use it. Our marriage could give you that opportunity."

Kat rested her arms on the railing and pushed her chin into her wrist. It was such a lovely evening and she didn't want to argue with him. She just wanted to sit there, soaking in the late-afternoon sun, her shoulder and thigh against his, smelling the sea and watching the waves kiss the shore.

"I don't want to argue with you, not tonight."

"Then don't argue, just listen."

Kat waited for Jonas to speak, turning her head to look at his profile. His sunglasses were pushed up into his hair and soft stubble covered his cheeks. Like her, he looked tired, played out. This project was sucking up his time and, from a few other discussions they'd had—Jonas was remarkably forthright with her about the inner workings of his business—he was putting out fires all over the country. There was a delay on a project in Toronto, one of Halstead's directors was in the hospital after a heart attack and a major investor had just pulled out of a deal to build a new casino in Reno.

Jonas was also preparing to marry a woman he didn't love for reasons he'd never properly explained. Oh, she knew about him losing his inheritance, but Kat suspected that there was more to the story.

"I actually respect the fact that you are independent, that you've gotten to where you are by your own effort. I sometimes envy the fact that no one can question whether you did it by yourself or not. People assume I am the CEO of Halstead & Sons because of Jack. Where else would a Halstead be? There is no doubt that you can do this, that you can hold your own."

There was a but coming...

"But, dammit, Kat, you make life so hard on yourself. You're exhausted, stressed, mentally and physically played out. And when I notice that, I get pissed because I can, with very little effort, lighten your load. You seem to treat this deal as if you are the only person benefiting from it, but this is a two-way street. I need you as my wife as much as you need my money."

"Will you tell me why?"

Jonas caught and held her glance, his eyes steady. "I might. If you consider taking a little more help from me."

"What sort of help?" Kat asked, suspicious.

"I'll cover Cath's medical expenses as agreed, but I'll also cover your current expenses and your studies. That way you can give up your job but still have income coming in. I'll give you a credit card you can use for emergencies. I know you won't use it but it'll make me feel better if you have it."

Kat hesitated, a part of her wanting to say yes but so damn scared that she'd take this deal and then he'd rescind on his promises. She'd been burned by empty promises before. "I don't know, Jonas. You're asking a lot."

"I'm asking you to let me help you," Jonas replied, his voice calm and steady.

"I don't accept help easily."

Jonas released a small smile. "Yeah, I kind of realized that. Why not? Your ex?"

Kat nodded. "I went into our marriage as blind as a bat. He said he wanted to marry me, that he wanted to take care of me, that he loved me. I believed him."

Kat felt Jonas's eyes on her face but kept staring at the ocean, not wanting to see pity. "The first month we were married, the first time we had to pay our bills, he told me he expected me to pay my way. He said that if I wanted this marriage, and him, I'd show him how much I loved him by being an equal partner. All our living expenses were split exactly fifty-fifty. Well, I paid fifty percent of the mortgage but his name was on the deed. I paid money toward his car but he didn't pay anything toward mine. When I tried to argue my case, he withdrew and became icy cold. Being shut out like that was torture."

"I understand. My father was a master at that. He started freezing me out as a punishment, but soon his icy reserve turned into a habit. By my teens I'd learned not to care."

Kat heard the pain in his voice and touched his hand in comfort. He didn't pull away so she continued her story. "I wanted us to be happy, for him to be happy, so I acquiesced. To give Wes what he wanted, I had to work two jobs, one of them at El Acantilado."

"What a douche," Jonas said, his voice filled with outrage.

"I should've left him, but I wanted the marriage to succeed so I worked and studied and scraped up enough money each month to meet his terms. Then he complained that I wasn't spending enough time with him. I couldn't win. Then my dad died and, as I told you, everything went to my stepmom. I couldn't pay for school and I asked Wes to help me but he refused. Cath stepped up with the cash but Wes still expected me to pay exactly what I had been paying, between school and his demands, I was financially squeezed. Then came the ring incident…"

"What ring incident?"

Kat swallowed, the hurt as sharp today as it had been four years ago. "The only item I had of my mom's was an art deco ring, a square-cut sapphire surrounded by rectangular-cut diamonds. Not big or terribly valuable but it was given to her on her twenty-first birthday and my dad gave it to me on my twenty-first birthday. It had both mine and my mom's initials engraved on the band."

It hurt to talk about this but she needed Jonas to understand. "I had a car payment due and I couldn't swing it. It was the second one I'd missed and they were threatening to take my car. Wes kept some cash at home and I was desperate so I borrowed the money, leaving an IOU in its place. A few days later, I looked in my jewelry box and saw that my ring was gone. I confronted Wes and he told me that I had no right to take his money and that he'd replaced it by selling my ring on the internet. He said he hoped I'd learned my lesson. Three hours later, my stuff was packed up and I was living with Cath.

"That ring was the only link I had to my mom and he treated it like it was a used appliance, like it was nothing important," Kat whispered, feeling the all-too-familiar waves of grief, pain and mistrust. "I still check internet sites, hoping someone has put it up for sale, but no luck. It's futile, but I keep trying, hoping to find it."

"Give me your ex's name and address and I swear I'll make his life a living hell," Jonas said, his voice low with anger. "After I rip his head off and shove it where the sun doesn't shine."

Kat smiled at the image before sobering again. "Thanks to him, and to my dad, as well, I have a hard time trusting people. I can't rely on anyone to keep their word."

"I'm not him, Kat. I'm not going to change my mind. I'm not going to offer my support and then withdraw it, leaving you floundering. I mean what I say and I follow my words with actions. I know you find trust difficult, but you can trust that."

She wished she could. She wanted to. But her lack of trust was now a habit that would take time to change. "Anyway, getting back to your generous offer… Can I think about it? Can we talk about this again?"

Jonas's expression was pure determination. "And we will." He pulled out his wallet, flipped it open and withdrew a card. He tucked it into the back pocket of Kat's jeans and when she opened her mouth to argue, he lifted his eyebrows. "No, we're not arguing about this. You run into a problem, you use the card. The rest of my offer we can discuss later but I need to know you have some sort of backup plan."

"I—"

"Change the subject, Kat."

Kat knew she wouldn't win this argument. Okay, so she had one of his credit cards, but she was never going to use it so arguing about it was pointless. She'd just leave it in her purse unused until he asked for it back.

Kat unfolded her arms and echoed Jonas's actions, placing her hands on the concrete behind her and leaning back.

"So, if you don't marry, Jack will disinherit you," she said, changing the subject and putting the spotlight on him. It was his turn to open up and Kat wondered if he would.

"Yep. I'll be out in the cold," Jonas replied, sounding remarkably sanguine.

"You make it sound like that doesn't bother you, but since you're prepared to take the drastic step of marrying me, I know that's not true."

"I'm not scared of starting over, of doing my own thing, of building something new," Jonas told her. "In fact, that would be awesome."

"It would?"

"Sure. It would be all mine, built with my own sweat and tears, knowing that I was a hundred percent responsible for its success or failure. There's a freedom in that, Kat."

He sounded wistful, Kat realized, and she had an inkling of how being born into a legacy, as part of a successful clan, might mess with your head.

"Yet you are still marrying me to inherit your grandfather's shares."

"Yep. Loyalty to family is a bitch."

Kat cocked her head. "You once said to me that it was more important to you to keep the shares out of someone else's hands. Your dad's?"

Jonas looked shocked at her guess and even if he said nothing else, gave no further explanations, she'd know by his expression that she'd hit the nail on its head.

"What happened to cause such a rift between you two?"

Jonas stared at the beach far below them, his neck and back muscles tense. "What makes you think we have issues?"

"When I heard you speak to him at the engagement party, your voice changed. You were trying too hard to show the world, your grandfather, that you didn't hate Lane. He was a little better at concealing his loathing for you, but it was there. What happened?" Kat asked.

Jonas linked his hands behind his neck, his biceps bulging. "I was working my way up the ladder and Jack was CEO, but my dad, who was the chief financial officer, was making a lot of the decisions. Because I wanted to prove to them both that I was as good as them, I was working sixteen, eighteen, hours a day, moving from department to department. I was working in the finance department at the time and Jack told me to analyze the books. Using my fancy degree, he wanted me to tell him where we were wasting money and how we could improve the bottom line. My father knew what I was doing but, not having quite the same

attention to detail and work ethic as I do, didn't expect
me to dig as deep as I did."

Kat lifted her hand to her mouth, immediately knowing where he was going with the story. "You found
something—"

Jonas released a harsh laugh. "I found at lot of things.
Kickbacks, siphoned funds, fake companies. He did it
all and sucked millions out of the company coffers."

Kat felt sick. "Oh, Jonas. So what did you do?"

Jonas lifted one shoulder in a hard shrug. "I did what
I needed to do to save the company. I told him to resign
or else I would expose him and charge him with fraud. I
told him if he did go quietly, then I'd keep his treachery
from Jack. He could also keep his position as a Halstead
director and the enormous salary that came with it, but
if he ever opposed me, on anything, I'd expose him. I
had him between a rock and a hard place, and because
I had so much proof, he agreed."

"That must have been such a hard thing to do, Jonas.
I've read articles written about Jack and I know he's a
stickler for loyalty, demanding it from his employees
and his suppliers. Loyalty to your grandfather or loyalty to your dad—you must've felt like you were being
ripped apart."

Jonas slowly nodded. "I did. He resigned. I stepped
into his position and went on to become the CEO. He
still blames me for edging him out of the company. He
acts as if I was desperate for the job, desperate to worm
my way into Jack's good graces."

"He stole from the company!" Kat cried.

"Yeah, he's conveniently forgotten that part of the
story," Jonas said, his voice as dry as bone.

"But why did he steal? It's not like you Halsteads
are short of money."

"Gambling. He was addicted. That was another part of the deal I made with him. He left the company and he got treatment. He just transferred his obsession with cards into an obsession with art. As long as he stays far away from Halstead & Sons, he can do whatever the hell he likes with his money."

Kat bit the inside of her lip, still confused. "I still don't understand how this links with you having to marry."

Jonas rubbed his hand over his lower face. "Oh, that. Jack said that if I don't marry he's going to give his shares to Lane. If he does that, then Lane will have controlling interest of Halstead and he could cause a lot of trouble if he decided to resume his duties. One of two things could happen. I'd get fired and he'd have carte blanche to raid the company of its assets or I'd murder him and be sent to jail and then he'd raid the assets."

"Neither would be a good outcome."

"I want this company, Kat. I want people to look at it, and me, with respect again."

"They do," Kat protested.

"To an extent. But Jack's ruthlessness and my father's cutting-corners attitude are remembered. I want our name to be trusted. To do that, I need complete control, hence my need for a wife." Jonas stood, dusted his hands off on his pants and held out a hand to haul Kat up. "Do you know what else I need?" he asked when she was on her feet.

Desire replaced the bleakness in his eyes and Kat found herself edging closer to him, wishing she could follow up their conversation with a hug. She wanted to comfort him but she also wanted to feel that hot, hard, muscled body pressing into hers. Her breasts flat against his chest, his thigh between her legs, hands on her butt, mouth teasing hers.

"What?" She forced the word out, conscious of her pounding heart.

"Food. And sex." And there it was, what they both wanted but couldn't, shouldn't, have. "But that's still off the table, right?"

Nodding her head in agreement was one of the hardest things she'd ever done. After they'd both opened up emotionally, she wanted to be with him physically even more than before. But she managed to agree that they should abstain, with great reluctance. It was the smart thing to do and she prided herself in being a smart woman.

Jonas muttered a quiet curse and led her into the old hotel. "Damn. Let's get some food. Then I'm taking you home, you're going to pack a bag—you don't need much, just shorts, tees and a swimsuit—and we're going to the airport. Do you have a passport?"

"Yes…" When his words sank in, Kat stopped walking. "A bag? Airplane? Passport? Where are we going? I can't go anywhere!"

Jonas just looked at her, still handsome in the shadows of the building. "Why not? You're not working this weekend and you need a break. I'm giving you one."

"B-but—" Kat spluttered. "I need to—"

"Cath is at the clinic and can't have visitors until the end of next week. You don't have any pets, nor do you have any obligations. Come with me to Saint Kitts, I need to check on a development there. It'll take an hour tomorrow morning, maybe two, and then we can spend the rest of the weekend doing absolutely nothing."

Oh, it sounded like heaven.

"Just say yes, Kat. Don't think, don't analyze, just say yes," Jonas said, his deep voice washing over her.

"Yes, okay. Let's go to Saint Kitts." Kat wondered who this woman was who was speaking on her behalf.

Was she crazy? She had obligations. She was supposed to be staying away from temptation so she didn't sleep with this too kind, way too sexy billionaire. She was Katrina Morrison and she didn't make impulsive decisions to jump on her fake fiancé's jet to head for the Caribbean at the last minute.

But, apparently, today she was that woman.

Jonas, Kat at his side, stood on the ridiculously green, springy and expansive front lawn and looked at the 18th-century restored sugar plantation. He liked the property, with its landscaped gardens and breathtaking ocean views, but he wasn't sure if he liked it enough to add it to the Halstead portfolio. The inn was turning a profit, but that wasn't good enough.

Kat, dressed in white shorts and a blue-and-white-striped cotton shirt with the sleeves rolled up, flipped through the folder he'd handed her to read. It contained financial statements, assets registers and sales forecasts…everything he needed to make a decision on whether to shell out a hefty chunk of change for the property.

"What do you think?" he asked Kat. "Should I buy it?"

Kat held the folder to her side and slowly turned in a circle, taking in the gray-and-white building with its wraparound balconies, the view of the cloud-shrouded mountain, the gardens and the amazing view of the water. When she stopped, a tiny frown appeared between her arched eyebrows. "It had a major restoration three years ago—roof, plumbing, pool, gardens. The rooms need redecorating and some of the furnishings need to be updated. The restaurant needs more experienced chefs. Most of the changes you'd need to do are cosmetic. But—"

She shrugged, deep in thought. "Those changes won't make a difference to the bottom line. Bookings are steady. The pricing is in line with what the other accommodation establishments are charging."

Her eyes lightened when she was excited and involved, Jonas thought. She loved this. She loved looking at the figures, making sense of them, matching the figures against the product. That big brain of hers was wasted as a restaurant hostess. Damn, if he wasn't going to marry her, he'd give her a job at Halstead tomorrow.

"I'd rebrand the property," Kat suddenly stated.

Jonas lifted his eyebrows. "You would?"

Kat nodded. "I'd spend money redecorating and reduce the number of rooms, make them bigger, more expansive, more luxurious and romantic."

"Less rooms, less income."

"Not if you charge a ridiculous amount for each room," Kat said, her voice rising in excitement. "I'd market this as a very luxurious wedding and honeymoon venue."

"There are other wedding venues on the island," Jonas pointed out, playing the devil's advocate.

"There isn't a venue with these views that will be this luxurious. I think it could work."

He did, too. It was a fantastic idea. Jonas took his phone from the back pocket of his jeans, dialed a number and kept his eyes on Kat. "Sian? Take a look at the plantation house on Saint Kitts. I want cost projections, payback periods, sales forecasts on what returns we'll get if we have to convert the place to a luxury wedding destination. Have the figures on my desk by Monday. Thanks."

Kat couldn't contain her wiggle of excitement. "Seriously? You think my idea has merit?"

He chuckled at her enthusiasm. "I think your idea has a lot of merit and that is why Sian is going to spend the weekend crunching numbers."

Kat winced. "That doesn't sound like fun for Sian."

"Sian gets paid a very hefty salary to do her job," Jonas replied. "Speaking of how to spend the weekend... Work is over. Let's start ours."

"All I'd like to do is lie on the beach, swim and lie on the beach some more," she said.

Kat shoved her hands into the back pockets of her jeans, her spine arching. The fabric of her shirt pulled over her small but perfect breasts and Jonas felt the blood draining from his head. So, maybe bringing her to the islands wasn't the smartest idea he'd ever have because... Crap. Sun and sea and sex went together like ice and cream. He'd managed, by the skin of his teeth, to resist her back in the States, so why had he thought he could do it here?

Inviting her to Saint Kitts had been impulsive, but they'd made a connection at Cliff House and he'd wanted to spend more time with her. He'd wanted to show her a place he loved. Obviously, if his brain had been working, he would've realized that Kat in a bikini would be more temptation than he could resist.

Kat fell into step beside him as they headed for the small parking lot and his rented, open-top Jeep. "Where are we staying, by the way? Somewhere close to the beach?"

Jonas stopped, scanned the water and lifted his

hand to point to a small island across a narrow straight. "We're going to Nevis. It's smaller than Saint Kitts, less commercial."

"Do you own a hotel there?" Kat asked as they resumed walking.

"I own a small house on Nevis. It's situated on a cliff and you walk to the end of the garden, down some wooden steps onto a private beach. It's isolated and quiet, and it's my favorite place in the world."

Kat stared at him, her eyes round. He could see the confusion in her eyes, the desire. She knew that being alone together would be dangerous, that there would be so many chances for them to end up in bed together. They were in the Caribbean, with warm seas, hot days and nights, minimal clothing. It wasn't rocket science.

Why had he risked inviting her again?

"Or," he said to give her a way out, maybe to give himself a way out, "we can stay here." He gestured to the house behind them. "The owners offered us two rooms for the weekend."

Please let me take you to my home. I need you.

Kat touched her top lip with her tongue, her eyes smoking over with heat. They both knew this was about more than a place he wanted to share with her.

If she said yes, they'd both be saying yes to much more than a temporary marriage.

"Let's go to your cottage," she eventually said, putting him out of his misery.

He had to make sure. For both of them. "I'm putting sex back on the table, Katrina. Do you understand that?"

Kat's blue eyes darkened. "On the table, on the beach, in a bed. It all sounds good to me. I'm tired of resisting what we both want."

Relief filled his chest. "Thank God. Okay, we need

to head to the beach. I'm going to ask one of the local fisherman to ferry us across."

Kat's smile punched right through his gut. "What? No jet plane?"

"Impractical and expensive." Jonas returned her smile and slid his fingers around her hand. "Besides, crossing the Narrows in a boat is so much more fun."

They reached the rented Jeep and Jonas watched Kat climb up into the passenger seat, all long hair and longer legs. He wanted to taste her creamy skin, feel her amazing smile on his skin, get lost in the blue of her eyes. He'd wanted that for weeks. It was a testament to his determination that he'd held out this long.

He was finally, finally, going to make love to this amazing, vulnerable, smart, sweet woman. Jonas felt his heart stutter and stumble.

Do you know what you are doing, Halstead? She could mess with your head. This could go deeper than sex, could mean more than a weekend fling. She could become someone you want for more than a temporary marriage.

Jonas shook his head, hoping to dislodge his crazy thoughts. *You've had flings before*, he told himself. *You know how to do this.*

Yeah, but he'd never had a fling with Katrina Morrison. She was different from anyone he'd ever met before. And she'd be moving in, as his *wife*, very soon.

Even so, he could handle this.

Maybe.

Nine

Kat, her mind churning, her body pulsating, allowed Jonas to lead her across the front porch with its 180-degree ocean views and into his charming and traditional Caribbean-style home.

Kat heard the thump of bags hitting the floor and watched as Jonas walked over to the windows and opened the shutters, allowing dappled sunlight and a cool breeze to enter the room, raising goose bumps on her skin.

Or the goose bumps could be because of the way Jonas was looking at her. Dressed in black cargo shorts, a hunter green T-shirt and flip-flops, he looked more like a surfer than a CEO, sexy enough to dissolve any second thoughts she had.

"Are you sure this is what you want?" Jonas asked.

"This is what I want." Kat forced the words past her dry lips. Jonas started to walk toward her but stopped when she lifted her hand. "This is what I want until we get back to Santa Barbara. This is what I want for the next two days. It might not be what I think is best later on. Is that okay?"

"Two days with an option to renew?"

She huffed a small and nervous laugh. "Exactly."

Jonas started walking toward her again.

Kat hadn't seen anyone this sexy for a long time. Okay, never. It had been so long since she'd had a lover...

So damn long.

Kat's hand flew up again and Jonas stopped a meter away from her. The jumping muscle in his cheek was the only indication of his frustration. "Yeah?"

"It's been a while," Kat said, feeling embarrassed. "I'm not on the pill and I don't carry condoms. Even worse, I don't know if I remember how to do this."

Jonas stepped closer and placed his hands on her hips. She noticed tenderness in his eyes. Man, she wanted—craved—some tenderness. "I know how to do this and I have protection. I'll make this good for you, Kat, I promise."

Kat nodded, her hands resting on his chest. Her heart felt like it was about to burst. "I know, but I don't know if it'll be good for you," she said, her soft words muffled.

Jonas tipped her chin up with his knuckle. "Sweetheart, you're in my arms and it's already amazing. Your kisses rock my world so I am not worried."

Jonas looked at her mouth, bounced his gaze up to hers and looked at her mouth again. "Any more questions? Because I'm dying here."

Jonas didn't wait for her answer. His mouth met hers and he didn't bother with soft and sweet, he just hurtled straight to demanding and desperate.

His tongue delved into her mouth, swirled, retreated and dived in again. His kiss was fine wine and Belgian chocolate, bungee jumping and coral sea diving. It was heat and happiness and hunger.

Kat loved being kissed by him, but she wanted more, so much more, so she pushed her hips into his, sighing when her stomach encountered the hard length of him.

Yeah, she wanted more.

Instead of dialing it up, Jonas stepped away from her, his fingers the only part of him touching her. He ran them down her cheek, over her jaw. What was the problem? Why was he stopping?

Kat didn't know she'd spoken the words aloud until Jonas answered her question. "I'm stopping because if I don't, I'm going to last two seconds and that's not how I want this to go."

"I can do fast," Kat assured him, already missing his hard body against hers, his mouth fused with hers.

Jonas shook his head. "Nope, it's not going to happen that way, Kit-Kat."

Kat's heart melted at hearing Cath's pet name for her on his lips. It made her feel special, wanted, a little…loved.

No, this was sex, not love. *Don't you dare get the two confused, Kat.*

"Let's take this to the bedroom," Jonas said, bending his knees to hook an arm around the backs of her thighs. He lifted her and held her against his chest, easily carrying her across the room and down the hallway.

Kat played with his hair and nuzzled his jaw. In the bedroom, which was decorated in soft greens and white with a high ceiling, Jonas dropped her to her feet in front of a free-standing, white, wood-framed mirror.

He stood behind her, big and dark, his face a mask

of concentration. His hands rested on her shoulders and Kat watched, fascinated, as his fingers danced over to the open V at her neck. Those big hands undid the buttons of her shirt, slowly revealing more of her skin to his hot gaze.

"Watch me touch you, sweetheart," Jonas commanded, his eyes blazing pure green fire.

When her shirt lay open he pulled it off her shoulders and down her arms, revealing her lacy white bra to his intent gaze. Jonas kissed the side of her neck as he cupped her breasts, easily covering them with his big, broad hands.

Kat lifted her arms and gripped the back of his neck, her arching back lifting her nipples into his palms. Jonas groaned and swiped his thumbs over the hard nubs.

"Look at your eyes," he said, his words a low growl in her ear. "Look how they go a deeper, darker blue. *So* sexy."

She flicked her eyes to her reflection but her attention was snagged by the look on his face. Passion and concentration, all his attention focused on her, his only aim to give her pleasure.

Jonas dropped his hands from her breasts and pulled back, and she felt the fastenings to her bra open. She tried to turn but Jonas held her against him, meeting her eyes again in the mirror.

"No, like this," he insisted. Slowly—so, so slowly—using one finger, he pulled one cup down, revealing her right breast, her nipple rosy and hard and begging to be touched, kissed. Jonas groaned, ground his erection into her lower back and yanked the bra off her, dropping it to the floor.

"Going slow is killing me," Kat muttered, moving his hands back to her breasts, silently asking for more.

"It'll be worth it, I promise." Jonas's hands skimmed down her breasts, over her flat stomach to dip beneath the band of her shorts. Kat covered his hands with hers, dragging her fingertips over the backs of his hands and up his wrists before snapping open her shorts and pushing the fabric down her hips and thighs to the floor.

Jonas whispered a low curse in her ear. Her gaze flew to his face but his attention was on the tiny triangle between her thighs. "You are so damn beautiful."

Kat looked at her body in the mirror, practically naked and standing in his arms. Her breasts were high, her stomach flat, her legs long. She looked the same as she always did, but not. She looked, she realized, animated, as if she was glowing from the inside out, as if Jonas had flicked on all the lights inside her.

She looked like a woman who was desperate for her lover's touch. And she was. She yearned to know his secrets, to taste his soul. All the worries and risks that had held her back before now seemed like nothing in the face of this desperation.

Jonas ducked his head, placed his open mouth on her neck and slipped his hand under the fabric of her panties, his finger unerringly finding her sweet spot.

Kat felt the sparks, then the bolts of lightning, the heavy heat in her womb.

She also felt peace, like this was right. Jonas touching her, pleasuring her, was the only thing she was supposed to be doing right now.

"God, Jonas…" Kat murmured. "That feels so good."

"I'm glad, honey."

Jonas pulled his hand from between her legs, spun her around and covered her mouth with his. Her panties slid down her legs and then Jonas was pushing two fingers back inside her and placing his thumb against her clit.

Kat wound her arms around his neck, holding on because her legs were no longer able to support her.

The white light behind her eyes intensified and Kat pulled her mouth away, panting. "I'm so close. I need to come, Jonas."

She didn't care that she sounded crazy. She needed this release.

"Trust me, you will." Jonas looked around the room, smiled and walked her over to the windowsill, placing her bare butt on the cool wood. He shoved the shutters open and Kat felt the salty air on her skin, heard the waves crashing on the beach below. "Yeah, this will work."

Jonas dropped a hard kiss on her open mouth before reaching up and pulling his T-shirt over his head.

That chest, Kat thought, pushing her fist into her sternum. Wide, muscled, with a light smattering of hair that crossed ridged stomach muscles in a perfect line.

Her gaze dancing across his body, Kat held her breath as Jonas shucked his shorts and underwear. There he was, masculine, straight and hard. Kat lifted her hand to touch him but Jonas shook his head.

"Later. This is still about you."

"Me touching you is what I want," Kat murmured as he dropped to his knees in front of her, his wide shoulders pushing her thighs apart. Oh, God, it was too much, too intimate…

"Trust me, Kat."

She would. She did. Kat relaxed.

"I keep saying it but it's true. You are truly stunning."

No one had ever called her lady parts stunning. Kat

had barely finished the thought when Jonas kissed her, his mouth on the most secret part of her. Embarrassment scuttled away as sensation swamped her. This was lovemaking like she'd never experienced before.

Jonas pulled back and sat on his heels, his big hands moving to her torso, his gaze scanning her body. Kat dropped her head back as his finger—that clever, amazing, lightning-infused finger—explored her belly button, went lower, touched her bead and slid into her hot, wet passage. Then a second finger joined the first, his tongue swirled around, and every inch of her body hummed.

His fingers curled into her as his mouth loved her and she flew away on fireworks of pleasure. Light—pure and pulsating—flashed behind her eyelids and her body tensed, every inch of her poised like a free diver on a cliff, a base jumper on a building's ledge. And then she was flying...

Feminine power rushed from a place deep inside her until a dazzling display of fireworks erupted from her innermost core. Pleasure swirled and twirled, each revolution less potent than the last until the whirlwind stopped and she could breathe again. Panting, she hunched over, a light sheen of sweat on her skin.

Jonas placed a light kiss on her inner thigh before sitting back on his heels to look at her.

"I never...I can't... Wow."

A long, slow, smile crossed Jonas's face. "Good?"

"Amazing. Thank you." Kat suddenly realized she was recovering from a hell of an orgasm and he was still rock-hard and waiting.

Jonas just looked at her, waiting for her to make the next move. They had yet to make love, she realized. The past fifteen minutes had been his gift to her. She wanted togetherness now. Oneness. The giving and receiving of physical love.

Kat stood, held out her hand and watched as Jonas rose, in one fluid movement, to his feet.

He took her hand, curling his fingers around hers. "You're mine until we land in Santa Barbara," he stated, his tone suggesting that she not argue.

"I'm yours," Kat agreed, holding his volcano-hot gaze. "So, are those condoms anywhere close?"

There was a wave behind her. She was lying face-down on the board and she was paddling. So far, so good. When she felt the board rise, she had to pop up— *Pretend you're doing a pushup*, Jonas had told her—she had to stand...now!

Kat pushed up, wobbled into a crouch and the board skittered out from under her as the wave crashed over her head. Spitting out a mouthful of briny water, she planted her feet in the sand and pushed her wet hair out of her eyes.

She sucked at surfing.

Kat turned around and watched Jonas fly down a wave. She pulled a face. Her fake fiancé and current lover did not suck at surfing. He looked as at home on a surfboard as he did in the boardroom, on a construction site, on top of her, sliding into her.

Of all the things Jonas did well—of which she knew there were many—making love to her, she was convinced, was what he was best at.

She loved being with him, spending time exploring their passion. Sex with Jonas was off-the-charts amazing. But Kat also enjoyed just being with him. Hanging out in his kitchen, watching him cook, which he, annoyingly, also did really well. Cuddling on the hammock strung between two trees, him reading while she lay with her head on his shoulder, watching the endless blue ocean. Easy conversation and teasing laughter, drinking red wine while walking on the beach at midnight.

They'd only been here a day or two, but she loved this life, so far away from the craziness of what they were doing in Santa Barbara. This island life was relaxed, uncomplicated and easy. Out of the glare of society and flashing cameras, away from the demands of his life as CEO of an enormous company and Cath's illness, Kat felt more like herself than she had for…so long. Years.

She liked the Nevis version of Kat. She really, really, liked this laid-back, Nevis version of Jonas, and she knew that if they weren't leaving tomorrow, if they stayed here, she'd fall in love with him.

Maybe she was a little, or a lot, in love with him already.

It couldn't go anywhere, though. They were marrying under crazy circumstances. She was marrying him for money. He was marrying her for control over his company's future. For a marriage to succeed it had to be based on love first and last; it couldn't be complicated by "if you do this, then I'll do that." As she knew, making a marriage work was tough enough before adding any extra complications.

Kat looked up at the cliff, picturing the house behind the trees. It was her dream house—small, cozy, compact. Simple. She could live a simple life with Jonas the Surfer.

A life with Jonas the CEO Billionaire would not be so straightforward.

Kat sat with the board between her legs, telling herself it was salt burning her eyes and not tears. She knew, thanks to her wretched marriage and her father's death, that not everything in her life would last forever, but this...

This overwhelming feeling of contentment she was experiencing bobbing on a clear Caribbean sea, watching her lover surf—this she wanted to keep forever. But life didn't work that way. She'd have to let this dream, this contentment, trickle through her fingers when they left Nevis behind.

Something would go wrong when she left the island, when they went back to reality. Of course it would. They couldn't have it all. Well, maybe Jonas could, but she couldn't. She was setting herself up for a big fall if she thought he'd solve all her problems. People lied. People misrepresented the truth. They changed their minds, changed their perceptions.

Nothing was cast in stone; everything could go sideways on her. It was better to keep her distance, to keep scanning the horizon, to keep giving herself time to dodge those missiles that would blow up her life. This wasn't a fairy tale, Jonas wasn't her prince and she wasn't going to end up in a castle sipping mimosas for breakfast.

She didn't want to be a princess. She just wanted to protect her heart. Was that wrong?

Later, much later, when she and Jonas were over, when they'd both received what they'd needed from each other, when they'd fulfilled their bargain, she'd remember this moment. She'd remember this feeling of love and contentment seeping from every pore.

She'd remember and she'd smile, grateful she'd felt what it was like to be—mentally, physically, spiritually—in the right place, loving the right person, at least once in her life.

She'd remember. And she'd try not to mourn.

* * *

Kat plastered a smile on her face and walked into the ornate lobby of the Grenada Theater, silently cursing Jonas for asking her to meet him at the black-tie fund-raiser instead of picking her up at her apartment.

She recognized many of the attendees—many of them had dined at El Acantilado—but she didn't know them well enough to strike up a conversation.

Kat took a glass of champagne from a tray carried by a smartly dressed waiter. She lifted the cool glass to her lips as she moved to the edge of the crowd, putting her bare back against the wall and hoping Jonas would soon arrive.

He'd been delayed in Toronto and was running late, or so his text had said. Kat pushed away her doubt; Jonas didn't lie. If that's what he said happened then that's what happened. She couldn't keep allowing her past to influence her future, she thought. Jonas wasn't Wes…thank God. Her first husband and her almost-second husband were completely, utterly different.

Staring down at her gold sandals, Kat realized this would be their last formal engagement before their wedding a week from today, which would be under snow-white tents on fields at the Polo Club.

She was getting married…

To a man she'd barely knew and who she'd hardly spent any time with lately.

Jonas had made love to her twice on the flight home from Saint Kitts, but when the plane had landed on US soil, Jonas her sexy surfer disappeared and Jonas the CEO returned. Now, three weeks had passed since they'd loved, played and laughed in Nevis and, despite attending social events, he hadn't, not once, made an attempt to kiss her. Underneath the longing and lust, she was grateful. They couldn't go back. This was their real life. And if they attempted to recreate their time in Nevis, tried to relive their fun-filled days and nights, they'd tarnish the memory of that amazing weekend.

No, it was better this way. In Santa Barbara, Jonas and Kat weren't the same people who'd loved each other senseless in the Caribbean. To keep her heart intact, to get through the next week, their so-called honeymoon, the next year, they had to be different people. If she was lucky, they'd skate through their business-deal marriage with no major issues. If luck deserted her, then she'd deal with whatever came her way and soldier on.

It wasn't like she had a choice. Cath needed her to make it to the altar.

Nothing could go wrong now and nothing would. She and Jonas had a deal, well discussed and thought out. Each had a copy of the signed contract, for goodness sake! The only way the wedding could be derailed was if either of them bailed, and neither would. They had too much skin in the game.

"Kat."

Kat lifted her head and smiled at Sian, Jonas's assistant, glad to see someone she knew. "Hi. I'm so glad you're here."

"Jonas wanted to make sure that you got his message that his flight was delayed," Sian explained. Her gaze traveled up Kat's body and she twirled her finger, silently telling Kat to turn around. Kat complied.

"Now that's a hell of a dress," Sian said.

It was, Kat admitted. It was a shimmering gold, floor-length gown with an extremely thigh-high slit that exposed her legs. It plunged down the front and down the back, just skimming the top of her butt. Kat felt nearly naked but Tess, who was her self-appointed and bossy stylist, wouldn't allow Kat to wear anything else.

You and Jonas agreed that he would pay for the designer dresses you needed for formal occasions, and this special screening of Swan Lake *is black tie all the way. Wear the damn dress.* Tess had been wearing her don't-argue-with-me-or-I'll-hurt-you look, so Kat had worn the dress.

Without, as Tess had insisted, any underwear.

Pray to God that Kat didn't get into an accident on the way home.

"Oh, did you hear that Jonas bought the plantation inn you guys looked at in Saint Kitts?" Sian asked.

He did? Kat felt a knife pierce her heart, hurt that he hadn't told her he was going to buy the property. "Oh," Kat replied, looking down into the gold liquid in her glass. "That's nice."

"He's upgrading, per your suggestion, to a super-luxurious honeymoon destination. He also said you are a natural at property development and if things were different, he'd employ you tomorrow."

Oh, wow. That was a hell of a compliment. But the words would've meant so much more if he'd said them to her face.

Sian moved so she stood next to Kat, her back also to the wall. Now feeling more comfortable, they looked at their fellow guests, making chitchat and low comments on shoes and dresses they liked.

"Mariella Santiago-Marshall is wearing Gucci. I love the color on her. You have to be careful with that shade of tangerine."

Kat followed Sian's gaze and saw Harrison's wife, who looked amazing in a pink-and-orange sheath, her black hair pulled off her face and diamonds dripping from her ears and wrists. Mariella, her hand in Harrison's arm, looked around the room, caught Kat's eyes and smiled at her, lifting her hand in a small wave.

"The Queen just acknowledged you," Sian said on a laugh. "And Jonas has finally arrived." Kat swung her head toward the door but Sian placed her hand on Kat's arm and her fingernails pushed into Kat's skin. "Whoa, look! Oh, I wonder what that's about."

Kat turned her gaze back to Harrison and Mariella. Harrison had turned away from Mariella, his broad shoulder blocking her view of his cell phone, a little smile on his face. If she hadn't been watching carefully, Kat would've missed the hurt and fear that crossed Mariella's face, the flash of anger at being dismissed and ignored.

Trouble in paradise? Maybe.

"That wasn't a business call," Sian said, still watching the Marshalls as Kat turned away to find Jonas.

Talking about trouble, six foot two of sexy was heading her way. Kat barely heard Sian's words because she was watching Jonas walk toward her, the crowds parting to get out of his way. He ignored the greetings of people he passed, his eyes never leaving Kat's face. Kat felt every inch of her skin heat; saw the passion and desire blazing in his eyes.

"Holy crap," Sian said from what felt like a place far away.

Kat looked into Jonas's intense expression and it was as if she could feel his mouth, his skilled lips, moving across her jaw, down her throat to pull a nipple between his teeth. Kat felt Sian take her glass from her hand and Kat placed both her palms on the wall behind her, hoping to support her shaky legs.

She could feel the heat in his eyes. She wanted to

step into that desire and burn with him. Sian, the ornate red-carpeted lobby, the wrought-iron staircases, the elite of the West Coast faded away. Just she and Jonas remained, caught in a space and time that was solely their own.

Jonas reached her and, shielding her from the rest of the room, placed his index finger in the very low V of her dress and tugged.

"I blame your super sexy body and the memory of how you felt in my arms for my inability to concentrate. The memories of you, under me, me in you, have distracted me every minute of every day. I blame you entirely for my exceedingly low productivity these past few weeks.

"I want you," he added. "I've wanted you every minute since we left the islands and I'm damn tired of fighting it."

Kat swallowed, unable to look away, desperate to have his mouth on hers. She needed him, again. Now. "I know. I feel exactly the same way. Let's put sex back on the table." Kat placed her hand on the lapel of his jacket and felt the thud-thump of his racing heart through the fabric. "Take me home, Jonas. I want to be with you. I *need* to be with you."

Jonas gave her a hard nod, gripped her hand and led her through the now quiet lobby, ignoring the amused, shocked and envious looks directed their way.

She didn't care what they thought. Jonas, what he could give her and what she could give him—that was all that was important.

Ten

His limousine was still parked outside the theater, his driver sharing a quick smoke with one of the parking valets. Jonas, keeping Kat's hand in his, called his driver's name and the man sprang into action, running around the car to open the door. All the saliva left Jonas's mouth as Kat bent to climb into the car, the fabric of her dress clinging to every luscious curve. He realized she wasn't wearing any underwear and his semi-hard erection hardened to steel.

Jonas followed her into the car, issued a terse instruction to the driver to take him back to his hotel—it was closer than her apartment—and hit the button to bring up the privacy screen. He half turned and looked at Kat. He'd just pulled her out of a black-tie event and everybody there, his grandfather and Harrison Marshall included, knew exactly how he intended to spend the rest of his night.

He didn't give a rat's ass. They could think what they liked. All he knew was that he'd been denying himself since their return from Nevis. And once he'd seen her there, he could no longer remember why. There was no way he could sit through *Swan Lake* with Kat's perfume in his nose without going slowly insane.

Jonas glanced at his watch. He'd managed three weeks, six days and eight hours without touching her and it was three weeks, six days and eight hours too long.

"Are you okay?" Kat asked, her voice soft and a little worried.

"I'm fine." Jonas ran the tip of his finger from the delicate V in her throat to the scooped edge of her dress. "This dress… Holy crap."

Kat sent him a look from under her eyelashes that was part wicked, part innocence and all hot. "Do you like it?"

"I think it's frickin' sensational." Jonas pushed the thin strap holding the triangle of fabric off her shoulder. One more swipe and her perfect breast lay bare. Jonas swallowed and, unable to resist, ducked his head to take her nipple into his mouth, lathing the responsive bud with his tongue. Fire licked a path from his mouth to his groin and blood pulsed into his dick, hot and hard. He felt Kat's hands in his hair, holding his head to her, heard her soft whimpers.

He pulled back, looked into her eyes and fell. Hard. "God, I've missed you."

"I've missed you, too. I miss Nevis," Kat said, her voice trembling, and he heard the truth in her words, felt them because he missed Nevis, too. He missed the simplicity they'd found there, the lack of drama.

Kat held the back of his neck, pulled his head down

and her lips moved over his, at first hesitant and then more confident. Her hand slipped under his jacket, between the buttons of his shirt, to find his bare skin, as her agile tongue dipped into his mouth, sliding against his.

Possession, need, desperation flooded his system and he wanted more, needed her now. He couldn't wait. Jonas pushed his hands under the nearly indecent slit of her dress and pushed the expensive fabric up and over her smooth, bare hips. God, so sexy.

"Lift up," he muttered against her mouth, his hand on her butt. Kat lifted, the material bunched behind her and Jonas opened the snap to his trousers and pulled down the zipper. Before he could free himself, Kat's hands were in his underwear and his vision started to tunnel. He needed to get inside her.

Jonas looked out through the tinted glass, saw that the car was crawling along State Street and, if they hurried, they'd have time.

Slow and sexy would be for later, he needed to take the edge off.

"Jacket pocket, wallet, condom," he growled against her lips, his hand sliding between her thighs to check if she was as ready for him as he was for her.

Cash and cards dropped to the seat of the vehicle, his wallet bounced off the floor and Kat used her teeth to open the condom. Then, thank God, he felt the heat of her fingers on him as she rolled the latex down. As she finished, he gripped her waist with both hands and lifted her onto him. Kat squeaked as her hot core connected with his hard shaft and her eyes closed in an expression of bliss.

"Kit-Kat," he groaned as she slid her wet heat against

him, "we don't have much time. We need to do this fast."

Kat gripped him in one hand, positioned him at her opening and pushed down at the same time as he launched his hips upward. Jonas's eyes flew open to check whether he'd hurt her, but Kat's eyes were fixed on his, her bottom lip between her teeth, her hands clutching the fabric of his shirt and she was riding him. Small movements, bigger movements, swirling around him in a dance that was part torture and all pleasure.

Torture and pleasure, that adequately described these past few weeks. Pleasure being with her, torture never being alone with her. He'd missed her, missed her more than the fantastic memory of great sex. He'd missed her laugh, her little frown that appeared when she was concentrating, her sexy laugh. When he was with her he felt calmer, stronger, better.

"Ah, sweetheart," Jonas muttered, lifting his hands to cover her breast, thumbing her nipples to give her as much pleasure as possible.

Kat responded by moving faster and Jonas, following where she led, pumped his hips. He needed her to come before he did but he had no control around this woman.

"Kat, I can't—"

Kat slammed down on him, her mouth an inch from his. "You don't have to." Jonas felt her clench around him, felt the ripples deep inside her.

Wrapping his arms around her to keep her still, he pistoned his hips, driving upward and into her, and felt like his head was about to spin away. His orgasm roared from his balls up his spine and into his brain and his vision faded.

This. Her. Kat.

He couldn't wait another three weeks—he couldn't

wait another three damn hours—until they did this again.

Something had changed and shifted inside him somewhere between Nevis and the back of this car and, as a result, something had to change between them. He couldn't live with her, pretend to be her husband and not have her in his bed.

Something had to change, Jonas thought again as Kat rested on his chest.

He just wished he knew what.

Through the open doors leading to the balcony area of his penthouse suite, Jonas, lying in the huge bed with Kat draped across his chest, watched the first signs of a new day. The pinks and oranges of what promised to be an awesome sunrise broke through the night sky. Despite feeling exhausted from making love with Kat throughout the night, he'd been unable to sleep.

Jonas looked down at his lover, at the delicate hand on his chest, the colors of her fire opal echoed in the sunrise. He touched the ring with the tip of his finger, thinking that this wasn't how he wanted her to wear his ring.

This wasn't the way it was supposed to be.

Jonas gently picked up Kat's arm, placed it on her hip and pulled his other arm out from under her. He didn't want her to wake up, not yet. If she opened those amazing eyes he wouldn't be able to stop himself from taking her again. He needed time to think.

They'd attended a few social engagements together but he'd deliberately limited their alone time, thinking that he needed some time to work out what had happened between them in Nevis. Obviously he was wrong.

Kat rolled over and buried her face in his pillow.

Jonas snagged a pair of running shorts from the chair next to his bed and pulled them on. He walked through the French doors onto the balcony, placed his forearms on the railings and looked out to sea.

Being fake engaged to Kat was killing him. The lies, the pretense—it was sucking away at his soul. Having that time in Nevis, when everything had felt so real, just made the pretense harder to pull off. He was so tired of manipulating and being manipulated, doing deals, considering the consequences of all his choices.

He'd spent the last fifteen years of his life dodging bullets, trying to live up to his grandfather's expectations, trying to keep the veneer of his family intact. Keeping his father's theft from his grandfather had been a stupid move, he now admitted. Lane did the crime; he should've had to face the consequences. Jack would've disinherited him, that much Jonas was sure of. Jack was intolerant of theft and couldn't stand disloyalty.

At the time, Jonas had thought he was protecting Lane, but really, he'd been scared to be the bearer of bad news. He'd thought that Jack might blame him, that Lane's decisions would impact Jonas and Jack's relationship. Jonas had also hoped that protecting his father would draw him and his father together, that Lane would feel grateful to Jonas for saving his skin. He'd hoped they'd finally be the father-and-son team he'd dreamed of in his childhood. It hadn't happened like that. His so-called help had just pushed them further apart.

Lane loathed him and Jonas understood why. When Lane looked at his son, he couldn't pretend that he'd left the company because he needed a new challenge, because he'd wanted to explore a world beyond that of Halstead & Sons. Jonas had seen Lane's dark underbelly and because Lane couldn't snow Jonas, he couldn't completely snow himself.

How could Jonas have ever thought they would forge a stronger relationship built on deceit, on theft, on disloyalty?

But wasn't he doing exactly the same thing with Kat? There was something between them, something powerful that was trying to form, but their foundation was rocky. Wasn't there an old Bible analogy about building your house on sand and not rock? That's what they were doing, building on sand...

In fact, his whole life was built on sand. It kept shifting for Jack's whims, and Jonas was so tired of shifting sands.

He wanted something different... But what?

Jonas stared at the rising sun, the bands of pink-and-orange ripples tossed on the sea, his mind running fast and hard.

What did he want? Halstead?

Yeah, he wanted the company. He loved what he did, but he wanted it free and clear, on his terms, no one else's. He wanted it if, and only if, Jack thought he was the best person for the job, only if Jack thought Jonas's track record as CEO warranted him taking over the company. If Jack was going to force Jonas into marriage and rule from the grave, he could take Halstead and shove it. Jonas had enough money of his own to walk away, to start again. He could renovate houses, do smaller developments, start off slow. He wasn't scared of hard work and, damn, he'd be free of the red tape and BS that went with dealing with Jack and the shareholders.

He also wanted Kat, in his life, in his heart, in his bed. But if he told her he wanted a clean break, that he wanted to live and work without the manipulation of Jack and the guilt of his past, that he wanted to live that life with her, she wouldn't believe him. Thanks to her moron ex, she wouldn't believe that he would keep his promise to pay for Cath's care, that he had more than enough to take care of them both and start a new company with Kat at his side.

He could walk away from Halstead, but if he bailed out of this deal with Kat, there would be consequences. He'd have to honor his debt to her; Cath was already at Whispering Oaks and she was making progress. Not much but some. There was hope. He couldn't jeopardize her treatment; that wouldn't be fair. He had the six million to honor his debt to Kat, too, but that wasn't the problem. The problem was her stiff pride.

She'd only agreed to this crazy deal because there was something in it for him, because he needed her as much as she needed him. If he tipped the scales, she would refuse to take his cash. She wouldn't let him pay for Cath's treatment.

If he backed out of their deal, she'd refuse to continue her studies. Kat would continue working at El Acantilado and it would take her forever to get her degree and move into a job she loved. He couldn't do that to her. She deserved to be happy. She could see the light and he didn't want to shove her back into darkness.

But he couldn't go through with the marriage as they'd set it up. He had to break the hold Jack had on him. He had to do that to survive, to regain his self-respect. That was something being with Kat had taught him. But he also had to make sure Kat was taken care of and to do it in a way she wouldn't reject.

He might lose her; he accepted that. But he'd had honesty with her in Nevis, and he wouldn't settle for less. He'd rather lose this half-real situation now and hope they could start over than lose her forever because they hadn't built their relationship on truth. If they were meant to be together, if she loved him even a little, then they would find their way back to each other.

They would find their way back to each other. They had to, because if they didn't then he was properly screwed.

Jonas heard her soft footsteps behind him and sighed when she wrapped her arms around his bare waist and placed her cheek against his spine. Pushing his arms back, he held her hips, closing his eyes. How could he allow her to leave his life? How was he going to let her go? He didn't know. He just knew that he had to do it.

Kat placed an openmouthed kiss on his spine before sliding under his arm to face him, her back to the rising sun and the view. She was dressed in his button-down shirt, her dark hair and the white shirt a perfect contrast, her blue eyes still sleepy. Messy hair, a pillow crease in her cheek. To Jonas, she'd never looked more beautiful.

He brushed the back of his hand against her cheek. "Hey."

"Hey back," Kat said, turning to look out at the sea. "It's such a beautiful morning."

"It's not as beautiful as you," Jonas said and he saw surprise flash across her face. She didn't believe him. She didn't even trust what he said. How could he expect her to trust that he'd do as he'd promised once he backed out of the deal? She wouldn't.

A long, taut silence stretched between them and Jonas didn't know how to break it.

Kat did it for him. "What are we doing, Jonas?"

"What do you mean?"

"This. Us. You yanked me out of the theater and

we've made love all night after three weeks of avoiding being alone with me. We've always been attracted to each other but…" Her words trailed away.

"But?" he asked.

"But now that we're back in Santa Barbara, this was supposed to be business. Adding sex to the mix just complicates the situation."

"We made love, Kat, you know it and I know it," Jonas said, throwing the statement out there to see how she would react.

She tensed, panic hitting her eyes. "Are you insane? Why are you saying that? We agreed that we wouldn't get personal!"

Her reaction was one of horror and fear. Friggin' *perfect.*

"What is it with you men?" Kat cried, her face flushed with anger. "Why can't you just keep your word, keep it simple? This is why we weren't supposed to get physical, Halstead! It complicates everything. You are not in love with me. I am not in love with you. We're just experiencing an emotional hangover from too much amazing sex."

I am not in love with you.

Right. He got it. At least he had one question answered. He was, apparently, the only one who'd developed feelings, the only one who wanted more than what they'd agreed to.

Crap. Hell. Dammit.

Kat tipped her face up to look at him and it felt like her eyes were drilling down into his soul. What would she see? Would she be able to read him? Kat's eyes widened and she gasped, horrified. "You're having second thoughts. You don't want to get married."

It was his crappy luck that she'd pick up on his reluctance to marry but not on his deepening feelings. Jonas, normally verbally quick, couldn't find the words to explain that he wanted something different, that he still intended to honor their agreement. Kat didn't give him a chance to say anything. Her eyes turned stormy as fury tightened her muscles. Her right hand clenched into a small fist and Jonas wondered if that fist would connect with his body.

"You bastard!" Kat shouted, her hands slapping against his bare chest. "I trusted you! I trusted you to do this. I trusted you to keep your word. I trusted you! Do you not know how hard that was for me? I never thought I'd trust anyone again but I trusted you!"

"Kat, you don't understand…"

Big tears she didn't acknowledge ran down her cheeks. "I can't believe you are bailing on me!"

"Kit-Kat, calm down. We can talk about this, find a solution."

Kat pushed her fist into her sternum and looked at him, her eyes filled with betrayal. "Oh, God, you really don't want to do this, do you?"

Jonas shook his head. "No, not like this—" He wanted her. He wanted it all.

But she only heard the word *no* because she spun around and flew back into the bedroom.

Jonas followed more slowly, hoping she'd let him explain. Jonas winced when Kat ripped his shirt apart, buttons flying. She pulled her gold dress from the chair, slid it over her head, grabbed her clutch and her shoes and stormed out of the room.

"Will you please calm down?" Jonas asked, and she nailed him with a scorching look. Wrong thing to say. She looked like she was planning his murder.

"Stop talking to me," Kat told him, heading for the front door.

"We can talk about this, find a way forward."

Kat stopped at the door leading to the hallway, her hand on the knob. "The only thing I want from you is for you to show up at the Polo Club on Saturday, in your tux. We'll get married, as we agreed, you'll pay me, as you agreed, and we'll spend the next few months ignoring each other. Got it?"

"Kat—" Jonas shoved his hands into his hair. He wished he could make her listen. But, he realized, Kat was in a full-on temper and nothing he could say, or do, would get through to her.

"We'll talk when you calm down," Jonas said as she yanked the door open and stepped into the hall. "Do you have money for a cab? I can call my driver."

Kat's eyes held the power of a million hurricanes. "Be there on Saturday. Marry me. Pay me. Surprise me by doing what you said you would. That's all I want. That's all I'll ever want from you."

Ouch.

I am not in love with you…

Jonas watched her walk away from him, barefoot, and felt like there was a knife lodged in his back.

"I'm not doing it."

Jack looked at Jonas, his white eyebrows pulled together. "You're not doing what?"

"Marrying. Dancing to your tune. Giving in to your blackmail," Jonas told his grandfather.

They were in the study at his grandfather's Santa Monica beach house and for the first time in his life Jonas felt free.

"Excuse me?" Jack asked, his tone as cold as the ice cubes he dropped into his bourbon.

"Don't pretend you didn't hear what I said," Jonas retorted. He placed his hands on the back of one of Jack's wing-backed chairs and gave his grandfather a hard stare. "I'm not marrying. Do what the hell you want with your shares. Give them to my father, sell them. But know this—I will not work for Lane, not under any capacity."

"You'll lose the company then," Jack replied, his voice now bland.

"I don't give a crap," Jonas told him. "I'll go out on my own. I'll do something else, *anything* else, but I won't work for that thief again."

Jack looked at him over the rim of his glass, not even slightly surprised by Jonas's hot announcement.

Jonas lifted a finger and pointed it at his grandfather. "You knew he stole funds from the company!"

"It's my company, of course I damn well knew!" Jack replied, annoyed. "The point is when were you going to tell me? And why the hell did you cover it up? Why did you let him skate?"

He knew that, too? Jonas shook his head. He'd thought he'd been so clever keeping it from Jack, yet the wily old man had known it all. Games, Jonas thought, manipulations. He was so tired of it all.

"Probably for the same reason you ignored it. It was easier to let him walk away than to charge him. It was less of a scandal to say that he resigned." Jonas rubbed the back of his neck.

"Why didn't you tell me, Joe?" Jack asked and Jonas frowned at the sadness he heard in his grandfather's voice.

Jack sat in his chair behind his desk, shaking his

head. "I thought we were a team, that you trusted me. Obviously you didn't, probably still don't." It was time to tell the truth, Jonas realized, to wipe the slate clean. "I wanted to protect you. I wanted to protect him."

Jack shook his head. "That was my job, to protect you," he protested.

"He's your child."

Jack's expression turned fierce. "You've been more mine than he was. You were always my first priority, my first concern," Jack stated, his voice a soft growl.

"Then why the hell did you insist I marry? Why did you put terms on the shares, on my future?" Jonas demanded, his voice cracking with emotion. "Why would you do that? Haven't I done enough, shown enough loyalty, been good enough?"

"Absolutely," Jonas agreed. "I did it to force you to stand up to me, to choose yourself and what made sense to you. If you had told me to go screw myself nearly three months ago, I could've told you that I'd never pass my shares on to anyone but you, that I was proud of you for finally standing up for yourself."

"I stand up to you all the time! I disagree with you constantly!" Jonas said, his voice rising.

"About business, sure. About your personal life? Not so much. Jonas, you were prepared to marry a stranger because you thought that was what I wanted! It should be, always, about what you want! I wanted you to realize that."

Jonas shook his head, pushing his hand through his hair. "Could you not have just told me that?"

Jack had the temerity to grin. "Not half as much fun. So, are you still going to marry your girl?"

He wished. "No. I love her but she doesn't love me," he reluctantly admitted.

"How do you know?" Jack asked, sounding genuinely interested.

This was the first non-business conversation they'd had in years, Jonas realized.

I am not in love with you...

"She told me that she didn't."

"So make her."

If only it were that simple. "This isn't the caveman era, Jack. Women do make up their own minds these days."

"Well, whether you marry you or not, the shares will be yours."

"I'm not sure I want them now," Jonas replied, the words flying out. He felt as shocked as his grandfather looked. He held up his hand. "I'm not saying that out of spite, Jack, I just don't know if Halstead is what I want to do any more, whether it's part of my future. I can't think of much more than sorting out this mess with Kat," he added.

Jack nodded, looking remarkably sanguine.

"You don't look annoyed. Why aren't you annoyed that I might not want the company?" Jonas asked, frowning.

Jack shrugged. "You're my grandson, you'll do the right thing. For yourself and for the company. Either way, I'll live with it."

Jonas scowled at Jack. "If you die and leave my father the shares, I swear to God I will dig you up and beat you back to death. We clear?"

Jack just smiled and lifted his glass. "Have a drink, Jonas, you sure as hell need one."

Eleven

Kat, hiding out in Tess's apartment, placed her heels on the seat of her chair and wrapped her arms around her shins. She glanced down at her cell phone, saw that her tally of missed calls from Jonas was now at twenty—five for every day they'd been apart.

Kat had taken some vacation time from the restaurant and it had been freely given. Her manager assumed she needed time to make wedding preparations. Since Kat was still answering questions from Mariella Marshall about their "exciting day" and because the tabloids and society columns were still talking about their Cinderella story, Kat presumed the wedding was still on.

She couldn't understand why because Jonas had clearly told her he no longer wanted to get married. Four days later and she still couldn't understand what she'd done to cause his sudden turnaround.

What was it about her that caused the men in her life

to flip out on her? Why couldn't they keep their promises, do what they said they would?

Oh, she was pretty sure Jonas would honor the financial promises he'd made to her. He was still paying for Cath's treatment. But in his touch, in the emotion she saw in his eyes, she'd thought they might have a chance, that he could be someone she could trust with her precious, battered heart.

Kat remembered her question to him—*You really don't want to do this, do you?*—and the image of his shaking head, his guilt-filled eyes. The memory of his heartfelt no was another punch to her heart.

God, why hadn't he just chosen one of his celebrity eye-candy girlfriends for this charade? Why her?

And why did she have to fall in love with him? Why was he the only man who'd managed to slip under the barricade she'd so carefully constructed?

Why couldn't he love her? She was bright and reasonably attractive, albeit stupidly stubborn. And even if he didn't want to remain married to her, why was the notion of marrying her now so unpalatable that he couldn't stand to be hitched to her for a mere ten months? Judging by what he had to lose, that was nothing!

What had she done, said, that made the risk of losing his place at Halstead & Sons an attractive option?

The questions kept bombarding her. Why couldn't she find a man to love her, someone who would put her first, always? Wes hadn't, and she'd been easily and quickly replaced in her father's affections by June. To Jonas, she'd been a way to save his company, a six-million-dollar deal to keep shares worth a billion or two.

She'd loved Wes, adored her father, but what she'd felt for them paled in comparison to how she felt about Jonas.

She beyond loved him.

She loved him with all the harnessed power of the sea, the pull of the moon, the solar flares of the sun. He was everything she wanted and all that she needed. Yet Kat had told him she didn't love him to protect herself. If he couldn't keep his promises, she had to let him go.

And if he wasn't going to stick to their deal, she had to speak to him, to cut the ropes that still held them together. She'd sell the exquisite dresses he'd bought for her online and she'd return his ring. She'd ask him for a payment plan so she could pay off the money he'd already outlaid for Cath's treatment. She'd find the rest of the cash she needed—somewhere.

She could do this. She'd be okay. She'd survived Wes's harsh and warped version of love and her father's neglect. She'd survive Jonas, as well.

The wedding was in three days. It was now or never. Kat picked up her phone and started to type. It was a simple message, three words. Can we meet?

His reply was equally brief. Your apartment. Thirty minutes.

Kat nodded and dropped her phone to the floor. By the end of the afternoon, probably within the hour, she would be saying goodbye to another man she loved.

This was, she thought as tears started to fall, starting to become a habit.

Kat flew out of her car and rushed up the concrete path to her front door, tears still streaming down her face. Through the mist she saw Jonas walking down the steps, his face slack with shock, his eyes red-rimmed.

Kat reached him and threw herself against his chest. "Is it true? Can it be? Please tell me it's not true. I heard it on the radio… They said…"

Jonas's arms held her against him, one hand on the back of her head. "Kit-Kat." He breathed her name into her hair, his grief and worry in every syllable. "Yes, it's true. Harrison had a horrific car accident this morning."

Kat grabbed the lapels of his suit jacket. "Don't tell me he's dead, Jonas! He can't be."

"Let's go inside and I'll tell you what I know."

Kat, her heart weighing a million pounds, led Jonas up the stairs to her apartment and opened the door. He followed her inside and, after tossing a folder onto the coffee table, shrugged off his jacket, pulled off his tie and rolled up his sleeves.

Kat sat on the edge of the couch and stared at her shaking hands, her thoughts going to Harrison in the hospital—her charismatic, funny, driven, kind boss now a shell of the man he'd been the day before.

"He refused to allow me to pay anything toward my rent," Kat said, her voice dropping into the silence between them. "He told me I was doing a great job and he wanted to reward me. So he told me I could have my apartment for free, as part of my compensation."

Jonas sat next to her, his elbows on his knees. "He's a good guy."

"He's a great guy," Kat corrected. "Without him, without my job…" Kat turned her head to look at him. "What happened? Tell me."

Jonas pulled in a deep breath and ran his hand over his face. "He was speeding. You know he has a lead foot. Team that with one of the fastest supercars known to man, it's not a good combination."

"But he's such a good driver. I mean, I heard he could've raced professionally, he was that good," Kat protested.

"Yeah, I don't understand, either. He knew the road,

knew the car, and while he was speeding, he was, apparently, not going that fast," Jonas replied. "His car spun out, flipped… He was thrown from the car, which happened to be a good thing. They rushed him straight into surgery."

Kat forced herself to ask the question, not sure she wanted to know the answer. "Is he going to live?"

Jonas shrugged. "He came through the surgery and he's in intensive care. The next few days will tell that story. It doesn't look good, Kat."

"How do you know all this?" Kat asked.

"I spoke to Gabe, his nephew," Jonas replied.

"Dammit." Tears slid down her face again. "He can't die, Jonas. He has so much to live for. Mariella, his kids, his businesses, his staff. He has to be okay."

Jonas placed a hand on her back and Kat had to restrain herself from leaning into him, from looking for his comfort, from soaking in his strength. Her boss was lying in a hospital bed, battered, bloody, hooked up to machines and fighting for his life. His family would be mad with worry. Mariella would be beside herself. Harrison had friends, from all parts of the world, thinking about him, sending him good energy.

If she were in the same situation, who would be worried about her? Tess and Cath? A few work colleagues? She didn't have parents, children, a husband or a lover.

She didn't have Jonas.

Oh, God, she wanted to love him, to be with him. She wanted to be his wife in all the ways that word meant. Not for a few months but forever.

She loved him.

But he didn't want her. Not like that. He wanted out. And could she blame her? This was a crazy situation, one that never really had much of a chance of working. It wasn't his fault he didn't love her like she loved him.

You can't force love…

She had to do this. She had to let him go. If she didn't do it now she didn't know if she ever could.

"We need to talk about Saturday."

Jonas sent her a look that she couldn't interpret. He stood and walked to the window, leaning his shoulder into the wall and looking out onto the street.

Kat started to speak but stopped when Jonas held up a weary hand. "One of the many reasons I've been trying to call you was to tell you that we can't get married on Saturday. It can't happen."

Before she could respond, Jonas spoke again.

"I'm not saying that only because we argued, Kat, there are other, practical, reasons why the wedding can't go ahead. Mariella is coordinating the wedding, and now that Harrison is in ICU, she will be out of action. Even if someone else from MSM Event Planning took over the function, society would expect us to postpone the event. I've known Harrison since I was a kid. He and my grandfather are good friends. Many of his friends are ours and nobody would enjoy themselves. Out of respect for him and his family…"

Kat nodded. She dug her fingers into her waist and said the words that would both break her heart and set them both free. "You should use this extra time to talk to your grandfather. Tell him this isn't going to work. This was a crazy idea and—"

"Jack and I came to an agreement. My being married is no longer a prerequisite to inheriting the shares."

Kat stared at the carpet beneath her feet, fighting the wave of sadness that threatened to pull her under.

She had to say the words, get them out. "Then there's no reason for us to marry."

"I'll admit that my reasons for setting us on this crazy path are no longer valid," Jonas said. He sounded like he was picking his words carefully, like he was trying to let her down gently.

Jonas flicked a glance her way and in the depths of those green eyes she saw an emotion she couldn't identify. It took all of Kat's strength to put a tiny smile on her face. "Well, then, that makes this decision simpler."

Jonas lifted a dark eyebrow. "Really? How?"

"You don't need to get married anymore and you'd save a bundle of cash by calling this off."

Jonas rubbed his fingertips over his forehead. "I never said I wouldn't provide the money I promised. Besides, how else would you pay for Cath's treatment, Kat?"

Kat lifted her heels to the seat of her chair, hoping she was hiding her terror from him. She had no idea how she would pay for it, but that was her problem now, not his. Something would come up; it had to.

"If you could give me a payment plan, I'll repay you as much as I can as soon as I can."

"For God's sake!" Jonas slapped his hand against the wooden frame of the window. "When are you going to realize I don't give a crap about the money? In all this time, have you learned nothing about me?"

I know that you are kind and honorable and you have a big heart. I know that the woman who finally gains your love will be immensely lucky.

"I'm just trying to do the right thing, Jonas," Kat told him, her voice quavering. "I'm trying to make this as easy as possible. I'd like us to walk away as friends."

"Friends?" Jonas repeated the word before thrusting his hand into his hair. "You've got to be freakin' kidding me." He looked at his watch and grimaced in frustration. "I hate to cut this little breakup conversation short, but I have to go. I promised Jack I'd go with him to visit the Marshalls at the hospital. They'll need the support of their friends."

He'd said "breakup," so that made it official. They were over.

Do not cry, Kat. Do not!

Jonas placed his hands in the pockets of his pants and nodded to the folder on the table between them. "It's all in there, Kat. I assumed this discussion would go this way so I made some plans."

Of course he had, he was the CEO of an international company. Making plans was what he did. Kat looked at the folder but didn't reach for it. Even though she'd asked him to come here to end this farce of a relationship, she couldn't bear to see the folder's contents, knowing the papers inside would sever her connection with Jonas.

"Knowing your independent, don't-help-me attitude, you'll probably curse me ten ways to Sunday. But I can't walk out of your life unless I know you will be okay. I had to do it this way, Kat, because giving you the freedom to be happy, to start a new life on your terms, is *that* important to me."

You loving me is all that's important to me!

Kat didn't care about the contents of the folder; she cared about him. About being with him, loving him. Kat opened her mouth to tell him so, but her words stuck in her throat. She was important to him, she reminded herself, but not important enough to marry.

Kat nodded, wishing he'd stay, wishing she was

brave enough to lay her heart on the line. But she wasn't and Jonas, full of honor and integrity, needed to leave.

"'Bye, Kit-Kat."

Her eyes filled with tears and Kat couldn't reply. It took all her willpower to let him cross the short space to the door. He stepped into her hallway and Kat felt like he was dragging her heart behind him. How could she just let him go? How could she allow him to walk out of her life?

Because he didn't want to stay and she couldn't ask him to. Jonas desired her but could never love her and she couldn't settle for less. Not again.

She was worth more than that. He was her fantasy but she wasn't his.

Jonas stopped by the front door, sent her one last look and slipped out of her life.

When the door snicked closed behind him, Kat slipped to the floor and cried.

"Harrison is still in a coma. He's been moved from St. Aloysius Hospital to an undisclosed private clinic. His situation is unchanged."

Kat disconnected the call to her manager and pushed her hair behind her ears. It was her day off and she'd begged him for a shift because she needed to keep her mind occupied, but Jose had refused. This was, he told her, supposed to be the first day of her honeymoon and he'd already arranged the schedule.

Her honeymoon. Kat pulled a face. She and Jonas had talked about going back to Nevis, agreeing that was where they both wanted to be. Instead, she was stuck in her small apartment with nothing to do. Cath was back home and doing relatively well on her new regimen. Kat could visit but Cath would interrogate her about Jonas and she'd be forced to admit they were no longer engaged. That they weren't going to get married.

Apparently, Kat and Jonas were the only two people who knew that their wedding was not simply postponed, as his press release stated, but canceled. Why hadn't he told the world they were over? Conversely, why hadn't she?

Because she didn't really want it to be over and when the news of their breakup hit the public domain, that would truly be the end.

Kat sat on her couch and eyed Jonas's folder, the one he'd left when he'd walked out of her life seventy-two hours before. She hadn't opened it, knowing it would be another confirmation of Jonas's unwillingness to marry her, to create a life with her.

No matter what his press release said, their relationship was over. It was time to accept it, to deal with it, Kat told herself. To do that, she had to face the contents of the folder. So Kat forced herself to pick it up. She placed it on her knees and felt the tears well.

You need to do this. You have to do this. You can't live in this state of limbo forever.

Kat bit her lip and flipped the folder open. The papers were all perfectly aligned and Kat skimmed through them. There was an agreement between Jonas and Whispering Oaks. He'd deposited six million dollars into their account and any monies not used for Cath's treatment were to be donated to cancer research in both her mom's and Cath's names.

Kat placed her hand over her mouth, trying to subdue her sobs. Oh, Jonas. She flipped to another page and saw he had covered the costs for her to go back to school full-time to finish her MBA. He'd prepaid the rent and utilities on her apartment so she could stay there for another year without having to work at the restaurant and he'd bought her a car, a sensible, compact, secondhand SUV with low mileage that was waiting to be collected at a reputable car dealer.

So generous but not over the top. So Jonas. He'd kept his word, down to the letter, as per the original prenup, and he had done it in a way—cleverly, she admitted—she couldn't refuse.

Jonas. She now had everything to make her life easier, but what she most needed was as far away as the moon. She missed him; her cells, her organs, her mind ached for him. She had so much love to give him and nowhere to put it.

Kat sighed, her fingers tapping the pile of papers. Feeling a ridge under what should be flat papers, Kat lifted the last page of the bulky car insurance papers to see a tiny velvet bag and an envelope with her name written across it. It had been tucked into the corner pocket of the folder.

Kat eyed the envelope while she pulled open the tiny velvet bag, tipping the contents into her palm. The big, square-cut sapphire flashed at her; a deep navy blue that took her breath away. Kat held the ring between her finger and thumb, instantly recognizing the symbolism.

The sapphire was a lot bigger and a deeper blue than her mom's ring, but the design was exactly the same and had her and her mom's initials engraved into the band.

Kat reached for the envelope and ripped the flap open. She pulled out the card and scanned Jonas's hastily penned words.

Kit-Kat,
It's not your mom's, but maybe it will go a little way toward easing the sting of losing her ring.

Unfortunately, the sting of losing you, of what could've been, is going to stay with me forever.
Jonas

Kat read his words and read them again. He didn't want to lose her? He wanted more? Was that what he meant? Could he, possibly, love her?

What did he mean?

Words…words always got in the way.

But if she believed, as she'd always said she did, that people showed how they felt through their actions, then she didn't need his words. Wes had told her, over and over, that he'd loved her, but his actions had proved his statements false. Her father had loved her, but his actions had proved he'd loved June more.

But Jonas, through what he'd done over and over, had expressed his love for her. It was in the way he'd looked at her and in the way he'd touched her, in his concern for her driving a rust-bucket car, needing to know that she was safe. He'd provided the money for Cath's treatment because Kat's worries were his, her family as important as his own. He'd told her he loved her by going to the effort—even though he was a busy man running a huge company—to track down a close copy of her mother's ring.

He hadn't said the words but his actions whispered his love.

She'd just forgotten how to listen. From now on, she *would* listen. She didn't need a marriage, temporary or otherwise, to hear the truth. A marriage agreement wasn't the promise she'd really wanted him to keep, she saw that now.

Instead he'd kept all the important promises. The ones about listening to her and taking care of her because he cared. And for every day he gave her, if he gave her any, she'd listen, and she'd tell him, with words and actions, how much she loved him in return.

She wasn't going to waste another minute. Kat picked up her cell phone and started to track down her man.

Jonas had felt emotionally battered before but nothing compared to the hell he was currently experiencing five days after walking out of Kat's life.

It will get better, he told himself.

Someday soon it will hurt a little less, and you won't miss her as much.

Jonas, sitting on his surfboard, looked up to his house on the cliff. Returning to Nevis was like returning to the scene of the crime shortly after losing your lover in a knife fight. It was bloody and painful and messy.

Jonas pushed his wet hair back from his face and eyed an incoming wave. Too small, not enough energy.

Not a bad analogy for his life, he thought. He felt small; he lacked energy. Waking up was hard, going to sleep was worse. Staying away from the booze was the hardest of all. But drinking himself into oblivion was too cliché and even though he was in Nevis, hiding out, he still had internet service and a company to run.

A company that was now fully his. The morning after their heart-to-heart conversation, Jack had filed the papers to transfer the shares to Jonas. He'd soon be the majority shareholder of Halstead & Sons. No more interference, no more monthly breakfast meetings—although Jack had hinted that he'd like those to continue.

But the business and Jonas's improved relationship with his grandfather meant little without Kat in his life. Funny how he'd run from the gold diggers and kept his shield up with every woman he'd met, but the simple act of removing a clothing tag had spun Kat into his world. And, while his heart felt like it had been cleaved in two, he couldn't—wouldn't—regret the time he'd spent with her. The past three months had been the best of his life.

Jonas glanced at his watch. It was time to head back to shore. He stretched out on his board and started to paddle in. He supposed he should think about dinner, that he should eat. But food now tasted like cardboard so he probably wouldn't.

Jonas looked toward the stairs leading to his house and frowned when he saw a figure walking down the steps. His steps. He was still far out but the form was female—dark hair, long legs.

He recognized that body, that brightly colored bikini top. He'd pulled that halter top off her torso once or ten times right here in Nevis. Jonas, his heart starting to pound, pumped his arms and his board shot through the water. He kept his eyes on Kat, whose face was covered by a pair of oversize sunglasses. Those had to go, along with her hot-pink top and ripped denim shorts and anything else she was wearing.

She was here and he was never letting her go again.

When he reached the shallows, Jonas pulled his board under his arm and jogged to the beach, stopping only to rip off his ankle cord and toss the board to the sand. He started to run, needing to know why she was there.

Was she here for him or had something happened to Cath? To Harrison? Jack would have called if Harrison had passed on and Jack's calls, and Kat's, obviously, would have been the only ones Jonas answered. There had been none from either of them. Had Kat come to personally deliver some bad news?

God, no.

Jonas stopped and placed his hands on his thighs, not wanting to face whatever she had to say. He didn't think he could take much more heartbreak.

Kat walked toward him and stopped when she was a few feet away. She pushed her hands into the back pockets of her shorts and rocked on her heels.

"I love you."

Jonas heard her words but didn't understand what she was trying to say. So he focused on the one thing he did understand. "You cut your hair."

Kat ran her hand over her funky new hairstyle and lifted an eyebrow. "I fly for hours to tell you that I love you and the first words out of your mouth are about my hair?"

"My brain is spluttering," Jonas admitted. He ran his hand through his hair and sent her an uncertain look. "Are you sure?"

"That I love you? Well, I used the credit card you left me to pay for the ticket," Kat said, pulling her lip between her teeth. "It was hard, but I did it."

Jonas straightened, his hands on his waist, dissecting her words. He'd forgotten that he'd left a credit card with her for emergencies. She hadn't used it once and he'd never expected her to, not with her insistence on independence.

She'd used his card to come to him, to tell him that she loved him. He was that important to her...

Holy crap.

That small gesture told him everything he needed to know. Light, happiness, goddamn relief, slid into him, loosening his knees and causing his throat to constrict. Before he lost his composure, he stepped up to her and ripped the sunglasses off her face. "These are hideous. Say it again."

Kat tipped her head back to meet his gaze, her eyes reflecting wariness and fear. She expected him to reject her and Jonas felt his heart wobble. But he needed to hear her say it again while he looked into her eyes, just to make sure he wasn't losing his mind.

"I love you. I'll keep telling you until you believe me."

Jonas held her precious face in his hands, his thumbs on her cheekbones. "I love you, too."

Kat's hands settled on his waist as she closed her eyes. "Thank God, I thought you might, but I wasn't sure."

Jonas pulled her into his body, her chest pushing into his, her stomach against his fast-growing erection. "How could you not be sure?"

"You didn't tell me," Kat pointed out, love turning her eyes luminous. Jonas started to apologize but Kat placed her fingers on his lips. "But I looked at what you did for me and it was all there. Thank you... Thank you for everything. Cath's treatment. The car. For paying for my studies. The ring. God, the ring."

Jonas looked down at her hands and frowned when he saw the fire opal on her ring finger and the sapphire on her other hand. "You're still wearing my engagement ring."

Kat looked down, lifted her eyebrows and nodded. "It appears I am."

"Why?"

"Why am I wearing the ring?" Kat asked, smiling a little at his question. "Well, I like it and I like being engaged to you. And I figure that until you officially call off our engagement—until our breakup is splashed across tabloids and society columns—then I intend to keep wearing it."

Jonas felt the tension slide from his body. Kat was here. She loved him and his world was perfect.

He smiled. "Well, FYI, hell will ice over before I call off our engagement." He dropped a hot, brief open-mouthed kiss on her lips, knowing that if he started to kiss her he wouldn't be able to stop. But he had some-thing he had to do first. They needed to start again...

Kat's joy flashed over her face and pulled her mouth into a wide smile. Then her smile turned to confusion when he took her hands in his and tugged the rings off her fingers.

"What are you doing?" Kat asked him, perplexed.

Jonas didn't answer. He just dropped to one knee, water still streaming from his body, sand clinging to his calves and thighs.

"No qualifiers, provisos or deals," Jonas said, squint-ing up at her. "This isn't about my company or my grandfather or a temporary agreement. From that morn-ing on the balcony of my hotel room, I knew I wanted this but I didn't know how to tell you. So... Just you and me, flat-out honest. I love you. I don't want to spend another day without you. Will you marry me?"

"No qualifiers, provisos and deals. Flat-out honest." Kat nodded, her hand on her heart. "Yes."

Jonas's heart sighed as peace and contentment settled over him. He opened his hand and looked at the two rings on his palm. "Choose one for your engagement ring, or if you prefer, we can have something made." He grinned. "Warning, it will probably be expensive."

Kat looked from his face to his palm and back again. She picked up the sapphire ring, slid it back onto the middle finger of her right hand and then picked up the fire opal ring.

"This one. It was the first ring you gave me and the only one I'll ever need. Though a matching wedding band would be nice."

Jonas, his fingers trembling, slid the ring into place and stared down at her hand. When he lifted his head and spoke, he heard the tremble in his voice. He didn't care. "You are my everything, Katrina. The wealth, the success—it means nothing when you're not in my life. You *are* my life."

Kat wound her arms around his neck and kissed the side of his neck. "I'm so happy to be here, with you. Being with you is all I'll ever need."

Jonas wrapped his arms tighter around her, happy to stand in the setting sun, the cool breeze on his back and Kat dropping kisses on his neck.

This was peace. Ecstasy. Acceptance. This was who he was supposed to be—the person who loved Kat.

The CEO, the heir, the successful property developer...he was all those things, of course, but being Kat's lover, friend and husband would forever be his most important jobs. And as her lover, he'd woefully neglected his duties lately.

Jonas bent his knees, scooped Kat up and started to run for the stairs. He couldn't wait another minute to peel that bikini top off her breasts, shove those denim shorts to the sand.

At the steps Jonas stopped, looked around and remembered this beach was private. He didn't need to wait any longer than he wanted.

He dropped Kat to her feet and slid his hand under her hair to tug at the strings holding her bikini top in place. Kat surprised him when her hands went for the tie holding up his board shorts. She needed him as much as he needed her and he wanted to weep from joy.

Kat's fingers brushed against him but he grabbed her hand and lifted it to his mouth, his lips settling on her open palm, his eyes connecting with hers.

"I love you, Kat. Every stubborn, independent, sexy inch of you. I'm going to make you so damn happy."

Kat's eyes, full of emotion, held the sheen of tears. "Nothing is more important to me than you knowing how much I love you." Kat touched his face. "I think our brand-new engagement is off to a pretty good start."

It was, Jonas thought, because their foundation was, finally, rock-solid. Jonas flashed a wicked grin and guided Kat's hand to where he most wanted it to be.

On a private beach with the woman he loved, who loved him in return—and who also happened to be sexy as hell. What was a man to do?

So Jonas did all of it. And more.

* * * * *

He looked up from the last bite to find Jill staring at him.

"That hit the spot," he said.

"I can tell, and you weren't kidding when you said you would eat those pancakes fast." She was obviously amused.

"Good food and good company. Nothing better after a long night."

A long, frustrating night, in this case. He hated the damn cast on his wrist and the fact he could be out of commission for weeks, if not months. He really hated that he didn't know Jill well enough to kiss her good morning. Or good night. Or all day.

Where the hell had *that* thought come from?

"I bet I know exactly what you're thinking, Houston Calloway."

Only if she could read minds, and he sure hoped she couldn't. "Huh?"

"You're lamenting the fact you're injured."

He wasn't too injured to stop fantasizing about her.

* * *

Expecting the Rancher's Baby?
is part of the Texas Extreme series:
Six rich and sexy cowboy brothers
live—and love—to the extreme!

EXPECTING THE RANCHER'S BABY?

BY
KRISTI GOLD

First Published in Great Britain 2017
By Mills & Boon, an imprint of HarperCollins*Publishers*
1 London Bridge Street, London, SE1 9GF

© 2017 Kristi Goldberg

ISBN: 978-0-263-92836-5

51-0917

Our policy is to use papers that are natural, renewable and recyclable products and made from wood grown in sustainable forests. The logging and manufacturing processes conform to the legal environmental regulations of the country of origin.

Printed and bound in Spain
by CPI, Barcelona

Kristi Gold has a fondness for beaches, baseball and bridal reality shows. She firmly believes that love has remarkable healing powers, and she feels very fortunate to be able to weave stories of love and commitment. As a bestselling author, a National Readers' Choice Award winner and a three-time Romance Writers of America RITA® Award finalist, Kristi has learned that although accolades are wonderful, the most cherished rewards come from networking with readers. She can be reached through her website at www.kristigold.com, or through Facebook.

To my daughter, Kendall—I am so proud
of the woman you've become. And to my
dear friend and fellow author Kathy D. for all
the brainstorming on this particular book.
Couldn't have done it without you…again.

Many thanks to my daughter, Kendall,
MLA, ATC, LAT, for all the endless technical
questions during the making of this book.
Any errors in interpretation are definitely my own.

One

He wore his cowboy charisma like a practiced charmer, but the storm in his dark eyes told Jillian Amherst this rugged risk taker wasn't completely immune to pain.

When Houston Calloway strode across the first-aid tent, his black hat tipped low on his brow, the licensed athletic trainer in Jill noticed the gash in his well-worn jeans above his right knee, and that his right hand was wrapped around his left wrist below the cuff of the red shirt. Had she not been a professional, she would have only noticed his confident gait, the shading of whiskers surrounding his mouth and his above-average height. But she *was* a professional and always had been.

Besides, as a member of an elite rodeo medical program, Jill had treated the likes of him before. In fact, she'd treated *him* before. Several times. The ever-popular rodeo superstar had enough bull-riding championship trophies to fill a football stadium and several

concussions on his injury résumé. He also had a penchant for being an uncooperative patient, something
she'd discovered the hard way over the past two years.

Jill rolled her chair back from the counter, swiveled
completely around to face him and suppressed a frown.
"What is it this time, Mr. Calloway?"

He worked his way onto the exam table across from
her without an invitation. "Got my left hand caught in
the rope when I was trying to get my right hand free,
and I took a horn to my leg. But I made it to the buzzer."

Good for you, she thought as she stood. "Are you
right-handed?"

"Yep."

"That's a plus. Any chance you fell on your head
again?"

He cracked a cynical smile. "Not this time."

"That's new and different. Are you sure?"

"Yep."

Doubting she could believe him, Jill held up a finger. "Follow my movement without turning your head."

He grumbled and scowled. "I told you I didn't fall
on my head. I landed square on my feet and if you don't
believe me, ask Henry."

Like she'd really believe a rodeo clown wouldn't
cover for him. Jill lowered her hand in resignation, but
stared at him straight on. "Okay. Fine. For now. But I'll
be watching you for any latent signs. You've already
had two concussions that I've treated, and who knows
how many you had before that."

That earned Jill a frustrated look. "Why are you so
bent on giving me grief, Jilly?"

Only one person had ever been allowed to call her
by that name, and the loss of that special someone still
hurt her to the core. She shook off the memories and

faked a calm demeanor. "Why are you so determined to annoy me with that Jilly thing?"

He inclined his head and studied her. "It fits you better."

"Well, I don't like it and I suspect that's why you do it."

He had the gall to grin. "Would you feel better if I let you call me by a nickname?"

Jill grabbed for a little levity to defuse her frustration. "Overly confident?"

"Hmm…" He streaked his right hand over his stubbled jaw. "Overly Confident Calloway. Has a nice ring to it, but it's too long. I was thinking more along the lines of Handsome."

Shocker. "How about Crazy Calloway?"

"Been called that before. Charming?"

This exchange could go on all night if she didn't put a halt to it now. With that in mind, Jill morphed back into medical mode and turned to retrieve a pair of disposable gloves, then approached the table to inspect the cut beneath the slit in his jeans. "You're lucky. Your leg was protected from certain doom by denim. This is superficial and nothing a little antiseptic and a bandage won't cure. Now let me see your wrist."

He gingerly held the appendage out for her to examine. "Probably just a sprain," he muttered.

She pressed the fleshy part of his palm next to his thumb and immediately heard a litany of oaths. "I hate to be the bearer of bad news, but in my opinion you have a scaphoid fracture. You'll need to confirm that with an X-ray."

"I don't have time for a fracture."

She shrugged. "You're going to have to make the time if my assessment is correct."

He frowned. "How much time?"

She reached behind her, grabbed an antiseptic packet and tore it open. "That will be up to a doctor to decide."

His jaw tightened when she began to dab at the cut. "Give me a hint," he said.

After discarding the damp pad in the appropriate bin, Jill applied a plastic strip to the abrasion. "Best case scenario, three months. Worst case, six months."

Surprise passed over his expression before turning to anger. "If I'm laid up for even three months, I might as well forget making it to the finals in December."

Always chasing those championships, as were most of the cowboys who came to her for aid. "If you don't comply with any treatment you might need, you could complicate matters."

He released a rough sigh. "Can't imagine this being any more complicated than it already is."

Oh, if he only knew…and now he would. "If you go back to riding before the fracture heals, you could suffer a ruptured tendon."

"It's my left hand. All I have to do is hold it over my head to balance."

"And if you lose your balance, you risk landing on it again. I assure you that would not be pleasant."

He swiped his arm across his forehead. "None of this is pleasant."

"No, it's not, but it's unfortunately a risk you take when you climb onto a raging animal. Do you have someone who can drive you to an emergency room?"

Houston looked even more defeated. "My brother took off in the rig to hook up with some old girlfriend."

"Which one?"

He scowled. "Hell if I know who she is."

Suppressing a smile, she stripped the gloves off and

tossed them into the bin behind her. "I meant which brother."

"Tyler."

Jill had treated the bronc rider once or twice, only he had always been polite and accommodating, unlike his big brother. "I'm sure if you give him a call—"

"I did before my ride. He told me to find a way back to the motel and I'd see him in the morning."

"You might try calling him again."

"Did that, too. It went straight to voice mail, which means he's tied up for the night. Literally."

Clearly he'd run out of brother-based options. "Surely you can find one of your rodeo cronies to give you a ride."

He slid off the table and groaned. "I was the last entry so everyone's probably headed out. I should've done the same thing and would have if Henry hadn't convinced me to come in here to see you. I could have just as easily waited to see my doctor at home."

A new nickname for him came to mind—Foolish. "It's a long way from Fort Worth to South Texas. It's never wise to delay treatment."

"I can have my private plane here in two hours. Problem solved."

Not quite. "Sure. You could do that, and if you have any blood-flow issues, they can fit you for a prosthetic hand when you get there."

He blew out a long breath. "Since you put it that way, guess I better call a cab and get this over with, although I figure it's probably going to be a waste of time."

Jill couldn't trust he wouldn't bypass medical care and opt for the plane trip, leading her to the last resort she'd been trying to avoid. "Look, there's a satellite ER two blocks from here. You'll be in and out much faster that way, and if it's only a sprain, you can tell me 'I told you so.' I'll take you there and drop you off at your hotel after you're finished with the exam."

He seemed seriously perplexed. "Why would you do that for me?"

Her answer would reflect her strong sense of responsibility, and possibly a serious lack of wisdom. "I can report my findings to the staff while I'm there and make sure you actually go inside."

"No one waiting for you at home?"

The next response would indicate the sad state of her life. "No. Tonight I have nothing better to do aside from grabbing something to eat and settling in to my motel room. If you accept my offer, we can go as soon as I close up here."

Houston mulled that over for a moment and smiled in earnest. "Tell you what. If you'll do this for me, I'll buy you breakfast since I'm sure we won't be done before dawn."

Heavens, she hoped that wouldn't be the case. Spending all night in a waiting room as a favor for a cranky cowboy wasn't her idea of a good time.

At 5:00 a.m., with his wrist and thumb bound in a cast, Houston followed the demanding athletic trainer through the double glass doors and into the warm September night. As he trailed behind her toward the sedan, he realized he'd never observed this side of her before. He'd never really considered that she was taller than most women. He'd never seen her shiny auburn hair out of a ponytail, never noticed the way it swayed against her back when she walked. He'd sure as hell never paid much mind to how well she filled out her jeans, but then again, she was usually facing him when she tended his wounds.

But he had witnessed the impatience in her green

eyes on several occasions when he'd put up a good
argument as to why he didn't require her attention. He
sure wouldn't mind her attention now…

Whoa, Calloway.

He had no business lusting after a member of the
rodeo medical staff, even if she happened to be a really
good-looking member.

Once they reached Jill's sardine-can car, Houston
practically had to fold himself in half to slide into the
passenger seat. Having a damn cast on his wrist didn't
help much.

Jill settled behind the wheel, turned the ignition and
asked, "Where to now?"

"We need to find someplace to eat."

She sent him a sideways glance. "I'm too tired to eat."

"Well, I could eat a whole side of beef. And don't
forget I promised you breakfast."

"Maybe later."

For some reason he wasn't quite ready to part company with her. "I know you're itching to tell me 'I told
you so,' and you can do that over a cup of coffee."

She sighed. "I've had at least four cups of coffee over
the past five hours."

"That leads me to believe you won't be falling asleep
soon."

She shifted slightly to face him. "You have to be the
most persistent man I've ever met."

"Persistence pays off most of the time." He tried on
a persuasive smile. "Come on. Join me. I promise to eat
fast and talk less."

She put the car in Reverse and guided it out of the
space. "Oh, all right. We can go to the diner next to
my motel."

"Where are you staying?"

"The place where everyone tied to the rodeo stays," she said.

"The Buckout Inn?"

"The one and only."

He couldn't imagine her taking a room in a dive populated with crude cowboys. "That's where I'm laying over, too."

"No four-star penthouse suite?"

He stretched his legs out as far as they would go in the cramped sedan. "Nah. I'm more of a down home kinda guy."

"A down home kinda guy with a private plane."

Apparently she wasn't all that impressed. "Technically, the ranch owns the plane. I just use it now and then."

She sent him a skeptical smirk before pulling onto the street. "Ah. That explains it."

As they drove down the Fort Worth streets in silence, Houston couldn't seem to stop stealing covert glances at Jill. He took note of how well she filled out that white tailored shirt stamped with her name right above her breast. Nice, full breasts. And if she caught him staring at that immediate area, she'd probably slam on the brakes and kick his ass to the next curb. Good motivation for avoiding that. He didn't care to call a cab at the moment.

A few minutes later, they arrived at the deserted diner and claimed a booth near the window. Houston scanned the menu for a few minutes while Jill checked her cell. He raised his gaze to find her frowning.

"I'll be back in a minute," she said as she grabbed her purse, slid out of the booth and stood.

Houston figured she either planned to climb back in the car and leave him, or she needed to make a call. "Do you want me to order something for you?" he asked as she walked away.

"A glass of orange juice," she said without looking back.

Must be the phone theory, and that pleased him. He couldn't quite put his finger on it, but something about Jillian Amherst intrigued him. He decided to spend the meal trying to peg exactly what that *something* might be, provided she cooperated. First, he had to make a call, too.

After fishing his cell out of his front pocket, Houston pulled up his contacts and chose the number listed as The Tyrant. He waited through two rings before Dallas answered with, "What do you want at this time of the morning?"

"You're always up by five."

"Yeah, and Luke had us up until two."

"Sorry, but this is kind of important. I had an accident last night and—"

"Did you fall on your head again?"

"Nope. Got my hand tangled up and it's fractured, so I'm pretty much done for the next couple of months. Since I can't find Tyler, I need you to send the plane this afternoon."

"Fine, but you'll have to arrange for transportation to the airport. I'd say having you at the ranch might be a good thing, but not if you only have the use of one hand."

He started to argue that he could do more with one functioning hand than some men could do with two, but thought better of it. "It's my left hand and I can still manage."

"I damn sure hope so. And while I have you on the phone, I need to talk to you about Fort's latest demands."

Houston didn't have the time or energy to deal with

Worth's twin. "Look, can it wait? I'm having break-fast with someone and she should be joining me at any minute."

"You must not be too banged up if you're with a woman."

"She's not a woman." Hell, that sounded weird. "I meant she's not a date. She's the rodeo's athletic trainer and she took me to the ER."

"Oh, yeah? How old is she?"

"Why does that matter?"

"Does she have a lot of experience in the medical field?"

"You could say that. She's tough as hell but she knows what she's doing."

"Then see if she might consider the job here."

Sleep deprivation had obviously robbed his brother of his senses. "You don't know a damn thing about her."

"Right now I'm pretty desperate. I've made a few calls but athletic trainers are in such high demand, there aren't a whole lot available around here. At least not any who are qualified to manage a program or who are will-ing to move to the middle of nowhere."

Houston could debate why Jill might not be a good fit, then he realized having her around wouldn't be so awful since he wouldn't be her patient, or her boss. "I'll ask, but don't get your hopes up. She seems pretty happy with her current position."

"Okay, but I expect you to use your powers of per-suasion. By that I mean persuade her that it's a good opportunity without trying to seduce her. I'll have the plane there by four."

Before Houston could respond, Dallas hung up the phone in time for Jill to return to the booth, sporting black-framed glasses. "Sorry," she said. "My contacts were killing me. I had to take them off."

"You look good with glasses." And she did—smart and sexy.

She released a short laugh. "Oh, yeah. You know the old saying about women in glasses never getting passes."

"That old adage has never been in my verbal repertoire."

Her eyes went wide with surprise. "Verbal repertoire? I'm impressed."

He leaned forward and smiled. "I might look like a hayseed, but I don't just climb on the backs of cantankerous bulls. I have a degree in business with a minor in marketing."

"Really? I suppose that comes in handy with all those energy drink ads featuring your smiling face that I keep seeing everywhere."

Hell, he didn't like thinking about those, much less talking about them. "They made me an offer I couldn't refuse."

She opened the menu and turned her attention to the limited offerings. "I'm sure it helps pay the bills, like all the expenses involved in owning a private plane."

At least she'd said it with a smile. "Yeah. That, and horses and entry fees."

After setting the menu aside, she finally focused on him. "Those entry fees are pricey, especially for the cowboys just starting out. I don't know how they manage the rodeo life and a family, like many of them do."

He leaned back and sighed. "I learned a long time ago that a wife and kids and rodeos aren't a good mix. I've seen a lot of relationship casualties over the past fifteen years."

"I'm sure you have, and I assume that's why you haven't gone down that path."

"You'd be right about that." At least partially. Truth was, he'd never met anyone he'd wanted to settle down with, or anyone he'd be willing to give up the life for.

A young woman with a lopsided blond ponytail arrived at the table, set two glasses of water before them and hid a yawn behind her hand. "I'm so sorry. It's been a long night. Someone didn't show up for their shift so I pulled a double, which wouldn't be so bad if I didn't have class in four hours."

"I remember those days," Jill said. "I use to wait tables in college to avoid student loans."

"You do what you have to do to make ends meet without borrowing money," the sleepy young woman replied. "But times like these have me reconsidering."

Jill sent her a sympathetic smile. "I hear you. But rest assured it will be worth it when you don't have any debt after you get your degree."

"I hope so. Are you folks ready to order?"

"I'll just have some wheat toast and a glass of milk," Jill answered. "And some honey if you have it."

Houston frowned. "That's it? Remember, I'm buying."

"I'm a cheap date." A faint blush colored Jill's cheeks as she handed the menu to the waitress. "Not that we're on a date. And I'm not cheap. I'm just not hungry."

He chuckled. "Glad you clarified that," he said as he regarded the now smiling server. "I'll take the Western omelet with a side of pancakes and bacon. And if it's not too much trouble—" he glanced at her name tag "—Ashley, just bring me a whole pot of coffee. I'm going to need it."

The coed grinned. "No problem at all. I'll have that out shortly."

Jill took a sip of water and shifted slightly in the seat. "I hope I'm not boring you so badly that you need a whole pot of high-octane caffeine to stay awake."

Not hardly. He didn't find anything boring about her mouth or her eyes or the way she rimmed the top of her glass with one fingertip. He sure as heck didn't see anything boring about the slightly dirty thoughts that little gesture brought about. "You're not boring me at all. I've learned a lot about you in a short amount time."

She rested her elbow on the table and supported her cheek with her palm. "Such as?"

"You don't like nicknames. You don't eat enough to feed a parakeet. And you worked your way through college waiting tables, although I have a hard time picturing you slinging hash in a greasy spoon."

She straightened and smiled. "Who said I worked in a diner?"

"I just assumed—"

"Assumptions aren't always accurate. Actually, I was a cocktail waitress in a casino."

He wouldn't have guessed that in a million years. "Where?"

"Vegas, where else? That's where I discovered rodeo in relation to athletic training. I interned with my current company and that landed me a job after I received my master's degree."

And he thought nothing about her would surprise him. "Let me get this straight. You worked your way through undergraduate and graduate school by working in a casino and managed to get by without financial aid."

"I did. The money was very good. Being objectified on a nightly basis was not. But I did what I had to do to survive."

The idea of some drunk groping Jill didn't set well

with Houston. He started to ask why her parents didn't help her pay for her education, but he decided that wasn't any of his business. "I admire your guts, Jill. I had no idea you could make that much serving booze. Exactly how much did you make?"

She frowned. "If you must know, on average, fifty grand a year. Some of my fellow servers made twice that much working full-time."

Damn. "I can only imagine what you went through, particularly during the rodeo finals."

Finally her features relaxed. "Nothing a good pair of glasses didn't cure."

That wouldn't have deterred him, or most of the guys he knew. "Congratulations on being resourceful, and thanks for allowing me to get to know you better."

"I know you a bit better, too."

"Oh, yeah?"

"Yeah. You want people to know you're not just a bull rider. You like the finer things in life but you downplay your wealth. You eat like a field hand and, most important, you're an incorrigible flirt."

She definitely had him dead to rights. "Am not."

"Are, too. I saw you trying your best to charm that poor, exhausted waitress with a wink and a grin."

He immediately jumped into defensive mode. "I didn't wink. I only smiled at her. In my book, that doesn't qualify as flirting. I was being polite, like my mama taught me."

She held up her hands, palms forward. "Hey, don't get your chaps in a twist. I didn't say it was a horrible trait. It's just part of your personality. Something that is second nature to you. And it's obvious you know how to contain it. You've not once ever attempted to flirt with me to get your way."

Did she want him to flirt with her? "Would it have worked?"

"Absolutely not."

Figured. "If you think about it, you've only seen me at my worst. Banged up and pissed off."

"And cranky."

He grinned. "Cranky Calloway. That's the best one so far."

They shared in a laugh until Ashley came back with the tray filled with his food and the requested pot of coffee. For the next few minutes, Jill picked at her honey-covered toast while he shoveled his food down like it might disappear. He looked up from the last bite of pancakes to find one pretty amused athletic trainer staring at him.

Houston pushed his plate away and sat back against the booth. "That hit the spot."

"I can tell, and you weren't kidding when you said you would eat fast."

The way she wet her lips brought about all kinds of questionable thoughts. "I guess you're going to tell me it's not good for digestion."

"No. I was going to say I'm glad you enjoyed it."

Her mouth held his fascination, and man, oh, man, he liked a woman with a great mouth. He also liked her slightly upturned nose and the dimples creasing her cheek, one more prominent than the other. He liked the way her slender hands moved when she spoke, and the intensity in those green eyes peering at him from behind the glasses. "Good food and good company. Nothing better after a long night." A long frustrating night, in this case. He hated the damn cast on his wrist and the fact he could be out of commission for weeks, if not months. He really hated that he didn't know her well enough to kiss her good morning. Or good night. Or all day.

Where the hell did *that* come from?

"I bet I know exactly what you're thinking, Houston Calloway."

Only if she could read minds, and he sure as heck hoped not. "Huh?"

"You're lamenting the fact you're injured."

He wasn't too injured to stop fantasizing about her. "It is what it is, and I've had worse. Dallas is going to be happy to have me home to work on Texas Extreme, although he's going to question what a one-handed cowboy can accomplish." In fact, Dallas already had.

"I'm sure you'll improvise," she said.

He could improvise when it came to her needs. Too bad he wouldn't have the opportunity to show her if Dallas offered her the job. Then again…

Houston could just hear his mom now, warning him to remember his raising and to never disrespect a woman. Unfortunately his lying, cheating dad hadn't followed that advice. He shook off those sorry memories and cleared his throat. "You're right. I'll manage."

Jill dabbed at her mouth and set the napkin aside. "Exactly what will your role be at this rodeo fantasy resort?"

"I plan to be the bull-riding instructor, as soon as I get this contraption off my wrist."

She moved her plate to one side and pushed her glasses up the bridge of her nose. "When is this venture supposed to be up and running?"

Should've been long before now. "We were supposed to be ready to go by next month, but now it looks like after the first of the year. We were warned about constructing a project this big. Expect delays and an increased budget. We've got both."

"You *are* going to have medical facilities, aren't you?"

No surprise she'd ask about that, and it was the perfect lead-in to Dallas's request. But he still wasn't sure he wanted to bother with doing Dallas's bidding. "We have a building, with nothing in it yet."

She perked up like a pup. "You should definitely utilize athletic trainers, if not full-time, on a contract basis. You'll need someone to manage that, and of course, they would also be in charge of ordering supplies, including safety gear. How close is the hospital?"

"They just built a new one off the interstate, about ten minutes or so away from the ranch."

"Excellent. You'll have an emergency room staff readily available, and you should have quick access to EMTs, just in case. Also, I suggest you might want to…"

Houston just sat back and watched Jill talk so fast he only heard half of what she was saying. He didn't like that he was starting to lust after a lady who wouldn't give him the time of day under most circumstances. More important, he hated to think he might be forced to see her on a daily basis and not be able to explore all the possibilities with her.

But that was okay. He could control himself around her if this whole employment thing came to pass.

"I'm sorry," Jill said, garnering his attention.

"Sorry for what?"

She let go a low, sexy laugh. "I'm sorry for rambling on about my ideas for your business. Once I let the passion take hold, I have a hard time stopping it."

Houston downed half a glass of water in response to the fantasies rolling around in his mind. Like *that* would help extinguish the heat building below his belt. He seriously needed to get a grip on his libido. "Nothing wrong with being passionate about your work. It's the best way to get ahead in life. Do what you love and love what you do."

"For you that's rodeo," she stated.

"Yep. And ranching." *And making a woman feel really good all night long.*

Jill took a quick check of her watch. "Wow. It's almost dawn. Way past bedtime."

Not if he had any say-so in the matter. *Down, Houston.* "Guess that's my cue that it's time to go."

She put her palm over her mouth and yawned. "I could use some sleep, and I'm sure you should grab a few minutes before Tyler returns. Are you heading back home today?"

"Yep. I hadn't planned on it, but with a bum wrist, looks like I don't have a choice. What about you?"

"I'm laying over here until next weekend, then I'll move to a motel near Mesquite."

That meant she was free for the week, a good thing if she agreed to the interview, provided he asked her about it. Houston pulled out his wallet and tossed a fifty onto the table. "Let's go."

Jill eyed the bill for a few seconds. "Don't you need to wait for your change?"

Houston slid out of the booth and came to his feet. "Nah. She needs the money more than me."

"Very generous, Mr. Calloway," she said as she stood. "I'm sure Ashley will appreciate your contribution to the college fund."

Knowing he still had the job offer hanging over him, Houston trailed behind Jill as she headed out of the glass door and started toward the car. "I can walk from here," he told her before she climbed inside the sedan. "I could use some fresh air before I enter that musty room."

"Suit yourself," she said with a slight smile. "And

if you need any advice on your medical facilities, feel free to give me a call or a text." She set her purse on the hood, pulled out a card and offered it to him. "Here you go. If I don't answer immediately, it's probably because I'm trying to put a broken cowboy back together."

He'd been that broken cowboy before, and she had always been an expert at trying to put him back together. She was an asset to the rodeo sports medicine program. She'd be an asset to any program. Hell, anyone would be lucky to have her, in a medical sense. Any other sense, for that matter.

It occurred to Houston that he wasn't quite ready to say goodbye to her yet. Not until he posed the question that could lead to a favorable response, at least for his brother, or a literal slam of the door before she drove away, leaving him to eat her dust as easily as he'd eaten breakfast. But if she agreed to consider coming to work for Texas Extreme, he could still look at her, even if he couldn't touch her. Even if he'd have to take several cold showers a day until he went back on the road. Damn Dallas for putting him in this predicament.

"Before you go, Jill," he began, "I have something else I need to say. Actually, it's an offer."

She looked more than a little leery. "What kind of offer?"

"One that I'm hoping you can't refuse."

Two

The comment robbed Jill of her speech, but only momentarily. "If you're about to proposition me, you can—"

"Do you want me to proposition you?"

She didn't intend to hesitate even a split second, but she did. "Of course not."

"Hey, relax. I have a proposition for you, but I promise it doesn't involve scooping you up and carrying you into the motel for a little predawn delight."

That stirred up a few inadvisable images in her muddled mind. "What a relief."

"Besides, that would be tough to do with my hand in a cast," he said, topping off the comment with a wily wink. He leaned back against the car, as if he had no intention of going anywhere. "First, a couple of questions."

So much for getting that snooze any time soon. "All right."

"Where is your home base?"

"Actually, I don't really have one. At least not a place of my own. I list my permanent address as my parents' house in Florida."

"You travel that much?"

"Most of the year. I live in hotels and motels and the occasional corporate apartment. I don't even own a car, so I have to rely on rentals, like that sedan you're polishing with your behind. Why?"

He shifted his weight from one leg to the other. "When you were gone earlier, I called Dallas. And when he found out you were with me, he suggested you might be a good candidate for the medical position at Texas Extreme."

That threw her for a mental loop. "He's offering me a job?"

"He wants to interview you first. It's my understanding you'd have full control over the medical program, hire anyone you want and make all the decisions."

She considered several problems with that setup and prepared to bat all his arguments away like a practiced tennis player. "Thanks, but I like the job I have."

"You'd have your own apartment. A brand-new apartment."

"I have no problem traveling. Makes life less boring."

"He'll double your salary."

He'd just served up a surprise backhand. "How can Dallas promise that if he doesn't even know how much I get paid?"

He pushed away from the car and smiled. "Doesn't matter. We can afford it."

That she didn't doubt. Still, she realized one serious obstacle remained, and she planned to lob it right to him. "No offense, Houston, but I'm not sure I could work for you."

"Not a problem. You wouldn't be working for me. You'd be working for Dallas. Besides, I'll be back on the circuit before you know it and you won't have to deal with me."

Having Houston's brother as a boss could be a major concern if Dallas Calloway happened to be as stubborn as his younger sibling. And she would still encounter Houston on a regular basis until he took off again for the next rodeo. That wouldn't be for another two to three months.

But double the salary? She'd be foolish not to give it some thought. She might be a bigger fool if she accepted without knowing all the particulars. "Look, I'd be lying if I didn't say I wasn't tempted, but—"

"I can tempt you even more."

Jill reacted to the deep grainy quality of his voice with unwelcome goose bumps. One more reason she should walk away from him and his blasted offer. Maintaining complete professionalism in his presence could be difficult outside the rodeo circuit considering his persistence, the fact that he wouldn't be her patient and this idiotic attraction to him that had begun to rear its ugly head. "I believe I have enough to make an informed decision, and my answer is—"

"A ride on a decked-out plane, complete with a fully stocked bar, in case you're nervous about flying."

"I'm not nervous." The slight tremor in her voice betrayed her, but it had nothing to do with the flight. "I can't count the times I've been on a plane."

"A private plane?"

If he only knew. "Actually, I have."

He cracked a crooked smile. "Yeah, but you haven't been on mine."

Why did everything that spilled out of his mouth sound suggestive? "And your point?"

"I just thought that since I'm done for the season, and you don't have to be anywhere until this weekend, we could mosey on down to the ranch so you can take a look around before you decide. We have plenty of places for you to stay overnight."

Overnight? No way. "I believe I've heard enough and I really don't think—"

"Pack an overnight bag, and I'll see you at four in the lobby," he said as he started across the lot toward the motel. "And FYI, I won't take no for an answer."

Wouldn't take no for an answer? Ha. Maybe that worked for most women, but Jillian Elizabeth Amherst wasn't just any woman, a fact he would soon learn. She'd spent a good deal of her adulthood telling people no, from pesky men to her own parents.

Come on, Jilly. Take a chance, for once in your life.

Jill shoved aside her onetime best friend's words and allowed caution to come into play. She had a decent life, a satisfying job. She liked the travel even if she didn't care for the solitude at times. She didn't really desire to have a permanent home or a larger salary, although she wouldn't reject extra money in most cases. But she surely didn't need the hassle of trying to avoid a cowboy who had begun to capture her fancy, and imagination. She worried she might not *want* to turn him down, if the opportunity presented itself.

That reason alone led her to the appropriate decision. When Houston Calloway walked into that lobby this afternoon, he wouldn't find her there.

Houston was kind of surprised to see Jill standing there, a blue canvas bag hanging over her shoulder, a larger suitcase at her feet and a ticked-off look on her face. She struck him as one of those organized people, and she probably didn't appreciate the fact he was ten minutes late for the rendezvous.

"Not much on punctuality?" she said as he approached her, confirming his suspicions.

"Sorry," he muttered. "I overslept."

"I didn't sleep at all."

She'd said it like that was his fault. "Why not?"

"Aside from having to turn in my rental car, I kept rolling your offer around in my mind, weighing the pros and cons. Instant insomnia."

No shock there. "Fair enough. Now follow me."

After picking up her suitcase, Houston escorted Jill out of the lobby to the black limo waiting at the curb. The driver opened the rear door and took the suitcase while Jill climbed inside. She claimed a spot on the lengthy seat on the far side of the limo, while he sat opposite her to maintain a wide berth between them. Otherwise he'd be battling the urge to coax her down onto the gray leather.

Like she'd be open to that. And he sure as hell didn't understand why he'd suddenly become so damn attracted to a woman who'd been a burr in his butt for two years. Maybe it was just the challenge and the chase. Maybe he'd gone too long without female attention. Maybe it was those dimples and that shiny auburn hair and the way that peach-colored T-shirt enhanced her finer attributes. And damn she smelled good, like the lavender his stepmom, Jen, planted everywhere she could find a scrap of dirt. Jillian's finer qualities, coupled with her no-BS attitude, presented a mighty fine package. He could so take her on one, hot ride…

"Nice ride," she said, breaking through his fantasies.

"Only the best. The bar's fully stocked if you want a drink."

"No, thanks. When I drink, which is extremely rare, I don't ever do so before seven."

He could use a shot of whiskey, but he'd refrain in order to maintain some control over his libido. "Did you have any lunch?"

"I grabbed a sandwich a couple of hours ago."

When she flipped that thick hair over one shoulder, he wanted to grab a cab and get out of there before he forgot his manners. "We'll have dinner with the family tonight," he said. "That would be a welcome change of pace. I tend to have a lot of fast food."

"I hear you. Nothing better than a home-cooked meal."

"I agree," she said before glancing out the window.

Houston still couldn't quite get a grip on the fact she'd agreed to accompany him in light of all her earlier arguments against it. He sensed Jill might be questioning that decision when she shifted and turned her attention onto the smoky glass partition separating the front from the back. The conversation died during the twenty-minute drive to the private airport and didn't resume even when they boarded the D Bar C corporate jet.

They settled into the beige leather seats kitty-corner from each other in the main cabin near the onboard bar. Jill stared out the window without speaking, leading Houston to wonder why she would find a hangar so damn interesting.

He snapped his seat belt closed and cleared his throat. "How does this plane compare to the others you've been on?"

She tore her gaze from the tarmac and looked around. "About the same," she said before finally looking directly at him. "Plush seats. Full kitchen with white marble counters. The ultimate in technology, right down to the WiFi. I assume the sleeping quarters are in the back."

"Yeah. Feel free to stretch out after we take off."

She rifled through her bag, took out a magazine and began to flip through the pages. "No, thanks. I'm fine right here."

All talk ceased as they taxied down the runway, and once they leveled off midair, Houston got up and grabbed a beer from the bar fridge. "Want anything to drink? I make a mean gin and tonic."

"No, thanks," she said without looking up.

"Glass of water?"

"No, thanks again."

Jill seemed bent on ignoring him, and that royally ticked Houston off. He took a swig before settling back in the seat. "Did I do something to piss you off?"

She sent him a fast glance and went back to flipping. "Not today."

"What is that supposed to mean?"

After closing the magazine, she looked at him straight on. "I'm sorry. I'm tired. I didn't intend to take it out on you."

He suspected there was more to it than fatigue. "Are you sure something else isn't bugging you?"

"If you must know, my mother left me a voice mail and I listened to it right before I left the motel room. She reminded me that my sister is getting married next weekend and I'm expected to attend. Sometimes her demands rub me the wrong way."

Houston decided Ms. Amherst had some serious mama issues. "You don't sound too excited about the nuptials."

"I'm not. I've never been that close to Pamela. She'd didn't even invite me to be in the wedding party. But I'm five years older and let's just say she's always been the favored child."

He sensed a sorry story there. "Why is that?"

"Pamela is a conformist. She went to college at my parents' Ivy League alma mater, and she had the good fortune to find the perfect, wealthy, shallow guy. I'm sure she'll go on to be surrounded by lots of socialites and have two point five children and a membership to the best country club in the country."

The resentment in her tone took him aback. "Not your scene, huh?"

"Not hardly. I'm the rebel of the family. I went to school in Sin City and didn't take the time to meet any guys, let alone get engaged to one."

That was one helluva bombshell. "You didn't date a single soul in college?"

"I was focused on my career, although I did consider seeking out a professional poker player just to add fuel to the family fire."

They both laughed for a few seconds before Houston posed another question to keep the mood light. "Don't you think bringing home a cowboy would've done the same thing?"

She mulled that over for a moment. "I wish I'd thought of that. My mother would have been completely beside herself, but at least she might have stopped trying to set me up with some rich, boring, misogynistic narcissist every time I went home."

Man, she didn't mince words. Big words. But he'd started to relate a little more to the always serious athletic trainer. He wasn't a stranger to complicated family dynamics, and he was curious to confirm if they shared another aspect in their background. "Correct me if I'm wrong, but it sounds to me like you come from money."

She folded her arms beneath her breasts and sighed. "Yes. A lot of money. I had a trust fund that I didn't bother to touch because it came with conditions."

That explained why she worked her way through school. "Conditions as in Ivy League schools and no cowboys?"

"Exactly."

A short span of silence passed before Houston decided to end the quiet for a second time. "I'm glad you let me in on the family problems. For a minute there I thought you were mad at me for forcing you onto a plane."

Her smile came back out of hiding. "You didn't force me, and no, I'm not mad at you. I *am* a little mad at myself for not declining the invitation. This could be a total waste of both our time if your brother isn't interested in hiring me. Provided I actually want the job."

"Or it could be a win-win situation. You'll have a better salary and a permanent place to land, and I'll earn some points with Dallas."

She frowned. "Are you holding some sort of competition?"

"Yeah. See who can find the prettiest prospective employee."

"That's rather sexist, Calloway."

"I'm kidding, Amherst. Dallas thinks I haven't been doing enough for Texas Extreme, so I figure finding someone as qualified as you to head the medical team will help prove my worth."

"Ah. Now I know your true motives. I could be a notch in your bedpost. I meant notch in your belt buckle.

Or is it just belt? Never mind." Her face looked a little flushed. "What is Dallas like?"

"I thought you'd probably met him."

She shook her head. "No, but I do know his reputation as an all-around champion cowboy."

"Do you know Austin?"

"Again, only by reputation. I did catch a glimpse of him during the national finals when I was interning, but I never had the chance to meet him."

"Is that his rodeo reputation or his reputation with the ladies before he got hitched?"

"His rodeo reputation. With you, I'd say both."

Ouch. "Aw, come on now. I'm not a player."

She narrowed her eyes and smirked. "That's not what I've heard."

"You can't believe everything you hear in the rodeo world. People like to exaggerate."

"I'm sure."

He didn't care for her cynical tone, or that she believed he was some skirt-chasing cowboy. That would be his half brother Worth, and the minute she met him, she might change her tune. Compared to Worth, he'd look like a saint. "To set the record straight, I had a girlfriend for a couple of years."

She leaned back and crossed her jeans-covered legs. "Really? What happened to the relationship, if you don't mind my asking?"

He did mind a little bit. "She got tired of me being gone all the time."

"She wasn't into rodeo?"

"Nope. She was a city girl from Dallas. She lived in a downtown loft and unfortunately tennis was her sport."

Her green eyes went wide. "Unfortunately? What's wrong with tennis?"

Open mouth, insert boot. "I take it you play."

"Yes, but not much since my boarding school days."

That nearly shocked him speechless. His family had always been well off, but they'd never shipped him off. "Like a live-in school?"

Jill looked like she wished she could take it back. "Yes. All-girl college prep academy, thanks to my mother's insistence. I concentrated on my studies, and not on boys."

He'd begun to wonder if she'd never had any exposure to the opposite sex. Nah. Not possible with her looks and smarts. "Surely you had a boyfriend at some point in time."

The way she lowered her eyes for a second told Houston he might already know the answer. "I've dated a little," she finally said. "But with my bachelor's degree, grad school, internships and a demanding job, my schedule hasn't allowed for much of a social life for the past few years."

He'd be glad to help her change that, but she probably wouldn't be game. Then again, if it didn't work out between them and she did go to work for the ranch, that could cause a lot of issues. "I imagine it would be pretty hard to have much of a social life with all the traveling, particularly in your line of work."

"Most men don't seem to have that problem."

He couldn't resist yanking her chain. "Isn't that a little sexist?"

She rolled her eyes and smiled. "Oh, please. That's the way it is. Men have an uncanny way of finding a woman in every port. Or in your case, arena."

"You're jaded."

"I am not. I only tell it like it is."

"Nope. You've been wronged by someone, most likely a cowboy."

She raised her hand like she was taking an oath. "I swear I have never been involved with a cowboy. I *have* been a silent observer during my tenure as an athletic trainer and I've seen it all. Broken hearts. Heated arguments. I've even treated the casualties resulting from cat fights."

He chuckled. "Gotta love those cowgirls."

"Let me add that I've also examined more than a few jaws resulting from cowboy fights, even if that's not in my job description."

"But not with me."

She grinned again. "No, not you. You're more inclined to fall on your head when you fall off a bull and then argue with me when you don't want to hear my advice."

He studied her a moment and had a surprising revelation. "I've got to be honest with you, Jill. When I first met you, I didn't like you much."

She laid a hand above her breasts. "I'm stunned."

"That's sarcasm, right?"

"Yes. You didn't like it when I ran you through concussion protocol."

"True. And I didn't particularly like that you seemed to treat other cowboys nicer." Now he sounded like some jealous jerk.

"You don't like anyone telling you what to do," she began, "and most of my patients tend to be much more cooperative."

Damn if she wasn't right about that. "Fair enough. But you tend to make a big deal over a bump on the head, at least when it comes to me."

She unbuckled her seat belt and scooted forward, her

hands clasped together in her lap. "Look, Houston, I'm only tough because I care."

"You do? Well, ma'am, I'm mighty honored to know that."

"I care about every athlete I treat," she added quickly.

"Even the annoying ones?"

Her smile traveled all the way to those great green eyes. "Yes, even the annoying ones."

When Jill yawned, Houston realized he was being selfish by keeping her from sleeping. "Are you sure you don't want to go to bed?"

"We don't know each other *that* well."

Finally, another glimpse of her sense of humor, although he didn't find the stirring below his belt funny at all. His "bed" question might've been totally innocent, but the images hanging out in his head were pretty damn wicked. "You know what I mean. You're about to fall asleep where you sit, which you can. Just press the button on the right side and the chair leans all the way back."

She blinked twice. "I'm fine. Really."

"You can barely keep your eyes open." He stood, stepped to one side of her seat and depressed the control, reclining the back of the chair and raising the foot rest at the same time since she refused to do it herself. "There you go."

He expected her to protest, but instead she muttered, "Thank you."

For some reason, Houston's feet remained glued to the floor as he continued to hover above Jill, leaving them in close proximity. She wet her lips and looked like she might want to say something, or do something, but she just sat very still, her gaze locked on his. He seriously wanted to kiss her, long and hard, but his mom's words about honor kept him from acting on impulse. Jill had been right. They didn't know each other that well, but if he had his way, that would change, if only to find out if his attraction to her was legitimate. He probably wouldn't get his way, so he should just stop thinking about that now.

"Have a nice nap," he said as he moved back to his seat.

"I will," she answered before closing her eyes completely.

Houston downed the rest of his now-warm beer and continued to watch Jill. He knew by the rise and fall of her chest, her slack features, she was out. She was also a pretty sleeper. Angelic. Sexy. So much for not thinking of her in that way.

He rested his head back against the seat and allowed his imagination free rein, at his own detriment. Every detailed fantasy made him more uncomfortable. Every questionable thought about what he wanted to do with her made him shift on the seat. And every time he tried to stop thinking about it, he met mental resistance head-on.

If he didn't get hold of his control, by the time they made it to the ranch, he'd have to ride in the pickup bed. *Bed*.

Damn. Asking Jill Amherst on this trip was definitely asking for trouble.

Three

"Buckle up, folks. We're about to land."

At the sound of the booming voice, Jill came awake with a start. She looked around to try to regain her bearings, and came in visual contact with a pair of golden-brown eyes. Now she remembered. Private jet. Persistent cowboy. Possible new employment.

She stretched her arms above her head and made sure her seat belt was secure as they started to descend. "How long have I been asleep?"

"Less than an hour," Houston said. "It's a fairly short flight."

As she braced for landing, Jill glanced out the window to see the roofs of several houses with pools and huge barns, and on the horizon, a huge multistory building surrounded by a massive amount of acreage. "Where are we landing?"

"The ranch. We have our own airstrip."

Of course. "It looks like suburbia in the middle of nowhere."

"We've all built our own houses, so I guess it would look that way. People in these parts like to refer to the D Bar C as the Cowboy Commune."

She brought her attention back to Houston. "Clever. I look forward to seeing the commune up close and personal."

The tires bumped and the plane screeched to a halt, followed by a resounding "Yee haw" coming from the vicinity of the cockpit.

"Who in the world was that?" she asked.

"That's Frank, the wannabe cowboy pilot," Houston said. "I forgot to warn you about him."

She wondered what other surprises awaited her. "I appreciate his enthusiasm." And she was happy that she hadn't been bucked out of the airplane.

After releasing her seat belt, Jill grabbed her bag and stood. Houston followed suit, but before she could take a step toward the exit, he said, "Just so you know, my family's kind of unconventional."

She would save that conversation for later. "Not a problem. You should meet mine."

Without waiting for a response, Jill headed out the now open door and sprinted down the stairs into the very warm Texas evening, Houston following behind her. She spotted a huge, black double-cab truck parked across the airstrip, a red Texas Extreme logo emblazoned across the side. And leaning against that truck, a guy with ham-hock biceps and sun-streaked hair. He wore a lemon yellow T and jeans and aside from the worn cowboy boots, he looked a bit out of place against the rustic backdrop.

The minute they made eye contact, he looked some-what surprised to see her. Not as surprised as she was to see the likes of him on a ranch—a surfer dude. Definitely not the typical rodeo guy, which led her to believe he must be either a friend or employee of the Callo-way boys.

"Hey, brother," the stranger said as he pushed off the truck.

Brother? Seriously? A brother with a serious air of confidence, Jill decided when he strode toward them, all the while keeping his gaze trained on her.

"Hey," Houston replied as he took the bags from the rowdy pilot with the handlebar mustache, who looked more like a gunslinger than an aviator. "Jill, this is Worth, the youngest of the crew."

"I'm a minute older than Fort," Worth said with a frown. "That makes me second to the youngest, and it's nice to meet you, Jill."

She'd known about Dallas, Austin and Tyler, but Fort and Worth had never entered any conversation she'd had about the Calloways. "Nice to meet you, too."

Worth sent her a slow grin. "I didn't know you were bringing a girl home, Houston."

Houston shoved a black canvas bag at Worth. "She's not with me, and she's not a girl."

"Okay, she's a woman and I saw her get off the plane with you."

"Yeah, but she's here to see Dallas about a job."

Worth turned his smile on Jill. "How long are you going to be here?"

She sensed the man was an incorrigible flirt. "Only one night."

"Would you like to go with me to—"

"No, she wouldn't, Worthless," Houston snapped.

"Take our bags to my house. And tell Mom to set an extra plate for dinner."

Worth looked as confused as Jill felt. "I'll drive you to your place."

After handing over a set of keys to his brother, Houston picked up Jill's luggage and started toward the truck. "We'll walk," he said as he put the bags in the bed.

Worth saluted. "Aye, aye, captain. I live to serve."

After Worth climbed back into the truck and drove away in a fog of dust, Houston turned to Jill. "I want to apologize for his behavior. He only has two things on his mind—women and chasing women."

Information she'd already gathered herself. "He seemed nice enough."

"He's a twenty-seven-year-old teenager."

"A year older than me," she said without much thought.

"Maybe chronologically, but not on a maturity level."

"Does he work here on the ranch?"

"Yeah, but he owns a yacht-chartering company on the gulf coast."

That explained the surfer look. "And apparently he has a twin."

"Yep. Fort, but he doesn't have anything to do with any of us."

Interesting. "Why is that?"

"It's a long story."

One she might never know. She did have an important question involving the rest of the family. "When you asked Worth to tell your mother to set an extra plate, it made me wonder if anyone knows I'm here."

He looked a little sheepish. "Only Dallas, but the rest will real soon, now that Worth knows."

"I don't want to inconvenience anyone."

"It's not a big deal," he said. "We have guests dropping by all the time.

Now follow me and I'll show you around."

"I'm looking forward to it." She wasn't exactly sure how she felt about being the surprise for the evening, or staying in Houston's house, but then again, it shouldn't matter. She was here on business, and she'd established that from the beginning. She didn't believe that Houston was the kind of guy who had to be reminded of that. Besides, he'd never held her in high esteem, although he had thought enough of her to present what could be a great opportunity. Provided she got past the initial first impressions. She had a feeling this could be an interview by committee.

They continued down a narrow paved road while Houston pointed out various landmarks, including the massive lodge in the distance, the new rodeo arena, complete with indoor and outdoor space. Then he pointed at the rock and cedar building adjacent to those facilities. "That's the medical clinic. I'll take you on a tour after dinner."

Clinic? She'd been expecting a glorified tent. "I'm pleasantly surprised. It looks top-grade."

"Right now it's empty," he said. "That's where you come in."

"If Dallas thinks I'm the right fit."

"He will."

Confident much? "*If* I decide it's something I want to undertake."

He grinned. "You will."

She'd learned from experience that debating with Houston Calloway would do no good, so Jill concentrated on meeting him stride for stride as they took a left turn at a bend in the road. The first of the residences came into view, a white rock and cedar single-story rambling ranch house set back from the road on their right. From the looks of the place, she guessed this place belonged to a matriarch, until Houston said, "This one's mine," shattering all her assumptions.

"Wow," she said as they headed up the driveway toward the three-car garage. She took note of the silver crew-cab truck, the typical rodeo cowboy's mode of transportation. Admittedly she was a little stunned to see the champagne-colored Mercedes parked next to it.

"Great," Houston muttered. "We have a guest."

"Old girlfriend?"

"Nope. New stepmom. That's her car."

"Worth's mother?"

"Yeah. Jenny. I've got to warn you, she's one of a kind."

"In a good way?"

"Most of the time."

Jill wasn't sure how to take that until the door opened to a woman with teased blond hair and a sunny smile. She wore a red polka-dot dress, covered by a white frilly apron that looked like a throwback from fifty years ago.

"Come in," she said with a sweeping gesture. "We're so glad to finally meet one of Houston's special friends."

"She's not a special friend," Houston corrected as they stepped inside the entry. "She's a prospective employee."

"Whatever you say." She turned her attention to Jill. "I'm Jenny, Houston's stepmama. And you are?"

Jill shook her offered hand. "I'm Jillian Amherst, but most people call me Jill."

"What a lovely name," Jen said. "For a lovely girl."

"No offense, Jen," Houston began, "but what are you doing here?"

"No offense taken, sugar. When Worth told me you'd brought home a guest, we decided to bring dinner home to you. Dallas, Paris and the baby are on their way. Now Austin and Georgie might be along a little later because Chance just took a tumble off the fence."

Jill immediately launched into medical mode. "Is he all right?"

Jen waved a dismissive hand. "Oh, certainly, sweetie. This is a daily occurrence with that seven-year-old. He's a walking accident waiting to happen."

Houston finally closed the door behind him. "How long until dinner?"

"That depends on how long it takes you to fire up the grill," Jen said.

Houston's expression turned stony. "We're having a barbecue?"

Jen looked at him as if he'd grown a second eye. "Of course. It's Labor Day weekend, sugar. I brought the burgers and all the fixins' plus a few hot dogs. I even have one of those fake patties for Paris. Your mama will be here in a bit with the apple pie."

Funny, Jill hadn't given much thought to the holiday. In fact, she hadn't remembered the date when it came right down to it. "That sounds great. I'm on the road so much, I can't remember the last time I celebrated a holiday."

"Well, that ends today." Jenny waved Jill toward the lengthy hallway to the right. "I'll show you to your room while Houston gets after that grill. Otherwise, we won't be eating until midnight."

As the enthusiastic stepmother began leading her away, Jill shot a glance over her shoulder at Houston. He sent her a sympathetic look before disappearing from the foyer.

So much for being rescued, Jill thought as she followed Jenny down the corridor, which seemed to run the length of the house.

Jenny paused at the end of the hall and opened a door. "Here we are. Your accommodations for the evening."

Jill walked into the tastefully appointed room to find her bags waiting at the foot of the queen-size bed covered in a rich purple satin comforter. She didn't peg Houston as a purple kind of guy, but then she doubted he had anything to do with the decor.

"I decorated this room," Jenny said, upholding Jill's conjecture. "In fact, I decorated all the boys' places, otherwise they'd be covered in cowhide and wood."

"You did a great job."

"Just wait till you see the bathroom," Jenny said as she practically skipped across the room to open another closed door.

Jill came up beside her and peered inside to see a white Cararra marble tile shower with matching countertops on the vanity. As impressive as it was, she had to admit it looked a lot like other bathrooms she'd known in her lifetime.

Determined not to disappoint Jenny, Jill turned and smiled. "It's very beautiful. I'm extremely impressed by your eye for decorating."

"Oh, thank you, sugar. Now before we go back out into the crowd, we need to have a little chat."

She could only imagine what that might entail. "Go ahead."

"First of all, you need to know you're going to be immersed in testosterone tonight. The Calloway men are a virile bunch. They can hang their jeans on the bedpost and get a woman pregnant."

That created quite a visual in Jill's mind. "Believe me, I deal with that every day in my job. Not the jeans thing, but the testosterone."

"Well, just so you're forewarned." Jenny grinned. "I can't wait for you to meet Paris and Dallas. You know, Paris worked for Dallas in exchange for marrying him."

Jill would swear she'd read that scandalous novel before, and although she wished she had more details, she decided not to prod. "Interesting."

Jenny sighed. "Oh, sweetie, it was. But then they fell in love, married and had a precious little boy eight months ago."

"What a wonderful story."

"And when it comes to Austin and Georgie, that was a love story decades in the making. They were high school sweethearts torn apart by family feuding and unavoidable circumstances."

"Obviously it all worked out."

"Yes, but not before they reunited for one magical night and conceived Chance. Of course, Austin didn't know about him for a good six years."

She'd read that book, too. "That must have been quite the bombshell."

"It almost tore them apart for good. Thankfully we banded together and talked some sense into the boy. And now they're living in wedded bliss as Romeo and Juliet, without the poison and dagger."

Jill was suffering from serious information overload. "I can't wait to meet them all, too."

Jenny hooked her arm through Jill's. "Then let's get to it."

Jill pondered what she'd gotten herself into. Correction. What she might be getting into if they came to an employment agreement. Right now she only worried about getting through the introductions.

They made their way through the masculine great room, complete with black leather sofas and, unsurprisingly, cowhide chairs as well as a large stacked-stone fireplace grounding the room. The kitchen was all Jill expected—high-end appliances, concrete countertops and a butcher-block island the size of Rhode Island. She wouldn't be a bit surprised to see a butler. Oh, wait. That would be her family home.

"Just go on out back, sugar," Jenny said as she opened the huge stainless refrigerator. "I'm going to season the burgers and I'll join you in a few with some of my special drinks."

"Sounds great."

After walking through a set of French doors, Jill entered a backyard that could best be described as resort-like, right down to the pergola and the pool. She found Houston lighting the grill built into a second kitchen built out of stone, a barbecue master's dream.

When Houston glanced at her over one shoulder, he smiled slightly. "Did Jen give you the grand tour?"

She pulled back a cushioned wicker chair from the round glass table nearby. "Yes, she did. She also gave me a recap of your brothers' love stories."

He lowered the lid on the grill and faced her. "I can only imagine what she said."

"Let's just say it was enlightening."

"No surprise there. Where is she now?"

"She's getting the burgers ready and making some kind of special drink."

Houston raked back the chair across from her and sat. "I have to warn you about that. Drink it slow and don't have more than one."

"Does she add something else?"

"Yeah. Tequila."

She'd expected maybe some sort of fruit. "I took a few tequila shots once back during my college days."

"Did you enjoy it?"

She grinned. "I don't remember."

"I've had a few of those nights."

"That was my one and only. I'm too much of a control freak to get drunk."

"Sometimes letting go of a little control is a good thing."

She rested her elbow on the table and supported her face with her palm. "Not when it comes to booze."

"Maybe I wasn't referring to booze."

Normally she would ignore the comment, but for some reason she had to ask. "Care to cite some examples?"

He leaned back and smiled. "Sometimes it's better to take a few risks. Follow instinct instead of logic. Do what feels good."

The overt sensuality in his tone drew her in like he was a human magnet and she was steel. "But what if feeling good in the moment leads to regret later?"

He leaned forward and kept his gaze trained on hers. "Life sometimes comes with regrets, but if you don't take a chance now and then, you're not really living."

Maybe he was talking about the job opportunity. Maybe he'd been speaking in generalities. Maybe she should move on and change the subject. "Just don't expect me to ever climb on the back of a bull."

"Nothing better than a good, long ride."

"I'd never last for the required eight seconds."

"Darlin', I've been known to go way past that."

"Really now?"

"Really. You just hang on tight, tune into your body and roll with the flow."

Oh, heavens. The images his words conjured up would make a Vegas showgirl blush. Images of tangled limbs and bare flesh and…

She didn't flirt. She didn't lust. Never. Okay, almost never. But Houston had an uncanny knack for making her fantasize about things she shouldn't even be considering. After all, he'd been a patient less than twenty-four hours ago.

Her attention went straight to his bandaged hand as a reminder, yet the thought of his good hand on her…

Jill brought her focus back to Houston's face and he sent her a knowing smile. She found herself smiling back and wondering what would happen next when he stood and rounded the table. He stared down on her a few moments before he braced his hand on the back of her chair, lowered his lips to her ear and whispered, "Just let me know if you want to take a chance and take that ride."

She shivered slightly before she snapped back into reality. Two could play this game. *Don't count on it*, she intended to say. "Are you sure you can handle me?" came out of her mouth. Apparently he had channeled her inner vixen and she hadn't even known she had one.

He grinned again. "I'm up for the challenge."

Before she could respond, an attractive blonde woman stepped out the patio doors, a precious sandy-haired baby on her hip and a tall, handsome man following behind her.

"Hi, Houston," the woman said. "Dallas told me about your poor hand. Does it hurt much?"

"Naw." Houston held up the cast. "It's going to come in handy when I need to hitchhike."

"It's not going to come in handy when you have to do some work around here," the presumed brother muttered.

Houston turned back to Jill. "This is Dallas and his wife, Paris," Houston said. "This is Jillian Amherst."

Jill popped out of her seat like someone had lit her bottom on fire and worried she might looked guilty, as if she'd been caught doing something nefarious with Houston. "It's nice to finally meet you both."

Dallas stuck out his hand for a shake. "Good to meet you, too."

Paris smiled and said, "Welcome to the zoo and this is our little monkey."

"He's also known as Luke," Dallas added.

Clearly the Calloways had run out of Texas city names for the next generation, unless...

"In case you're wondering," Paris began, "it's not short for Luckenbach."

At least that answered Jill's question. "He's a handsome little guy. How old is he?"

"He'll be nine months on October first. I won't be a bit surprised if he's walking before then."

"Neither will I," Jenny said as she breezed onto the patio with a tray of amber-colored drinks and bowls filled with salsa and chips. "Thought you might all like to have some appetizers and drinks before dinner."

"I think I'll have a beer," Houston said. "Otherwise I might burn the burgers."

"Luke is still nursing," Paris began, "so I'll have to pass."

"A beer sounds good to me," Dallas chimed in.

Jenny leveled her gaze on Jill. "Surely you'll try one of my famous mint juleps, sugar."

Refusing the offer would simply be rude. "Of course."

While everyone stood there and watched, Jill took one tumbler and sipped some of the concoction. She should have known by the smell alone that the drink would curl her toes. And her board-straight hair. When her eyes began to tear, the crowd began to laugh. Most of them.

Jenny frowned before she turned her smile on Jill. "You'll get used to it, honey. By the third or fourth swallow you'll be clamoring for another one."

Most likely she'd be passed out under the table. "I do like the fresh mint. It tempers the alcohol."

Jenny patted her cheek. "Spoken like a true Southerner. Are you from the South, sugar?"

"Nothern Florida," she answered around the burning in her throat.

"Why, that's Southern enough in my book."

The door opened again, this time to a petite olive-skinned woman with long dark hair, and at her side, a little boy she couldn't deny. "Sorry we're late," she said. "Chance decided to take a dive off the fence."

"I didn't dive, Mama. I fell off a little."

She ruffled his thick dark hair. "You scared the heck out of me."

"Where's Austin?" Houston asked.

"Unsaddling the horse. He'll be along in a minute." She eyed Jill for a few seconds before she spoke again. "Hi. I'm Georgie, Austin's wife, and you are?"

"I'm Jill." She still remembered her name, a good thing.

"Jill Amherst," Houston added. "She's here to talk to Dallas about the medical job."

Georgie eyed the glass still clutched in Jill's hand. "And you decided to get her drunk with one of Jenny's drinks before the interview?"

"Oh, hush now, Georgia May," Jenny scolded. "Now why don't you and Paris and the kiddos join me in the kitchen while these three talk business?"

"Good idea," Paris said. "This little guy is getting heavy. Is your kitchen child-proof, Houston?"

Houston scowled. "What do you think?"

"Probably not," Paris said. "I'll just keep him away from all your pots and pans."

Once the women filed out, Jill was more than happy to be seated again, although she found herself taking another drink of the julep. Then another. Nerves, she supposed. And not very wise.

She slid the glass to one side and prepared for Dallas Calloway's inquisition, when Paris emerged from the house holding two beers that she placed on the table.

"Here you go," she said, then patted her husband's back and kissed his cheek. "Go easy on her, okay?"

Dallas smiled up at Paris. "If she can survive Jen's drink, she can handle a few questions."

Jill wasn't so sure about that, especially when Houston got up from the table. "Since this is Dallas's thing, I'm going to feed my horse real quick before I have to go back to grill duty. And, Dallas, like your wife said, cut her some slack."

Dallas frowned. "To hear you two tell it, I'm some kind of a jackass."

Houston grinned at Jill. "There's only one kind, brother."

With that, he walked back into the house, leaving Jill alone with a virtual stranger. She wasn't too crazy about the abandonment, and when Dallas trained his blue eyes on her in a serious stare, something suddenly dawned on her. A temporary escape to gather her wits. "I should probably retrieve my résumé. It's in the guest room."

"No need for that," Dallas said. "Let's just keep this casual."

Casual she could handle. "Sounds good. What would you like to know about me?"

"Ever worked around horses?"

That she didn't expect. "Actually, I used to ride when I was younger. Competitively, but it's been a long time." Yet it seemed like yesterday when the accident that claimed her best friend had caused her to quit.

"What did you compete in?"

"Hunter and jumper competitions."

"Does Houston know this?"

"No. Why would he?"

"When he mentioned you might be interested in the job, he told me you'd known each other for a couple of years."

"We have. He'd fall off the bull and I'd fix him up."

"So you've only had a professional relationship."

"Strictly professional." Aside from a few recent ridiculous fantasies she'd had about him.

"That's good," he said. "Mixing business with pleasure can create a whole lot of problems. It usually doesn't turn out well for all parties involved."

According to Jenny, that didn't hold true in his case. "I assure you I will maintain absolute professionalism where Houston is concerned."

Dallas gave her a half smile. "I'm not worried about you at all. I don't necessarily trust Houston when it comes to being around an attractive woman."

"Believe me, Dallas, Houston isn't interested at all in me."

Four

Thanks to the sexy redhead back at the house, he was hotter than a firecracker in the desert on the fourth of July. Hotter than the grill he should be manning right now. But unless he pulled it together, he'd have to hide behind that grill all night to preserve his dignity.

Houston put away the pitchfork and considered taking a dip in the horse trough outside. Or getting the hell out of Dodge in his Dodge truck.

His gelding, Skip, raised his head from the hay bag in the stall long enough to nicker when Houston walked by. "I know, I know. Man up. But damn, she's one good-lookin' woman. Like you'd care about that. All you care about is eating, so get back to it and stop staring at me."

"Talkin' to horses now about your love life?"

Houston's gaze shot to the barn's entry to find his younger brother standing there, grinning like he'd won the lottery. "Shut up, Worth."

"Kiss my ass, Houston. Just because you've got it bad for a little gal you can't have doesn't mean you've got to take it out on me."

He brushed past Worth and strode down the drive leading to the house, ignoring Worth's laughter. Or trying to. But he couldn't ignore that his brother was quickly catching up with him. "Hold up, Houston. I think I know the answer to your dilemma."

He stopped and spun around on the heels of his frustration. "If you're going to suggest that I just go for it, I can't. She might very well be an employee here, and Dallas would skin me alive if I even looked like I might be interested in Jill outside of business. And there's the fact that she's barely given me the time of day since I met her two years ago."

"And that's the problem, Houston. You live for the chase and you can't stand it if she doesn't respond. That's why you need to act like you don't care one way or the other about her. That will take care of Dallas's worries and your girlfriend will soon be eating out of your good hand."

Of all the stupid assumptions. "She's not my girlfriend, dammit, and how do you know that's not what I've been doing?"

"Because I know you. You bring out the charm and toss out some innuendo and expect her to run to your bed. You're better off playing hard to get."

Houston started walking again. "You're mistaking me for someone else."

"Who?" Worth asked, meeting him stride for stride.

"You."

"Oh, hell, Houston. That's how we all operate. The apple doesn't fall far from the tree."

That just pissed him off. "I'm not a damn thing like

our dad." Fed up with his brother's counsel, Houston quickened his pace and didn't look back, even when he reached the house. He tore open the door, walked through the deserted great room and into the kitchen to get another beer. When he heard the back door open, he glanced back from the refrigerator to see Worth leaving through it. Only then did he peer out the window to see Dallas flipping burgers and Austin crouched down nearby, talking to his son. Houston's mom and Jen were lounging by the pool, drinks in hand, while Jen talked nonstop. Fortunately, he could only see the back of Jill's head. *Unfortunately*, he discovered Worth had taken a seat beside her.

After releasing a rough breath, Houston popped the top on the can, took a long drink, geared up to face his current object of interest and vowed to intervene if his baby brother even leaned an inch her way.

Before he proceeded, he paused a moment to ponder Worth's words. Ignoring Jill would be the wisest course. Yeah, that's what he'd do—be polite but disinterested. No inappropriate comments. No suggestive looks. No damn fun whatsoever.

Armed with a plan, Houston pushed through the door and immediately homed in on Jill, seated, who was holding his nephew while Paris and Georgie looked on. When she caught sight of him, she smiled, showing off those damn cute dimples. All his good intentions threatened to blow away like the smoke coming from the barbecue.

He could do this. He could bypass the women and convene with the men. He could talk about rodeo or any kind of sport that didn't involve the bedroom, although that's exactly where his mind wandered. Luckily, his body didn't react. Yet.

He joined Dallas and held out his functioning hand. "Hand over the flipper. I'll take it from here."

Dallas shook his head. "I've got this now. If we'd waited for you, we'd all starve. What took you so long?"

Thoughts about the woman at the table behind him. "Just wanted to give you enough time to have a talk with Jill. How did it go?"

"Pretty good." Dallas lowered the grill's lid and turned toward him. "I think she'd be a great fit. She's a smart lady and seems to know her stuff. Greg Halbert told me she did."

"Who the hell is that?"

"Her boss."

"When did you call him?"

"Two weeks ago, before you dropped her name."

Now he was *really* confused. "I'm not following you, Dallas."

"I decided to check with the rodeo sports medicine programs to see if they could suggest any candidates for the job, like maybe an intern or two. Ben immediately mentioned Jill and said she was the only one he'd trust to run a program like ours. Then he threatened my jewels if I hired her away from him."

Great. "Does Jill know about this?"

"I'll let her know if she agrees to take the job."

"Do you think she will?" Damn, he sounded like an enthusiastic kid waiting to see if he'd gotten selected as a baseball all-star.

"I'm not sure, but I believe she could be leaning that way. She said she'd give me an answer by tomorrow before she heads back to Cowtown."

She wouldn't be heading back if Houston had his way. *Remember the "I don't care plan," Calloway.* "If she turns you down, we can always find someone else."

"Easier said than done," Dallas said. "Athletic trainers of her caliber and with her experience are snapped up pretty quick."

"Didn't realize that."

"Ben did mention some guy named Mike who's been in the business for twenty-five years. I could get in touch with him if this doesn't work out with Jill."

Houston didn't want some guy named Mike filling the position. Any guy for that matter. Truth was, he wanted Jill to go to work for them. He wanted *her*, plain and simple, right or wrong. Wise or not.

"Could you not say hello to your mother, *mijo*?"

Damn. Nobody got anything past Maria Calloway, and no doubt she'd make a big deal over his injury. Might as well get it over with.

He turned around, muttered, "Sorry, Mom," then leaned over and kissed her cheek. "I just figured you and Jen were having one of your usual talks. I didn't want to interrupt."

"Jenny was doing all the talking." She lifted his hand to inspect his cast. "My son, you are a *torpe*."

"I'm not a klutz, Mom. Just unlucky sometimes."

"At least you'll be home for a while now, yes?"

"Yep." Unfortunately, and not because he didn't like being around family. He just didn't care for being off the circuit. "Did you meet Jill? Dallas might hire her to head up the medical team."

Her dark eyes narrowed as she flipped her gray-and-black braid over her shoulder. "I did meet her," she said, adding in a lowered tone, "*Ella es muy bonita*, so you best keep your lust to yourself."

Assumptions traveled fast on the ranch. "Just because I brought her here doesn't mean I'm lusting after her."

She patted his cheek. "*Mijo*, if the sun rises in the

morning, you'll be lusting after a woman who looks like that."

Houston followed his mother's gaze to Jill, still sitting at the table, looking pretty as you please. And the only one who remained at that table with her happened to be his worthless brother. He said something to her, she laughed and Houston fumed.

He downed the rest of the beer and crumpled the can in his fist, itching to throw a punch. But that would be playing right into Worth's hand. It would also prove that what everyone else was thinking about him happened to be true—he had a belly full of lust for one beautiful athletic trainer.

Damn if he didn't, and he couldn't do a thing about it.

Houston didn't utter one word to Jill during dinner. In fact, he'd barely looked at her at all. Right now he seemed preoccupied with the conversation he was having with Worth by the pool. Clearly not a friendly conversation, in light of the body language. She knew all about sibling spats and wrote it off to a difference of opinion. Hopefully her ability to handle the workload wasn't up for debate during their discussion.

Jill turned her attention to Austin and Georgie's son sitting in a lawn chair, away from everyone else, looking a little forlorn. She might have assumed he could be bored, until she noticed the way he held his right arm. Her mind went back to Jenny talking about Chance's fall, and that only heightened her concern.

She raised her hand to get Georgie's attention and waved her over. "Got a quick question for you," she said when Georgie arrived at the table.

"Sure. What's up?"

"Jenny mentioned something about Chance falling off a fence this afternoon. Did you see how he landed?"

She could see a touch of panic growing in Georgie's eyes. "It happened so fast, and I was in the paddock treating a mare right before we were heading over here. When I ran over to Chance, he was kind of on one side. Why?"

"I've seen him favoring his arm a little."

Georgie whipped around to study her son. "I swear he never said a thing about anything hurting, and I asked him at least ten times. And you'd think since I'm a veterinarian, I would have noticed something."

"Don't worry," Jill said, bent on calming the nervous mother. "Children have been known to conceal their injuries from adults, especially little boys who want to be tough."

"That's my son, a chip off the old Austin block." Georgie attempted a smile before it rapidly disappeared. "Do you think it could be serious?"

"It could be nothing more than a bruise or a sprain. I could do a quick exam, if that's okay."

"I would so appreciate that," Georgie said in a grateful tone.

"Not a problem. It's what I do."

Georgie turned to her son and called, "Chance, come here for a minute."

The boy slid out of the seat and trudged over to his mom. "Are we going home now? I'm tired."

"In a minute," Georgie said. "Ms. Amherst wants to talk to you."

"Call me Jill, Chance," she said. "Does your arm hurt, sweetie?"

He shrugged only one of his shoulders, the first confirmation of her suspicions. "A little."

Jill swung the chair from beneath the table but remained seated. "Do mind if I take a look at it?"

He responded by shaking his head and moving in front of her. "I'm just going to touch your shoulder a little," she told him.

Chance looked more than a bit wary. "Is it going to hurt?"

Probably, but this was the only way she could diagnose the problem. "I'll be really gentle."

Jill ran two fingers along his clavicle and felt the deformity after very little exploration. When the boy winced, her suspicions turned to confirmation.

"That's all, Chance. You're a very brave young man." She looked up at Georgie. "He definitely has an injury to his collarbone."

Georgie's brown eyes went wide. "Oh, no. What do we do now?"

Jill stood and rested a palm on Chance's head. "Take him into an ER tonight for an X-ray to make sure I'm correct."

"And if it's fractured?"

"Most likely they'll put him in a splint until it heals." She didn't dare mention the dreaded S word—surgery—which could be a possibility.

Chance tugged on the hem of Georgie's T-shirt. "What's a splint, Mama?"

Jill jumped in when Georgie hesitated. "It's a wrap that goes around your shoulder to help it heal."

Chance suddenly looked somewhat excited. "Is it gonna look like that thing on Uncle Houston's hand?"

"Not exactly, but close. You'll have to wear it until the doctor tells you it's okay." She glanced at Georgie. "Kids tend to heal faster than adults, so it could be as little as three weeks but usually six at the most. The doctor will probably instruct you to put some ice on it for a while."

Georgie gave Jill a quick hug. "You're an angel. Can I call you later if I have any questions once we get back from the ER?"

"Of course. Definitely let me know how he does."

"I will." Georgie regarded her son. "Tell Jill thank-you, honey."

"Thanks."

"You're welcome, sweetie. Get plenty of rest and you'll be back to climbing fences before you know it."

"Not if I can help it," Georgie muttered as she set out in the direction of her husband.

Soon after, Jill gave a final reassurance to the entire concerned family and said goodbye to them all as they cleared out, leaving her alone to remove the dinner remnants from the outdoor dining table since Houston had once again gone MIA.

She carried the plates and utensils into the almost clean kitchen—thanks to the mothers—and began loading the dishwasher, all the while wondering why Houston had brushed her off all evening for the most part. In fact, she only recalled him asking her to pass the mustard. Had it not been for his mother, stepmom and sisters-in-law, she might have spent the time alone in the corner, incessantly rolling the offer around in her mind. But she did appreciate the warm hospitality, the camaraderie, and found being around a good-hearted family quite refreshing. Dinner with her parents usually involved pretentious food and conversation centered on stocks, gossip and noncompliant children. She wondered if Houston recognized how lucky he'd been to be born into such a caring, down-to-earth group of people. She wondered if she'd even see him again to ask.

Jill suddenly sensed a presence behind her before she heard a deep, sensual voice asking, "What's a good-looking girl like you doing at a kitchen sink?"

Five

A dish tumbled out of Jill's hand and into the stainless-steel farm sink. She thanked her lucky stars she hadn't broken it when she nearly jumped out of her skin. "You startled me," she said as she placed the last plate in the washer. "I nearly shattered your china."

She sensed him moving closer, although little space separated them. "It's not exactly china, but you managed to rescue it, just like you rescued my nephew. That makes you an honest to goodness hero."

After drying her hands on a towel draped across the counter, Jill finally faced him, bringing them into even closer proximity. "I simply assessed the situation and made a recommendation. Nothing heroic about it."

Houston reached over and ran his fingertips down a strand of her hair, taking her by complete surprise for the second time in a matter of minutes. Had the seduction started?

"You had soap suds in your hair. Or maybe it was whipped cream from the pie."

So much for seduction. And why was that oddly disappointing? "I didn't have any pie, but I did rinse the dishes."

"Thanks for that, and since it looks like you're done, do you want to take a tour of the medical building?"

"I'd love to." She'd love to not feel so shaky around him. So aware of the scent of his cologne. The blanket of whiskers surrounding his mouth. The fact he was all alpha male and probably possessed plenty of talents in the bedroom...

"So are you ready to get after it?"

Her gaze snapped to his. "Excuse me?"

"The tour."

Good grief. *Get over it, Jillian.* "Lead the way."

She followed Houston out the front door and into the South Texas night. They walked the drive back to the main road serenaded by a chorus of cicadas. Only a slight breeze blew, providing little relief from the September heat.

Jill looked up at the sky highlighted by a host of stars and sighed. "The full moon is gorgeous tonight."

"Yeah, it is."

She glanced to her right and found him staring at her. "What's wrong?"

"Not a thing. You have a great profile."

"I have a nose that should be on a child."

"It's cute."

"It's my Irish heritage."

"But you have a darker complexion for a redhead."

She could almost hear what he was thinking—*if you're really a true redhead.* "This is my natural color, and I have some Spanish thrown into the gene pool on my mother's side. That accounts for my skin tone. How about you?"

"My mom is a fourth-generation Mexican American, and my dad's lineage is Old Norman French. It sounds pretty sophisticated for a bunch of cowpokes, doesn't it?"

She couldn't help but smile. "It's always good to know where you come from, but I'm surprised you, Dallas and Austin don't look much alike."

"That's because we have the same father, but not mother. Their mom died in a horse accident when they were pretty young. My mom ended up being their nanny, married our father and had me and Tyler shortly after that."

Not quite as convoluted as she thought it might be. "Okay. Then I assume your father divorced your mother, married Jenny and had the twins."

Houston swiped a hand over his jaw. "Not exactly."

Perhaps she'd been mistaken about the convoluted concept. "You don't have to explain if you don't want to."

"The truth will come out sooner or later when you come to work for us."

If she came to work for them. "I'm all ears."

"My dad met up with Jen in New Orleans on a business trip. He ended up marrying her but he failed to divorce my mom. He spent most of his adulthood living a lie and working hard to cover it up."

Jill swallowed hard around her shock. "Then he was—"

"A bigamist. We found out at the reading of the will after he died. Learning you have twin half brothers and a stepmom was one helluva surprise straight out of a soap opera."

A colossal understatement. "You all seem to get along well, but I am a bit confused as to why Jenny would choose to live here, and why your mother would even allow it under the circumstances."

"Jenny came down a few summers ago to introduce us to Worth. They never left. And even though it seems like Jen and my mom don't get along, they're really pretty close. I'm sure they have a good time burning my dad in effigy for all his many sins."

She'd love to be a bug on the wall during some of those conversations. "I think it's great you all get along."

"All of us but Fort. He's still mad as hell at my dad and the brothers. We added Jen to the list after she decided to stay."

"Maybe he'll come around eventually."

"Not likely, but it's his loss. There's nothing more important than family and friends. You don't know how much you appreciate them until they're gone."

Jill surmised that even in light of all his father's transgressions, Houston still missed him. She found that quite honorable—the willingness to forgive. If only she had the capacity where her own mother was concerned.

They walked the rest of the way in silence and arrived at the elaborate clinic a few minutes later. Jill stood by while Houston keyed a code into the pad. He opened the door and stepped to one side. "Here ya go. Your future place of employment."

She frowned at him. "You're jumping the gun a bit, aren't you?"

"We'll see after you take the tour."

Jill entered the building and moved into a large empty space with several windows and white tiled floors. Beyond that, she spotted several closed doors along the back wall. "This is a very blank canvas."

"And that's where you come in," Houston said. "Two of the rooms over there are for treatments. The other two are bathrooms, and in the corner a break room."

Evidently they'd thought of everything, except furnishings and equipment. "I'd like to see the treatment rooms."

"Sure. Follow me."

Their footsteps echoed in the expansive area as she trailed behind Houston. When they reached the closest room, he opened the door and once again, moved aside for her to inspect the premises.

She automatically went to the counter with the built-in sink and ran her hand over the stainless steel top. "Nice. Lots of room, too."

"And storage." As he reached around her to open the upper cabinet, his arm brushed against her arm and his injured wrist came to rest on her waist. Did he intend for that to happen, or was it simply an inadvertent gesture? Regardless, he didn't move his hand, and Jill remained glued to the spot, unsure what she should do next.

Speaking would be good. So would acting casual. Disinterested, as if a virile man's palm on her person was an everyday occurrence. "This will come in handy for all the supplies."

"You'll have free rein to order anything you think is necessary."

She thought it necessary that he give her some space before she did something stupid, like melt right into his fantastic arms. "That's good to know. Mind if I turn around now?"

"You don't need my permission to do that."

"I do need you to step back a little, otherwise I'm going to be rubbing, uh, bumping against your..." Manhood? Manliness? Oh, my. "Belt buckle."

"Rubbing and bumping. Sounds like one of those old-time disco dance moves, or a great time on a Saturday night."

Smooth, Jill. She couldn't believe she'd actually she used the word *rubbing.* Freud would have a field day with her. Houston was having a darn good time, too, if the amusement in his tone and the suggestion in his words was any indication.

Finally, he dropped his palm from her waist and moved back. She turned around to find him grinning like a well-practiced bad boy. "You're really having fun with my faux pas, aren't you?"

"Well, yeah. I'm used to hearing nothing but medical speak coming from that pretty mouth of yours. I have to admit I enjoy knowing you're not all business all the time."

"No, but only when it's appropriate and not in a professional setting."

"You're on my ranch."

"We're in a clinic. Granted, a clinic that's barely more than four walls and a couple of restrooms."

He sent her a mock frown. "Are you criticizing the accoutrements?"

"*Accoutrements?* Big word for a cowpoke."

"I know a few big words. I did graduate from college."

"Your major?"

"At first, female anatomy, but the extra homework took too much time away from the rodeo team so I changed it to business."

I will not laugh. I will not laugh. She laughed. "How long have you been using that line?"

He brushed her jawline with a fingertip. "First time. I'm just trying to keep you in a good mood."

She was in the mood all right, but not exactly for joking around. She'd always heard the term *palpable tension* but she hadn't experienced it...until now.

That realization, and the possibility of making a foolish mistake with an attractive-to-a-fault man, prompted her to make a more prudent suggestion. "We should head back to the house now. I need to take a shower."

He winked. "As a matter of fact, so do I."

Oh, boy. Oh, *man*. "I suppose you're going to say if we shower together, we could conserve water."

He moved beside her and leaned a hip against the cabinet, one elbow resting on the counter. "Nope, I wasn't, but if that would make you feel more welcome in my home, I'm game."

Oh, boy, did that unearth some unbelievable mental pictures. "I'm feeling quite welcome as it is, and I'm sure you make enough money to pay the water bill."

"Leave it to you to go from fantasies to finances."

She playfully slapped at his arm. "Okay. Stop trying to flirt with me."

"Hey, you were the one who wanted to take a joint shower." He winked. "That's still on the table if you change your mind."

She pointed at the open door. "Let's go. Now. Before I..."

"Before you what?"

Before she kissed him like some smitten buckle bunny. "Before I fall asleep on my feet. I'm still trying to recover from Jenny's drink."

He pushed away from the counter. "You didn't even finish the drink, but then you are a lightweight, Amherst."

"And you can be a pain in the butt, Calloway."

"It's part of my charm. Too bad you don't appreciate it."

There, Jill thought. Back to their usual insulting banter. The world was now tilted correctly on its axis. All was good and right.

Still, something had changed between them. Subtle, but still apparent. A sensual connection, she feared. Now that she acknowledged exactly how this might go if she wasn't incredibly careful, Jill pledged to keep their liaison platonic and their relationship somewhat contentious, as it had been in the past.

But after spending practically the past twenty-four hours with Houston Calloway, and liking it, only time would tell if she could rewind that clock.

If he could turn back time, Houston would do it, just so he could watch Jill walk back into the room. She wore a loose, light blue T-shirt stamped with "Quick Responder" and white shorts that gave him an eyeful of her long, long legs. She still had on a bra but she didn't have on shoes and he was kind of surprised to see pink painted toenails. Hell, even her feet were sexy. Her hair looked sexy, too, pulled up into a high ponytail and obviously still damp. If he'd coaxed that shower out of her, he would've made sure she was downright wet.

Stop lusting, mijo...

What a fine time for his mother to jump into his head. Probably not a bad thing. He'd already blown Worth's advice about ignoring her right out of the water like a duck decoy. Time to regroup. Time to put the plan back into action.

When Jill walked right up to the sofa and studied him head to toe, the plan began to slither away again.

"It's so weird to see you dressed in shorts and a T-shirt, Calloway."

"I could say the same about you, Amherst." Although he wouldn't call it weird. He'd call it damn good.

"Is that your bedtime attire?" she asked.

For him naked was bedtime attire, a fact he would keep to himself for the moment. "Nah. I usually wear my chaps, but I sent them out for a good cleaning."

"That would be really weird." She smiled, sat at the opposite end of the couch and curled her legs beneath her. "Have you thought about being a cowboy stand-up comic when you retire from the rodeo?"

"Nope, because I don't plan to retire anytime soon."

She tightened the ponytail and adjusted the throw pillow at her back. "How long have you been competing?"

He had to stop and think about that. "I guess I rode my first bull when I was fifteen, so that would be almost sixteen years."

"So you're thirty going on thirty-one."

"How old did you say you were?" he asked.

She tried to look insulted but failed. She just looked damn beautiful. "Didn't your mother teach you it's impolite to ask a lady her age?"

"Yeah, but first of all, I recall you said you're a year younger than Worth. Second, I've never understood why that's such a big deal."

"Me, either. And to refresh your memory, I'm twenty-six."

"Dallas mentioned you used to ride horses."

She brought her knees up and hugged them to her chest, giving him a glimpse of the back of her thighs. "I did ride. A long time ago."

"What made you stop?"

When she shifted slightly, Houston figured he'd hit a nerve. "It's sort of a sad story."

Sad he didn't need, but he sensed she need to talk. He did have to be careful not to push her. He wouldn't want anyone to pressure him when it came to his secrets, and he still had one he'd never told a living soul. Not even his own mother. "I've got all night to hear the story, but only if you want to tell it."

"Actually, it's not all bad," she said. "That long-ago event drove me to help others."

He wondered if it involved her having some sort of bad accident. That would sure explain why she was so protective and persistent when it came to her patients. "How did that come about?"

She hesitated a split second before speaking again. "I guess it all started when I was around five and I learned to ride. Two years later, I wanted something more challenging than going around an arena, so I learned how to jump. I remember how exhilarating it was that first time."

"I remember feeling the same way when I stayed on a bull for eight seconds." And the first time he'd had sex. Something he didn't need to consider right then.

"Well, I guess we have that in common," she said with an uneasy smile.

They had more in common than he cared to admit. "I guess so."

"When I was about fifteen," she continued, "I was heavy into competition, and so was my boarding school roommate and best friend, Millie. We used to spend weekends going to events together, and we practiced almost every day together at the school's stables. She was such an incredible person. So full of life and much more daring than I ever was."

"She took higher jumps?"

"No. She used to sneak out the window and meet up with boys from the nearby military academy."

"Did you ever go with her?"

"Not hardly. My mother drilled me my entire formative years about the dangers of teenage sex. 'You'll get a disease, Jillian' or 'You'll get pregnant, Jillian.'"

"No 'You'll go blind, Jillian'?"

"Luckily, she never said that, the only thing that saved me from total sexual frustration."

After she blushed and looked away, Houston inched closer and touched her shoulder to reassure her. "Hey. Don't be embarrassed, Jill. When nature calls, you best answer or you *will* go blind."

She tried to smile but it fell flat. "Funny, Millie used to talk about that. The nature thing, not the going blind thing." She paused and sighed. "When I lost her, I felt like a part of me went with her."

Houston could only speculate why the relationship ended. "Did you two have a fight?"

"She died."

That he hadn't expected. He also couldn't help but notice the lack of emotion in her tone, but the pain in her green eyes spoke volumes. He could be entering dangerous waters, but he had to ask. "What happened to her?"

"We were competing one Saturday during the summer when we were home on break. Her horse balked at the jump and she was thrown." She paused to take a breath. "But in usual Millie fashion, she stood up, brushed herself off and got back on her mare to finish the course. Everyone thought she was okay. I thought she was okay. But it turned out that wasn't the case at all."

The first sign of tears began to appear in her eyes,

leading Houston to grab a tissue holder from the coffee table and offer it to her. "You don't have to keep going, Jill.'"

She laid the box in her lap and lifted her chin slightly. "I'm okay. I need to tell you everything, although I'm not sure why." She drew in another deep breath and let it out slowly. "I talked to her on the phone that night. We were supposed to sleep over at my house but she complained about having a headache. She told me she was going to take a pain reliever and go to bed early. The next morning, the maid couldn't get her to wake up. They rushed her to the hospital, but it was too late. She'd had a brain bleed. She passed away that afternoon."

He reached over and took her hand. "I'm sorry, sweetheart. That had to be tough."

"It was. Very tough. I realized later that if someone with medical knowledge had been present, they would have known what to look for. They would have assessed her to see if she had a concussion. At the very least, they would have kept her from getting back on the horse. Although we have no way of knowing for certain, continuing to ride and jump could have caused a secondary impact, which could have led to the bleed. Someone should have been there to tell her not to take certain pain medication."

He'd had a lot of experience with the "could haves" and "should haves," so he understood exactly where she was coming from. He also understood why she was so protective of her patients, and he felt kind of bad how he'd treated her in the past. "Second-guessing can be a bitch, can't it?"

"Definitely. I still do it from time to time, but the experience has made me a very diligent athletic trainer. I take nothing for granted when it comes to taking care of athletes."

Houston realized that with every cowboy or cowgirl she'd treated, and possibly saved, she'd had her best friend in mind. "One thing's for sure. Loss changes people, sometimes for the better." But not necessarily in his case.

"I was never quite the same in so many ways, but I still have great memories." She snapped a tissue from the holder and dabbed at her eyes. "We called ourselves soul twins, Millie and Jilly. We both had rich parents and one obnoxious sibling, only she had a younger brother. He's still a spoiled jerk."

Now he knew why she didn't like him calling her Jilly. That had been reserved for a longtime friend. "So you stayed in touch with her family?"

"Not by choice," she said in an angry tone. "Jilly's brother is marrying my sister next weekend."

His life might be a soap opera, but hers sounded like a well-heeled incestuous mess. "Tough break."

"They deserve each other. Millie deserved to live. Not a day goes by when I don't think about her. When I don't wish I had told her how much she meant to me."

Houston could seriously relate to that. When he thought back to what he'd said and done the day before his father died, it made him sick. It also disturbed him to see her hurting that badly, so he did what instinct dictated—he scooted to her side and put his arm around her.

He wouldn't have been surprised if she pulled away. Rejected the gesture. Instead, she rested her head on his shoulder. They stayed that way for quite a while, until she finally raised her head. The look she gave him was all too familiar, and he'd bet his last buck he knew what she wanted. Trouble was, he worried about the repercussions of answering her request. But when she cupped his jaw with her palm, and pulled his mouth to hers, only a fire on the living room floor could have stopped him.

He brought her into his lap, all the while thinking this wasn't a good idea. She was vulnerable and her motivation for doing this had a lot to do with her emotional state. But when she snuggled up against him, all bets were off.

Houston tried to keep the kiss light, keep it controlled. Keep it restrained. Jill had other ideas. She met his tongue stroke for stroke, wriggled in his lap and he'd begun to believe she had no intention of putting an end to the torment until he gave her what she wanted. What he wanted. But at what cost?

He reacted as any man would, with a strong stirring beneath his shorts and the need to touch her. As he ran his palm up her thigh, he felt her shiver, and he knew he had to find the strength and some way to stop before he couldn't.

His pocket began to vibrate, followed by a classic country honky-tonk song. He could ignore it, or view it as a good excuse to halt this craziness before they reached that point of no return. Answering the call would be the better part of valor. Saved by the bell or, in this case, a ringtone.

With that in mind, he gently slid her off his lap and groaned, then fished the phone out of his pocket.

Austin. Normally he'd curse his brother's bad timing, but not tonight.

He cleared his throat before he answered. "Hey, Austin."

"Hey, Houston. What's up?"

Bad choice of words. "Not much. What's going on with you?"

"Georgie told me to report to Jill after we took Chance to the ER."

Houston felt like jerk for not remembering his nephew's injury. He glanced at Jill to see she had her hand pressed against her lips, looking slightly shell shocked. He wasn't sure she was in any shape to take the call. "She's busy right now. Tell me what the doctor said and I'll relay it to her."

"Chance has a fractured collarbone, just like she said. He has a splint, also like she said, and he's going to be back to normal in a few weeks. Tell Jill we owe her one."

Houston owed her an apology for letting things get out of hand. "I'll let her know, and I'm glad he's going to be okay."

"So are we. And, Houston, just a few words of advice."

Great. More brotherly advice. "About what?"

"We all really like Jill, and we'd like to have her as part of the team. Try not to screw it up by making a move on her."

It could be too late for that. "Message received. Tell the kid to hang in there and I'll see him tomorrow. We can compare injuries."

"Will do."

After hanging up, Houston set the phone on the table and regarded Jill again, who thankfully looked a bit more composed. "That was Austin. He said your diagnosis was correct and they wanted to thank you for helping out."

She clutched a pillow to her chest. "I'm just glad he's going to be okay."

"Are you okay?"

"That's still up in the air after what I just did."

"You weren't alone. I could have put a stop to it."

"Why didn't you?"

"Honestly? I didn't want to. But just so you know, I wasn't going to let it go any further."

"We shouldn't have gone there at all, but it really was my fault. I don't know what came over me."

"You were running on emotion. You were just looking for comfort."

"But that's not like me at all."

"It was only a kiss, Jill. No big deal."

"Well, that makes me feel better. I realize it's been a while since I've kissed anyone, but I didn't think it was that bad."

Not in the least. In fact, it was real good. "Do you hear me complaining?"

She finally smiled. "No, but I really hoped you would break out into song. I thought you had until I realized it was your phone."

"If I was going to sing to you, it wouldn't be a song about my tractor."

They both laughed then, and that helped ease the burden Houston was carrying around because he hadn't shown a scrap of restraint. But all humor disappeared when Jill's expression turned serious again.

"This could really complicate everything," she said. "I can't accept the position if I know this is going to be a problem."

He wasn't ready to throw in that towel just yet. "It won't be a problem at all as long as we maintain the boundaries."

"No more kisses."

"That's probably best." But now that he'd sampled her skills, it wouldn't be easy.

"We operate on a strictly professional level from this point forward."

Unacceptable as far as he was concerned. "You wouldn't be working for me, so I don't see any reason why we can't be friends."

She pointed at him. "Friends with no benefits."

Damn. "If that's what it takes for you to come on board, then that's what we'll be." Now for the all-important question. "Does this mean you're going to take the job?"

She pushed off the sofa and stood. "It means I'm going to bed. I'll let you know my answer in the morning."

He came to his feet. "You're going to keep me in suspense until then?"

She strolled across the room and paused at the opening leading to the hall. "You're a tough guy. You can handle waiting a little longer."

With that, Jill disappeared, leaving Houston to question their agreement. He didn't care much for science, but he could recognize chemistry between two people. Could he be only her friend without wanting more? But in reality, that would only be until he hit the road again to return to the rodeo. Still, spending a couple of months with a woman he wanted, and couldn't have, would be torture. Then again, she could turn down the job. Problem solved.

He'd worry about that tomorrow. Tonight, he planned to go to bed and let the fantasies about Jill Amherst fly.

Six

Jill hadn't slept more than four hours last night. Instead, she'd relived the kiss a hundred times, and tried to disregard how Houston had made her feel. But she couldn't ignore the guilt over laying her feelings bare, and making the first inadvisable move. She could chalk her conduct up to emotional upheaval, or the very real fact her attraction to him had grown due to his kindness. And this morning she would have to confront the reason for her restlessness. Putting it off would only delay the inevitable.

On that thought, Jill climbed out of the bed and went through her normal routine, twisted her hair into a low ponytail, then dressed in khakis, casual flats and a blouse. Once in the great room, she followed the scent of coffee into the kitchen and came across Houston seated at the center island, dressed in a light chambray shirt and denim jeans. He didn't bother to look up from the laptop before him when she entered the room.

"Mind if I have a cup?" she asked on the way to the coffeemaker.

He still hadn't even ventured a glance at her. "Help yourself. Mugs are in the cabinet next to the sink. Cream's in the fridge and sugar's in a canister next to the coffeepot."

Jill located the cups and ignored the white one that said Bull Riders Stay on Longer. After pouring the brew into an innocuous blue mug, she joined Houston at the island and slid onto the stool opposite him.

Since he still refused to look at her, she decided to start the conversation with small talk. "Catching up on current events?"

"Catching up on circuit standings and checking out a new ad campaign."

"Ad campaign?"

"Yeah. I did some advertisements for a company that makes compression wraps."

"What kind of advertisements?"

"Internet and a few TV spots but mostly billboards."

His face splashed across an oversize roadside sign could distract more than a few female drivers. "Is it a national campaign?"

"Yep."

His apparent inability to even venture a glance at her was somewhat frustrating. "I just wanted to say how much I appreciated your friendship last night. You really are a good listener." And a phenomenal kisser, which she would not mention.

He closed the laptop's lid and finally met her gaze. "No problem, but I'm still pretty mad at myself this morning."

Here we go. "You didn't do anything but listen to my story."

"But I wasn't acting too gentlemanly. You were hurting and I should have realized that. I feel like I took advantage."

She'd *wanted* him to take advantage. "I kissed you, remember, not the other way around."

"Yeah, but I sure as hell didn't protest. If Austin hadn't called, it might have gone further, and we both might have regretted it."

True, it would have been a huge misstep. Perhaps a pleasurable one, but a mistake all the same. "Lacking a little in the willpower department, are we?"

He cracked a crooked smile. "It's your fault for being so damn sexy."

Sexy? "You're forgiven."

He slid off the stool and stood. "Finish your coffee and let's go."

"Where?"

"I have a few more places to show you around the ranch."

"You haven't even asked if I've reached a decision."

"I feel like you're still on the fence, so I'm hoping what you see this morning will push you over to our side."

He'd nailed it. She had yet to make up her mind. Making out with Houston should have convinced her to walk away. Or run. Yet she couldn't allow a moment of weakness to ruin what could be the opportunity of a lifetime.

After taking another drink of the coffee, Jill came to her feet. "Just let me change into my sneakers and we can go."

"No need," he said. "We're not going walk."

"Are we traveling by truck or horseback?"

"Neither. We'll take one of the ATVs because it's already hot as hell outside."

The joys of South Texas weather in late summer. Fortunately when they climbed onto the two-seater and took off, it generated enough breeze to offer Jill some relief. Yet by the time they stopped in front of the mountain-sized lodge behind a van, she felt as if she'd been in a sauna, dressed in a parka.

"They're still doing some finishing touches on the lodge," Houston said after the climbed out of the vehicle. "I swear the damn thing will never be finished."

Jill highly doubted the Taj Mahal was built in a day. "It's a big place."

"Yeah, it is. I'd take you inside but I don't want to get in the workers' way and force any more delays."

That disappointed her. "I understand."

"That's not what I want to show you anyway. Follow me."

She did, past the lodge's front facade and around the corner. He opened a gate to a courtyard with a pool in the center of what appeared to be a series of apartments. "What is this?"

"Where you'll be living when you come to work for us."

She decided not to correct him on the "when" thing and opted to enjoy the tour. They crossed over the deck and Houston paused at the first unit, pounded a code into a keypad and opened the door.

Jill stepped into an amazing living space open to an equally stellar kitchen, complete with gorgeous black slate appliances, gray cabinets and marble countertops. Beyond that, a sliding glass door revealed a private, fenced-in patio.

The whole place was awe-inspiring given they were

KRISTI GOLD

87

employee quarters. She'd expected something less elaborate and more along the lines of a bunkhouse. "This is extremely nice."

"It's only one bedroom," Houston said. "But it's a nice bedroom."

He pointed out a half bath in the small hall, then led her to the sleeping quarters that looked a hundred times better than the motels Jill had occupied in the past two years. Attached to that, a spacious bathroom with a huge soaking tub and a stand-alone shower, all decked out in marble opulence.

"Jen decorated this one and one other," Houston said. "The rest are more in line for male support staff."

She imagined barn wood and leather. "It's great, but I don't have any furniture."

"Not a problem. You can pick out what you want."

This all seemed much too good to be true. "I admit this is fairly tempting."

"Good. I have one more thing to persuade you."

"I can't imagine what that would be."

He started across the room. "Believe me, you'll be impressed."

She noticed the impressive fit of his jeans, his confident gait and the width of his back as she walked behind him. The fact she noticed all those attributes nudged her back into relying on her head, not her desires. She had to weigh the problems that could arise should they cross a line they had no business crossing. Still, they had established the friendship boundary last night, and it seemed Houston was determined to abide by the terms.

After they returned to their transportation, Houston drove back up the road and stopped at an expansive metal barn adjacent to the lodge. She trailed behind him down the stable's alley, where he paused at one stall.

"I'd like you to meet Gabby," Houston said. "She's a good old girl."

Jill inched her way to his side to see a bay mare sticking her muzzle between the railings. "She's beautiful."

"She's the only Thoroughbred on the place. Tyler traded for her when a couple nearby wanted a quarter horse gelding for their son so he could learn to rope. She's supposed to be a great English horse."

"And I doubt any of the Calloway boys ride English."

"Not a chance." He turned and smiled for the first time today. "But you do, and I figure you could take her out for a ride now and then."

Jill put up her hands, palms forward. "Wait a minute. I haven't ridden in over a decade." Not since the accident.

"Then it's way past time you get back on and remember how great it feels to ride."

She lowered her eyes to study the pavement beneath her feet. "I don't know if I want to remember."

Houston touched her face, causing her to look up. "I wouldn't force anything on you, but maybe you should start moving forward, not backward. Take a few chances. Get busy living. And I'll be here if you need a little push in that direction now and then."

A solid truth rang out in his words, and Jill realized she had been holding back in so many ways. She'd subconsciously crawled into a social cell, burying herself in her career to keep from feeling. The same routine day in and day out, holding everyone in her life at arm's length. Change wouldn't come easy, but the time had come to try.

"I guess I could get back on a horse again, but first things first. I have a lot of work to do around here."

His expression brightened. "Does that mean—"

"Yes. I'm ready to join the Texas Extreme team."

Houston grabbed Jill off her feet and swung her around and she felt petite for the first time in her life. She also felt winded and wild and even a little nervous, particularly as he lowered her down his body, slowly. When he kept his gaze trained on hers, she experienced a spark along with a touch of heat. He didn't immediately let her go. She didn't automatically wrest herself out of his arms. They simply stood there a few moments, until the horse nickered, as if she'd nominated herself as their equine chaperone.

Jill came to her senses and stepped back. "Don't do that again, Calloway. I can't do my job if you break my ribs."

"At least you could heal yourself."

"Very amusing." She wrapped her arms around her middle. "So what's next?"

He sent her a sly smile. "What do you want to do?"

She thought of several answers, none that would be suitable, or wise. "I suppose I need to break the news to my boss. Fortunately I'm not on the schedule for three weeks, so he should have time to find a replacement."

"Guess I should go tell Dallas the news, unless you want to do it."

"You have my permission. Besides, if it weren't for you, I wouldn't be here."

His expression went suddenly solemn. "I'm glad you're here, Jill. We're all glad you're here. Welcome to the Calloway family."

That took her aback. "I wouldn't go that far, Houston. I'm just an employee."

He smiled again. "Believe me, they'll see it differently. In fact, I won't be a bit surprised if they throw you a party."

As it turned out, Houston had been right. He escorted Jill to the main house later that evening, where they were met with a round of applause and a spread of food laid out on tables on the front porch.

Jen stepped forward first, as usual. "We're so glad you're with us, Jill!"

Houston stood back while one by one, the women hugged Jill, except for his mother, who only briefly patted her on the back. Maria's behavior didn't shock him. She'd always been cautious when it came to women, especially if she thought they had staked a claim on one of the sons for all the wrong reasons. Particularly him. She'd be proud to know he'd barely touched Jill since that mind-blowing kiss. Except for that unplanned grab-and-go earlier in the barn when he'd wanted to kiss her again. And not being able to do it was killing him.

Dallas came out onto the porch next, followed by Austin, Worth and, bringing up the rear, Tyler. He had a bone to pick with that brother over his abandonment in Cowtown, but he'd wait until later. Or not, he thought, when Tyler walked over to Jill and pulled her into a bear hug.

Houston instantly moved forward like he was protecting his territory. But Jill wasn't anyone's property, and she sure as hell didn't need protecting.

Try telling Tyler that, Houston thought when his brother draped his arm around Jill's shoulder. "This woman is the angel of the rodeo," he said. "She rescued me more times than I can count."

Jill glanced at Houston before returning her attention back to Tyler. "How is your knee, by the way?"

"It's great, thanks to you. PT saved my season last year. You saved my season."

Disgusted by the scene, Houston turned his back, grabbed a plate from the table and began filling it with taquitos and chips and some sort of round thing with spinach. Normally he'd complain that this wasn't enough stuff to feed a squirrel, but he'd pretty much lost his appetite. Besides, he needed to occupy his good hand in order not to punch Tyler.

What the hell was wrong with him? Jill was free to do as she pleased with whoever she pleased. He had no call to be jealous or mad or even concerned. But he was. He still wanted to be her friend, and he also wanted benefits. A lot of benefits…

"Do you want to go over your benefits while you're here, Jill?" Dallas asked from behind him.

"We can cover that later," she answered.

Houston wanted to cover her in a few ways she wouldn't forget. With his working hand. With his mouth. Talk about some mighty fine benefits. But she might prefer to be tied up with Tyler, and that thought made him angry all over again, although that made no sense whatsoever. He'd never viewed his younger brother as competition, but then they'd never competed over a woman before.

He turned to find Jill occupied with another guy, only this one didn't wear a cowboy hat and ride bucking bronc. This one had a pacifier in his mouth and a fistful of her hair. She looked like a natural mother with a baby in her arms, all the more reason for him to steer clear. Had a lot of rodeo left in him before he traveled down domestic drive. She might want a man who'd give her lots of babies before that old biological clock began to drive her crazy. He wasn't ready for the responsibility of changing diapers and planning for a kid's college fund.

Jill claimed a spot on the glider next to Paris. "Does he sleep all night?" she asked.

Paris took a squirming Luke from Jill and smoothed a hand over his head. "Most of the time."

"And when he doesn't," Austin began, "I get up and walk him around until I'm sleepwalking."

All the confirmation Houston needed to avoid the parent trap. He couldn't very well tend to an infant when he still ran the circuit. And he wouldn't quit the circuit until he was good and ready, in about ten years.

He took a seat in a rocker and picked at his food while the rest of the crowd filled their plates. Once everyone settled into their seats, Jen announced, "I believe I'll make some juleps for this celebration." When she was met with a chorus of simultaneous noes she looked highly insulted. "You people are no fun," she said. "I suppose I'll just have to make my famous lemonade."

"Good idea," Maria said. "And don't go sneaking in some vodka."

While the conversation continued, Houston hung back to watch for any sign Jill was tiring of all the questions. Then his mom pulled her chair closer to the glider and he immediately sensed trouble.

"You said you're from Florida. What city?"

"Ocala. It's about eighty miles north of Orlando."

"What do your parents do?"

"My father is an investment banker. My mother is a social butterfly."

Maria leaned back. "So you're rich."

Houston couldn't stay silent any longer. "That's enough, Mom. She's not on trial here."

"It's okay," Jill said. "Yes, my parents have money. So did their parents and their parents' parents."

"Are you an only child, sugar?" Jenny chimed in.

"Actually, no. I have a younger sister, Pamela, and that reminds me…" She looked directly at Dallas. "I forgot to mention that Pamela's wedding is next weekend. I'm supposed to attend, but if you'd prefer I stay here, I'd understand."

"We wouldn't hear of it," Jenny said before Dallas could open his mouth. "It would be blasphemous for a woman not to attend her sister's wedding. She wouldn't have nearly enough time to replace a bridesmaid."

Jill looked away for a minute. "I'm not in the wedding party. She's left that to ten of her closest friends."

"That's terrible," Georgie said. "I don't have any siblings but if I did, they sure would have been in my wedding."

Jill smiled. "Believe me, it's not a problem. We've never been close, or haven't been in a long time."

"Regardless," Jen began, "I'm sure your mother would be disappointed if you didn't show up."

He could see a hint of anger in Jill's eyes. "My mother would be disappointed if I didn't show up to meet a whole slew of husband candidates from the local country club. I would miss seeing my father. However, if you absolutely would prefer I stay, Dallas, you'd be doing me a favor."

"I have a better idea," Paris said. "What if you take one of the brothers along with you as a pretend boyfriend? That way you could see your father and get your mother off your back."

Jen clapped her hands together. "That's a wonderful idea, Paris. We have three available, all very hand-some and single."

Worth stepped forward. "I can rearrange my sched-ule and go."

Tyler punched him on the upper arm. "No way. You'd get run off before the end of the reception for flirting with all the female guests. I'll go."

The more the banter between the brothers continued, the madder Houston got. Truth was, he didn't trust ei-ther Worth or Tyler any further than he could hurl them.

And when Jill sent him a *save-me* look, he figured it was time he stepped in.

"Neither of you will go," Houston said, drawing ev-eryone's attention.

"I agree," Dallas added. "We can't count on the two of you not to make a move on her before the plane took off."

"I still think it's a wonderful idea," Jenny said. "And I also think it's best that Jill choose which brother to take."

"I'm the logical choice," Tyler added. "But Jen's right. It should be her choice."

Worth inched toward Jill and winked. "Sometimes it's not about logic."

"You're all crazy," Maria said. "You haven't even asked the *chica* if she wants an escort."

All eyes turned to Jill, who just sat there, mouth agape.

Not a problem. He'd go ahead and speak for her. "If anyone is going to take her to Florida, it's going to be me."

"Have you lost your mind, Houston?"

"No, and would you slow down, dammit?"

Jill quickened the pace as she strode across his drive-way. If she had her way, she'd beat him into the house and hide away in the guest room until he gave up.

But he was too fast for her, she realized when she reached the porch and he clasped her arm, bringing her to a stop and turning her around before she had a chance to open the door.

She'd been only a few feet from escape. "Look, I'm tired. Can't we just discuss this in the morning?"

"Give me ten minutes to argue my case."

"Five minutes."

"Fine."

She moved into the great room and glanced at the couch where they'd had the monumental talk the night before. Where she'd crazily kissed him. She opted to keep going through the kitchen and onto the patio to avoid a repeat performance, as if the sofa held some sort of magical powers of persuasion. That would be the cowboy behind her.

Once outside, Jill chose a deck chair by the pool while Houston selected the one beside her. She stared at the backlit blue water and under normal circum-stances, she might take a dip. But she found nothing normal about taking a pretend boyfriend home to meet the folks.

She shifted toward Houston and said, "Your five minutes start now."

He leaned back and crossed his long, jeans-covered legs at the ankles. "First of all, although I didn't come up with this plan, Jen has a good idea. If you don't want the hassle of your mother trying to set you up with some guy, it makes sense for you to bring your own. Second, both my younger brothers would be draped all over you like a cheap shirt."

"And you wouldn't," she said in a simple statement of fact, and hopefully without any disappointment in her tone.

"Not unless we agreed to mutual draping."

Oh, that grin and those deadly eyes. "Interesting concept. The BYOB, bring your own boyfriend, not the draping. But this isn't a sorority mixer, Houston. This is a wedding."

"You have a point, but have you thought about doing it just for fun?"

She'd never been one to do anything only for fun, and that had kept her out of trouble. "I can't imagine pretending you and I are a couple being all that much fun, especially if we slip up."

"We'd have to make sure that didn't happen."

"How do you propose we do that?"

He rubbed his stubbled jaw. "Well, we'd have to act like we like each other."

"Which would involve a certain amount of affection, I assume."

"We could hold hands. I could kiss your cheek now and then."

"Are you going to chase me on the playground, too?"

He smiled. "Sure, as long as you let me catch you now and then."

"Maybe." Had she really sounded that coy?

A span of silence passed before Houston spoke again. "Here's something else to consider. You said your mother wouldn't approve if you brought a cowboy home."

"Or a professional poker player."

"I could say I play poker when I'm not competing."

"Double whammy. I like that."

"There you go. You'd be sending the message to your

mom that you're going to make your own decisions when it comes to who you choose to date, and maybe she'll stop trying to fix you up."

"Or I could just tell her to stop fixing me up."

He looked confused. "Haven't you told her that before?"

"Truthfully, yes."

"How's that working for you?"

"Not well."

"Point made."

Yes, he had made a few valid points, and seeing her mother's reaction to having a cowboy in the house would be priceless. However, that would only be a temporary fix to her mother's matchmaking efforts. Still, it could be worth it…

Jill had one important question to ask her possible escort. "What's in it for you, Houston?"

He shifted in the seat. "Just helping out a friend. Besides, I don't have anything better to do this weekend. And who would want to turn down a trip to Florida?"

Any man who'd ever met her mother. "You *do* realize I'm being forced to make two major decisions in one day."

"One down, one to go."

"This one might be tougher than the last."

He pushed out of the chair and pulled her up, right into his arms. "Let's practice."

"Practice what?"

"We need to see if we can do this pretend thing. If you cringe every time I touch you, it won't work."

She'd never cringed around him. Exactly the opposite. "I can handle it, Houston."

He nudged her closer, pressed his palms on the small of her back and lowered his voice. "We're on a dance floor with your family looking on. I tell you they're watching. What do you do now?"

"Tell them to stop ogling us?"

He tipped her cheek against his shoulder. "You relax. You pretend you like being in my arms."

She wouldn't be pretending. "Okay."

He tucked her hair behind one ear and kissed her cheek lightly. "You look up at me and smile. I lean over and whisper—" he brought his lips to her ear, causing her to shiver "—'I could use a beer.'"

With the spell now broken, she batted her eyelashes and spoke through a fake smile. "Do I look like your servant?"

"I didn't know you were into role playing."

She should probably yank out of his arms, but she felt like someone had cemented her to his chest. "Only if you're *my* servant."

"I'm game if you are."

The tension between them created a clear and present danger. Jill wanted to tell him to shut up and kiss her, but she didn't have to. He brushed his lips across hers, once, twice before he swooped in. He kept it gentle, kept it soft, kept her wanting more with each sensual stroke of his tongue. He slid his hands down to her bottom and pressed against her, sending the unmistakable message that this little mouth action had raised the sail. She could relate. The heat and dampness she experienced was almost foreign to her, and she knew if this interlude didn't end, they could be tossing away the no-benefits clause.

As if Houston sensed the same thing, he broke all contact, cleared his throat and stepped back. "You passed the test. I'm convinced."

Jill was only convinced of one thing—she hadn't

wanted it to end. "You do realize if I agree to this, we can't have a lot of that happening."

"But we can have some of it?"

"Yes…no…" Heavens, her mind had been blown to bits. "We have to be sensible. After we return to the ranch, it's back to business as usual." Which sounded like anything would go in Florida. "We'll discuss this further in the morning."

"Sounds like a plan."

When Houston crossed his arms and pulled off his shirt, Jill was momentarily rendered speechless. "What are you doing?"

"I'm going to take a swim. Wanna join me?"

Oh, wow, did she ever. But she wouldn't. "I'm heading for the shower," she said as she began to back away.

"Suit yourself, but you have a giant bathtub at your disposal right here."

She also had a man with a monumental set of muscles and an amazing chest standing before her. "I'll pass, but you go ahead and enjoy your *bath*."

The minute Houston began to undo his buckle, Jill spun around and hurried into the house. But extreme curiosity or feminine insanity sent her to the small window to peer out into the yard. She caught a glimpse of Houston's bare butt before he dove into the pool, and it was more than enough to spark her imagination.

She had absolutely no idea what had gotten into her. Well, actually, yes she did. Houston Calloway had crawled right under her skin. And now she had to decide if she would allow him to accompany her home.

She could choose the path of least resistance and go alone, or she could take a chance and let whatever happened happen. She could be cautious, or she could be carefree.

Deep down she recognized she would have to be strong if she accepted Houston's offer, and she wasn't certain she possessed that much strength. For that reason, she leaned toward nixing the whole plan and going the safe route.

That would probably be best for all concerned. The wisest course, and she'd always given a lot of credence to wisdom. She saw no reason to veer from that now.

Yes, she did. Perhaps the time had come to pull out all the stops. To finally learn what she'd been missing. To take a risk with a man she could trust. Yet she had no way of knowing if Houston was that man.

In order to find out, she could learn through personal experience, or she could search for a few personal references. And she knew just where to go for those.

"That was so much fun!"

Jill slid onto the bar stool across from Paris and set two bags on the ground beneath the small round table. "It was tons of fun, but I feel bad that you had to be gone from the baby so long."

Paris shrugged. "Dallas could use some dad time with him, and now that he's eating solid foods, Luke isn't that dependent on me. Besides, it's time someone else did some diaper duty."

They shared in a few laughs before Jill set out on her information gathering. "Dallas seems like a natural father, and so does Austin. Frankly, I can't see Houston ever assuming that role."

"I can," Paris said. "He actually watched Luke for me a couple of times when I had a meeting with the lodge's contractor. He didn't seem flustered at all, and had he been in town more, I'm sure he would have babysat whenever I asked."

Jill tried to picture Houston with an infant, without success. "I'm glad to know he has that side to him, but it doesn't quite gel with the whole tough-guy persona."

Paris waved at a middle-aged woman seated in the corner of the restaurant before bringing her attention back to Jill. "You know what they say. Don't judge a book by its cover, or in this case, a cowboy by his bull riding."

She recognized that in many ways, she had misjudged him over the past two years. He'd proven he was more than an irritable, injured rodeo rider. She'd even seen a few signs he had a wicked sense of humor and an inherent sensuality. Granted, she hadn't let herself see him in any other light to maintain professionalism. But now that he wasn't her patient, she'd begun to open her eyes. "I guess we're all guilty of prejudging people before we get to know them. My mother has the market cornered on that, though."

"Mine, too, at times," Paris said with a smile. "Tell me something, Jill. How are things between you and Houston?"

Jill swallowed hard. "What do you mean?"

"I mean he's a great-looking guy, and you're two consenting adults. You're staying in his guest room and—"

"Not after today," Jill interjected. "The apartment furniture is going to be delivered this afternoon."

"True, but that still leaves the past two nights in that big house, all alone with a hunk. I know it's really none of my business, but is there any chance you two might be experiencing a little chemistry?"

Had they ever. "What makes you think something like that would be possible?"

"Because you're a beautiful woman, and I know how irresistible the Calloway brothers can be. It took me less than one kiss with Dallas before I was ready to follow him anywhere. If you're attracted to Houston, and he's attracted to you, which I suspect he is, you should go for it."

Jill could use a sounding board, even if she didn't necessarily agree with Paris's advice. "If some chemistry is brewing between us, and I'm not saying it is, I don't believe it would be professional to act on it since we'll be working together as colleagues."

"Nonsense," Paris said. "Dallas hired me to design the lodge on the condition I marry him so he wouldn't lose control of the ranch, thanks to some ridiculous terms in his dad's will. We tossed professionalism out the window before the ink dried on our license."

She recalled Jenny mentioning that little tidbit, minus the dirty details. "So you didn't exactly go the traditional route, huh?"

"Not hardly. We met, married and then fell in love. Ass backward, as Dallas likes to say."

"I'm glad it worked out for you and Dallas, Paris, but I don't see Houston and I having that sort of relationship."

Paris narrowed her eyes and stared at her. "You don't see it or you're fighting it?"

Clearly Jill had guilt stamped on her face. "All right, I'm fighting it. For many reasons. First of all, I'm fairly sure Dallas wouldn't approve."

"He doesn't," Paris interjected. "He's not happy you've been bunking down at Houston's house. But he doesn't have any room to talk for all the reasons I cited earlier about our start in life together. Besides, I'll handle him if anything with you and Houston arises, if you catch my drift."

Jill sighed. "I've never been that spontaneous. Aside

from taking a career path against my parents' wishes, I've almost always walked the straight and narrow. I've never engaged in sex for the sake of sex." Never really engaged in it, period.

"Well, maybe it's time you take the chance, Jill. Take a little seduction out for a spin. You have a good start with those dresses you bought for the wedding. Houston's going to flip when he sees you in them."

So would her mother, Jill acknowledged. "I'm not sure seducing Houston is such a hot idea."

Paris grinned. "Oh, it could be very hot. And you shouldn't hesitate to take care of your needs with a man you know you can trust."

Aha! A personal reference. "How do I know I can trust him?"

Paris leaned over and patted her hand. "Because he's a Calloway brother, and they've been taught well when it comes to how to treat a woman. They have their mothers to thank for that."

Not exactly what she'd been led to believe. "According to Houston, Worth and Tyler are both serious players. And Houston enjoyed that reputation on the rodeo circuit."

"They're all charming to a fault, yet always respectful," Paris said. "Of course, their father was charming, too, but a total failure in the chivalry department. I believe that was also a contributing factor to their strong sense of honor. Heck, most of their former girlfriends still speak highly of them, to hear Maria tell it. Therefore, I can honestly say I believe Houston would never intentionally do anything to hurt you."

Maybe not physically, but he could damage her emotionally. If she let him. Which she wouldn't.

Jill had a lot to consider, and only a few days to

do it before she might find herself spending an entire weekend with Houston at a wedding. Fortunately, she would be able to spend that time without him and assess if "going for it," as Paris had suggested, would be the best course or one massive mistake.

Seven

This whole "fake boyfriend" idea could very well wind up being one major mistake.

Houston determined that when, with less than a half hour until their scheduled landing in Florida and meeting of the parents, Jill still looked as nervous as a cat on a car radiator. "Are you going to be okay?"

She shot Houston a look that said she didn't appreciate the question. "I'm fine."

Yeah, right. "You look like you're about to jump out of your skin. Are you regretting having me with you?"

"No. I just don't like turbulence."

He recalled a couple of bumps, but that was it. "You're worried about facing your folks with me in tow."

She glanced away. "Maybe."

"No *maybe* about it. You've barely spoken a word since we boarded the plane. That was over two hours ago."

"I've been mentally rehearsing how I'm going to explain you."

"Apparently you've been doing that all week. I've barely seen you for more than a few minutes."

"I've been busy picking out furniture, stocking the kitchen, dress shopping with Paris, not to mention ordering first-aid supplies and all the medical equipment. You know, part of the job Dallas hired me to do?"

He didn't want a countdown of her activities. He wanted an explanation. Besides, she'd left going out of her way to ignore him from the list, and now that she'd moved out of his guest room, he'd found he missed the company. *Her* company. But he had all weekend to make up for lost time, before they returned to the reality of the ranch and she went back to ignoring him again.

Jill raked her gaze down his T-shirt and jeans and boots, a fair exchange since he'd been eyeing her short blue sleeveless dress since he'd picked her up this morning. Man, what he wouldn't give to run his hand underneath it. Or take it off completely.

"Did you bring any formal clothing?" she asked, disrupting his dirty thoughts.

"Yeah, a suit and a tux. Wasn't sure how fancy this shindig was going to be."

"You'll need both, the suit for the rehearsal dinner tonight at the country club and the tuxedo for the wedding tomorrow."

He narrowed his eyes and studied her head-on. "What would you have done if I hadn't brought either?"

She shrugged. "Winston would have taken you shopping."

He'd had a blue tick hound by that name at one time. "Who the hell is Winston?"

"You'll meet him soon enough."

The plane jolted, causing Jill to dig her nails into his arm, right above the cast. "We're in for some rocky weather," Frank said over the loudspeaker. "Just make sure you stay belted in. Shouldn't last too long."

"Great," Jill muttered. "A late summer storm. A sign of what's to come, I'm sure."

He patted her hand still clamped to his arm. "Stay calm. Cowboy Frank knows what he's doing."

She finally released her grip and sighed. "I was referring to the storm we're sure to encounter when you meet my mother, Hurricane Helen."

He'd deal with the fallout when the time came, even if he had to bring out his charm arsenal. "You haven't said a whole lot about your dad."

She leaned back against the headrest. "He's a good man. He rolls with the flow while my mother runs roughshod over him. He likes to keep the peace."

His own dad had been inclined to disturb the peace, but he'd always treated everyone fairly…except when it came to Maria and Jen. He'd totally screwed them around.

Jill straightened and leaned forward. "Do you have any white wine at the bar?"

"Sure." He released the belt and stood. "I'll get it."

"Not now," she said. "There's still lightning outside. Wait until we're sure the turbulence is over."

He figured it had only begun and might continue throughout the weekend. "Sweetheart, I've spent a lot of time sitting on top of mean, two-ton animals and their only goal is to throw me on my ass. I can handle a moving aisle."

"All right, tough guy."

"Glad you see it my way."

He sidestepped to the small refrigerator, opened the

door, leaned over and located the miniature bottle of chardonnay, a staple they'd kept stocked for Jen. After uncapping it, he poured the wine into a plastic stem cup and returned to his seat without incident.

"Here you go," he said as he handed her the flute and a cocktail napkin. "A little liquid courage. Peanuts or pretzels to go with that drink?"

"No, thanks. Aren't you going to have anything?"

"Nope. It's not even noon yet."

She checked her watch. "I totally forgot the time."

He stretched out his legs and laced his hands on his belly. "Don't worry about the time. Your secret's safe with me."

She sipped the wine and smiled. "All of my secrets, I hope, are safe with you."

His mind reeled back to the night on the sofa, and the liplock by the pool. "If you're talking about what happened between us a few days ago, I don't kiss and tell."

"At least that last time it was on you, not me."

She'd been all up against him, and that he hadn't been able to forget. "You enjoyed it and you know it."

"It was okay."

That might've offended him if she hadn't been lying. "Women don't moan when it's only okay."

She took a long drink of the wine this time. "I did not moan."

"Maybe it was more like a purr."

"I don't purr, either."

"Yeah, you do." And he wanted to know how she sounded when they really got down to business. He could forget about that right now because the chances that would happen were slim to none.

Jill downed the rest of the chardonnay and handed him the cup. "I'll have one more please."

"Do you think it's a good idea to show up on your mother's doorstep three sheets to the wind?"

She grinned. "Couldn't hurt, but I'm not going to get drunk on two glasses of wine. Relaxed maybe, but not intoxicated."

Her attitude put him in a not-so-great position. "I could refuse to serve you for your own good."

"Then I'll get it myself."

He didn't want her lack of judgment to come back to haunt him, but under normal circumstances, the alcohol content in wine wouldn't likely get a sparrow drunk. Even so, she was a self-proclaimed lightweight in the booze department. "Go ahead, but don't say I didn't warn you."

Jill looked perfectly steady when she slid out of the seat. Houston, on the other hand, felt a little light-headed when the hem on that fitted dress rode high up her thighs as she crouched down in front of the fridge. "I don't see it."

He streaked both hands down his face. "It's in the shelf in the door."

"Oh, there it is."

Yeah, there it was—a woman who had him feeling hot and bothered. To make matters worse, when she started to work her way past him, the plane lurched and Jill landed the hand not holding the wine on his upper thigh. "Sorry," she said as she straightened. "That could have been a disaster if I'd spilled this all over you."

It could have been real revealing if she'd moved her palm a little higher. He wasn't the least bit worried about flying through a storm. He worried he might meet his demise if he didn't get some relief soon. Death by permanent woody.

"What's so funny?" Jill asked when she reclaimed her seat.

He hadn't realized he'd been smiling. "Not a thing. I was just thinking about how impressed I am you landed on your feet. You should try riding a bull sometime."

"Don't hold your breath."

He couldn't resist challenging her. "You're right. You're not tough enough."

She drank more wine and laid a dramatic hand above her breasts. "Someone release those orange butter cups from the ceiling. The cabin's filling up with testosterone and I need some oxygen."

He laughed to keep from groaning. "You beat all I've ever seen."

"Well, I try. Believe me, I'm surrounded by testosterone-ridden cowboys on a regular basis. It usually doesn't faze me."

"Usually?"

"It didn't until I've gotten to know you better."

His ego puffed up like a rooster in a henhouse. "Is that bad or good?"

"I'm not sure. I mean, you're not my type. Frankly, I don't have a type. I really haven't had enough of a social life over the past few years to find out."

"Only you can change that by getting out there and taking a few chances."

"You're right." After finishing off the wine, she leaned over him and set the glass on the counter, putting them too close for Houston's comfort. "But I could use some help."

He could, too, he realized, after she brushed up against him. "What kind of help?"

"Well—"

"Tie yourself down, folks" boomed from the overhead speaker. "We'll be on the ground shortly."

They both secured their seat belts before Jill continued. "I've decided to take this weekend and be less guarded, more carefree. Stop listening to my mother's warnings. Throw caution to the wind."

Houston had no idea what that entailed, but he was damn sure going to find out. "What exactly does that mean ? Aside from showing up tipsy for the nuptials."

She playfully slapped at his arm. "I'm not tipsy, and before I answer your question, I have one for you. Would you say we have chemistry?"

His body had been telling him that for almost a week, loud and clear. "Yeah. You could say that."

"Good. I thought it was just me."

"Are you serious? It's all I can do not to climb all over you whenever you walk in the room."

Her eyes went wide. "Seriously?"

"Well, yeah. Could you not tell that when I kissed you by the pool? Or when you kissed me?"

"Look, Houston, I'm not naive. I just don't have a lot of experience when it comes to male-female relationship dynamics."

He'd gathered that, but he couldn't believe she didn't see in herself what he saw in her. "You're a beautiful, sexy woman. Any man would be crazy not to want to be with you."

"Yes, they're all lined up at my door back at the ranch."

She honestly didn't get it. "Don't forget that my

brothers almost came to blows over who was going to escort you here."

She smiled. "Until you intervened."

"Yep. I wasn't going to have those two hounds dogging you the entire weekend."

"You're not going to dog me?"

Not if he could help it, though that was up in the air at the moment. "I'm not going to do anything you don't want to do."

"Would you kiss me again if I asked?"

"Yeah."

"Would you touch me if I asked?"

Oh, hell yeah. "Anywhere you want me to touch you."

When the plane began to descend, Houston figured the conversation would have to continue on the ride to her house. Jill had other ideas.

"Before we land, there is one thing I have to tell you," she said.

He could only guess what that might be. "Shoot."

"When I said I've had little experience with men, I should have said I've had no measurable experience."

Houston's mind began to reel over the implication. No way. No how. Not a gorgeous woman like her. "Are you telling me—"

"I'm saying, to use an antiquated term, that for all intents and purposes, I'm a virgin."

To say Houston still looked stunned would be a major understatement. Jill had less than ten minutes to bring him out of his stupor before they met the welcoming committee. Fortunately Winston had closed the partition dividing the Bentley's front and back seats, allowing them some privacy. "I know this little tidbit has come as quite a surprise, but—"

"You could say that. I don't know many women who haven't taken that step by the time they're in their midtwenties. Heck, I don't believe I know *any* women who haven't had sex before." He reached over the console and took her hand. "All this means is you're discriminating when it comes to men. And for that reason it scares the hell out of me to even consider us having some kind of weekend fling. You deserve better."

She deserved to make that decision on her own. "I don't have any expectations, Houston, other than having a good time. If anything happens between us, I accept that we'll go back to being friends and occasional adversaries."

He remained silent for a time before asking, "Why me? Aside from the chemistry thing."

"I've asked myself that quite a bit. The answer is I'm sure you know what you're doing, and I can trust you to respect me."

"Just so you know, I don't take any of this lightly. My mother has always told me that women are to be treated well. My father showed me how if you ignore that, you only create heartache. I don't want that to happen to you."

Exactly what Paris had told her. "In your estimation, I might not be tough enough to ride a bull, but I'm emotionally stronger than you realize."

"How do you know how you're going to feel if you've never had sex before?"

"I'm not totally innocent, Houston. I've been on dates with guys who had roving hands."

"And none of them succeeded in getting you into bed?"

She refused to believe he was that obtuse, only amazed. "A few tried, all failed. It never really felt right."

"But you honestly think it would be right between us?"

"As hard as it is to believe, yes, I do. And I do because I'm not that college student anymore. I have needs and I want to explore all the possibilities. But if you're not willing—"

"I didn't say that."

Her optimism began to climb. "Then you will consider it? No pressure, of course."

He seemed to mull it over for a few moments before he responded. "I'll consider it, but only on one condition."

Her optimism threatened to fall off the cliff. "What would that be?"

"If we get into some of this exploring, and you want to back out, you only have to tell me and it's over."

She didn't foresee that happening. But then she hadn't predicted she would ever ask him for some sensual attention. "That's fair."

When the car slowed, Jill glanced out the window and realized they were pulling into the lengthy drive. "Looks like we've arrived at the esteemed Amherst estate."

"Then I guess it's time to start the show." He tipped her face toward him and smiled. "Want to get in a little practice?"

"Do you really have to ask?"

"Yeah, I do. I want to make sure you haven't changed your mind."

"In two minutes?"

"Stranger things have happened."

Yes, as in she'd propositioned him. Her mother would

be so proud. "I would like nothing better than to engage in a little lip practice with you."

He kissed her then, softly at first, then more deeply. She was so engrossed in the moment, she didn't realize they'd stopped, or that Winston had opened the door. She didn't realize they had an audience, either, until she heard the familiar voice.

"Oh, my stars, Jillian Elizabeth, why on earth are you kissing that cowboy?"

Eight

Jill abruptly ended the kiss and leaned around Houston to discover her mother on the top step beneath the portico, standing as stiff as her strawberry blond bob hairdo and sporting her patent disapproving look.

After leaning back against the seat again, Jill muttered, "Hurricane Helen is about to be unleashed. Let the destruction begin."

Houston sent a quick glance in her mother's direction. "How does she even know I'm a cowboy when I'm not wearing my hat?"

"Big silver belt buckle, jeans and boots. Dead giveaway."

"Hadn't thought about that."

Jill wondered what he thought about the queen of the manor. In light of Helen's glare, he probably wished he hadn't agreed to come. "Climb on out and let's get this over with. And it's best if initially you let me do all the talking."

"Whatever you say."

After Houston exited the Bentley, he offered his hand and helped Jill out. She adjusted her dress and walked right up to Helen with the cowboy in residence trailing behind her. "Hello, Mother."

"You haven't answered my question." She pointed a finger at Houston. "Who is this man?"

Jill glanced back as if she'd forgotten he was there. "Oh. Him. I picked him up on the way from the airport." She clasped Houston's cast-wrapped hand and lifted it up. "He was hitchhiking. You couldn't miss the thumb."

Helen's mouth gaped open. "You picked up a stranger? Winston, what were you thinking?" she shouted at the driver now bent over the trunk, unloading the bags.

The white-haired, goatee-bedecked family fixture leaned around the car and smiled at Jill. "I was only following Miss Jillian's instructions."

Time to set the record straight before Winston found himself in the unemployment line. "I'm not serious, Mother. This is my guest. He's also my…my…"

"I'm her fiancé." While Jill froze on the spot, Houston offered his good hand to Helen, which she promptly ignored. "Houston Calloway. Pleasure to meet you, ma'am."

Fiancé? This time Jill was a victim of the verbal stun gun. So much for Houston letting her do all the talking. Oh, joy. She might as well play along. What better way to thwart her mother's usual matchmaking? "Yes, mother, meet your future son-in-law."

Helen continued to disregard Houston's extended hand and turned her ire on Jill. "You might have said something when we spoke last. I had no idea you were dating anyone, much less engaged to a man we've never met."

Houston wrapped his arm around Jill's shoulder and gave her a squeeze. "It was kind of a spontaneous proposal, ma'am. Or maybe I should start calling you Mom?"

Helen looked no less unhappy over the situation. "Mrs. Amherst would be best since I don't know you at all."

"Works for me for now," Houston said with a grin. "Once you get to know me, you're gonna love me."

"Houston asked me to marry him while we were on the plane," Jill interjected. "I was very surprised."

"Yeah, she was, and real excited." He looked at her and winked before bringing his attention back to her mother. "I still don't have a ring yet, but we'll take care of that soon. Unless you have some kind of family heirloom you want her to have. That sure would save me some time and money."

Helen lifted her chin. "No, I do not. And I would prefer you not mention any of this to your father right away. His health hasn't been too good of late."

Jill felt a bite of panic. "What's wrong?"

"His heart," her mother replied nonchalantly.

"I don't remember you mentioning *that* to me when you called, Mother."

She waved a hand in dismissal. "He doesn't want anyone to make a fuss. Now come this way, but take care not to disrupt the wedding planner's staff." She sent a pointed look at Houston's feet. "And please wipe your boots on the mat. They polished the marble this morning."

Houston tipped an imaginary hat. "Yes, ma'am."

They walked through the foyer and into a flurry of activity. One woman was draping greenery and white flowers on the banister while a man moved around her mother's prized furniture in the parlor to their left. Houston and Jill followed Helen past the library and into the den at the rear of the house, the only living space where Jill had ever felt comfortable. All the antique settees and chairs and expensive accessories had never held any appeal.

When Helen said, "I'll return shortly," and started toward the kitchen, Jill showed Houston to the white leather sectional, where they sat side by side.

He draped his arm over the back of the sofa and surveyed the most comfortable room, aside from the all-white color pallet. "Nice digs."

"Nice job of acting," Jill said in a lowered voice. "I can't believe you actually told her we're engaged. What were you thinking?"

"Sorry. It kind of shot out of my mouth when she kept looking at me like I was pond sludge."

Jill couldn't contain her smile when she remembered her mother's reaction. "The shock on her face was kind of amusing. You're one of the few people to ever put her in her place."

"When do you want to tell her the truth?"

She had to think about that for a moment. "Not until after we're ready to return to the ranch. After I reveal all, we'll need to make a quick escape."

"Good plan. You can tell her we broke up when you found out I don't have a dime to my name."

"Or that you already have a wife and kids." Mortification rushed through Jill when she realized what she'd said. "I'm so, so sorry. That was insensitive in light of your father's history."

"Don't sweat it. It's not that big of a deal anymore."

She surmised that attitude was the product of self-preservation. "Anyway, I appreciate your covering for me in such a creative way."

Houston chuckled. "You can thank me later, sweet cakes."

Sweet cakes? "You're welcome, honey bun. And whatever you do, don't tell her you have money."

"Sure thing."

"Don't mention a word about the new job."

"Not a problem, and don't worry, I can handle Helen. You ain't seen nothing yet."

Jill was left to speculate about his intentions when her mother reentered the room holding two crystal glasses. She set coasters in front of them and placed the drinks atop the copper disks.

"I took the liberty of serving you some of Penelope's famous raspberry tea," Helen said as she pulled up the club chair closer to the sofa. "I assume you like tea, Mr. Calloway."

He shrugged. "Call me Houston, and tea will do, unless you have a beer. Or whiskey."

Her mother looked slightly appalled. "We don't serve alcohol this time of day."

Jill found it amusing that Helen had discounted her three-martini lunches with the bridge club, a fact she decided not to point out.

Houston planted his palm above Jill's knee. "Then tea it is."

Helen eyed his hand before raising her condescending gaze to his. "Tell me, Mr. Calloway. What do you do for a living?"

"Well, Helen, I pretty much herd cows and slop pigs. Tend to the horse, that kind of thing."

Her mother looked as if she'd eaten a pickle. "Then you live on a ranch?"

"Yes, ma'am. A working cattle ranch in deep South Texas."

"It's an hour south of San Antonio," Jill said.

"And about seventy miles from the Mexican border," Houston added. "The livestock pretty much outnumber the people in those parts."

Helen's green eyes went wide. "Jillian, where on earth are you going to work if you're in the middle of nowhere?"

"I'm not sure yet."

"She doesn't have to work," Houston said. "Except for maybe feeding the chickens."

Jill scraped her brain for a way to end the inquisition before they dug a deeper deception trench. "Where's Daddy?"

"Outside. Are you certain you're cut out for ranching life, Jillian?"

So much for the subject-changing tact. "Actually, I—"

"Sure she is," Houston broke in. "She's one tough little lady. And as far as making her own money goes, she doesn't need to. I don't have much, but I do have a two-bedroom house and enough money to put food on the table and raise a passel of babies."

And Jill hadn't thought her mother could look any more stunned. "A passel of babies?" Helen repeated.

"Yes, ma'am. At least four, maybe five." Houston popped a kiss on Jill's cheek. "I like to keep my women barefoot and pregnant."

Helen eyed him suspiciously. "Your *women*?"

"Woman," Houston corrected. "There's only one woman for me, and that's this little gal here."

If he squeezed her any tighter, Jill might actually wince. "Any other questions, Mother?"

"I'm sure I will think of more as the weekend wears on."

The sound of footsteps drew everyone's attention to the den's entry. When Jill spotted him, she instantly hopped off the sofa and rushed to him. "Hi, Daddy!"

He pulled her into a long hug before taking a step back. "My, my, ladybug, you're still as pretty as ever."

Jill noticed he wore his traditional white tennis clothes and she found that disturbing. "Dad, are you sure you should be on the court considering your heart issues?"

"I don't have heart problems. I have acid reflux."

They both shot a look in Helen's direction before Jill said, "Mother told me—"

"Don't listen to your mother, ladybug. She exaggerates everything."

"I don't necessarily believe your doctors, Benjamin," Helen said. "They barely ran any tests."

"They ran every test known to humankind," her father retorted before spying Houston. "Who is this young man?"

Houston stood, stepped forward and extended his hand for a shake. "Houston Calloway, sir. I'm Jill's—"

"Friend," Jill added.

"He's her fiancé," Helen stated with a good deal of disdain in her tone.

She hated lying to her father and decided to set him straight when they had a moment alone. "Mother didn't want us to mention it—she led us to believe you might have a cardiac arrest."

"Ignore your mother's flair for the dramatic. This is very welcome news." He gave Houston's hand a hearty shake. "Welcome to the family, son. Just don't tell me you plan to marry tomorrow. One wedding in this house is quite enough."

Jill would wholeheartedly agree to that. "Don't be concerned, Dad. Houston and I plan to have a long engagement."

Houston frowned. "Aw, now, sweetheart. I'm thinking the quicker we get married, the better."

Helen's eyes went wide. "What does he mean by that, Jillian? Are you expecting?"

She was expecting to have the lies come back to bite her on the backside, but she resented her mother drawing that conclusion. "Why, Mom? No one would ask me to marry them if I wasn't?"

"That's not what I'm saying," Helen retorted. "I believe we have a right to know if our daughter is pregnant out of wedlock."

At the moment, Jill had no desire to correct her mother's supposition. "We'll discuss it later. Right now we'd like to get settled in."

"Where shall I put these, Miss Jillian?"

Jill looked beyond her father to see Winston hauling the luggage into the den. But before she could respond, her mother popped out of the chair and said, "Jillian will be staying in her sister's room. Mr. Calloway will be in the pool house, unless he's arranged for a hotel room."

"Nope," Houston said. "I'm a little short on cash, but I could find a cheap motel if I'm going to be putting you out."

Ben patted Houston on the back. "Nonsense, son. You're part of the family now."

Jill had one burning question to pose. "What's wrong with me staying in my old room?"

"It's been turned into a guest room," Helen began,

"and we have guests occupying every suite. You and Pamela can share her room for a night and get reacquainted."

She'd rather eat garden sod. Jill also refused to allow her mother to dictate the sleeping arrangements. "I'll be staying in the pool house, as well, Winston."

Helen looked mortified. "You certainly will not, Jillian. It only has one bedroom."

"If you seriously believe I'm pregnant, and I'm not saying I am, why can't I stay with Houston? I can't get knocked up twice."

Helen lifted her chin and folded her arms tightly across her middle. "Pregnant or not, it wouldn't be proper."

"Come on now, Helen," Jill's father chimed in. "They're adults. I recall a time or ten when you and I occupied the same room before we married, and we know how that turned out."

Helen crossed her arms tightly and huffed. "That is not going to happen beneath my roof, Benjamin. End of story."

Her dad sent Jill a sympathetic look. "Sorry, ladybug. The hurricane has spoken, and considering her stress level, it's best not to unleash her."

Jill nixed further protests out of respect for her father. Besides, she could still find a way to spend the evening with Houston without anyone's knowledge. "Fine." She turned to Winston. "If you'll just take the blue luggage upstairs, I'll show Houston to the pool house."

"As you wish, Miss Jillian."

When Jill turned back to her mother, she sensed another lecture coming on and quelled it immediately. "Before you say anything, I assure you the sanctity of the pool house will remain intact." For the next few hours. "What time is the dinner tonight?"

"Seven o'clock sharp," Helen said. "Do you have an appropriate dress for the event?"

"Yes. Red-and-white gingham with matching ruby-red shoes. Grab your luggage and follow me, *fiancé.*"

She heard Houston chuckling while he gathered his bags and followed her as she marched through the sun room. When she headed out the doors that led to the pool deck, she spotted a huge white tent in the distance, set up near the lake.

"So that's where the magic is going to happen," Houston said from behind her.

"Yes. It's a nice backdrop for a wedding."

"I meant the pool house."

This time she laughed. "I suppose that remains to be seen."

He came to her side and matched her steps. "You can always sneak out after everyone's gone to bed."

Clearly he'd read her mind back in the house. "Provided my mother doesn't post a guard at my sister's bedroom door."

"I could always climb up and carry you out the window."

"Banner idea. I'll have Winston fetch a ladder."

She opened the door to the blue-and-white cottage, expecting to see that the decor hadn't changed since she'd left home. In reality, it had. The furnishings had all been updated in muted tones of white and gray with a pop of lime green in places. She assumed they'd renovated it when they'd turned her room into guest quarters. As much as she hated to admit it, that stung like a hornet and only cemented how far removed she'd become from her family.

"This will work just fine," Houston said as he stepped inside.

"It's nice enough." Jill walked to the bedroom and surveyed the space. "I'm not sure how much you're going to like this."

Houston slid his arms around her from behind. "Haven't seen that since I shared a room with Tyler when we were kids."

"Those twin beds are a monument to my mother's contempt for all things sexual."

"Yeah, I figured that out pretty quickly. I can't figure out why you didn't deny the whole baby thing."

"Hey, you set it up by adding that whole 'the quicker the better' thing."

"I figured she'd just think I couldn't wait to make you my bride. I didn't know she'd actually go straight to the baby thing."

"Of course she would, and for all the reasons I stated to her." She looked back at him and grinned. "That said, it was kind of cool to get engaged and pregnant in less than an hour."

He was uncharacteristically quiet for a few moments. "Have you ever talked to your mom about her attitude?"

She faced him and thought back to her formative years. "No. She did all the talking."

"Maybe you should broach that subject while you're here."

"Why?"

"Because people who have negative opinions about sex usually have something in their past that's influenced them."

He'd made a good point that she should seriously contemplate. "If the sex subject comes up before the end of the weekend, and I'm sure it will, I'll consider addressing it then, when I tell her there's no baby or impending wedding."

"Good idea." He pulled her into his arms. "You don't hold sex in contempt, do you?"

She shook her head and swallowed hard. "Fortunately it doesn't appear to be genetic."

"Damn fortunate." He brushed his lips across her forehead. "This cowpoke would sure like to kiss this lady."

"This lady would like to be kissed."

He lowered his head and paused. "You don't think they have surveillance cameras in here, do you?"

"Knowing Helen, it's entirely possible. However, my father would draw the line at voyeurism."

"Good to know."

As Houston kissed her soundly, Jill put all her concerns about family issues away. She didn't care about the sleeping arrangements or enduring social events with pretentious people. She only cared about Houston's hands roving down her back, the undeniable heat when he backed her against the wall and pressed against her. She couldn't claim she wasn't surprised, and excited, when his hand came to rest on her breast. She was also taken aback by her immediate reaction to his touch when he used his fingertips to work her nipple into a tight knot. His skill told her this wasn't his first time at first base. Not exactly her first time, either, but he'd obviously been playing the game for some time.

When Houston breezed his lips down her neck and began toying with the back zipper, Jill reacted with a little shudder and a bit of caution. With a bedroom so close, she recognized how easy it would be give in to sexual oblivion. But with her parents nearby, they would be risking discovery.

"What are you doing, Houston Calloway?" she said in a raspy tone.

"I want to take off this dress, and it's damn sure not because I want to borrow it."

She wanted him to take it off. Honestly, she did, but… "Do think now is the right time with my mother lurking in the shadows?"

"Probably not." He released his hold on her, moved to one side and tipped his forehead against the wall. "I'm so jacked up right now I could take you right here. But this isn't how I want your first time to be."

The fact he'd considered her feelings, and not the prospect of getting caught, buoyed her spirits. "I appreciate that," she said as she readjusted her clothing. "Although in reality, I wouldn't have objected to a little more foreplay."

He straightened and half grinned, half groaned. "Darlin', if you want foreplay, just wait for what I have in store for you tonight."

While Houston waited next to the white limo, he wasn't sure what to expect tonight. Rubbing elbows with a bunch of stuck-up people wasn't his idea of a good time. Country music and barn dances were more his style. But for Jill's sake, he'd make do and be a perfect gentleman. He'd behave himself in public and keep his hands to himself. No one would ever know that getting Jillian in his bed, even a twin bed, would be first and foremost on his mind.

That plan was pretty much shot to hell when Jill emerged from the mansion wearing a low-cut, little black dress and matching high heels, her hair piled high on her head, leaving her neck fair game. But the way she looked at the moment—a little pissed off—probably meant she had no desire to make out in the back seat of a moving vehicle.

After the driver opened the door, Jill slid inside and he claimed the spot beside her. Houston questioned why they didn't immediately move. "Are we waiting for someone else?"

Jill crossed her legs, inadvertently hiking up her hem. "No, thank heavens. We're the last to leave."

"Bad day?"

"Boring day. How about you?"

"I watched a little baseball, took a little nap. Oh, and Penelope brought me a tray of sandwiches."

"Were they good?"

Not nearly as good as Jill looked, and smelled. "They were about as big as my banged-up thumb, but they were okay. They had some kind of cream cheese stuff and, best of all, no poison."

She finally smiled. "Lucky for me."

He shrugged out of the jacket and tossed it on the seat across from him. If he had his way, that wouldn't be the only article of clothing coming off tonight. "How did it go with your sister?"

"It didn't. She was flitting about the house and, when she saw me, muttered a greeting, then went out to the tent for the wedding run-through."

"Did you go?"

"I didn't feel the need to rehearse sitting in the audience."

He immediately noticed the bitterness in her tone. "You didn't see her when you were getting ready tonight?"

She shook her head. "No. Apparently she decided to dress at her maid of honor's hotel room. I'm sure alcohol was involved, which could be interesting during this little soiree."

Doing what he wanted to do to her, right then and

there, could be damn interesting. He decided to be subtle, not come on too strong. For those reasons, he laid his palm above her knee.

"You look real pretty tonight, ma'am."

"You look nice, too. Very handsome. You clean up good, Calloway."

Maybe so, but he was having some fairly dirty thoughts. "How many people are attending this dinner?"

When he drew slow circles on the inside of her leg, she released a ragged sigh. "I'd guess a hundred or so of my mother's closest friends."

He let his fingertip drift upward, but not too far. "I like an intimate gathering."

"I like..."

"You'd like what, darlin'?"

She closed her eyes and her legs opened slightly. "Um...I'm not sure."

He pressed a kiss on her temple. "How are you feeling right now?"

"Very warm."

"Want me to tell the driver to turn up the air-conditioning?"

Her eyes snapped open and she frowned. "I'm not exactly *that* kind of hot."

He ran his palm up the inside of her thigh. "Oh, yeah?"

"Oh, yeah."

"You feeling a little turned on tonight?"

Without verbally responding, she wrapped her hand around his neck and pulled his mouth to hers for a long, deep kiss. "Does that answer your question?"

"Pretty much."

Considering that kiss his cue to continue, he leaned over and grabbed his coat, then draped it across her lap.

Awareness dawned in her expression, and she shuddered when he slid his hand back beneath her skirt.

Houston rimmed the edge of her panties with his fingertip, and really wanted that scrap of lace gone. But before he did that, he decided to test the waters by pressing his palm between her legs. He encountered a good deal of dampness and heat. And after just a couple of strokes in a prime place, Jill made a small sound in her throat, grabbed his arm and shook like the devil.

Without much effort on his part, she'd gone off like a rocket. Even though it pleased him to know he'd given her some pleasure, he was seriously feeling the effects.

Jill leaned back against the seat and muttered, "Wow," right when the car pulled up to the country club's front door behind several more sedans. "I didn't expect that to happen."

He kissed her cheek. "Neither did I, sweetheart. But your quick-to-fire reaction isn't all that surprising."

"The pitfalls of celibacy." She smiled but it quickly went away. "This isn't at all fair to you."

"I'll be fine, if you give me a few minutes."

She sent a pointed look at his groin. "Oh. I see."

His predicament was hard to miss. "Yep. Unless you want me to be the sideshow at dinner, we're going to have to sit here a little longer."

Jill looked out the rear window. "We don't have much longer, but I have an idea." She brought her focus back to him. "Just think about the fact that you're going to be hanging out with Hurricane Helen all night."

He'd be damned if that didn't do the trick.

Houston felt secure enough to put on his jacket in preparation for a night with the presumed in-laws. He figured if he could take on a rank bull, he could handle the Amherst family. Besides, he was more than curious to meet Jill's sister.

When they finally worked their way inside the entrance, he saw women in fine dresses and men with expensive watches. The net worth of this crowd had to be in the billions.

Jill slipped her arm through his, signaling the pretending had begun. She led him toward Ben and Helen, who were being greeted by several guests. He had no trouble spotting the bride-to-be. He noted only a slight resemblance to Jill. Her hair was much redder and she was a whole lot shorter. He'd classify her as fresh-faced pretty, where Jill was more refined and, yeah, elegant. She stood next to a tall, lanky guy with brown hair who kept looking at her like he'd won the prize.

As they waited for the crowd to clear, Houston's first impression of the couple happened to be they were damn young. His second—they actually looked real glad to be together. Maybe it was all just a front to please the folks. Or maybe he was too jaded to believe in ever-after. He had his own father to thank for that.

Jill began to move forward and murmured, "Time to put on our happy faces and get this over with."

Houston wanted to get it over with and get a beer, or a shot of whiskey. Probably the best whiskey money could buy. Free whiskey, in this case. Nothing wrong with that.

When Jill released his arm to hug her dad, Houston hung back and waited until he was properly introduced. Her hesitancy to embrace her mom wasn't lost on Houston, nor was the coolness when she greeted her sister. He wasn't the least bit surprised to see her shaking the groom's hand, like he was more stranger than longtime acquaintance. There was so much not-so-great history in the group that someone could write a family self-help book on the spot.

After Jill waved Houston over, Ben gave him a hearty handshake and Helen gave him a fake smile that caused the devil to land on his shoulder. He immediately pulled the female hurricane into a bear hug, and wished he had a camera to capture the stunned look on her face.

"Houston," Jill began, "this is my sister, Pamela. Pamela, my fiancé, Houston."

She didn't smile, didn't offer her hand, and that plain pissed him off. "Nice to finally meet you."

"Likewise," she said without a scrap of sincerity in her tone.

The groom stuck out his hand. "I'm Clark Hamilton," he said. "Helen told us you're a rancher."

Houston returned the gesture and said, "Yep. Born and bred Texan."

Clark grinned. "I envy you. I always wanted to live that cowboy lifestyle."

Pamela elbowed him in the side. "Be serious, Clark."

He frowned at his bride. "I am serious."

"It's a hard life," Houston said as he slipped his arm around Jill's waist. "But it has its rewards. Nothing better than a long day of working the land and coming home to a good woman."

Clark rubbed his jaw. "And you can make a decent living at it?"

If the guy only knew. "Yeah, if you're willing to take a few odd jobs when times get hard."

Houston then noticed a tall blonde woman with a phone standing nearby, several other young women gathered around her, staring at the screen. He couldn't imagine what all the fuss was about, until the blonde and her girlfriends made their way toward him.

"Excuse me," she said. "Are you Houston Calloway?"

Damn. His first instinct involved denial, and his second involved backing out the door. He figured it was too late for either. "Yeah."

"I told you that was him," she said to one of her friends. She then held up the screen to proudly display an internet ad featuring him. The one that had just shown up on billboards throughout the country. The one where he was shirtless with a blue compression band around his bicep. Oh, hell.

Houston turned to discover Ben looking a little rattled and the happy couple looking more than a tad bit shocked.

And Hurricane Helen looked more than ready to blow as she faced her oldest daughter with a glare. "Jillian Elizabeth Amherst, why in heaven's name are you marrying a porn star?"

"I assure you, Dad, Houston is not a porn star."

Her father downed a shot of bourbon and patted her cheek. "I know that, ladybug. Are you really surprised your mother went there?"

Jill glanced from her seat at the bar to Helen, who was surrounded by a few of her favorite gossips, most likely doing damage control. "I guess I shouldn't be shocked. She has a way of making something as innocuous as an ad campaign into something lurid."

"That she does," he said. "And your young man might not be a porn star, but right now he looks like a rock star."

She followed her dad's gaze to Houston standing near the dance floor, a bevy of bridesmaids hanging on his every word. Unwelcome jealousy bit into her when she saw one petite blonde whispering something

in his ear. "Do you think they're asking him to auto-
graph their cell phones?"

"I think they're treading on your territory, ladybug.
I also think you should walk over there right now and
take it back."

Jill turned around and took a sip of wine, knowing full well she had no real claim on him. "He knows
where I am. When he's finished with the fawning, he'll
find me."

"Honey, he's your man, and you need to let him, and
all those women, know that. Ask him to dance."

Heavens, she hadn't danced since her senior cotil-
lion, and she wasn't sure she remembered how. "Houston doesn't seem like he cares to dance."

"He seems as if he'd like to be rescued. I've noticed
him looking over here several times."

Jill glanced Houston's way and received a smile
from him for the effort. "You're right, Dad. I'm going to
march over there and reclaim my *man*." And if Houston
took exception to the intrusion, too bad. He'd started the
phoney fiancé scheme and she intended to keep it going.

After drinking the last of the chardonnay, Jill slid off
the stool and hugged her father. She then strode across
the room as fast as her heels would let her and walked
right up to Houston. "Excuse me, honey, but I'm here
to honor your request for that dance."

His expression said *What dance?*

"Sure. Now?"

She hooked her arm through his. "Yes, now. It's a
lovely, romantic ballad. What better way to celebrate
our love?" She sent a pointed look at the blonde who
didn't seem pleased at the interruption. "So if you'll
excuse us, ladies, I'm going to steal my fiancé for the
rest of the evening."

As the women scattered, Houston led her onto the dance floor and regarded her again. "I'm more into country dancing, but I guess I can wing it."

"Just put your arms around me and move in time to the music. That's all there is to it."

But that wasn't all, she realized, when he pulled her close. As she rested her cheek against his chest, the warmth of his body, the hint of his clean-scent cologne, had a magical effect on her. The music continued to play, a slow, sultry romantic tune, Houston held her closer, pressed a kiss on her temple and for a moment Jill felt as if they were a real couple, falling in love.

Yet that was only a fantasy, and a farce. A show for the family's benefit, and it had done its job, Jill determined, when glanced to her left to see her mother and father looking on. Where Ben looked pleased, Helen looked skeptical. And not far away, she noticed Pamela and Clark dancing, too, only their affection seemed sincere. She predicted her sister would be pregnant in a matter of months, and that would make her Aunt Jill. An absentee aunt. Maybe the time had come to make amends with Pamela, or at least try. Question was, how did she erase all the years of resentment? How could she reconnect with a sibling she barely knew? Obstacles that she might not be able to overcome.

When Houston whispered, "Are you okay?" Jill realized she had tensed in his arms.

She relaxed a bit and met his worried gaze. "I'm fine. Just ready to get out of here."

"Looks like a lot of people already have."

When the song ended, Jill surveyed the room and realized the crowd had thinned quite a bit. "If we hurry, we might be able to claim a limo all to ourselves."

He brushed a kiss across her lips and grinned. "I'd be up for a little more limo foreplay."

"You're a bad, bad boy, Calloway."

"You're a damn sexy woman, Amherst. Now let's go before someone notices us leaving."

The minute Houston took Jill's hand and led her off the floor, she heard, "Ladybug, wait up."

Being the dutiful daughter, Jill faced her father with a smile. "We were just leaving, Dad."

"That's why I stopped you," he said. "Your mother insists on staying and conducting the postmortem on the event. In other words, discuss everyone ad nauseum with the bridge club. Personally, I want to go to bed, so do you mind if I accompany you?"

How could she say no? She sent Houston an apologetic look before saying, "Of course, Dad."

So much for canoodling in the car with her cowboy, but then again, they had all night to spend together.

Nine

Dressed in khaki shorts, gold sandals and a sleeveless coral blouse, Jill knocked on the pool house door and waited for Houston to answer the summons—if he hadn't already taken off for Texas.

A few seconds later, he opened the door wearing worn jeans and a T-shirt, no shoes and an unreadable expression. "Are you sure you want to be seen with a porn star?" he asked without a touch of amusement in his voice.

"Leave it to Helen to make that assumption," Jill muttered. "And I'm really sorry for any embarrassment she might have caused with her accusations."

"Not a problem. I've been called worse. Besides, I probably sold a few of those compression wraps in spite of the questionable PR."

At least his tone had lightened somewhat. "I think we've cleared everything up fairly well." Everything but the bogus engagement and presumed pregnancy.

"However, I won't be a bit surprised to see several smit-ten bridesmaids sporting those wraps at the wedding in honor of the shirtless internet cowboy in attendance."

"I hope not," he said. "Helen would have my hide for messing up the dress code."

Speaking of Helen… "Do you mind if I come in be-fore the troops come home and catch me sneaking out here to see you?"

He eyed the overnight bag in her hand. "Do you plan to stay awhile?"

A sudden bout of insecurity blanketed Jill, and she suddenly wondered if he'd changed his mind about the overnight due to the debacle. "Only if you'd like me to stay."

Finally, he smiled. A sexy, devious smile. "I can take you for a few hours, and you can take that any way you want."

The somewhat suggestive comment suddenly spurred Jill's confidence, and fantasies. "Sounds like a great way to spend the night."

"You bet it is."

The second Jill stepped inside, Houston reeled her into his arms and kissed her soundly but ended it all too soon. "I found a few beers in the fridge. Do you want something to drink?"

She had a sudden crazy craving. "Actually, I know what I want, but it's not a drink."

"Same here, but I thought we might wait a bit to make sure the family's all tucked into bed. Once I get started, I don't want any interruptions."

She set the bag on the nearby chair, stood on tiptoe and kissed his chin. "Actually, this has to do with dessert."

He winked. "Darlin', you can call it whatever you'd like."

"I'm referring to a literal dessert." She wrested herself from his grasp, strode to the fridge, opened the freezer and pulled out the treat before she faced him. "My mother's favorite, although she swears she doesn't eat them, hence hiding them away in the pool house."

"An ice cream pop?"

"Yes. Strawberries and cream, to be exact. It's the last one."

"Are you sure you want to take it then?"

"Of course. Why not?"

"Because you're gonna risk resurrecting the wrath of Helen if she finds a bare freezer."

"She can buy more, and frankly I'm in the mood to live a little dangerously."

"Has my risk taking rubbed off on you?"

"Not exactly, but the night is young, so we have plenty of time for rubbing." Without waiting for Houston's response, Jill crossed the room, sat on the couch and patted the spot beside her. "Come here and I'll share it with you."

Houston walked to the fridge to procure a beer. "I'll come there, but I don't need any ice cream." As soon as he dropped onto the sofa beside her, he said, "Now let's make a deal."

"What would that be?"

"We don't talk about what happened tonight."

"Are you referring to the unfortunate advertisement thing or the thing in the limo?"

"The advertisement thing, but I don't mind discussing the limo incident." He set the bottle down on the coffee table, rested his arm on the back of the sofa and laid his palm on her leg. "I figure we might want to re-enact that scene a little later, this time without clothes."

Holy Toledo, what an image. "I might be game for that."

He frowned. "Might be?"

"Your odds are good." After pulling the protective paper from the ice cream, Jill sucked the rocket-shaped pop into her mouth, and for some reason, Houston grimaced. "What's wrong?"

His golden-brown eyes seemed to turn a shade darker. "Do you want me to be honest?"

She took another quick lick. "Sure."

"I'm thinking it would be a whole lot easier on me if your mother's favorite dessert was a piece of cake, not a frozen ice bomb on a stick. Watching you putting your mouth on it is making me damn hot and real bothered."

Awareness dawned when her gaze came to rest on the obvious bulge below his waistband. "Oh, I see."

He shifted on the cushion. "I'm sure you probably do. It's kind of obvious."

"Just a little bit."

Feeling wild and somewhat wicked, Jill laid the ice cream on the wrapper resting on the table, then straddled Houston's lap. He sent her a grin that shamed the stars. "Lady, are you trying to drive me crazy?"

"Yes. Is it working?"

"I'm about as close to the edge as I can be without falling over the cliff."

She didn't intend to push him completely. She did plan to drive him further to the brink. But when she leaned forward to kiss him, he guided her hips and pressed her down against his groin, reclaiming the control she would gladly relinquish at the moment. Leaning back, he used his one good hand to work his T-shirt over his head and tossed it aside, giving her an up close view of the stellar chest that had held a large group of women captive earlier that evening. A panorama of muscle and taut skin and a thin stream of hair that disappeared into his jeans. Talk about happy trails.

"Your turn," he said. "Unless you're too shy."

She'd never considered herself to be that reserved, but she couldn't claim she wasn't a tad self-conscious. She also couldn't resist a good challenge.

With that in mind, she began unbuttoning the blouse, slowly, keeping her gaze trained on his eyes. Two more buttons and a bra stood between her and flesh-to-flesh contact.

She paused before releasing the placket completely. Was this really happening? Was she seriously about to finally end her self-imposed celibacy with one of the sexiest men in the country? Heck yeah, she was...

As long as the person rapping on the door would go away.

"Ignore it," Houston grumbled.

Jill made an effort to do that very thing, honestly she did, but the knocking didn't stop. In fact, it only grew louder.

When she climbed off Houston's lap and began re-doing the blouse, Houston groaned. As an afterthought, she grabbed a throw pillow from the club chair and tossed it at him. "You might want to cover your current predicament, in case my mother's on the threshold."

"Or I could just wait for you in the bedroom."

"Stay put. I'll get rid of her fast."

"And I'd buy tickets to that."

After a brief mental pep talk, she opened the door, not to her mother, but to her sister still wearing her pink cocktail dress and matching heels. And before Jill could utter a word, Pamela brushed past her and entered the pool house like a Texas Tornado. A regular chip off the old storm.

Pamela spun around and faced Jill, her back to the sofa where Houston still sat, shirtless, apparently unnoticed by the flustered sister. "I thought I'd find you here," she said. "You should have left me a note."

Since when did she have to answer to her sibling? She didn't bother to close the door in hopes that Pamela would take the hint. "If you're here to scold me, consider me scolded. I'm sure you're anxious to get to bed and get some rest before the big day, so have a great night."

"Actually, I came here to tell you I covered for you with Mother."

"Did she do a bed check?"

"No. She sent me upstairs to tell you she had something to discuss with you. When I found you gone, I told her you had a headache and you'd talk to her tomorrow."

"And I'm sure she asked if I was alone."

"Of course."

"Well, thanks, Pamela. Sleep well."

"That's not all."

Great. "All right. What else?"

"Are you going to be here all night?"

"That's the plan."

"Good, because I need the room all to myself."

Her sister's selfishness never ceased to amaze her. "I promise I will not grace your inner sanctum until tomorrow morning so that you have privacy to prepare for the nuptials."

"I need my privacy because Clark's here." Pamela moved to the still-open door and said, "It's okay. You can come in."

Lovely. A prewedding party in the pool house. Jill didn't recall sending out any invitations.

Clark stepped inside, hands in pockets, looking a little uncomfortable. "Hey, folks."

"Hey, Clark," Houston said from the sofa, his first words since the disruption. Fortunately he'd put on his shirt. "Anyone else out there in the yard?"

Clark grinned. "Not unless the hurricane saw me drive in."

"Hi, Houston," Pam said before she punched Clark's arm. "I told you to turn off the headlights."

He caught her hand and continued to hold it, either out of affection or self-preservation. "I did, but your mother has a built-in radar."

Jill simply wanted everyone to vacate the premises so she and Houston could continue their alone time. "Well, it's good to see you both, and rest assured I won't say a word about your sneaking the groom into your bedroom for some prehoneymoon playtime."

"Good, because you owe me one," Pam said.

"Excuse me?"

"Remember that time you and Millie sneaked out at midnight to go to Billy Haverkamp's house for a party?"

She did, though she'd prefer to forget it. "Yes. And your point?"

"I never told a soul about it, even the part where you came home drunk and threw up."

Jill ignored Houston's chuckling. "And I thanked you profusely before I found out you told Clark and he told his mother and his mother told ours."

"Sorry about that," Clark muttered. "I didn't know you were both going to be grounded almost the entire summer."

That fateful summer when she'd lost her best friend. Jill glanced at the clock hanging above the kitchenette. "If we're finished with the trip down memory lane, it's almost eleven o'clock, which means you only have an hour before you'll have to go your separate ways."

Pam looked perplexed. "Why?"

"It's bad luck for me to see the bride on the day of the wedding." Clark brought his attention to Jill. "Before we go, I need some advice."

"You might want to talk to me about that," Houston said.

Clark smiled as he wrapped his arm around Pamela. "It's about the wedding. We have a chair reserved in memory of Millie. Pam thinks we should put flowers there, but I believe it should be more personal. Do you have any ideas?"

Jill's emotions began to rise, putting a definite damper on the evening. Yet she did have a good suggestion that would do the memorial justice. "Do you still have her championship ribbons?"

Clark glanced at Pamela. "Yes. They're still hanging on a bulletin board in her room. Everything is still there. Mom didn't have the heart to change it."

Jill's heart did a nosedive. "Then I'd use those ribbons. They meant so much to Millie."

Clark surprisingly drew her into a hug. "Thanks, soon-to-be sister-in-law."

Clearly she had misjudged him. The jury was still out on her sister. "You're welcome. I know you miss her as much as I do."

Pamela sighed. "I miss her, too." She gave Jill a meaningful look. "I miss the you before Millie died. The you who used to help me with my homework and took me to riding lessons and watched movies with me. You changed so much after you lost Millie that I barely remember my big sister."

The truth in Pamela's words stung like a scorpion. "I didn't realize how much that affected you."

"It did," Pamela said. "But I just want that sister back now."

This time Jill made the first move and drew her into an embrace. "I'm sorry, Pam. We'll start over."

Pam moved back and sniffed. "We better. If we'd done this sooner, I wouldn't have had to ask Cousin Tisha to be in the wedding. I would have asked you instead. But most important, I want to spend time with my niece or nephew."

Jill started to set her straight on the pregnancy misunderstanding but decided to save it for another conversation, after the wedding. "I promise to stay in touch."

"We'll hold you to it," Clark said. "Right now we're going to leave you two alone to go back to doing whatever you were doing before we interrupted."

With the sudden change in the mood, Jill hoped that was possible.

After Clark and Pam said their goodbyes and left, she turned to Houston, who was standing next to the sofa. "That was interesting, to say the least."

"I'd say it was pretty enlightening. Come here."

Jill walked easily into his outstretched arms and they stood there for a time, her head on his strong shoulder, holding each other. Houston seemed to know what she needed, and she found that to be a wonderful and welcome surprise.

After a brief span of silence, Jill pulled back and stared into his eyes. "What now?"

"That's up to you. If you want to go to bed to get some sleep, I'm okay with that."

"I'm not," Jill blurted out. "I need to be with you."

"I need that, too, but only if you're really ready."

She did need the closeness, the intimacy. She needed him much more than she should. "I trust you can make me very ready."

His grin arrived, slow as warm maple syrup, and just as sweet. "Darlin', you can count on that."

Without warning, he swooped her up into his arms, causing Jill to panic. "You're going to injure your wrist again, Houston."

"Not if I'm careful, which I am." He nudged the bedroom door open. "You'll figure that out real soon."

After he deposited her onto the bed, he whipped off his T-shirt and his hand came to rest on the button securing his fly. "You still have time to back out."

She leaned back and supported her weight on bent elbows. "Never. Continue."

Jill held her breath as Houston lowered his zipper, and released it slowly when he shoved down his jeans and boxers. *Oh, wow. Oh, my.* He was extremely happy to see her.

After removing his pants completely, he threw them onto the adjacent bed and smiled. "Your turn. I'd help you, but with this bum hand, it'd take me all night just getting those buttons undone."

Now or never had arrived. She chose now. With one exception. "Okay, as soon as you shut off the light."

"No way."

"Yes, way."

"But I want to see you."

"There's enough light coming in through the window. I just don't want to feel like I'm in the spotlight the first time." Which sounded as if she planned to have a second time. Stranger things had happened, namely finding herself in a bedroom at her parents' home with a naked Houston Calloway. Who would've thought that? Not her.

Houston trudged back to the door and flipped the switch, but not before he gave her a good look at his remarkable butt. Good times.

With the room now washed in the slight glow from the guard light outside the window, Houston took a seat next to his discarded jeans and waited for the official undressing.

Jill scooted off the bed and stood on shaky legs. Her hands also shook when she unbuttoned the blouse, but she managed to get it off. She had little trouble removing her shorts. She sensed Houston's gaze as she reached behind her, unhooked the bra and slid it off. Only one barrier remained, and with only a mild hesitation, she hooked her thumbs in the lacy band and let the thong slide down her legs. After she kicked off her panties, she remained frozen on the spot, wondering and waiting for what would come next.

What seemed an interminable amount of time passed before Houston rose and took her hand. He then led her back to the too-small twin, threw back the covers and positioned them on the bed where they somehow managed to find enough space to lie side by side. "You're incredible," he said and then brushed his lips across her temple. "Incredible mind." He kissed her cheek. "Incredible conviction." He lowered his mouth to her throat. "Damn incredible body."

When he drew her breast into his mouth, Jill involuntarily lifted her hips from the sensations. She felt as if every nerve she owned came alive when he circled his tongue around her nipple, softly, slowly. After he paid equal attention to her other breast, he rose above her and kissed her with such tenderness. "It's not too late to stop, Jill."

She didn't care to stop. Ever. "I promise I'm still ready."

"Not quite, but you will be." He slid his hand slowly down her belly and kept going until he reached the apex of her thighs.

He used his fingertip like a feather, stroking her lightly, then more deliberately, until Jill felt as if she couldn't stay still. She closed her eyes, immersed in sensations much stronger than they had been in the limo. The orgasm hit her swift and sure and much, much too soon, yet Houston didn't let up until all her spasms subsided.

"You're plenty ready now," he whispered. "If you're sure you want to go through with this."

She'd never wanted anything more in her life. "I'm sure," she managed through her uneven breathing.

"Okay."

Houston left the bed and began to rifle through a bag on the floor. He came back and perched on the edge of the mattress. Jill heard what she gathered was the opening of a plastic packet and realized condom time had come. That led to a burning question. "Did you bring those along just in case?"

"I never assumed anything," he said. "But I'm always prepared."

Of course he would be. After all, she wasn't his first conquest. Probably not by a long shot.

Jill refused to let that hinder the prospect of being with him in every way. Of finally feeling like a normal, healthy, sexual being, though she recognized this first foray into lovemaking wouldn't be comfortable.

"I'm going to try not to hurt you too much, sweetheart," Houston said as he rolled the condom into place. "Just hold tight to me."

Exactly what she planned to do when he shifted on top of her. She gritted her teeth when he eased inside her, and clasped the sheet in her fist when he met her body's initial resistance. After a short thrust, he drew in a deep breath and stilled, giving her time to adjust to the pressure before he began to move easily, gently. "Damn, you feel good," he said in a harsh tone. "Too good to last long."

Jill could tell he was holding back, and she truly didn't want that. "I'm okay," she told him. "It's okay for you to let go. I can handle it."

Her words seemed to unearth something in Houston, a little bit of wildness and a whole lot of strength. She moved with him, the pain all but forgotten, as she ran her palms down the solid plane of his back and the pearls of his spine.

She kept going to his hips, relishing the play of his muscles until he tensed from his own climax. He muttered a few sexy oaths that would send Hurricane Helen into a tailspin, yet they enthralled Jill. When he rolled onto his back, he hit some part of his right arm on the wall and muttered a few more.

Houston then slid his arm beneath her shoulders and asked, "Are you okay, darlin'?"

"I should be asking if you're okay. Please tell me you didn't fracture your good arm."

"I'm fine. I just hit my funny bone, but it wasn't a damn bit funny."

"You actually tweaked your ulnar nerve, not a bone. It'll go away soon."

"Man, I just love medical pillow talk."

Jill couldn't help but laugh. "Sorry. Don't forget I'm a rookie."

He nuzzled her neck. "But you act like a pro."

"Yeah, right. I still have a lot to learn."

"I'm a good teacher."

Jill's defenses went on high alert. "I doubt we have enough time left this weekend for too many lessons."

"We still have tomorrow night."

Time to reveal what she'd decided earlier today. "Since the wedding's at four, if it's okay with you, I'd like to fly back to Texas tomorrow evening. That way I'll have all day Sunday to relax before I dive into work on Monday."

He remained quiet for a few moments before he spoke again. "Sure, if that's what you want. But I figure your family's going to be disappointed by your early departure."

"My dad, maybe, but not my mother."

"You need to work things out with her, Jill."

Where had that come from? "That's a lost cause, Houston."

"Only if you give up. Life is short and parents don't live forever. Believe me, you don't want things left unsaid, unless you don't mind dealing with a truckload of regrets."

Jill surmised he was speaking from personal experience. "Does this have to do with your father?"

"Yeah."

"Do you want to talk about it?"

"If I do, then you'll never see me in the same way again."

"Why don't you let me be the judge of that?"

He stayed silent for a few seconds, then sighed. "It's one helluva sorry story, and a damn heavy secret, but maybe it's time for me to tell someone. So here goes…"

Ten

He didn't know why he felt the need to tell her. He didn't know where to begin. In reality he did know— the day he'd dishonored his dad.

Houston scooted up against the headboard and waited a minute to corral his thoughts before he spoke. "My father called me one night and told me he was under the weather. He asked me to cancel my next event and come home to help out with the ranch. I told him that would mess up my points and I might not make it to the finals. I figured that would be the end of it."

"But it wasn't," Jill said from her place beside him.

"Not by a long shot. He told me I had my priorities screwed up, like he had any right to lecture me on priorities after what he did to my mom and Jen, although I didn't know about that at the time. Anyway, it's what I said to him before I hung up that's been eating away at me for seven years."

When he paused to take a breath, Jill touched his arm. "You don't have to continue tonight."

If he didn't, he might just keep it bottled up for the next thirty-one years. "No, I want to tell you everything."

She sat up and tipped her head against his shoulder. "I'm listening."

He hesitated a second before continuing. "He started lecturing me about responsibilities and how I needed to grow up and be a man, not a boy. Then he said, 'I love you, son, but I'm not getting any younger. I don't know how much time I have left.'" A direct quote that had been branded in his brain. "I was so pissed off I told him that with my luck, he'd live forever. He passed away two days later."

"Oh, Houston, I'm so sorry."

He sighed. "So am I. Sorry I said it. Sorry I can't take it back. No matter how many flaws he had, or that he spent a lot of time away from home, when we thought he was away on business, I still loved him. He taught all of us how to rope and ride and tend cattle. He came to our rodeos when he had time. He was stern, but fair, and he told us he was proud more times than I can count."

"I guess his downfall would have to be falling in love with two women."

"Three if you count Dallas and Austin's mom." He let go a cynical laugh. "I've never fallen in love with one woman." Until now.

The thought sent alarm bells sounding in Houston's mind. He might care for Jill, but love? Nah. He chalked up the foreign feelings to sex with a woman who'd never been with another man. A great woman who'd trusted him enough to give him what his mother would say was the ultimate gift.

He scooted back down in the bed, taking Jill with him. When he slid his arms beneath her shoulders, she shifted to her side and laid her head on his chest. "I hope you don't think any less of me," he said after a time.

"Of course not. You made a mistake and said things you didn't mean. I'm sure your father knew that."

If only he could believe that. "I did learn something. Life is damn short. It's always good to forgive your parents' sins and let them know you love them before it's too late."

Jill's silence told Houston she was taking the advice in. "You're right," she said. "Before I leave tomorrow, I'm going to try to mend my relationship with my mother."

"And tell her the truth about us?"

"Yes, though I'm not sure if she'll be relieved we're not a couple, or angry because I lied about it."

"Friends who enjoyed some mighty fine benefits."

"Oh, yeah. Mighty fine."

He kissed the top of her head. "I guess you'll just have to hope for the best, and prepare for Hurricane Helen to blow."

"Jillian Elizabeth Amherst, what do you mean you made all this up?"

Jill surveyed the area around the tent to see who had heard her mother's outburst. Fortunately the post-wedding champagne was flowing and everyone in attendance seemed more interested in that instead of their conversation. "I thought you'd be glad to know you're not going to be a grandmother."

Helen sent a quick glance at Houston, who stood off to the side a few yards away chatting up her husband, both out of the hurricane's immediate path. "And you're not engaged to him?"

"No. We're friends and colleagues. I'll be working on the ranch as their resident athletic trainer for a camp geared to aspiring cowboys."

"Yet you shacked up with him in the pool house all night."

So much for her sister covering for her. "What difference does it make? We're both adults."

"Clearly consenting adults, and there is no telling what you consented to."

Jill made an effort not to look too guilty. "I'm an adult, Mother. I don't need a nanny any longer."

"It appears you need a keeper, Jillian. Why did you lie to me in the first place?"

"Because I didn't want to come here and face a slew of prospective boyfriends lined up by you and your friends. Instead, I brought my own pretend beau."

"That is ridiculous. I've never lined up boyfriends for you."

"Never, Mother?"

Helen glanced away. "Perhaps once or twice. You rarely came home after you left for college."

She should have predicted that dig. So much for the healing process. "Anyway, I basically wanted to set the record straight and tell you we're about to fly back to Texas."

"Tonight?"

"Yes. I need to be back to prepare for work on Monday."

"You're going to miss the cake cutting and the bouquet tossing, not to mention the fireworks."

She'd witnessed enough fireworks for one weekend. "I'm sure I'll see all the photos."

"Are you going to say goodbye to your sister?"

"I already have." And they'd even hugged a lot and cried a little when they'd gathered by Millie's memorial chair covered in her riding ribbons and white roses.

"She made a beautiful bride and she's chosen a great groom."

Helen eyed her suspiciously. "You've never cared for Clark."

"You're right, back when he was Millie's bratty little brother. But he's changed for the better."

Helen wrung her hands and fretted for a few moments. "Well, have a good flight, although I hate the thought of your traveling in coach."

Boy, this was going to be fun. "I'm traveling in Houston's private plane."

Her mother's eyes went as wide as a balloon. "He makes that much money? He must be a very good male model."

At least that was better than the porn star assumption. "He's not a male model. He's a world champion bull rider and spokesperson for several sponsors. He's also a partner in an extremely successful ranching operation."

"Then he's rich?"

The enthusiasm in her mother's query was unmistakable. "You could say that."

"Why didn't you say so sooner? I would have welcomed him into our home with open arms."

Typical Helen. "Mother, I hope someday you'll realize it's not the size of a man's wallet that matters, it's the wealth in his soul. If Houston didn't have a penny to his name, he still has an abundance of honor. The woman who lands him is going to be one lucky girl."

Helen stared at her straight on. "You wish you were that woman."

The comment stunned Jill into momentary silence. "I never said that."

"You don't have to. I can see it in your eyes and hear it in your voice. You're falling in love with him, if you haven't already."

She couldn't quite wrap her mind around her mother's theory. "As I've said, we're only friends."

Helen hooked her arm through Jill's and led her farther away from Houston before facing her again. "I know his kind, Jill. He's a very handsome and charming young man, just like your father was at that age. Of course, Benjamin wasn't quite as rugged. Nevertheless, if you're not careful, you could find yourself in the same predicament I was at your age. Actually I was much younger then."

"What predicament?"

"Pregnant out of wedlock."

If the grassy lawn opened up and consumed her, Jill couldn't be more shocked. "I thought you and Daddy were married ten months before I was born."

"That's what we told everyone to save face. In truth, we eloped a month after I found out I was expecting you."

Now her mother's attitude had begun to make perfect sense. "And that's why you scared the bejeezus out of me when it came to premarital sex. I thought you had an aversion to it."

Helen shook her head. "Not in the least. Why, even now, your father and I—"

"Let's not go there, Mother."

"All right."

Jill did have a serious question that needed to be

asked. "Is that also why you resented me for most of my life?"

Helen looked sincerely taken aback. "I've never resented you, Jillian. I might have been ill-prepared to be a mother at twenty-two, but the moment I held you that first time, I knew that I could never love another soul as much as I loved you, aside from your father and your sister."

More stunning revelations. "It always seemed Pamela was your favorite."

Helen waved a hand, her trademark dismissive gesture. "Oh, pooh. Pamela was an easier child. You were more challenging. You climbed trees in your Sunday best and argued at the drop of a hat. But I've always loved you, even when you've disappointed me."

Well, she couldn't expect her mother's attitude to change overnight, but at least this verbal exchange was a start to understanding her motives. "You're referring to my career choice."

"Yes, I suppose I am, but you're obviously successful at it, although I don't fully understand how you get any satisfaction out of treating injuries. I'm proud of you and I still love you as much as I did on the first day we met."

The words that Jill had longed to hear for years. "Thank you, Mother, and I love you, too, even when I don't understand your need to judge people, and when you've harassed me about copulation."

Helen frowned. "I may not be perfect, Jillian, but I will always be your mother."

"Yes, and we still have a long way to go to mend our relationship."

"I'm willing if you are."

She was, too, more willing than she'd ever been. "I am, but right now I have to go back to work."

They shared a somewhat awkward hug before walking side by side as they approached Houston. "You take care with my daughter, Mr. Calloway. And if you're going to be associated with this family, I'd prefer that you don't pose half-naked again. It's going to take months to explain why my daughter's fiancé, *presumed* fiancé, would do such a thing."

Typical Helen, Jill thought, yet Houston responded with a winning grin. "You bet, Mrs. Amherst."

"Please, you may call me Helen," she said. "As long as you don't precede it with *Hurricane*."

"It's a deal, Helen without the hurricane." He regarded Jill then. "Winston put the bags in the car and the plane's ready when you are."

"I'm ready."

After giving her mother another fast hug and her dad a lengthy embrace, she crossed the lawn with Houston, walked back through the house and entered the Bentley for the ride to the airport.

"How'd that conversation with your mom go?" Houston asked after they'd settled into the sedan.

"Better than expected," she answered. "I did learn an interesting tidbit."

"She doesn't despise me any longer now that she knows I didn't put a bun in your oven?"

"Yes, and she's thrilled to learn you have a bank account, but that's not what I was referring to. I found out my father put a bun in her oven before they married. That bun is me."

Houston laughed. "Old Ben. Didn't know he had it in him."

"Apparently he did and still does, although I halted that topic with my mother before she scarred me for life. All in all, it went fairly well, although realistically we still have miles before we get back on track. She even told me she loved me for the first time in a long time."

Houston went strangely silent. "Did you say it back?"

After their conversation last night, she knew exactly why that seemed so important to him. "Yes, I did, and I told my sister and my father and even Clark, so all is right with the Amherst family for the time being."

He slid her hand into his and gave it a little squeeze, yet he failed to look at her. "I'm real glad for you, Jill."

They stayed that way until they reached the airport, holding hands and immersed in comfortable quiet. But Houston's continued silence during and after takeoff bothered Jill a bit.

"What's on your mind, Calloway?" she asked after she grabbed a soda from the fridge and reclaimed her seat.

"Nothing much. I was just thinking I kind of hate that the weekend's coming to an end."

"Technically not until tomorrow."

He locked his gaze on hers. "I meant our weekend together. I've had a damn good time."

She smiled. "So did I. That was one unforgettable night."

"In a good way, I hope."

"A very good way."

"Are you feeling any ill effects?"

"I was a little uncomfortable this morning, but I'm fine now."

His devilish grin came out of hiding. "It's always better the second time around."

He'd gone from sullen to sexy in five seconds flat. "Are you trying to compromise me, Calloway?"

"That depends, Amherst. Do you want to be compromised?"

She decided to leave him in suspense. "I'll let you know when we land."

"I don't want to wait to compromise you. We've got three hours to kill, a bed in the back and no one around."

Jill resisted the urge to climb out of the chair and tackle him. "Sounds interesting."

"Interesting enough to take me up on the offer?"

She didn't have to think twice. "I could use some benefits to go along with our friendship." A friendship that had taken a remarkable turn.

"You've come to the right cowboy for that."

How well she knew that.

Houston pulled her to her feet and led her into the back of the plane, where he opened a sliding door to compact sleeping quarters. The double bed, covered in navy and beige, practically took up the entire space with very little room on the sides. Obviously Houston was more than aware of that issue, Jill realized, when he sat her down on the end of the mattress.

"I like this dress," he said as he unhooked the back of the collar, allowing the blue halter bodice to fall to her waist. "No bra, huh? I really like it now."

Jill liked the way he made her feel when he finessed her breasts with his talented mouth. She liked the way he streamed his hands up her thighs. She seriously liked the sensual words he whispered in her ears as he reached beneath her skirt and slid her panties away.

And when he went to his knees and feathered kisses on the inside of her thighs, she grew excited with anticipation, and became slightly nervous. "Where are you going, Calloway?"

He lifted his head and grinned. "Where I assume no man has gone before."

"You would be correct."

His smile dropped out of sight, replaced by a concerned expression. "Do you trust me?"

"Yes, I do." And she did…enough to let him continue.

"Are you sure?"

"Very."

"Good. Now just relax and enjoy it."

Enjoy it, yes. Relax, no way. Not when he worked the dress up, parted her legs and his mouth hit the mark. This ultimate intimacy drove all thoughts from her mind. She tuned in to every nuance, every sensation until her body's natural course took over. The orgasm hit swift and sure and didn't last long enough for Jill.

As if Houston agreed, he didn't let up with the soft, steady strokes of his tongue and amazingly drew out another climax, leaving her trembling and struggling for breath. Wrestling with the fact she'd never felt this way before.

Jill fell back on the bed and closed her eyes, absolutely amazed that she had done that twice. Correction. Houston had helped her do it twice. She shouldn't be so surprised. Everything he endeavored to do, he did it well.

She opened her eyes to see him standing at the bed, shirtless, removing his jeans. She shimmied out of her dress and when they were both naked, he joined her on the bed, condom in hand.

He rolled to face her and smiled. "How do you feel?"

She touched his shadowed jaw. "Like I just had a double scoop of chocolate chip ice cream while on a cruise to the Caribbean."

"That good, huh?"

"That good."

"Are you ready to keep cruising?"

"I sure am." Feeling bold, she snatched the packet

from his grip, tore it open and removed the condom. "FYI, this is also a first for me, so be patient."

He looked somewhat wary. "No offense, but this isn't a good time to practice. If you put even a little nick in it—"

"Look, Houston, I put on gloves all the time without any issues. I can handle this."

"Yeah, but—"

"Do you trust me?" she asked as she nudged him onto his back and ran a fingertip down the length of him.

He groaned. "I guess I don't have any choice if you keep doing that."

"Then just stop worrying and enjoy."

She did a bit more playing and he did a bit more groaning before she finally had the condom in place, although it hadn't been quite as easy as she'd presumed it would be. Now that she appeared to be in control for a change, she straddled his legs and guided him inside her.

"You're just full of surprises, aren't you, darlin'?"

"Yes, I am," she said proudly. "And just because I'm a novice doesn't mean I'm not a quick learner."

She demonstrated that by moving slowly, all the while watching the change in his eyes and expression. Drunk on the power of seduction, she moved faster and noticed his respiration increasing.

Seeing the moment he reached his own climax was a true wonder to behold. Knowing she'd been responsible for it made her want to strut around the plane. Instead, she rested her cheek against his chest and listened to his heartbeat return to normal.

Jill stayed that way for a time before shifting onto

her back beside him. "You are in so much trouble," she said in a teasing tone.

"Why is that?"

"I'm starting to really like this."

He released a low laugh. "I've created a sex monster?"

"I wouldn't go that far, but I realize now what I've been missing." Making love with a skilled, careful man.

He rolled her into his arms, held her tightly. "If someone had told me a month ago that I'd have you in my bed, I would've said they were crazy."

Her heart sank. "I didn't know I repulsed you that much."

He pressed a kiss on her forehead. "Exactly the opposite. I used to find excuses to see you when I was on the circuit."

"Come on, Houston. You weren't injured that often."

"True, so didn't you think it was kind of strange when I used to show up in the tent with my friends and fellow bull riders and I didn't have a scratch on me?"

In hindsight, he had. Often. "I assumed you wanted to give me a hard time."

"I assumed that, too, but I didn't want to admit to myself, or anyone else, that I was damn attracted to you."

"You had a weird way of showing that."

"Not anymore." He topped off the comment with a light kiss between her breasts, putting her senses once more on high alert.

She rose above him and kissed his chin. "We still have a good two hours left, so did you bring any more of those condoms?"

"Unfortunately, no. But I've got plenty at my house, and a king-size bed. We could actually have some space for a change, although we don't really need much."

Jill needed to keep her head on straight. "That would break our rule about no fooling around on the ranch."

He touched her face gently. "Stay with me just one more night."

Logic told her to say no, but her illogical heart urged her to shout yes. "Okay. One more night. But after that, we go back to the way it was before this weekend. You harass me—I scold you."

His smile arrived, but only halfway. "If that's the way you want it, then that's the way it will be."

The disappointment in his tone surprised Jill. Did he want something more? A real relationship with potential for a future?

Wishful thinking, of course. Houston Calloway was a risk chaser who wouldn't welcome anything permanent at this point in time. In a matter of weeks, he would be gone again, immersed in the thrill of the rodeo, and all she would have would be the memories of a wonderful, wild weekend with a charming cowboy.

After he climbed off the mechanical bull, Houston realized he hadn't felt this satisfied since…well…last night with Jill in his bed. The vow they'd made to return to only friendship had gone up in smoke several times since they'd gotten back to the ranch. He chalked it up to uncontrolled lust, and he figured that need for each other would probably run its course.

But not soon, he decided, when he saw Jill standing in the opening of the enclosed training arena, her silky auburn hair piled atop her pretty head in a sexy ponytail. She wore a blue-and-white plaid shirt rolled up at the sleeves, a pair of great-fitting jeans and the brown boots he'd bought her two days ago as a surprise. She also sported a look that said she didn't exactly appreciate finding him on a moving animal, even if it happened to be a bad imitation of the real thing.

Houston strode toward Jill, intent on kissing that sour look off her face, regardless of the ranch hands milling around the area. He nixed that plan when she folded her arms across her middle and glared.

"Did you have fun with that?" she asked, not even bothering to hide her anger.

He shrugged. "Not really. The damn thing was going so slow even Chance could have ridden it."

"And that would have been wonderful with his cracked collarbone."

Damn, he couldn't win for losing. "Do you want to try it?"

"No, I do not."

She spun around and headed toward the clinic at a quick clip, keeping her back to him.

After he caught up to her, Houston clasped her arm and turned her around. "Don't get your feathers ruffled, Jill. I was just testing it out. No harm done."

"Maybe not now, but what about later, when you get back on a real bull?"

"I'm still a few weeks away from that."

"If you don't permanently injure yourself before then."

"I'm being careful."

"All signs point to the opposite."

He sensed something else might be behind her irritability. "What's really going on here, Jill?"

"Nothing, aside from the fact that I worry about you."

He winked. "Aw, darlin', what a sweet thing to say."

She rolled her eyes. "Of course I care. I don't want

you damaging your wrist more than you already have. Dallas made me promise I'd keep you out of trouble."

He wrapped his good arm around her waist and reeled her in close. "You shouldn't make promises you can't keep, although last night you definitely kept one promise I'm not going to forget for a long, long time."

Jill surveyed the area and frowned again. "Hush. Do you want everyone knowing our business?"

"Who cares?"

"I do. Now unhand me, you cad, so I can get back to work."

He brushed a kiss across her mouth before handing her a suggestion he'd been thinking about all morning. "I have a better idea. You should take a ride."

"Houston, seriously, I don't have time for afternoon delight."

Man, that conjured up a lot of great fantasies. Time to return to the original plan. "I meant a ride on a horse."

Now she looked alarmed. "I told you it's been too long."

"Yep, you're right. Way too long, and that's why you just need to do it."

Before Jill could protest further, Houston took her hand and led her toward the barn. She stayed silent while he led Gabby out of the stall and began to tack up the mare. "You'll have to ride Western," he said and he set the saddle on her back. "Hope that works."

"I haven't agreed to ride yet."

He fitted the bit in Gabby's mouth and adjusted the headstall. "You're dying to do it, so don't even bother arguing."

"You think you know me so well."

Better than he ever believed he would know her. "I know you need to prove to yourself that you can do it."

He turned to find her staring off into space. "I don't need to prove anything."

Time to bring out the big guns, in spite of the risk. "If Millie were here, what would she say to you?"

Her gaze snapped to his. "That's not fair."

Probably not, and he didn't want to cause her pain. He just wanted to move her into the present and out of the past. "Answer the question, Jill."

Her expression turned from anger to resignation. "She'd call me a wimp and tell me get on the damn horse."

Houston realized that might be the first time he'd heard a curse word coming out of her mouth. "Good advice. Just a couple of turns in the round pen. If you're not comfortable, you can get off and call it a day."

"Okay," she said as she took the reins from him. "But only for a few minutes."

Houston trailed behind Jill as she led the mare out of the barn and into the nearby pen. She stopped in the center of the circle to tighten the girth strap and adjust the stirrups, then hesitated with her hand on the saddle horn.

"Need some help climbing on?" Houston asked from his position near the gate.

She sent him a frustrated look over one shoulder. "No, I don't."

Jill mounted the horse with ease, proving her point, then cued Gabby into a walk. She made two rounds and Houston figured that would be it. Then she surprised him when she began to trot, bouncing up and down in the seat like a practiced English rider. He couldn't deny his surprise over how at home she looked on a horse. He also couldn't ignore the pleasure in her face as she kept going.

After a time, Houston decided a little encouragement was in order. "You should try a lope."

"No," she said. "But I will try a canter."

No sooner than she'd said it, she did it, as easy as you please.

Houston stood there and watched with pride as she rounded the ring again and again. He couldn't believe she'd agreed to this. He couldn't believe how thrilled she looked. He really couldn't understand why her happiness seemed to matter so much to him, but it did. *She* mattered to him, more than he cared to admit.

Maybe he just liked the fact she'd overcome some fairly sorry memories from her past. Maybe he wished at some point in time he could do the same, but that didn't seem all that likely.

A few minutes later, Jill dismounted and guided Gabby toward Houston, a bright smile on her face. "That was great."

So was the excitement Houston saw in her green eyes. "You're a natural, Jill."

She patted the mare's neck. "She's a natural. I'm just a passenger."

"Don't think for a minute she believes that. Neither do I."

She gave him a meaningful look. "Thank you, Houston. I'm not sure I would have ever gotten back on a horse if not for you."

He considered that one high compliment. "I didn't do anything aside from providing a vehicle. And you can ride her all you want while I'm gone."

Her frown reappeared. "Where are you going?"

Somewhere he didn't care to go, but business called. "I have to head out tomorrow to Los Angeles for a photo shoot."

"With your clothes on, I hope."

"I don't fly naked unless you're with me."

She laughed. "I meant naked photos."

"Nope. I'll be fully clothed in cowboy garb."

"Good to know. Now I need to get her unsaddled and get back to work."

He grabbed the reins from her and realized he didn't want to leave her now, or at all, truth be known. But he had no choice. He did have one thing he could control, if she was willing. "I'll take care of Gabby, on one condition."

"You and your conditions. What now?"

"Stay with me tonight, sweetheart. Your place, my place, it doesn't matter. I'm going to be gone for a while, and I'd like a good send-off."

For a second she looked torn before she smiled again. "All right, I suppose." She pointed at him. "But this has to be the last time, Houston, otherwise someone will find out, namely Dallas, and I'll lose my job."

He refused to let his brother interfere in his personal life. "Don't worry about Dallas. I can handle him." He brushed a wayward lock of hair away from her cheek. "Let's just concentrate on having one last wild night and making some mighty fine memories."

Jill stared at the reminder of her continued careless behavior for a good five minutes. She'd taken a huge chance on being carefree, and now she would pay for it. Maybe she'd been attacked by the cruel hand of karma, a self-fulfilling prophecy for allowing her family to believe she was pregnant. And now she was.

When the doorbell sounded, she immediately tossed the plastic stick into the bathroom's trash bin in a blind panic, ill-prepared to face the father of her unborn child.

She drew in a deep breath and attempted to calm down. After all, Houston had been gone for the past week, and she didn't expect him to return for another two days. But what if he'd cut the trip short?

If that happened to be the case, she didn't have to say anything yet, not until she figured out exactly what she would say.

When the bell sounded again, Jill walked slowly to the entry and peeked through the peephole. Her shoulders sagged with relief when she discovered Georgie, not Houston, standing on the porch.

She tried on a casual expression and opened the door. "Hey there. What a great surprise."

Georgie looked confused. "You asked me to stop by for coffee at nine. And it's two minutes after."

Darn if she hadn't done that very thing. "I'm so sorry. I've been distracted lately with all the staff issues and stocking supplies." And baby surprises.

"No problem. We can postpone until tomorrow."

Jill gestured her inside. "No way. I need some company." Badly. "Come in."

"Gladly," Georgie said. "I could use some girl talk."

That, Jill could absolutely provide, if she decided to reveal what she'd learned only minutes before. But wasn't that why she'd invited Georgie over in the first place, when she'd only suspected the pregnancy? She seriously needed some counsel from a woman who would know exactly how she felt at the moment.

After Georgie entered the apartment, Jill showed her to the kitchen dinette and put the coffee on to brew. "I hope you don't mind decaf."

"Decaf's fine. I've already had two cups of the real stuff, and no sugar, just cream."

Jill poured them each a cup, set the mugs on the table

and took the seat across from Georgie. She decided to begin with small talk. "How are the boys?"

"Austin's great and Chance is growing like a weed. But you would know that since you had dinner with us last night, so what's really up with you?"

Her uneasiness came out on a sigh. "It's about Houston."

Georgie's brown eyes lit up and she grinned. "I knew it! Paris and I both thought you two would hook up."

"It happened the weekend we went to Florida." And again two days later at her apartment, and once more at Houston's house, the night before he'd left for California, all details she preferred to omit.

"Austin said he saw you sneaking out of Houston's place one morning not too long ago."

So much for being discreet. "All right, we've been together a few times since, even though we swore we wouldn't do that when we came back to the ranch."

"Sometimes you don't have control over that powerful pull, Jill. It was always that way between me and Austin, even after we'd been apart six years."

"But you and Austin were in love."

"That's true, which leads me to an important question." Georgie's expression turned suddenly serious. "How do you feel about Houston?"

Good question. "Well, when I met him, I thought he was arrogant and reckless, and oh, boy, did he know exactly how to ruffle my feathers. But when we were in Florida, I saw another side to him altogether. He stepped right into the role of pretend boyfriend without missing a beat. And honestly, he's the first person who's taken on my mother, not at all an easy feat, but he did it without being snide." She looked away and smiled with remembrance. "He has this wicked sense of humor, and he's definitely a great listener. He even held me when I cried after I told him about losing my best friend years ago. I've told him things I've never told anyone."

"It sounds to me like you've completely fallen for him."

Jill's gaze snapped to Georgie. "We're becoming good friends. That's all."

Georgie sipped her coffee and sent Jill a cynical look. "Are you sure that's all?"

"I don't know." And Jill truly didn't, or maybe deep down she did. "I do know we have one huge complication hanging over us now."

"Houston's career?"

"Okay, two complications. He's determined to keep riding bulls until he has some kind of record for championships. I'm almost positive he has no intention of settling down."

"How do you know that for sure unless you ask?"

She might be forced to ask him when she told him about the baby. Or at least if he wanted to be involved in their child's life. Somehow she knew he would, even if their relationship never amounted to more than friendship. But what if it did become more? What if Houston wanted a life partner and a family? What if he wanted her to be a permanent part of that family?

"You mentioned two complications," Georgie said, dragging Jill back into reality. "What's the second one?"

Jill prepared to blurt out the truth and deal with the possible fallout. "I'm pregnant."

Georgie's brown eyes went wide with surprise. "Oh, my gosh. When did you find out?"

"Right before you got here. I asked you to come over so you could be here for the verdict, but I couldn't wait.

After what you and Austin went through, I felt like you would understand."

Georgie reached over and touched Jill's hand. "I do understand. I still remember that morning I found out I was pregnant with Chance. I also remember trying to reach Austin much later, only to learn he'd married someone else and then stupidly deciding not to tell him because I didn't want to rock the boat."

"You thought you were doing the best thing at that time."

"It was a stupid mistake. I didn't give Austin the opportunity to know his child for six years, and I've always regretted it. But that's where you and I can differ, Jill. You have no reason to wait to tell Houston."

The thought of his reaction only increased her anxiety. "I have no idea how to tell him. I mean, we used protection every time, and I can't even fathom how it happened." Although she suspected her lack of experience with condom application might be the culprit.

"It doesn't matter how," Georgie said. "It's done. Now you and Houston have to decide what to do about it."

Jill rubbed her palms over her face in an effort to erase visions of his possible reaction. "I'm afraid he's going to be furious."

"He might be mad for a time, but he'll be reasonable."

"I can't ask him to give up his career, but I can't stand the thought of him seriously injured, or worse. The prospect of losing him breaks my heart."

"That's because you're in love with him."

Jill wanted so badly to deny it, but she'd reached the point where she couldn't. "I guess you're right."

Georgie smiled. "I know I'm right."

"But how could it happen so quickly?"

"How long have you known him?"

"Two years, but—"

"And in that two years, did you ever feel excited when you saw him?"

In hindsight, she probably had, but professionalism had tamped those feelings down. "Possibly, but we spent most of that time arguing over his stubbornness."

"Let's face it. Adversity can sometimes breed passion, and you find yourself loving the very thing you thought you despised."

"I never despised Houston. I did hold him in low esteem a few times."

They engaged in a light moment with a bout of laughter before the atmosphere turned serious again. "Would you like some advice?" Georgie asked.

"I'm open to any you can give me."

"Don't wait too long to tell Houston."

"Where the hell have you been? I haven't seen you since I've been back."

When Jill spun around, Houston noticed she looked pale and tired. "Do you have to sneak up on me like that?"

"I didn't sneak up on you. I walked through the door. Now answer the question, Jill."

She eyed the cut over his eyebrow. "First, you answer a question. What happened to your head?"

He should've expected that. "A cow got caught up in the fence and I got head-butted by the heifer."

"You didn't fall off a bull?"

"Hell, no."

As predicted, she strode up to him and examined the bump. "Are you seeing double?"

He only saw the concern in her green eyes. He only knew how much he'd missed them, and her. "It's fine, dammit. I'm fine."

Jill walked to the counter and withdrew a packet, reminding Houston of the last time they were together at the rodeo. She came back to him and dabbed at the cut. "When is this crazy risk taking going to end, Houston? When are you going to realize people care about you and don't want to see you hurt?"

As bad as he'd wanted to see her, now she'd just made him mad. "I'm a rancher, Jill. Ranchers have to take risks now and then to save the livestock. It's all a part of the life. And I can tell you right now I've dealt with cattle catastrophes hundreds of times without getting hurt. Just like I've climbed on the back of bulls hundreds of times and didn't get a scratch."

"You're too reckless, Houston, and sometimes I believe it's not going to end before you seriously injure yourself, or worse." She threw the damp antiseptic pad into the trash with a vengeance. "I guess you really don't care, do you?"

He damn sure didn't care for her attitude. "You didn't answer my question. Why have you been avoiding me?"

She crossed the room and began stacking a few boxes into a cabinet before facing him again. "As you can see, I've been very busy in here. I've started making calls to line up a contracted staff. If you want to be up and running by January, I have to get everything organized."

He wasn't buying her excuses. "It's still September. That leaves you a good three months."

"You're not counting the holidays."

"You're not being honest. Something's bugging you and I figure it has to do with me."

"Your penchant for being hardheaded is bugging me, and I'm sorry you think I've been intentionally avoiding you, but as I've said, I've been busy."

"Too busy to come to dinner with the family last night?"

"Yes."

When she looked away, Houston could tell she wasn't being completely honest. "I find that kind of strange when, to hear Dallas tell it, it's been a routine with you since I've been gone. And now that I'm back, you've suddenly broken that routine."

"Houston, I can't…"

"Can't what?"

She sighed. "I can't be around you right now. Not without risking falling back into bed with you."

Finally, the truth. She'd been all he'd thought about, too, but it wasn't solely about sex. "So what if that happened? It's damn good between us, Jill. Why don't we just see where it goes?"

"I know exactly where it would go. We'd fool around now and then, and when your cast comes off, you'll go back on the road and I'll be left here with nothing but busy work and a broken heart and something even more important."

That threw his mind off-kilter. "You can't get your heart broken if we keep it casual."

She lowered her eyes and studied the floor. "It's gone beyond that. At least it has for me."

"I'm not following you, Jill."

"Are you really that obtuse? I have feelings for you. Strong feelings, and it's not because we had sex, although that was pretty great. I see in you a strong, kind, honorable man who isn't even close to being ready to settle down."

Before he'd met her, he might have agreed. "People can change when the time is right."

"When will the time be right for you, Houston? When will you ever stop running away from your guilt over your father while chasing the high you get from riding bulls? A high that could get you killed?"

"It's who I am, Jill."

"It's what you do, not who you are. You have an opportunity here to put your talent to good use, although I'll never quite understand the lure of climbing on a raging animal and hanging on. But you could be here full-time to mentor those wannabe cowboy while spending quality time with your family."

The conversation was getting way too heavy, and making him way too uncomfortable. "I'd never ask you to give up your job."

"Normally I probably wouldn't ask you to do it, either. Under different circumstances."

"What's different about our circumstances?"

"First of all, as I've said, I really care about you. Second, we're about to take on a huge responsibility, or at least I am. Whether you'll be willing remains to be seen."

"I'm just not ready to hang around here all the time. Not when I have the chance to get one more championship next year."

"I wasn't referring to that responsibility."

"Okay. Stop talking in circles and tell me what the hell you're talking about."

"I'm talking about an error we inadvertently made. My mother's prophecy, I suppose you could say."

Her words had done little to clear up the confusion. "Prophecy?"

"If you have premarital sex, you'll get pregnant."

Oh, hell. "What are you saying, Jill?"

"I'm going to have a baby."

He felt like his head might explode. "You're telling me that you got pregnant when we used protection every damn time?" Protection that he'd worried had failed the first time, thanks to his haste. Or the second time, thanks to her inexperience.

"Yes, that's what I'm telling you."

The impact of the declaration caused him to pace around the room before he turned to her again. "You're sure it's mine?" And that had to be the stupidest question to ever leave his mouth.

Jill obviously thought so, too, he determined, when she folded her arms across her middle and glared at him. "Come to think of it, maybe it was that groomsman I accosted underneath the banquet table at the wedding. Of course it's yours, and it really hurts that you would assume otherwise."

"I'm sorry," he muttered. "I'm just so damned shocked. How long have you known?"

"I suspected it about a week ago. I confirmed it with three positive pregnancy tests."

The timeline royally pissed him off. "You should've told me the minute I came back to the ranch."

"I had to think, Houston. I had to weigh all my options before we discussed it, and I've decided I want to raise this baby, with or without you."

His anger didn't come close to going away. "I'd never abandon my child, dammit. And I sure as hell don't want you running off with it. Austin didn't know he had a son for six years and I know what it did to him when he found out he'd missed all the milestones."

"Apparently everything worked out because they seem to be very happy."

"It almost didn't happen because she didn't tell him they had a kid until years after the fact."

"But I'm not deceiving you, Houston. I'm telling you now so you can decide how you want to handle this situation."

He didn't know crap because he could barely think. "You can't just lay this on me and expect me to come up with a coherent plan."

"I don't expect that at all. Right now I want you to go away and think about being a father and what that entails. You have to decide what's more important, continuing to risk your life or raising a child."

"But I—"

"Take all the time you need, Houston, and come back to see me when we can have a logical conversation."

He planned to do that very thing, but first he had to seek out the one person who could make some sense out of this. Not one of his brothers because they would only chastise him.

"I'll talk to you later," he said as he tore out of the building to head for the main house to find his mother.

A few minutes later, he discovered her sitting in the rocker on the front porch wearing her trademark flannel shirt, jeans and braid, a glass of sweet tea in her hand. He sat in the glider across from her and sighed. "Mom, I've got one big problem."

"I can see that, *mijo*. What's troubling you?"

He surveyed the immediate area, worried they might not be alone for long. "Where's Jen?"

"In San Antonio shopping. She won't be back for hours."

"Good. I don't need an audience when I say what I have to say."

"And I need to put the pot roast in the oven soon, so just say it."

"Jill's pregnant with my baby."

He expected his mom to be furious, but she just sat there, cool as a cucumber. "Your brother is going to tan your hide, Houston."

"I don't give a damn about Dallas. I only care about what I need to do."

She leaned forward and glared at him. "You need to man up and do the right thing. You need to accept that you're going to be a papa."

"What if I suck at it?"

"You might for a while, but you'll learn to be a parent, just like every parent that has gone before you, including me. My question is, how do you feel about the baby's mother?"

"I care a helluva lot about her. Not that she doesn't piss me off now and then. But damn, she's smart. And she's beautiful, inside and out. She doesn't take any BS from me, and when I'm not with her, I miss her like crazy. But she deserves someone whose life doesn't revolve around the freaking rodeo. She deserves better than me."

Maria leaned over and touched his face. "*Mijo*, in my opinion, there is no man better for her."

"You're biased."

"Yes, but not so biased that I don't see in you a man who only wants to love and be loved. I see a man who is nothing like his papa when it comes to the way he treats women."

He managed a smile. "You taught me that."

"And I taught you well. Not that I believe you haven't slipped up a time or two and broken a few hearts along the way. But this time, you must treat Jill's heart with care. She's a good woman, and she loves you."

"Why would you think that?"

"Because while you were away, and she was with us, you were all she talked about. Dallas noticed it immediately, and so did the rest of the family. He hasn't been happy about it, but the girls are thrilled. They consider Jill a part of this family, and so should you."

Houston leaned forward and studied the porch slats. "We haven't known each other for that long."

"Some would say two years is long enough."

"I meant really known each other. I don't want to let her down."

"If you love her, you won't. But if you don't have those feelings for her, then—"

"I do love her." There, he'd said it, and the earth hadn't opened up and sucked him into some dark abyss.

"There's your answer, my sweet boy."

"I'll have to give up the rodeo, Mom."

"I know, but think of what you'll be gaining."

The thought was damn daunting. He'd have a kid, and maybe even a wife. He'd be facing two o'clock feedings and college funds. First steps and first cars and, damn, first dates. And what if he had a girl? Oh, hell.

But he'd be waking up with Jill, and going to bed with her every night. He'd be sharing both good times and bad. He'd finally have someone who really loved him. Someone he could love back without any reservations.

That alone drove him to the decision he was bound to make. Now he just had to find the right time to tell her.

Jill didn't know when she'd see Houston again. Maybe in a few days. Maybe never if he headed for the hills. But less than three hours after she'd told him about their baby, she heard a series of forceful knocks.

She'd barely opened the door before Houston rushed in, tossed his tan cowboy hat onto the end table and dropped down on the sofa. "Okay, I'm ready to talk."

Considering his stern expression, Jill couldn't exactly claim she was prepared for what he had to say. But the sooner she got this over with, the better.

On that thought, she chose to sit in the small blue club chair across from him and folded her hands in her lap. "All right. I'm ready."

He hopped off the couch like a jackrabbit, as if he had too much energy to stay seated. "First of all, I'm damn sure not ready to be a dad."

Her heart sank like an anchor. "Okay, but—"

He held up a hand to silence her. "I doubt anyone is ever really ready until they dive in, headfirst. That said, I'm going to be involved in his life. I'm going to teach him how to rope and ride and herd cattle."

"What if it's a girl?"

He mulled that over for a moment. "It's not likely given our history. Austin has a boy and so does Dallas."

"There's always a first time. Would having a daughter totally freak you out?"

"Nope. Not as long as she's just like you. Smart as hell and as pretty as a bluebonnet, although that's going to be a problem when she discovers guys in her teens."

The compliment both pleased and surprised her. His fatherly attitude thrilled her. "Thank you for the praise, and for protecting our daughter."

"Or son," he added. "And you can count on me to keep them safe. The same goes for you. I wouldn't want any harm or hurt to come to the mother of my child."

"I appreciate that, but I'm fairly good at taking care of myself."

"Dammit, Jill, would you just let me be who I am? I want to protect you. I *need* to protect you. And I want to be around you all the time."

"I'm pregnant, Houston, not fragile."

He muttered a few oaths under his breath. "I'm not talking about your current state. I'm talking about our future together."

What in the world was he getting at? "I hope that we'll endeavor to remain friends while we're raising our baby. And should you decide to marry, I would like to know you'll choose a woman who'll accept our child."

"I don't want another woman, dammit. I want you."

Okay, this was insanity. "Want me in what way?"

He strode to the chair and pulled her up right into his arms. "I want you in every way, and not just because you're having my kid."

"You mean you still want the benefits."

"Yeah, but not just the sex benefits. I want you in my bed every night and every morning. I want you with me for all the family dinners and the boring charity events. Lately I've missed you like crazy and I damn sure don't want to go through that again."

Jill took a moment to reclaim her voice. "What exactly are you saying?"

"Are you really that clueless?"

She had her suspicions, but she needed to hear it. "Pretend I am."

"I love you, dammit!" he shouted.

"Well, I love you, too!" she shouted back. "Are we crazy or what?"

Houston gave her a knee-weakening kiss before saying, "Yeah, we probably are a little bit crazy, but there's nothing wrong with that. I love you something awful, Amherst. And I believe I fell in love with you, lock, stock and barrel, a year ago when you treated my groin injury after that bull kicked me good in the cojones."

She poked him in the ribs. "I love you, too, Calloway, even if you are such a guy. And I believe I started to fall in love with you during the wedding weekend, when you let me cry on your shoulder and you stood up to my mother by inventing some unbelievable story that somehow everyone believed. I really fell in love with you the first night you made love to me with such care and consideration. I knew for certain I loved you the day you encouraged me to ride Gabby."

He winked. "I'm that good, huh?"

Very typical guy. "I'll feed your ego like a zoo animal and say yes, but only if you'll continue to make love to me that way, and often."

"Just lead the way to the bedroom, darlin'."

First, she still had one more serious aspect of the conversation they hadn't covered. "Houston, it's important you know that I don't believe we should rush into a marriage until I'm sure this is what we both want."

"Sweetheart, I'm one hundred percent sure this is what I want, and I don't see myself changing my mind ever. But if you want to wait until next month or next year, that's fine by me. Just know your mother isn't going to be happy about it."

She brushed a kiss across his cheek. "To heck with my mother. At the moment, I just want to spend a lot of time with you. We'll put the wedding on hold for now."

"By the power vested in me by the state of Texas, I now pronounce you husband and wife. You may now seal your covenant with a kiss."

Her handsome new husband, dressed in a black suit and tie, wearing his trademark matching cowboy hat, winked at Jill and smiled. "Gladly."

Following the sweetest of kisses, Jill hooked her arm through Houston's and walked down the makeshift aisle in the Calloway's historic main house. Her gaze immediately zoomed in on her mother, who was dabbing at her eyes with a handkerchief provided by Jill's dapper dad. The whole hurry-up wedding had been her suggestion, and they'd appeased her.

Hurricane Helen, one. Happy couple, big winners.

But fortunately her mother had come through during the planning of the family-only holiday wedding, even if they'd had less than two months to get it all done. Jill had selected a white satin, strapless dress with an empire waist to cover the slight baby bump even though most knew about the baby, thanks to Houston's penchant for telling everyone they knew, and a few people Jill didn't know.

As they paused by the front door, the crowd soon began to gather to ply them with good wishes, hugs and kisses, while the Calloway brothers looked on. Maria and Jen stood by the red-and-green-bedecked Christmas tree, conversing with Helen, who appeared to be a bit stunned. Jill imagined Jen had just let her in on the secret ingredients in the mint julep her mother was now clutching like a life raft.

Little Luke was crawling around on the floor at his mother's feet, as his cousin, Chance, ran through the rows of chairs. Wonderful chaos as far as Jill was concerned. In a matter of months, she and Houston would be adding to that chaos with their own baby.

Paris soon emerged from the opening to the dining room and announced, "Food is ready, so come and get it."

As the guests began to file toward the table full of treats, Houston clasped Jill's hand, halting her progress. "Not so fast," he said. "I'd like a little alone time with my bride. Actually, I'd like to start the honeymoon in a few minutes."

Jill faked a frown. "I'm eating for two, remember? And frankly I'm starving."

Houston rested his hand on her abdomen. "How is junior today?"

"She's fine."

He chuckled. "What do you think about Laredo if it's a boy?"

"Sure. And if it's a girl, we'll call her Corpus Christi, C.C. for short."

"I'll have to think on that one."

Jill didn't have to think on her decision to marry this man, even if her head still hadn't quite stopped spinning. "I seriously do love you, Calloway."

"And I seriously do love you, Amherst…wait. Am I supposed to call you Amherst-Calloway?"

"You can call me anything, honey, as long as you call me to bed and ravish me."

He nuzzled her neck and whispered, "Go grab some food fast before I take you into the coat closet and have my way with you."

She touched his face and kissed him softly. "This is going to work, isn't it?"

He narrowed his eyes. "It worked well enough to get you pregnant."

"That's not what I meant."

"I know, darlin,' and the answer to your question is

yeah, it's going to work, as long as you're okay with being hitched to a cowpoke who's just a plain ol' rancher."

"I'm more than okay with that, and having my gorgeous, sexy, albeit stubborn, rancher's baby."

Only this time, they weren't pretending, about the baby or being in love, and Jillian Elizabeth Amherst wouldn't have it any other way.

* * * * *

Don't miss any of these sexy romances from
Kristi Gold!

THE RANCHER'S MARRIAGE PACT
AN HEIR FOR THE TEXAN
THE SHEIKH'S SECRET HEIR
ONE HOT DESERT NIGHT
THE SHEIKH'S SON

Available now from Mills & Boon Desire!

MILLS & BOON®

Desire™

PASSIONATE AND DRAMATIC LOVE STORIES

sneak peek at next month's titles...

In stores from 7th September 2017:

Billionaire Boss, Holiday Baby – Janice Maynard *and*
Little Secrets: Secretly Pregnant – Andrea Laurence

Billionaire's Baby Bind – Katherine Garbera *and*
Fiancé in Name Only – Maureen Child

One Night Stand Bride – Kat Cantrell *and*
The Cowboy's Christmas Proposition – Silver James

MILLS & BOON®

Why shop at millsandboon.co.uk?

Each year, thousands of romance readers
find their perfect read at millsandboon.co.uk.
That's because we're passionate about
bringing you the very best romantic fiction.
Here are some of the advantages of
shopping at www.millsandboon.co.uk:

* **Get new books first**—you'll be able to buy
  your favourite books one month before they
  hit the shops

* **Get exclusive discounts**—you'll also be
  able to buy our specially created monthly
  collections, with up to 50% off the RRP

* **Find your favourite authors**—latest news,
  interviews and new releases for all your
  favourite authors and series on our website,
  plus ideas for what to try next

* **Join in**—once you've bought your favourite
  books, don't forget to register with us to rate,
  review and join in the discussions

Visit **www.millsandboon.co.uk**
for all this and more today!